W9-BUV-686

Letting Go

Book One of

The Maryland Shores

May you enjoy The
love story as well as
The Chesapeake imagery!

Lauren

Lauren Monroe

Shore Thing Publishing

❋ ❋ ❋

Letting Go
Book One of The Maryland Shores

ISBN-13: 978-0-9912822-0-3 (eBook)

ISBN-13: 978-0-9912822-1-0 (print)

Copyright © 2014 by Lauren Monroe

All rights reserved, including the right to reproduce this book or portions thereof in any form whatsoever, including any reproduction or utilization of this work, in whole or in part in any form, by electronic, mechanical or other means, now known or hereafter invented, including xerography, photocopying and recording, or in any information storage or retrieval system. For information about this or regarding subsidiary rights, contact Shore Thing Publishing at shorethingpublishing@gmail.com.

This is a work of fiction. Apart from well-known, historical people, data and events, the names, characters, products, places, and incidents are either the product of the author's imagination and/or are used fictitiously, with no relation to anyone bearing the same name(s) and circumstances. Any resemblance to actual persons, living or dead, business establishments, organizations, events, or locales, known or unknown to the author, is entirely coincidental and used for characterization and other elements in this fictional narrative. West Riverside Hospital Center does not exist and has been created for the purpose of this novel.

Cover Photo by Shore Thing Publishing
Shore Thing Publishing
Queenstown, Maryland

https://www.facebook.com/lauren.monroe.novels

For comments or to contact, email shorethingpublishing@gmail.com.
Publisher is not responsible for websites or Internet content that has not been generated by the author or Shore Thing Publishing.

First Printing: January 2014

Patty & Kathy

Your enthusiasm and
encouragement
has meant so much.

I don't think I could have
completed this book had
each of you not loved it,
and conveyed that, so many times!

Table of Contents

Prologue

Graphic Artist: F/T mktg dept position. Team player. Generous salary/benefits. 4-yr degree and 5+ yrs experience, plus:

- Desktop publishing and writing skill.
- Proficiency with QuarkXPress and/or Adobe software.
- Physician/staff interaction daily to produce collateral material.

Maren tucked the email attachment into her 2002 Job Search folder. Disguised by a blind box, it came straight from Alicia Lewis, Director of Marketing, at West Riverside Hospital Center. She spotted it also in *The Washington Post.*

Her Mac G4 model housed the graphics programs. Her design degree hung on her wall. Maren knew she probably should apply. "Maren Mitchell." Startled, she grabbed the call before it woke her son. "I'm well Alicia. Yourself?"

"OK except our COO wants interviews for that position completed—someone here within two weeks," Lewis replied. "I dragged my feet, Maren, hoping you'd reconsider. I'm arm-twisting because we love your work."

Maren leaned back in her desk chair. Following 9/11, with magazine circulation down, page counts shrinking, advertising and PR budgets sliced in half—sometimes halved again—she felt like a fool for not giving Alicia Lewis a yes, like yesterday. The two of them had studied graphic design together.

"Well, thanks. I enjoyed the Buckle Up promotion and that patient education series." Maren didn't add how her stomach pitched and turned as a result. "How much interaction with staff are we talking?"

"Interviewing key people," Alicia elaborated. "For their expertise, you know how that goes?"

"Listen, learn and act astonished?" Maren chuckled, used to dealing with different professionals from many walks of life. This walk, however, might seem like a mountain hike.

"Telecommuting? Dylan's only in first grade."

"Better if you could work from home two out of five days—more perhaps?"

"Potentially. He's got the flu today. I don't have a ton of back-up."

"Poor Dylan…and you." Alicia knew first-hand balancing a sick child plus keeping some semblance of a work life.

"Stomachache, vomiting. Was about to check on him." Maren breathed in, her shoulders heavy. She'd been at her keyboard three hours already. "I promise a decision Friday. I've been so slammed with deadlines, and it's only Wednesday."

"We all have those weeks," Alicia told her hand-chosen candidate. "I can stall two days." Having seen Maren's resumé, no one else's came close.

"I appreciate that." Folders and screen icons stole Maren's eyes. Her Mac model provided a handy tax deduction to the graphic design business she began three years ago. "Friday. I promise."

"Friday it is, then. I hope Dylan feels better."

"Thanks. Bye, Alicia." Maren audibly emptied her lungs. Normal 32-year-olds didn't work themselves into knots dealing with doctors. They had ordinary squeamishness, not gut-wrenching, hold-your-breath reactions.

Medical subject matter hijacked her amygdala—that brain area responsible for fight or flight that drives you crazy if worry exceeds your capacity to squelch it. It hadn't until 16 months ago. The photograph one board member chose on the road safety campaign depicted an ambulance, red lights on alert, next to twisted, blood-singed metal meant to scare people straight. It had sent Maren straight to the restroom heaving. If she took this job, it might take pharmaceuticals just to get through a meeting, let alone an entire workday.

Chapter 1

"Mrs. Mitchell, sign here please."

Maren took the clipboard, hastily scribbling her signature on the consents. The pen color reminded her of body fluids. At least the ink flowed out blue.

"Thank you, ma'am. Can I get you anything?" the nurse asked.

"No, thank you," Maren replied as the woman went behind a desk. Finger combing her auburn hair, Maren remembered the mantra she cultivated from the support group she joined last year and ended over the summer. *Be still inside.*

She tried, as the group leader had prompted, to check out fearful thoughts and make sure she wasn't lobbing last year's stress into this moment's problems. Did people ever have to repeat a grief group like a college course?

From where she sat it all seemed frighteningly familiar. Bright lights, shrill pages, people starting and ending their shifts at 11 p.m. Every time someone slapped the wall with the coaster-sized square that opened the heavy double doors, Maren jolted. Her spine could have been that wall they hit. It rattled just the same.

The bent insurance card rested on her lap. This wasn't like her. Maren Mitchell kept everything neat and orderly. She rested her head against the wall, the chair just as uncomfortable as last year. *God, please, don't let him...*

Maren shook her head to lose that thought. Her son lay in surgery. No stitch in the forehead and little time for questions. When Dylan had ear tubes inserted, Mark helped. The last time Mark was here, he never left. Not alive, anyway.

These antiseptic walls closed in as the chilled air rushed out of the vents and the fear ran through her. Sniffing latex and disinfectant reminded Maren how good PR could gloss over despair, sometimes death.

She carried her little boy into triage around nine o'clock, outlining Dylan's symptoms in a curtained-off space. An ER doctor quickly ordered the necessary lab work and scans. With no back up in CT, they soon knew it was appendicitis and called in a surgeon.

The hours faded as fast as the light left these September evenings. Maren's disheveled sweater and the crinkled cardboard—familiar displays of her stress—reminded her of how little control she had for the past 16 months. She stared out the window sorry she had reacted with a stony glare to the registration clerk.

No guarantees now. Bad things could happen. She picked out a staff member by the designer scrub top worn against solid green pajama-like pants.

"Excuse me, where can I get an update on my son's surgery?"

The nurse, on her way home, didn't slap the elevator button, sparing Maren's nerves. "Your son's in good hands, Mrs. Mitchell. Do you have a friend or relative?" The nurse held the elevator door before it could ding. "Call someone."

Maren's appreciative nod convinced the nurse to go the rest of her way. As she stooped to retrieve the mangled card from the floor, Maren tucked the insurance information into her handbag. The rare pay phone, relegated to a corner, told how times had changed. Maren didn't have a cellular phone before 2001. Now she stored important contacts into her Nokia flip model.

To call her parents: Again? Last week, the electrician came the day a client rescheduled an all-important project. Her father delayed going into work to be at her house. Recently her mom forfeited lunch with a friend when the school nurse called about Dylan's nosebleed.

He freaked out because I freak out, Maren thought, vowing not to bother her parents, nor friends from church or her neighborhood. Instead, she put on her sweater pulling it closely across her chest. Maren felt she used her support system as thoroughly as one could. Any more and she might end up friendless.

People were a real lifeline after she lost Mark, consoling her and pinch-hitting with Dylan. But she was in no mood for platitudes tonight like the at-least-he-didn't-linger ones that assaulted her ears then. If it was God's will to take Mark at the prime of their lives, then God truly could miscalculate. Maren got up to pace. *I'm sorry, Lord...that's me, tonight. Please don't take Dylan, too.*

No one delayed a diagnosis tonight as Mark's parents suspected a year ago, costing their son his life. Maren had prayed as Mark got wheeled into surgery. *I'll do anything...give up anything...not Mark, not yet...please let him live.*

8

Two hours later, Mark was gone.

Hearing that he had "sustained multiple injuries" and "lost a lot of blood despite all of our efforts" stole the color from her skin. Those words flashed at her then, haunted her now.

Sometimes Maren felt bitter when she lay alone at night hearing stirrings that made her believe Mark was home, bursting through the door and back into her life. Now, Dylan was the only force bursting through the house. He kept Maren moving forward. *Be still inside.*

Repeated at midnight, *Larry King Live* scrolled names of those lost a year ago. "A very sad day," King termed it speaking with a 9/11 widow. Maren knew she wasn't the only woman suddenly plunged into single parenthood. This one-year anniversary of crashing jetliners rendered many into a second round of despair. The 12 months had taught Maren—and the world—that life was indeed unpredictable. Precious.

"Mrs. Mitchell." Maren's muscles tightened as her eyes focused on the man, scrub cap the color of a robin's egg in one hand, motioning her to take his lead toward the sofa. "Dylan's fine. His surgery went really well."

She felt her stomach loosen as she took in air. Dr. Kramer, the surgeon she met only briefly in the ER, stood in ordinary, pale scrubs, several inches taller than her 5'6" frame, hands resting on his hips, elbows at attention. It rattled her wondering if he thought her son's illness was ordinary.

"You can see him in recovery." This doctor slowed his speech afraid this child's mother didn't comprehend. "I'm admitting him to the floor…for tonight. Most kids have some pain with the air we use in the belly. It'll go away."

"You're admitting him where?" Maren's brown eyes edged in red, focused.

"Sorry, to the children's wing. Often, this might be same-day surgery but…that's pushing it…for a six-year-old. He certainly can't leave tonight."

"He'll be OK though? There's something else?" Maren's voice quivered, afraid the doctor could see fresh tears welling in her eyes.

He had, taking a seat next to her. His words became tender seeing her distress. "Nothing else. We'll monitor him awhile longer."

"What does that mean?" She retrieved an already sodden tissue from her sweater pocket.

"He's on IV antibiotics. We watch for complications, but I don't expect any." Kramer explained that with laparoscopic surgery comes reduced post-op pain.

"Thank you," Maren said, shoulders sinking as her eyes sent appreciation. "I really am grateful. It's late. He was so sick when I brought him in." When diarrhea started after vomiting, Dylan definitely had taken a turn for the worse.

She reached both her hands to her ponytail and felt oddly disoriented for not remembering how she'd styled her own hair.

"He ought to recover beautifully. I'm here, or my resident, if you have questions." Kramer looked around. They talked several minutes. Maren Mitchell raised herself off the sofa. The crumpled tissues she snatched, fallen from her pockets, showed her torment. "Anyone else with you tonight?"

Maren's eyes darted to the carpet before returning to Kramer straight on. "Dylan's father passed away last spring, in 2001. A terrible car accident."

"I'm so sorry," he said. Those tissues represented more profound stress. "You know, I can ask them for a sofa in Dylan's room, if you'd like. Do you need to go home first?" He wasn't sure if Dylan was her only child to attend to tonight.

"I'd really appreciate that. I'd like to stay." Maren heard a doctor snapping orders in the distance. The doctor who pronounced Mark's death? It stole the color from her face.

"I'll make the arrangements. Dylan will be groggy." Kramer studied her. "Will you be all right?" he asked. "Recovery is this way." His arm pointed. He got the distinct impression her presence here—or maybe his—frightened her.

"I'll be fine." Maren felt self-conscious as she retrieved her jacket and shouldered her handbag. "I'm sorry...quite the night. Thank you, Dr. umm..."

"Kramer," he offered her memory lapse. His shoulder tap spoke to her anxiety.

"Goodnight Dr. Kramer."

Working in this environment would be God awful, Maren decided as she grasped the blanket the nurse had given her and propped two pillows on the sofa next to Dylan's hospital bed. Dylan's IV ran out again and monitors beeped, yet he rested. His sleep, not hers, mattered most. In his hospital gown, a shock of his true brown hair spilled over his eyebrows. Somewhere around six a.m., she left her parents a message on their answering machine, fearing if she didn't she would certainly hear that she should have. Dylan was their only grandchild.

An intern, followed by a surgical resident checked on her son, within the past two hours jostling her subtle slumber. Maren picked up the *Post,* yet quickly saddened. Last year's tragic recap proved too heavy a read, especially today.

"How's he doing?" Kramer whispered, peeking inside the door and sparing any more 9/11 tributes. The clock read 8:15 when Maren glanced at the wall.

"He's hardly stirred." She got up securing loose strands with both hands into the ponytail she'd slept on overnight. Maren moved closer to the doctor, his stethoscope to Dylan's chest under the sheet. Her heart felt as if it might jump.

"He doesn't look in much pain," Maren said. At least Dylan's sleep wasn't disturbed. The resident and intern had seen to that earlier.

"It's Dr. Kramer...how ya feeling," he whispered to his young patient.

"OK," Dylan hushed.

Kramer smiled, tousled the child's hair. "Great, snooze away." He let the sheet drop into place and stepped away from the bed. "The anesthesia will start to wear off. I can prescribe something if he's uncomfortable." Kramer took note of the monitors and scribbled on the boy's chart before turning to Maren. "Sorry, that sofa close up doesn't look that comfortable."

"Don't worry about me," she answered, though honestly, his concern seemed genuine. "I just need a cup of coffee. Anything new I should know?"

"Looks good. Discharged maybe by evening, but I'll make that call later this afternoon. All systems have to return to normal, if you know what I mean."

"Discharge already?" She delivered this abruptly. Dr. Kramer—she remembered his name fully now—seemed like a man who wrapped his mind around many complicated details of his patients, patching them up and out before moving to other cases.

"If it was up to me, Mrs. Mitchell..."

"Call me Maren, please," she told him realizing her reaction. "I didn't mean how that came out. I am kinda tired." She paused. "He has to go to the bathroom successfully, is that it?"

"Exactly," Kramer ginned. "If my choice, Maren, I'd keep him longer. It's insurance. But let me see. Tomorrow is probably the longest he'll be here." Maren Mitchell looked far from relaxed, her eyes searching every inch of Dylan for confirmation he was healing on schedule. "I'm almost finished with rounds. If you really need coffee, I'll walk with you to the cafeteria." Kramer spotted her attempts to fake a smile. Her worry wasn't fading, and he wanted to reassure her of the boy's continued progress.

"Thanks." The invitation brought a slight curve to her lips, for the first time since Dylan had been admitted to West Riverside Hospital Center. "The idea of shipping him home though..."

She tucked the covers in tighter and kissed Dylan softly on the forehead. Usually, he'd smile. Maren loved seeing his toothy grin, with near perfectly shaped teeth. There would be no orthodontist in his future. Not now anyway.

"We'll talk about the timing if you want. Give me a minute to return this." Kramer stopped short of the door, absorbing some of the torture in her posture. "I'll meet you at the desk. Take your time." Maren planted another peck on Dylan's warm skin. To her, it looked like a long day ahead.

"You look stressed, Mrs. Mitchell." Kramer observed, sugaring his coffee. He looked up realizing Dylan was his patient, not the boy's mother.

"Maren...please," she reminded, biting her lip. "I don't like hospitals. The whole scene, I guess." Her eyes would have said 'I just miss Mark, terribly' if only eyes could communicate. "I have to say though, you've been kind, taking time with us. Appreciate the coffee." She'd been prepared with her wallet when he showed his ID and told the cashier it was on him.

"Sounds as if you've had a rough year."

"It shows, I realize. I don't mean to over-react."

"Well, places like this can be intimidating if you're not used to them." He watched her eyes dart, evade slightly.

"I worry. Maybe I've also had my share of bad luck or made poor choices in health ..." She stopped. She'd look rude if she continued where she was headed.

"What?" His curious tone urged her to finish.

"It's nothing really." She felt timid.

"No...go ahead."

"Well, my pediatric group wasn't the best choice. I like the woman we usually see, just not her abrupt colleagues. Or else my tolerance is really way off. So being here..." Maren closed her eyes momentarily. "I'm sorry."

Dr. Kramer raised the hot coffee to hide a cringe. "No need to apologize."

"That didn't come out right. Again," she admitted. "The doctor who brought him into this world, in Annapolis...loved her, too. I'm not totally anti-doctor."

Just half way, Kramer thought, with coffee cup shielding an erupting grin. "No really, social skills are a commodity." He laughed. "I have a friend. We trained together. He has a theory that some of us physicians either get that social deficit or we've crossed over to being human."

Maren Mitchell smiled. "Which are you?"

"You be the judge." He laughed again. "Sorry you had the difficult kind."

"Is difficult your friend's clinical diagnosis?"

"No, but..." Kramer leaned closer. "Jerk isn't an ICD-9 diagnostic code."

Maren Mitchell felt the tension escape with her laugh. Her son's doctor clearly could be as disparaging as she could be at times. She stared out the window trying not to say something amiss again or he'd think she lacked social graces.

"Café au lait in a hospital cafeteria. Wouldn't expect a French touch."

"Our marketing gurus. Next they'll open a sushi bar."

"Yeah, they're getting extremely active in that department."

"Oh no." Kramer eyed Maren quizzically as if he'd misspoken. "You say that with inside knowledge?"

"I've done consulting work in the office wing. In fact...contemplating a job offer."

"R-e-a-l-l-y?" Kramer pressed his back against the chair. "Interesting. Step up or lateral move?" The doctor paused to sip his steamy brew. "We need a few fresh faces around here, but you seem undecided."

"I am. I work from home now." She struggled with just how to put 'I'm an anxious mess with anything to do with medicine' into words and decided simply, she just wouldn't go there. "Clock ticks on my answering her, too."

"When do you have to do that?"

"Today is? Thursday? I think." Embarrassed, she shook her head but she had been a little preoccupied in the preceding 24 hours. "Tomorrow."

"Well, if my opinion counts, I'd say go for it. Then you can have all the French coffee you want. French coffee, not cappuccino?"

"Some days I need every kind. Went to France a college semester when I thought I might major in fine arts. My morning habit along with croissants, but my fine arts fascination fizzled by semester's end. Settled on marketing and graphic design, taking classes in art school— more career options with that path. Anyway, I'd love to go back. In another life."

"Speaking of getting back, I'll stop by later." Kramer pushed his chair, eyeing the clock. Swigged his last gulp. "Hope it's a little quieter for you."

"Thanks again." She waved him off, feeling a little calmer as she collected her handbag. On a scale of 1–10, her son's doctor had moved her from a fear-injected nine to a less apprehensive six. Coffee and kindness provided prescriptions she needed to contain painful memories, still raw.

Be still inside. Get through this day.

Maren stopped to get a stuffed animal from the gift shop. The nurses had already lined Dylan up with a pediatric patient bag filled with a coloring book, crayons, small play dough, and a book about staying in the hospital. Shortly after she got to his room, Dylan woke in the discomfort Kramer predicted, but the medication he left orders for helped that fade quickly.

Lunch delivered on a tray and Maren's quick errand home helped them pass a few hours. She sat coloring with Dylan on his bed as they heard a familiar voice.

"Maren, hi." She could hear his soft tone through the wide-open door.

"Luke. How'd you know we were here?"

"I checked the register. When I saw a Mitchell listed, I thought I'd better come up." She knew from her hospital projects and privacy rules that Dylan's name wouldn't be available to just anyone.

"You know me well, don't you?" Maren uttered with a yawn. "It's sweet of you to stop by. Appendicitis."

"How are you young man?" Luke eagerly extended his hand.

Pretending to be shy, Dylan only smiled. "Better," he replied.

"On the mend I hope?" Luke's eyes fixed on Maren who last year endured months of her own personal agony that then imploded into a fall season filled with hell for everyone else Luke worked with. September 11th knew no bounds.

"He's getting better. At least that's the latest report."

"How are you holding up?" Luke knew this environment couldn't be easy.

"Working on being positive. It's so good to see you." Unlike her son, seeing Luke's outstretched hand, Maren took it with a firm squeeze.

"You know I'm here if you need anything. Just call," he said.

"I really do appreciate it." The comforting touch helped. She hadn't let it go, until two more people stepped through the door.

"Mom...Dad." Maren moved to hug them. "Dylan, look who came."

"Hello Luke," Jack Cole said extending his hand. His wife Audrey touched Luke on the back acknowledging him. She bee-lined it to Dylan, depositing a hug and kiss on her grandson.

"Grammy, see this stuff." Dylan held up the crayons and play dough, some crumbled out of its container, while the rest had been formed into a blue whale staring out of the bag. Suddenly with his grandparents, whom he knew and felt comfortable around, Dylan propped up in his bed. "This one's for you." He offered Audrey one of his hand-colored pictures of a child attached to an IV.

"I love it. Look how well you stayed in the lines."

"I did another one," Dylan said showing Jack a picture of a bear with a stethoscope. Unsteady inch-high letters spelled "Grampy" across the top.

"Thanks, buddy. How ya feeling?" Jack tousled his grandson's hair while they all made him the center of their collective attention.

"It hurts," Dylan said. "Yesterday I threw up all over the carpet." That stain might have cured into the fibers by now.

"Bet that was awful." Jack knew from Maren's message how it landed them in the emergency department. Carpet was the least of his daughter's concerns.

"Maren, I'm going to head out. Good seeing you." Luke shifted focus to the Coles. Visitors were restricted to ideally no more than two people, and three was already a stretch of hospital policy. "I'll give you a call."

"We appreciate your stopping, Luke. That was sweet of you," Audrey said.

"Thanks Luke. I'll be in touch." Maren walked with him to the door as they parted company. Luke squeezed her hand again. She gave him a hug with outstretched arms as he left. Since the nurse's station—the hub of activity with doctors leaning over the counter and nurses in and out—was practically right across the hall, Maren left the door ajar only briefly.

She stepped back to Dylan's bed. Audrey and Jack Cole doted on Dylan as if he was the son they never had. Though they had hoped to fill their Annapolis home with more children, Maren was their only child. Their bond showed it.

Audrey had given up full-time teaching at the end of the last school year to substitute. At 57, she wanted to travel, do community service, and help their daughter who was suddenly a single, working mom.

Three years his wife's senior, Jack worked in finance for the State government. He had shifted meetings to make this visit happen. His career provided them a comfortable lifestyle, centered upon Maren, in younger years taking dance lessons, playing soccer briefly and landing as a varsity cheerleader in high school. When she wasn't studying or laying out the next yearbook, Maren often hoisted the mainsail and jib with her father on his 18-ft. daysailer.

"This has to be hard on you, honey. I wish you would've called us last night." Maren's father rubbed his daughter's back. She rested her head on his shoulder.

"I'm OK, Dad. I dealt with it." Maren shifted, looked at her father admiringly. "You always told me when I was little that no one would face my fears for me."

"I did. When you learned to ride your bike and the first time you trimmed the sail and managed the tiller on your own." The sight of a wide-eyed Maren flooded Jack's memory as he made a mental note to sail with Dylan now that they were all getting older and his boat was even bigger nowadays.

She grinned, putting her head back on him. "Well, maybe the message stuck. This place has taken the wind out of my sails, but everyone's been super nice."

"That's good. You know we can cancel tonight," Audrey offered.

"No Mom, you've had these tickets. I'll be fine," Maren insisted. "There's talk maybe he'll go home before morning."

"I know hospitals aren't your favorite, but if he has a chance to stay, that's probably best," Audrey said with a slightly tutorial tone. Maren appreciated her mom on so many levels, but occasionally felt as if she would forever be her student throughout life. Her parents had a very different tolerance for medical matters, making Maren wish she had it, too. Especially today.

"Any update?" her dad asked.

"Just that he's progressing. I thought his doctor might stop by, but I haven't seen him since early morning."

Maren's father detected a cord of frustration in her face and felt tension evident as she leaned against him. "Hospitals are busy places, Maren."

"I know, I know. I'm impatient."

Maren's mother asked if she got much rest, to which Maren replied, "a minimal amount." Her father offered to hunt down coffee but she kindly refused.

"You'd know where to find it, Dad. Still volunteering for church hospital visits?"

"Once a month or so. And yes, they do have decent coffee downstairs."

"You noticed that, too." Maren said. They smiled in unison. Like father, like daughter.

A brisk knock drew their eyes to the door, and white coat alone told them that Dylan's path might be decided very soon.

17

"Mom, Dad, this is Dr. Kramer," Maren said, pulling away from her father, to introduce them. "These are Dylan's grandparents, Audrey and Jack Cole."

"Pleased to meet you," Kramer acknowledged extending his hand to each of them before moving to Dylan's bedside. "The reports I got say Dylan's still in some discomfort. Sorry I haven't been in since rounds. He's more awake."

Maren thought he should be sorry for keeping them guessing the next steps. Her spine stiffened preparing her nerves if she got unsettling news.

Kramer listened with his stethoscope and offered for Dylan to try it. He took the instrument in one hand, making faces at the unfamiliar sound and turning Maren's frown upward. Kramer's fingers ran over Dylan checking for soreness.

"Ouch," he yelped. One word said what five might have solicited. With Wong-Baker FACES pain scales plastered in pediatric rooms, Kramer took the smiles and frowns chart from its hook and asked Dylan to point out his pain.

Frowning forcibly, Dylan indicated the hurts-even-more six on the scale.

"Sorry bud, all done," Kramer said. "He has more energy this afternoon, but he's feeling rough. Still, he needs to get out of bed some. Move around. That will help some other things move."

"What things?" Dylan asked innocently.

His doctor leaned over and whispered two words that Maren thought she heard correctly as "bowel movement."

"I have to poop for everybody?"

Kramer laughed. "Yes, even passing gas becomes a big deal around here." Dylan's mom, he thought, stood ready to correct her son's word choice. "No harm...I can write for something that will help with that."

"Dylan's not shy about some things," Jack added. "Most boys aren't."

Kramer grinned agreement.

"Grammy you can use this button and people get you whatever you want."

Audrey Cole laughed. Having taught elementary school, a child's discoveries never ceased to amaze her. "Don't wear it out, Dylan." She winked knowing full well that the contraption set a precedent that their daughter would have to contend with once Maren got him home.

"Dylan's won over the nurses," Kramer said. "And my chief resident and the interns. There are more notes in his chart than on my other cases." He cast a look at the grandparents. "So here I am adding more." That minor point hadn't escaped them, and they all shared a laugh.

"They've dubbed him adorable. That might change if he keeps calling them when I step out," Maren replied. "They'll want to tie his hands. So where do we go from here?"

"I put orders on for him to stay until tomorrow after what my resident wrote here. I'll stick with that plan."

"Hopefully we can sleep with fewer problems than last evening." Maren breathed more freely now. It gave her, Audrey and Jack their answer. "My parents were just heading to the Kennedy Center." She looked at her watch. "It's really OK if you need to leave. I don't want you to risk being late."

"Well, we wanted to stop by, but we'll see Dylan tomorrow," Audrey said, picking up her handbag she had deposited on the sofa. "Thank you Dr. Kramer. It was good meeting you."

"Yes, thanks for helping our little guy here." Maren's father extended his hand.

Kramer shook it and met Jack Cole's eyes. "He's a great kid. We'll get him out of here soon." Kramer looked at Audrey also. "Have a good evening."

"Thank you, we will." Kramer stood silent as the grandparents headed to the door.

"I'll walk you out." Maren took two strides. "Be right back. Say goodbye, Dylan."

"Bye Grammy and Grampy. Hey what's this?" he asked, pointing to the pager on Kramer's waist. Maren saw Dylan's doctor do a 180 and hand over his pager, figuring Dylan would soon master it just as he had the call button. For being only six, Dylan had a way of winning people over, and an even better way of commandeering their gadgets.

"Hang in there," Jack said awaiting the elevator. "Seems like a good report. Home tomorrow."

"Thanks Dad." Maren hugged them each a last time.

"You call us tomorrow, OK?" her mom reminded. "Get some rest."

Maren held onto that thought as the silver elevator partitions separated them and she walked back yawning as mid-afternoon settled in. Coffee would have been a good idea after all.

"Did you get out at all today?" Kramer asked her, securing the pager back to his belt. The September sun would have beckoned anyone outdoors.

"Yes, I went home to pick up some things before lunch," Maren said. "My parents had these tickets for the longest time and were hoping to have dinner in Georgetown. Always best to account for traffic."

"Especially on the Beltway," Kramer replied shifting focus to the watch on his left wrist. "No guarantees at this hour." Three o'clock started the afternoon rush. West Riverside Hospital Center was located south of Annapolis, far enough out of its boundaries to be a major hospital for communities along the Chesapeake Bay. "He'll be out before 11 tomorrow, if all goes well. How's that sound?"

"I can live with that." She smiled. Springing him would have been easier, she knew. This meant more documentation and for someone on this hospital's staff, a little haggling with utilization review at the insurance company.

Kramer set Dylan's chart down and motioned for him to use the TV remote on the bed table. Kramer mulled something. Maren looked his way. "Anything more I should know?"

"No worries," he replied. "More thoughts on the job you told me about?" Kramer nudged Dylan with his elbow pointing to a channel Dylan might like.

"Oh no. I completely forgot." Maren's eyes widened. She plopped onto the sofa that had become hers for the past day. "Alicia expects an answer." Maren dragged both hands through her long hair, that when not held back, lay just below her shoulders, loose strands framing her face, this afternoon.

"I guess it's not really my business, but…"

Extroverted curiosity, she thought. "Why I'm not jumping at this in a post-9/11 economy that's rocked advertising and marketing to its feet?"

"Well, economic headlines aside, I wasn't sure if you had another job." Kramer transferred from Dylan's bed and sat down next to Maren.

"You must not have children, Dr. Kramer?" No wedding band evident. No tan line to suggest one either.

"No. Someday. I do like kids."

"I can tell." Thankful for a concerned doctor, she gave him the benefit of the doubt shifting to a whisper. "What did the Queen call 1992—her castle burning, kid's marriages crumbling?" She shrugged. "Annus horribilis. Like my 2001... I guess not stellar for anyone."

"I'm sorry," Kramer said, voice softening. "Some years I vaguely remember who was president. Last year impossible to miss."

"Goes with a hectic job I'll bet."

"Side effect. '92-'93 was a blur. My fifth year of residency, never a free moment." He stopped his ramble, lowering an octave. "I can't imagine losing your husband so unexpectedly. Were you or Dylan involved in the accident?"

"No, that's partly why I cling to him so...if I lost him, after losing his father...with losing a big chunk of my work. All the changes, and worrying what this world has come to." She shook her head. "2003. Ring...it...in!"

Kramer brushed his hand on Maren's to punctuate what he had to say. "You won't lose him...not over this. His counts are good, no fever. Nurses told me he ate well. I had them take out his IV. Doubt he will back slide. He just has to..."

"Yes, I know." Maren took in Kramer's unwavering words. How many doctors were this kind? But then Kramer seemed a little suave and either tremendously confident that others thought as he did or would do as he directed.

With his dark hair and boldly handsome face, Kramer seemed to have the right phrases stashed in his white-coat pocket. The minute she'd asked two nurses when he might stop by, they all aligned to defend him much like the nurse had done when questioned last night.

Kramer reached onto his belt to silence his pager. "Gotta run. May the force be with you for a better night," he said, patting the firm surface underneath them. "If not, I guess you'll get to think about working here."

"Thanks. I brought a book if I'm up half the night." She feigned curving her lips as he strode away. If he was this persistent with everyone, Maren quickly wondered about taking—or not taking—the job. She rather liked keeping a safe distance. Dr. Kramer seemed personable, but he could confine his directives to the operating room. Was she being too harsh, too sensitive?

21

Working here would be a constant reminder of pain, accidents, blood…death. The last year had been filled with those images—from survivors pulled from under skyscraper debris to the burning embers of a plane in a rural field, and smoke billowing out of the Pentagon. In this very hospital, Maren would never forget the sick pit in her stomach when asked about donating Mark's organs that weren't destroyed by the accident's trauma. At first angered, she remembered how her minister had woven the gift of new life into Mark's funeral service, with the large framed photo of him beside his casket. It had helped.

As she contemplated her next career move, did she really need to create more impressions that she would have to manage day in, day out? If facing her fears had been a familiar childhood lesson, Maren felt she'd capitalized on that education multiple times.

Someone ought to grant her a graduate degree, she thought, because it had been such hard work managing her shakiness today and last night—unsteadiness she hadn't known since making funeral arrangements. Managing more might be pushing things.

Chapter 2

Despite her unease, Maren tolerated her second night on the sofa slightly better feeling more positive by sunrise. She considered herself a people person and found chatting with nurses eased the edges of her frayed nerves, both literally after such a stiff sleep and figuratively with her unwanted discomfort.

Today, however, was Friday. Maren had to make up her mind. Would she become one of them here at West Riverside? Rest helped, but she still teetered on the yes/no fence. People easily spend more than one third of a day in the workplace. How many set out to make themselves miserable?

West Riverside Hospital Center wasn't as advanced as Baltimore's Shock Trauma or large city medical centers. It was a smaller teaching hospital that on any given day saw its share of boating accidents, ordinary maladies, or small traumas unless the patient required life-flight transport elsewhere.

She got her own coffee and brought it to Dylan's room, fingering the paper cup and feeling a trace silly for avoiding the medical community. If the job here didn't work, she could resume projects in her established business. Yet, if she took it, she'd let go of what she built. Pride was at stake.

With the business, if she paid her State fee, her LLC remained intact. Yet she wished to actively create a future, beyond the one already shaped by Mark. The plan-driven saver, he left them with ample life insurance, in addition to the settlement Maren received from his accident. She promptly tucked that into a trust as soon as the check had arrived. On a salary, she could stash away extra income, hoping she never needed it. But what if she did?

Dylan grew antsy confined to his hospital bed or the pediatric playroom. The staff brought toys—a boat and some small people figures. Maren retrieved an *Arthur* episode and another DVD when she journeyed home yesterday. Nurses encouraged her to take an hour for herself—another sign that maybe she judged this place prematurely.

"Ready to go home?" Kramer inquired as he burst through the door, his white coat sailing in like a jib in front of him.

"Hi neighbor," Dylan greeted with a six-year-old howdy-partner cadence. Dylan looked at the TV set attached from the wall. He had put the DVDs to quick and unending use, at the moment watching the land of make believe.

Kramer did a double take. "Mister Rogers? My brother watched him."

"Either your brother is awfully young, Dr. Kramer or you're showing your... Oops, never mind."

"Mister Rogers is an institution." He re-directed her age guesstimate. "My brother is 14 years younger, and I'm not *that* old." He wasn't so sure why he rescued her since the blush of her cheeks matched her pink sweater atop crisp blue jeans. Maren Mitchell looked more refreshed than she had the day before.

She rolled with his humor. "Everything has...moved along, shall we say."

Dylan's bathroom success charted, he knew what she meant. "Yes, I'm releasing him." Kramer brushed Dylan's brown hair aside as he felt under his bangs and jostled his attention.

"This is the water, and these people fell off the boat," Dylan told him maneuvering the small craft across his blue hospital bed blanket. "Watch out! Splash!" The child diverted attention from his animated play to the DVD he had obviously watched more than once since being confined.

"They have lifejackets. What'd you do, Dylan? Catamarans are stable. When you come for your appointment, I'll show you pictures of my boat."

"You have a boat? Like this?" Dylan's eyes widened.

"Nah, a power boat. I used to have a sailboat. You remind me, OK."

"You lost your sailboat?" Dylan asked.

"No, my brother uses it now," Kramer answered sensing confusion in his young patient's mind. If they hadn't had this conversation, Dylan's pupils would have indicated something other than awestruck.

"My father owns a sailboat," Maren added. "I think Dylan feels your brother is a little kid with his own big boat."

Kramer laughed. "Either you're all kid or all adult. My brother's a grown up now. I could probably take it for a sail, if I wanted to."

24

He paused. "He certainly inherited your brown eyes." Looking straight into those, Kramer continued: "Most important: Play quietly the rest of this week. No sky dives off the sofa. No rough and tumble. Don't want to see you back here." He handed Maren a prescription pad note to be excused from school. "Use this if you need it. Otherwise, he's good to go during the day."

"No more shots or needles…and no school!"

Kramer winked at Maren. "Yes, yes and…maybe." Putting aside Dylan's chart, he spotted brochures lying near Maren's overnight bag, packed to leave. Without asking, he picked up two of the colorful pamphlets. Maren Mitchell certainly had talent. And her hands full, too, by the looks of this child's activity suddenly sparked to full throttle.

"I have some of these in my waiting room. Have you decided about the job? This is creative—takes the edginess out of difficult topics." Kramer glanced at Dylan's mom. "The colors…picked on purpose, I'll bet."

"Thank you. Yes, they were." Maren had refined the color palette her predecessors had used. No more blood-red bold or omen-evoking black headlines. For much of this series, she'd chosen calming pastels—pink if she needed it—that gave serious subject matter and disease prevention a lighter air.

Maren regarded Dr. Kramer somberly, her eyes urging him to listen. "I really appreciate all you've done. You've been very kind, making me reconsider my—avoidance." She hated to admit, but the last two days had brought some awareness. "I can't let this stuff get to me."

"It's understandable." Kramer appreciated Maren's brown eyes looking incredulously into his. "So, your verdict?"

"I'm calling the director as soon as we get settled back home. You all win, I guess." Maren threw both hands up into the air and let them fall without protest. "I never would have predicted this, but how bad can it be?"

A broad grin spread across Kramer's face with the feeling he'd helped to influence her decision. "You really make it seem as if you'll be working between the devil and the deep blue sea." Stepping back, Kramer showed off a gray dress shirt and aqua tie with fine black diagonal lines. The accent melded perfectly into dark black slacks, creating a stark contrast with his lab coat. She wasn't the only one who pondered a color palette.

"I wasn't always like this. I used to watch *ER* episodes." Mark had gotten her hooked when the popular TV series was a pilot. "It'll be a change in routine."

"Whatever you call it, it's good to have you on board." Kramer's eyes glinted with intrigue. For a brief moment, he lifted his chin and raised his heels as he emphasized, "Congratulations and welcome!"

"Say thank you to Dr. Kramer, Dylan. He's got to get going." It didn't look that way but surely he had other patients.

"Thanks dude." Dylan scooted his little behind off the bed, hand ready for a high-five. Kramer crouched a few inches to meet palms.

"And since you'll be staff," Kramer added, standing tall and extending his hand to Maren. "It's Steve, unless your boss insists on formality." They shook as if re-introducing themselves, his hands sturdy and sure. Given what he did for a living, Maren knew that mattered, but considered them differently as they enveloped hers, reluctantly letting go.

"Thanks for the welcome," she said licking her lips with cautious anticipation. Something else had flashed between them, like a charge—something new and hopeful. Maren would take hope. She needed plenty of it, in fact.

"A nurse usually calls to follow up. Have a good weekend." He backed himself several paces out the door.

"You, too," she shouted before she lost sight of his coat cast in the fast-paced, self-assured breeze his movement created.

A week ago Maren might have perceived such as bordering on arrogance, but the scent of his after-shave lingered and if her fears had let her watch those TV medical dramas, Maren was certain that at least one of the male characters could have been Dr. Steve Kramer. Yet, with her hefty dose of skepticism, she wasn't sure she believed in fictionalized medicine either. Fiction or non-fiction had the capacity to inject apprehension.

Seeing his shoulders strain against his white lab coat would certainly be one perk if that were the only reality of the job ahead. The one she was about to accept, and that brought her to this amazing cross roads of decision-making.

Priding herself on practicality, Maren knew that perk would only last about five minutes on any given work day. How she got through the rest would be her next substantial challenge.

Maren sat at her desk Friday afternoon in the home office created during Dylan's toddler years. Framed inspiration occupied the wall above her Mac computer. When Maren turned 32 last March, her mom gave her a beautiful blouse, skirt and scarf. Typically her father would defer to Audrey who would put his name on the gift also. This year was different.

Jack Cole had seen his daughter struggle the preceding months since the unexpected death of her husband Mark. Reflecting on their sailing days together when Maren was a child, he had chosen a poster prominently displaying heeling hull, beam, and mainsail that had caught the wind atop an equally powerful dose of encouragement.

"We cannot direct the wind, but we can adjust the sails."

Maren loved that quote by Bertha Calloway, an activist and historian. It said everything her father had wanted to impart to his daughter. So it hung proudly in the place where she sat for long hours toiling over text and images.

As she silently drew in the message, Maren made good on her promise to phone Alicia Lewis, who was thrilled and scheduled her interview for Tuesday. A formality since Maren was 98% assured the job.

Lewis wasn't kidding when she said hospital administration wanted someone quickly. Same day as her interview, Maren got the offer, signed it, and spent the rest of the week wrapping up client projects and scrambling together after-school arrangements. Until then, she'd made her work hours coincide with school, which Dylan went to thankfully, without needing the excuse Steve Kramer had written.

The last week in September, Maren started a weeklong orientation putting her at the hospital each day. Staff from various departments presented material regarding healthcare regulations, benefits and parking policy, privacy, HIPAA, as well as what constituted conflict of interest. She ended Thursday relieved she could continue some freelance work if it was out of the healthcare realm, and Lord knew she welcomed that prospect. She had stayed later that day to get her required TB test read two days after it had been administered along with the flu vaccine, and a blood draw to check titers for other required immunity.

"Maren, wait up." She heard the shout from several parking spaces away. Crisp air, the kind that makes one welcome fall's arrival, rustled the palette of leaves just starting to turn a few delicate shades of rust and orange on the trees.

"How's Dylan feeling?" Steve inquired moving his Ray-Ban sunglasses to his head and pocketing his car keys having caught up to her. His assigned spot was close to the building, but she read in the orientation packet that he'd just been named chief of surgery effective September 2002.

"He's doing well. Me: Major mother guilt. First week I haven't had as much contact with him." Maren looked across the lot. Her car farther from where they stood, she took strides toward it as he walked with her.

"They initiated you," Kramer remarked of the bandage and cotton ball below her short-sleeved shirt. Her light blue blouse was tautly held beneath the waistband of her navy slacks, belted in black, the same color as low-heeled pumps. Open-toed shoes weren't allowed she learned this week.

"I'll live. Congratulations on your promotion," she said smiling. "I didn't realize." But she recognized she knew little about the doctor who healed her son two weeks ago. "Change happens!"

"Yes it does. My new office is a mess. Fortunately, I have a secretary to help put it together. I refuse to give up weekends to empty boxes when I could be outdoors."

"Well good for you. Since it's Thursday, the weekend's almost here."

"And you...you've started I see."

"Last day of orientation tomorrow. I plan to work here Monday, Wednesday and Thursday with Tuesday/Friday working from home. Eight to four this week; shifts Monday to nine to five."

"Sounds very doable." He paused. "How 'bout we celebrate? You have a new job. Me too. I know of this French place. Not the kind you go to alone...unless of course, I'm intruding, in which case we can confine it to coffee." There was a sudden sheepishness about him. "I...I didn't know if..."

"If what?" Maren recognized reluctance, a trace of strain etched on him.

"If you were seeing anyone. I wasn't sure." His voice noticeably deeper, Maren studied to understand.

"What would give you the impression I'm seeing someone?" Paperwork she had to sign asked—brazenly she thought—for marital status. It had nearly killed her to check 'widowed.'

"During your stay a man asked directions to Dylan's room. I was at the desk. In fact, now I remember. I got called between patients, walked past his room at one point, and you were holding hands, hugging. Same day I met your parents."

"Ah, he took my hand. Sshh, I'll let you in on a secret." Maren leaned a little closer commandeering Kramer's left ear. The newly crowned chief of surgery looked a little flustered.

"He's married, too." She loved the shock settling into his blue eyes. "Steve, he's my minister…Luke. Has a wife, three kids, and a fabulous bedside manner. We love him. Absolutely love him!"

A sense of relief washed over Kramer. Jangling keys in his pant's pocket, he looked to the pavement, then back at Maren. "You're enjoying this aren't you? I should be better at this." He tried unsuccessfully to hide his meek grin.

Wondering how it could be that he wasn't better here, Maren decided she'd in fact had enough fun and glanced at her watch. A man this handsome had to have much experience hitting on a woman.

"It's a really tempting invitation," Maren replied. "I've just had so many things on my mind. Can I get back to you? I ought to look at the calendar at home." As she said this, she knew she needed to consult her internal chart of mood and readiness more than any wall calendar. Was this really happening?

"No rush. If we want to go this weekend, probably ought to make reservations by tomorrow." Steve handed Maren one of his newly printed cards. "My email and pager, but I can give you my cell. Do you have a pen handy?"

This time Maren couldn't conceal amusement. "Here," she said, reaching into her handbag. "And no I don't believe for a minute that you're really not good at this, Dr. Kramer."

"A man my age you mean." He lifted a brow and smirked.

"For the record, you brought up age this time," she pointed out. "My comment goes to experience. You've been married, right?"

"No, I haven't," he said smugly. "Now, what gives you that impression?" The tables had turned. He enjoyed watching her mind wrap around that newly divulged detail so much so that he leaned against her Ford Focus and thrust his hands deep into his pockets. His eyes never left hers, looking for his answer. A few awkward seconds passed. "Or, what are you *really* wondering?"

Her cheeks appeared to warm, and Steve Kramer didn't think it was from the September sun alone. Even better, if she had no interest at all, she wouldn't give a damn, he thought as he continued leaning into her vehicle, thereby keeping the conversation rolling.

"OK, I'm curious. Age? Relationship status? I get the impression you're well-liked around here."

"And that would mean?" He took his eyes away to scrawl the number hurriedly, handing her back his business card.

"That's an eight or a nine or some hieroglyphic?"

"An eight," Steve said now fumbling with the pen and crossing it out.

"I better get used to deciphering such chicken scratch."

"No problem asserting yourself for what you need," Steve replied. He handed her a totally different card confining his crumbled first attempt to his pocket. He wrote on this one deliberately slow. Something made him want to keep her even longer. The parking lot began emptying slowly around them.

"That skill might be necessary since you're dodging my questions. My demographics were an open chart with Dylan's name on it." Maren grinned, somewhat pleased with the assessment of her assertiveness he had just rendered, but still damn curious and slightly resentful that he had an edge on the information front. "I'll email or call you tomorrow, how's that?"

"I'll look for your reply," Steve said fingering his sunglasses before shielding his eyes from hers. "I'll check when sunset's expected. Won't want to miss that."

"Ah, I haven't said yes," she reminded him.

"Yet." He studied her, slightly parting his lips in another sheepish grin.

An irresistible one, Maren noted, more determined than ever to dig her heels into the pavement beneath them. "Here's my number," she said, scrawling it on a scrap of paper from her purse. "I should have my cards tomorrow."

Steve reached for her hand, the one that didn't hold onto her handbag shouldered on her right side. "Maren, I'm more than happy to entertain your questions. Have dinner with me. You'll get your answers. A gorgeous sunset, too." Maybe more he thought with another smile turned mischievous before he erupted in laughter.

"The devil you talked about is indeed in the details. Not in the deep blue sea." She shot him an all-too-knowing gaze. "Have a good evening. After-care closes in 20 minutes. I better get moving."

Maren reached into her handbag for her keys. Without asking, he took them from her and opened her car door. Maren tossed her bag to the passenger seat and slid in. Steve handed back the keys. "Likewise. Give Dylan my best."

"I will. Thanks." She pulled her car door shut and waved goodbye. To the man who liked to take charge; the one who also cornered her curiosity.

Ending orientation, Maren reviewed employee paperwork in HR, received her insurance details as well as her newly printed business cards with the title of marketing associate and discussed with her boss how the first week felt.

"I'll make it work," Maren said of the small office. "The department has these manuals, right?" Maren referred to the desktop publishing software they used.

"Yeah, we have the online help desk and database. Keep at home what you need for days you aren't here," Alicia replied. "Next week you'll get a better feel for the real schedule. How's Dylan adjusting?"

Like Maren, Alicia Lewis had studied partly at Maryland Institute College of Art, otherwise known as MICA in Baltimore, each obtaining their BA degrees elsewhere. When Maren and Mark were newly married, the two women remained friends easily commiserating about projects, deadlines, and life getting in the way.

"The typical complaints, not wanting to get up in the morning." Hands perched on her hips, Maren sighed. "If he hadn't been admitted, I wouldn't shudder every time he complained."

"A stomach ache isn't always a stomach ache, I hear ya."

"Yeah, but it turned out OK," Maren admitted about Dylan's appendicitis. "Staying here steered me into the department, Alicia. That and some nudging."

"Well, whatever it took. Did I prod too much?"

"No, I totally understand where you were coming from. Chatting with Dylan's doctor, I must have shown I hated hospitals or something."

Maren derided how that must have come across. "I let it slip that I had an offer," she said. "He encouraged me to seriously consider the spot...kept asking if I'd called you."

"There are some who appreciate us and others who see marketing as unnecessary overhead," her boss cautioned. "Get used to it. Who was it?"

"Dr. Steve Kramer. I'd rate him on our side overall." Maren didn't offer the wisecrack he made about the sushi bar. On a scale of being marketing minded, Maren put him at maybe an eight, on a 1–10 scale.

"I don't know him that well, but he's got a good reputation. Works long hours. Doesn't hang around, if you know what I mean. Works; leaves." Alicia turned to Maren. "Trust me, a few females around here might love to have been you in a conversation with him. He's single."

"I'm aware," Maren revealed. "He asked me out."

"No way," Alicia said incredulously. "Are you going?"

"I don't know. I put him off, but I promised a reply."

"I'm seeing that as your style, Maren. How many days did I have to wait for a yes?" Alicia Lewis shifted into a hearty laugh, standing in Maren's newly appointed office.

"You call it like you see it." Maren rolled her eyes. "Dylan in here was a legit excuse for my stall on that."

Alicia touched Maren's shoulder. "Of course it was, but I also sense it's hard to know what paths to pursue when you've had a year like you just had."

"Thanks, it is. My minister Luke always said not to make major decisions in the first six months, maybe a year after a traumatic event."

"Mark died May of 2001? Almost a year and a half ago, right?"

"So I'm being too cautious?"

"Maybe not terribly cautious, but you have to decide when you'll try new things. I know you loved Mark. The few times we went out after class, I could tell you made a great couple."

"I do miss him." Maren's eyes scanned the floor but nothing could steer her away from images of her late husband. Alicia had noticed the ease they had between them, and yes, the affection, too. "So much sometimes."

"What would Mark want for you, Maren? For Dylan? Think about that."

"Mark wasn't the kind to wallow. He was a doer. Problems got tackled. Straight on."

"So he'd want you to live a little and be happy?"

"Yeah…" Maren's voice lowered realizing what she said. "But how to do it and when? Foreign territory for sure."

"Step by step. There's no one right way." Alicia looked squarely at Maren. "Like this job, the opportunity presented itself. You seized it. I'm elated. I hope you will be. I know there's other stuff out there for you, too."

"Like dating? Ugh. I'm so out of sync with that scene."

"It's a lunch or dinner or whatever he asked you to. Step by step," Alicia encouraged. "I'm dating or I'd be jealous."

Maren's face fell blank. One ounce of curiosity confirmed. Steve Kramer was considered a catch, even by her own friend, turned boss. "How long have you dated Drew?"

"Six months. We met online," Alicia revealed. "So no worries." Alicia's smile seemed innocent enough. "Look, I have to clear my desk. Promised my kids I'd take them shopping tomorrow and to the park. So I'm not taking work home."

"Good for you," Maren said as Alicia started out of her small space. "Thanks for thinking this through with me."

"After my divorce, it took me some time. No one-size-fits-all guidebook. Have a good weekend." Alicia waved as she walked to her office.

"Thanks…you, too." Maren sat down at her desk. Still fairly sparse, they had given her a telephone, which she picked up, then set back down in order to find Steve Kramer's number as she dug into her purse before the dial tone ran out.

She picked up the receiver again, this time with his business card in her other hand, and punched in the now clearly legible digits of his cell phone number.

"Steve Kramer," he answered. It was about four p.m. He hadn't recognized the number on the caller ID, but knew it was an internal hospital extension.

"Maren Mitchell, Dr. Kramer. How are you?"

"It's Friday. It's getting better." Steve pulled himself away from his desk in the high-back leather chair. He planted one elbow upon the armrest, hanging onto his cell lazily with his left hand. He'd have to

33

commit her extension either to memory or enter it into his contacts. Or both, he thought.

"I promised I'd give you an answer."

"Yes, you did." Steve leaned back having an idea that if she was rejecting dinner outright, she'd have told him via email.

"If you're talking Saturday—tomorrow—I probably can do something. Dylan spends a weekend each month with my parents. They're chomping at the bit to spoil him, especially after his hospital stay, so they're taking him tomorrow."

"And you're telling me you can *probably* do something?" Kramer's voice conveyed that questioning tone.

Maren laughed. "I can make it."

He matched the chuckle. "Don't let me rush you. If you need a few more hours to decide." Steve's expression rose. He got the impression Maren Mitchell didn't do anything fast.

"A woman has to eat, and well, I do like French cuisine." She sensed the tease but wasn't about to let his ego swell. Flirting. Part of the dating drill, too?

"What time should I pick you up then? I was thinking 6:30 but maybe sooner, well before sunset."

"I can be ready by 5:30 or 5:45… not knowing how long it takes to get there." Maren gave Steve her address. He straightened his chair in line with his computer, quickly calling up a map search engine. He told her the name of the restaurant as he tapped her address into the keyboard.

"5:30. That way, we can have a drink on the observation deck. Nice views."

"Sounds good. I'll see you then."

Maren hung up the phone, letting go a breath she held bottled inside. "What'd ya know?" she muttered aloud. No one save the fake plant in the corner could hear her. That plant had to go, she thought, as she gathered her things, grabbed the sorry-looking semblance of plastic and silk, and closed her office door.

Saturday morning came quickly since Friday night hadn't afforded as much sleep as Maren and Dylan both needed. Still, Maren always liked driving to the home where she grew up, especially on a gorgeous afternoon with just enough sun peeking through a few cumulus clouds, which Dylan dubbed cotton ball clouds when he was only three. The description stuck.

Jack and Audrey Cole had raised their daughter in a community along the South River in Annapolis. To get there, Maren navigated streets, crossing creeks and small bays—inlets that people enjoyed as part of their way of life.

Dylan happily bounded into his grandparent's house with its three bedrooms, 2 ½ baths, and den with built-in bookshelves right off the foyer. Every spring the daffodils bloomed in the front, followed by black-eyed susans, the state flower, prospering each summer. Though it was slightly past their season, Maren loved how some of them hung on.

She wondered if her parents would keep the house after retirement, but that seemed like a dozen years away. She considered them young in years, active in lifestyle. She didn't like to impose, but they had grown accustomed to keeping Dylan once a month, especially in the last 12 in order to give their daughter a much-needed break from solo parenting.

Maren followed him with his backpack as Dylan insisted upon wheeling his own suitcase, which looked hardly more than a backpack, by her estimation. Some days, like this week in a new routine, she appreciated his independent streak; other times, it reminded her that her precious little boy was growing up.

It hadn't seemed that long ago that she and Mark had brought him home as a newborn. It would soon be a year and a half since they had lost Mark. Dylan was four then, not even in kindergarten. Not in the public school system. He hadn't known how to tie his own shoes, and he was much more shy. Back then, Dylan still had hit or miss accidents, and after losing his father, progress in potty training slid backwards.

That, thankfully, resolved. Today, rustling his bag to the front door, you wouldn't have known that just weeks ago, he was one sick little kid, either.

"Hi Grampy, Grammy," he said, knocking on and opening the door as he knew he was always welcome.

"Hi honey." Audrey kissed him and hugged Maren as she strolled in behind. "Much traffic?"

"Some people out shopping, but I stayed clear of the Navy jam." Navy Memorial Stadium could draw a crowd with college football fans.

35

"Dylan, you can put your things in your mom's old room. Your train table is in the spare room. I just made some iced tea. Come have some," she said leading Maren to the kitchen and a particularly sunny spot just beyond it where they could have a pleasant view of water in the distance. "How's work?"

"Next week will be the real test. This was just orientation, learning the ropes, getting shots." She took the glass, swallowing a refreshing amount. "Thanks, tastes good," she said. "Hi Dad."

Jack had just noticed her car and extra voices in their often too quiet home. "I heard you talking about your job."

"Yeah. It seems OK, but it's only been a few days."

"I'm proud of you honey for taking it," Jack told his daughter. Maren took note of the extra gleam in his eyes.

"I think Alicia instigated it, Jack." Audrey smiled. "These girls were always friends. It's good they kept in touch."

"Yeah, graphic design has helped keep my mind occupied. I'm glad for that."

"Anything we should know about Dylan? He's OK to play and do whatever these days?" Audrey might not ask such a question if Dylan hadn't been hospitalized weeks ago.

"I'd take him on the boat tomorrow but I'm committed to 18 holes of golf," Jack added. "Maybe before the season ends."

"Actually, he has some medicine for his ears. Instructions are on the bottle. He takes it without complaint." Maren put it in the refrigerator. "Has to be kept cold so don't let me forget it when I pick him up. He had his morning dose."

"What will you do the rest of the day? Running errands?" Jack asked. He could never figure why women spent time going here and there, sometimes void of clear purpose.

"No, Dad. I'll stop for groceries, but I have plans actually." She took another sip of iced tea, downed it, and suddenly saw both sets of parental eyes inquiring. Being an only child wasn't always the best thing when you became the singular focus. "I'm going out."

"Where?" Audrey asked. "Just curious. Someplace fun?"

Maren laughed. "Now I know where I got my innate inquisitive streak." She tried to mask the fraction of embarrassment. It still seemed odd. "I have a date. Just a friend from work." Audrey and Jack looked at one another, rather matter-of-factly. Not disapprovingly. They merely fell silent.

"What? You think it's too soon?" Maren's eyes grew a little wider, ping-ponged between them. "You met him actually. Dylan's doctor. We chatted at work, and we're celebrating my new job and his promotion."

Jack Cole smiled at Maren. "It's been a while since my little girl has been on a date, and no I don't think it's too soon. If you don't." He rubbed her back in recognition of the step this was after the year she had. "Of course, I wouldn't have thought you'd be going out with a doctor or anyone from a hospital, but then I never thought you'd work in one either."

"You and me both, Dad." Maren shrugged. The heaviness of that choice still weighed on her without total certainty it was the best professional call. She shared with him how the poster he'd given her had bolstered her decision to make the leap from freelancer to full-time employee.

"I don't remember him too well. Except that he was handsome." Audrey searched her memory. "He was good with Dylan, as I recall."

"He was. Seems nice. I hardly know anything about him. And please, Dylan doesn't know. It's not a big deal." Not quite a big deal. It was a milestone, however. "Speaking of Dylan, I better check on him."

"Maybe he and I can go outside," Jack said. "It's too nice to stay indoors. He can play trains tonight." Jack Cole enjoyed being the male figure Dylan looked up to this past year.

"He can play all he wants. Just nothing too terribly physical."

"I guess that topic might come up tonight." Audrey goaded her daughter. "Nervous?"

"I don't know. I shouldn't be; maybe a little."

"Where are you going?" she asked.

"A French restaurant with a great view. He made the arrangements." Maren gathered her handbag. "You really don't think I'm pushing it here, do you?"

"No honey," her mom reassured. "You're not the type to rush into things and you need to have a little time to yourself. You're too young to sit at home."

And too beautiful, her father mused as he walked into the next room. Jack had buried the unease fathers felt when daughters brought new men into their lives. Mark treated Maren well and through the years he had become a fixture in their lives, abruptly snatched away from them too.

"You sound like Alicia." Maren smiled. "Dylan, come give me a hug," she shouted up the stairs. Hearing his mom, he scampered down.

Maren stooped to hug him and plant a kiss on her son's forehead. "Be good."

"Mom…I don't get in trouble here," Dylan reminded.

That was for sure, Maren thought. "Bye Mom," she said kissing Audrey's cheek. "Bye Dad," she yelled out, walking into the other room to plant a kiss on him as well. "I'll be here around lunchtime tomorrow if that's OK?"

"See you then," Jack said, reaching out for his daughter's hand. He took it in his. "And Maren…"

"Yeah, Dad?" Maren had pulled away after the quick peck to his cheek but this gesture claimed her a little closer again.

"Have a good time." He winked his approval, smiling because she was not of the age where she sought it. But Jack Cole knew his vote mattered in Maren's mind. It always had.

"Thanks, Dad. I will." She let go and let the front screen door slap closed behind her.

Chapter 3

Steve pulled his black Jaguar convertible into Maren's driveway and picked her up as planned. They were both glad they bumped up the reservation to be seated in time for sunset.

Maren chose a grape colored short-sleeved dress tied at the waist, black pumps and gold seashell earrings as Steve hinted they'd be dining along the water's edge, but inside, at Rive Ouest.

He opened her car door holding her matching handbag and chiffon wrap while she smoothed her dress curling her body into the passenger seat. He had already put the top up on his car, once he'd arrived, but Maren couldn't help but yearn for a ride with the top down. It was a treat to ride in. Smooth leather: the look and feel of a recent purchase.

Arriving earlier than their reservation, Steve pocketed a large pager as they strolled along the observation deck and watched the late afternoon sky become layers of beige, yellow, orange, and purple set against a glimmering blue bay. They looked across the Chesapeake glimpsing land from their vantage point.

The pager vibrated in Steve's jacket. Their table ready, he and Maren followed the hostess who offered them menus.

"Look outside," Steve said, motioning at the sun setting. Their table was one of the few bestowed with both an eastern and western exposure where the sun slowly faded into the horizon. In the distance, ships lined up waiting to pass underneath the Bay Bridge. Their lights cast a sparkle onto the water around their hulls.

Each entrée tempted Maren, impressed at the menu design and use of ample French description. In her line of work, such details captured her eye.

"L'Angleterre," Steve ordered, pointing to his selection. Maren caught their waiter curve his lips as he took the large folder back into his hands. Maren had already ordered crab cakes, always her favorite.

"You just asked for Great Britain," Maren told him once they were alone. "Might take a while to locate."

"The word for lobster then?"

"Langouste, one translation anyway. I think he got the idea."

"That's all that counts." Steve recovered without embarrassment, observing how fluently that word rolled from her tongue. It added to his intrigue.

Maren enjoyed how Steve Kramer's blue eyes danced with delight at every menu item either of them mentioned, even if he struggled with pronunciation.

"How'd Dylan do once you got home last night?"

The two had an unplanned encounter Friday late into the evening, not even 24 hours ago, after Maren had called Steve to say yes to dinner tonight.

Dylan was in the ER again, this time having woken Maren with fresh tears, tugging at his ear. A forehead swipe alarmed her. She had scooped him up and driven him there before the night became intolerable, shortly before 10 p.m.

"He slept well. Today only whined a little before I took him to my parents. A quick recovery," she replied, nodding to Steve. "I just didn't want to wait until office hours."

"I'm glad you didn't. Or I might not enjoy your company this evening." He looked sideways at the lights more prominent in the dark, running bow to stern.

"I'm seeing a lot of West Riverside this month! How did you know we were in the ER? This time."

"You and Dylan are becoming frequent flyers," he said. "I saw 'Mitchell, Dylan' on the ER screen when I hung around to talk with another doctor." He paused. "I wait, too, sometimes."

"I can tell you command more respect," she shot back.

"You should, too. What was going on before I spotted you?"

Maren collected a kind thought. She wanted to keep the evening positive. Steve looked devastatingly handsome in a blue striped shirt and navy blazer atop grey pants. The blue and grey tie, precisely knotted, stole her attention just as his hand had when it glided her to the railing as they observed the sunset. What's more, Steve had secured what had to be one of the restaurant's best tables.

"I've never had trouble with the ER docs, mind you, but in Dylan's pediatric group, you deal with who's on call," she said. "We like the female we see, but I had no clue her colleague was there. After they registered Dylan—that didn't take long, this time—and saw that he went to that practice, they called him in. Lucky us." Her cynicism prevailed.

"That doesn't answer why he was grilling you." Their waiter brought their appetizers—stuffed escargot mushrooms for Maren, smoked salmon for Steve—and placed an enticing basket of bread and rolls between them. Steve started breaking his apart. "Please tell me he doesn't speak to you like that often."

"Welcome to my world. He's brusque, bullish, and tries to belittle parents. Want my theory on pediatrics?"

"Of course," Steve said, nodding to the sommelier that the wine met expectations. Maren enjoyed watching Steve take that first sip, waiting until their glasses were full, and they were alone again.

"If you can't stand being asked the same question multiple times and deal with ailments mundane to—your kind—but uncommon maybe to us parents—pick another specialty, by all means."

Steve nodded. Maren Mitchell had spunk, unafraid to render her opinion. "I have to agree. I didn't like his tone. Don't take that from anyone, but especially from *my kind*." He raised his eye.

"Trust me, the parent wanted to lob sarcasm. Now that I work there...you know what I mean." Steve nodded, realizing she also had a sensible level of self-restraint. Maren lifted her glass of chardonnay meeting his in the air.

"To health and career...and a beautiful night," he said gently, affecting the clang of their stemware.

"Yes. I can't believe I accepted this job. To finish the story, he was upset I hadn't taken Dylan's temperature. Anyone could tell he was feverish but he chided me with 'you were here two weeks ago' and 'don't you own a thermometer?'" Maren gave Steve the animated version imitating the arrogance she'd endured. He had to admit she looked enticing when slightly annoyed.

"He actually said that? Besides, that's what triage is for."

"Exactly. Thank you. He would have gone on had you not stopped by."

"Hope you didn't mind. When I first spotted the name, I thought he might be having a setback. They only listed the complaint as fever. But they hadn't paged me." Steve paused. "I thought I'd check on him." He left out the part about checking on her.

"Mind? Your staying made him leave." Steve realized he stalled after speaking with the ER doctor he needed. With Dylan down the

41

hall, Steve gave his abdomen a quick look and listen before the nurse brought Dylan's discharge papers.

"Well, he's healed. I made a note in his file. He could forgo his follow-up appointment…it's up to you."

"I just changed it to work out with my schedule. I don't mind bringing him." Maren knew that his post-op visit would merely put her mind at ease. "Anyway, long night. I had to look totally fried after orientation week, getting out the door earlier than we're used to."

"You looked fine. And tonight, lovely." He took his time delivering that, appreciating the sight of her. Maren's long auburn hair was loose in subtle curls lapping the top of her dress. She wore just a hint of make-up and lipstick, but to Steve, he was certain she didn't need any.

"In the future, call me, and if I can give Dylan a look, you won't have to take that attitude."

"Thanks. You have a lot of responsibility though. How'd you get to West Riverside?"

"I'll give you the short version. Grew up in Montgomery County, Bethesda-Chevy Chase area. Went to St. Mary's College graduating in the mid-eighties, same year the Mac computer came out. I insisted on one as a graduation gift." Steve paused at the indulgent memory. "Columbia and New York. I needed to broaden my horizons outside of Maryland."

"Culture shock from rural St. Mary's. Good call on the computer."

"The first model, no less. Oh yeah…big culture shock. Huge! Finished in '88. Got matched at UPMC. That's University of Pittsburgh Medical Center for my internship and residency."

"That would account for the black and gold on your car."

"My sister got me those license plate holders. If your dress matches team preference I'm in very deep trouble." He chuckled, sitting back to watch how she responded.

"You're safe. My college roommate at Western Maryland was a Steelers fan. I don't honestly follow football, but around here people are going a little nuts with purple. This wasn't a fashion statement." She sipped more wine and started on her salad. "How'd you get back to Maryland?"

"Oh, a fellowship at Hopkins. Worked in the city—when Baltimore was teamless—then I had enough city life and took a spot here."

"That's commitment." To her, that training path proved dedication. Determination too.

"Confinement. You went to Western Maryland?" She nodded. "Good private school. I'd have considered it, but I wanted water. Didn't they just rename it?"

"Yeah." A warm glow invaded the ivory of her cheeks. "When I saw the name change I wondered if anyone would make the connection."

"Your work will speak for itself. My turn: So you became a graphic designer, and..."

"I met Mark, my husband, in college. His family was wealthy—we won't go there—originally from Northern Virginia but they now live in Seattle." Steve noted how she said the word husband with tenderness rendered and how Seattle seemed a welcome relief.

"I think my in-laws felt Mark should have gone someplace bigger, like New England or even New York." She dismissed those ideas with her head. "We lived in Towson a short while. Actually met my boss Alicia when we took classes together." Maren tilted her water glass to her lips. Their entrées diverted them momentarily.

"Mark had a small town feel...like you, I guess. Even when he worked in Baltimore, he refused to live near the city, especially after Dylan was born. That's how we got here. He didn't mind the commute, but in the end..."

Maren noticed she had veered into personal history. Her crab cakes gave her an excuse to pause revealing anything more. The next part of her story was still sensitive. It hurt too damn much.

"So...that was a hefty professional track. No George Clooney-like, TV-type drama?" Maren eyed Steve as much to avoid where she last left off. "You promised answers if I came to dinner. Start talking, doc." She laughed out loud, wine in hand. Ready.

"I did promise." He didn't mind her calling him out. He enjoyed it, in fact. "Drama yes: Here and there. Lasting relationships: No."

Steve took another bite, pressed the cloth napkin to his lips and reached for his glass. Maren couldn't tell if he was thinking or deliberately changing the topic. His eyes looked unhappy. "Someone in med school. Three of us actually shared an apartment. Made New York somewhat affordable. Then, believe it or not, we all three landed in Pittsburgh. Better cost of living, but we still shared a place."

"The arrangement made it affordable. Isn't that what they all say?" Maren bobbed her chin processing this. "Two others?" There was a distinct glint in her brown eyes. "You're kidding me, right?" He hadn't responded immediately. "Really?" Maren questioned as she shook her head sideways.

"Apartment mate number two was a guy I'm still friends with— Paul Romano or Dr. Romano to you since he's staff, Ms. Mitchell." Tone mocked the indignant suggestion that he had lived it up with two women. "He's originally from 'the burgh' as they call it. Loved going back there."

Steve finished his glass of wine, and putting it down, seemed to unleash a memory. "They had this place called 'The Strip' and Paul would shop and make us these recipes from his grandmother, I swear. He's Italian through and through. Anyway, we definitely benefitted. If he goes back home, he still shops there and brings a few surprises."

"I'll bet you got benefits. The Strip, huh?" Maren sat back. "This just gets better and better."

Steve howled. "No…OK." He put both hands in the air as if to tamp down her concern. "You've got to know Pittsburgh. 'The Strip' is not a red-light club. It's this strip of warehouses where you buy fresh produce, meats, cheeses, bread, biscotti. Didn't name it, just loved it."

"I'll take your word for it." He seemed sincere enough to laugh at how incongruent the name and purpose seemed to the uninformed. She surmised he told the truth. A quick Internet search could confirm that if it didn't red-alert her parental controls. "So your relationship…wasn't serious?"

"Let's say, we went different paths." Steve appeared perturbed, and for a moment before he spoke again, she wondered if it was with that particular question. "After that, I …got busy building my career. Started seeing a nurse in Baltimore. She wanted more than I could give at the time. Ended another relationship last year. Wasn't going to work."

Maren listened, putting the pieces of Steve's life together. She certainly didn't mind being with him, and she imagined other women had made themselves plenty available, but that perhaps he wasn't the ladies' man that his handsome exterior suggested. "Surgery has been my commitment, no doubt about it. Looks as if it paid off or we wouldn't be celebrating, at least not for me."

"Well I'm glad we are. For your sake, this helped you to get away even a little while." Maren shifted her head, hoping to change the tone from serious.

"What? Those eyes. That grin."

"Well, I'm guessing at your age."

"Go ahead," he gestured with his hand to lob a number.

"Oh." Her grin grew wicked. "Should've known you'd make me pull for the details."

"It's way more fun that way. Come on…"

Her eyes did circles. "Thirty-eight?"

"Close. Very close." His face turned devilish, on purpose.

Maren's hand met the table with her napkin. "No fair."

Steve leaned across in a whisper. "Anyone ever tell you how good looking you are, especially when you're pissed off?" She hadn't but touched the surface of true annoyance, but he'd use any excuse to let her know she looked appealing.

"You are a little devil, aren't you?"

"I've always preferred fire in a woman to ice." He hadn't detected any of the latter in Maren, but as the night drew on he certainly saw a bit of the former. He'd stoke it, with pleasure.

"Something tells me you haven't hit 40. Thirty-nine?"

"Indeed, rolling into another decade in the spring. And you, Ms. Maren?"

"Work for it." She pushed back, careful to appear unruffled.

Steve leaned to retrieve his fallen napkin, and when he raised his head, it seemed as if he'd taken up the direct challenge.

"I was born in '63, the year of turmoil. Finished high school in '80. You're savvy about Mac computers. They came out in '84." He studied her reaction. She tried desperately to give none. "Dylan is six, born in '96. Sounded like you were married a few years before he came along?" She wasn't budging but visibly clamped her lips. "Thirty-four?"

"Close, but no."

Steve loved the way she enunciated the word "no." He'd dare her to a yes any day. "Thirty-two, born in 1970. The decade of folk rock, the Jackson 5, disco and Sonny & Cher."

"Yes, you'd be correct."

"I love robbing the cradle even more." His hand seized hers, rubbed it affectionately. "More conservative Karen Carpenter or sultry Donna Summer? Attitude, mind-set, behavior, that is."

45

Oh no, Maren mused. She wasn't making this simple. "Somewhere in between." She slanted him a glance. "You can ponder that one."

"Gladly," Steve said, raising his chin. A little clutch within her stomach told Maren that challenge didn't elude him. He might just run with it.

She turned toward the water glistening outside. "You mentioned to Dylan you have a boat. Not a sailboat, but some speed demon thing I'll bet." She paused. "Exactly. Speed demon suits the little devil in you."

"I do have a boat." Now Steve sat spine straight getting his second wind of the night. "I keep it at the yacht club. Combines speed and stability as it cuts through the water. But I used to sail, especially in high school and college."

"Really. My father owns a 30-foot Catalina. What made you pick a powerboat?"

"Versatility. Comfortable to take people out. Paul and I fish some. I haven't had it that long though. I'd put off getting it." Steve looked out the window with another ship visible, its long string of lights announcing it in the channel.

"Bought it gently used. My grandfather left us grandkids each a little stash. That's why I won't work weekends unless I'm on call. Freedom. Clears the mind."

Maren shared how she sailed as a kid and was surprised to learn that Steve, in his younger years, had taken fairly intense boating classes. Where he'd found the time she wasn't so sure.

Tempted by all five of the desserts offered to them, Maren settled upon crepes topped with lavender ice cream while Steve went for the raspberry brulée.

"Here, try a bite," Steve said, offering her some on his spoon midway through. He watched while she tasted it.

"That is good, too. Try the crepes." Steve did as directed, but their desserts brought the realization of the hour upon them. They'd remained longer than most dinner guests that evening enjoying coffee with dessert. Maren's eyelids hinted of fatigue. She revealed that they got the prescription filled and Dylan settled only after one in the morning.

Steve asked for the check and put his credit card inside the folio. "I better get you home. Big day Monday."

"Don't remind me. I still have a freelance project to finish, an appointment next week, some lectures the week after in Bethesda.

Schedule's filling fast. Thanks again. This was so nice." Maren stretched tossing her hair back. He loved the look of her silky locks flowing freely over the purple framing her neckline.

"I'm glad you could make it," he said, picking up the chiffon wrap she had draped on her chair, putting it over her shoulders.

Steve returned her to the two-story brick home she and Mark had shared. He figured they would have filled it with more children if Mark had lived. Maren told him, on the way, how much they enjoyed building it but vowed never to do it again. Their hard work showed. The house looked warm and inviting.

"Stay there, it's chilly." He came around, opened her car door, and walked her to the entrance where she sprung the lock quickly and invited him to step in while she turned on the nearest lamp.

"I'm glad we could do this. I don't know when I've been so relaxed," he said caressing a hair away from her face.

"Fabulous restaurant. Delicious meal. The view. You made great arrangements, Steve." Before Maren could say more, she felt Steve's other hand on her waist draw her close to him. His lips casually brushed her forehead before gently grazing her mouth. He cupped her chin looking deep into her brown eyes.

"Au revoir." He stood close enough that his whisper felt warm. Tingled her. "Did I say that right?"

"Perfectly," she managed. He hadn't let go of her. Maren broke the silence raising up to plant a quick kiss on his cheek, meeting him again to rub away the smidge of lipstick from where she'd deposited it.

Their eyes locked blue into brown. The fingers that had brushed his face now stroked his hair directly above his ear. He lowered his head to kiss her again, this time just a trace longer. His mouth felt firm but sensitive, meeting her needy lips that parted for his instantly.

Warmth shot past her neck, through her upper body that subtly touched his jacketed chest, down to her waist where he held her. If he hadn't, she might tumble she thought. This couldn't be happening.

He loosened his arms granting space between them. Steve's eyes softened, and his lips curved, ever slightly.

"What?" Maren asked, licking the lips he'd just kissed. Twice.

"I promised answers, but now maybe you've run out of questions. Damn."

"That's a dilemma," she said nodding up and down.

47

He sniffed. She wasn't making this easy, and he should have known better. "I need to market my services."

"You do not." She grimaced, gidily.

"Going through emails, there is one…from your boss I believe, asking if we need anything." He lifted his eyebrow, knowing just who should help him. "I think I need to let you go. We'll have to do this again."

"Yeah, that'd be nice." Her voice was all but hushed.

Steve kissed her quickly and released the grasp beneath his fingers. The tightness of her dress had caught his eyes hours ago, and he'd waited all evening to touch it, to feel the casual curve of her waist as it molded into her hips. "Goodnight."

"Bon nuit," Maren whispered, then closed the door, putting her forehead against the wood frame, as he trotted down her front steps. She had watched as he pulled up hours ago donning his dark Ray-Ban sun specs, with the top down on his Jag. She had admired his precision as he latched and secured the top back in place before exiting the convertible, then jogging up to her door.

Given his condensed life story, Maren didn't begrudge him a few pleasures like that hot car and the boat he said he used as an escape. He had devoted so much of his life—all of his twenties and beyond— to learning and perfecting his skills to make a difference for others as he had done for Dylan.

Steve Kramer had a respectable way of turning the focus onto others, not himself. That attention, that concern, forced her to question the judgments she formed over the last year. When she vented, disparaging "his kind," he took it in stride, not defensively. Yet this whole new environment—maybe his affection—scared her, too.

Sinking into her pillow that night, Maren gave thanks for all that was good—and there was plenty—and turned her thoughts to sleep. Out of the corner of her eye, she caught a glimpse of Mark's picture proudly propped on the dresser. She felt flushed remembering how she'd finished the evening. Maren could feel her heart rate rev as she resigned herself to sleep.

It was one kiss. OK, two. Three, if that last one counted. Be still inside.

Steve Kramer was now a colleague, someone she would encounter occasionally at work. Only he was all about medicine, and Maren knew what that did to her nerves. Internet searches dubbed it medical anxiety, and she'd bookmarked too many entries as proof on her web browser.

Dealing with the medical world during the day would take every ounce of emotional bravery. If only her fears would go into remission, but there was no known antidote short of facing these worries, one by one.

Steve, this man who made it his life's work, certainly knew how to connect outside of it, given how his last kiss wouldn't escape her mind. It had been brief, but in Maren's mind, it lingered much longer until she finally drifted to sleep.

Monday for Maren began meeting with Alicia, the rest of the marketing staff, and having her first discount secured with her name badge in the hospital cafeteria, grabbing iced tea at lunch. She took it upstairs to eat at her desk with a salad, carrots, and hummus she brought from home.

"The weekend: How was it?" Alicia demanded, not with any true authority. Purely personal, stemming from Friday's conversation. "Make that your date. Sunday inconsequential." Alicia slanted her head slyly.

"Really lovely. The food was out of this world, and the view spectacular."

"Will you go out again?"

"My mother asked me that when I picked up Dylan. You two have the same questions." Maren snickered though. Who wouldn't be curious? Roles reversed, she'd ask that. "I have no clue."

"You had fun?"

"Yeah, it felt odd at first. But nice getting out, being somewhere quiet to have an adult conversation, and ..." Her voice trailed off in a twinge of guilt.

"And...do tell."

"The attention was nice."

"How nice?" Alicia's voice lowered to a soft purr.

"Oh, he loved it. I put the moves on him, and the man could barely make it to his car, Alicia. He's been in the ortho ward since Saturday."

"Maren!" Her boss, but even more, her friend snorted. "I deserved that."

"Indeed, you did." Maren stabbed at her salad to finish it off, swallowing before responding. "I meant he's just very attentive, polite. Chivalry isn't dead." Flashes of Steve opening her car door, taking her hand, covering her shoulders melded into one pleasant memory.

"That's nice. I'm happy for you." Alicia crinkled the paper from the sundried tomato and chicken wrap she'd brought up from downstairs. "Whoever said modern women don't want a little of that was way off."

"Exactly," Maren concurred. "Now, I'll get back to work. Back here at 5:30 for Dylan's appointment so I'm leaving a half-hour early."

"I wonder who will get more attention?" Alicia bit back any more teasing as Maren's hand pushed the air. She wanted to finish up, Alicia could tell.

"Out of here. My boss expects work."

Even though Steve had pretty much discharged Dylan from his caseload following the ER visit, Maren kept the follow-up appointment. Dylan's get-out early from after-care ticket. Maren had to pry him from his friends, and he whined all the way back to the office wing.

"That doctor already saw me. Two doctors, Mom." Dylan fretted, feet kicking the back of the passenger seat, already taking his I-don't-want-to-be-prodded position. "Am I still sick? Will I die?" Dylan fumed. "This is stupey."

"Use a better word and stop kicking, Dylan. Lose the drama, too." Maren hated it when Dylan acted out in the car. It jolted her concentration.

Fears can often run through families, Maren had learned. She knew all too well how she modeled that fear, but she kept this appointment if for no other reason than reassurance that Dylan was OK.

Now she had misgivings, but wouldn't cancel—not on Steve or any provider without a better reason than running tight on time and meeting a first-grader's social demands. Maren Mitchell was too obsessive about things to no-show.

"Mister Rogers says always look for helpers," she offered Dylan in her most convincing voice. It was a message that the after-care program instilled especially after 9/11 and with the anniversary reactions weeks ago. "Remember how awful you felt the night you threw up? Steve helped you. Think of it that way." That was then; this was now.

50

Miffed, but with a major hissy fit averted, Dylan strutted into Steve's office. Brianna, Steve's physician assistant, seeing only one more appointment, asked if Steve wanted her to see the boy instead.

"No, I'd like to see him," Maren overheard Steve tell his PA.

The exam was pretty perfunctory since Steve had just checked him out in the ER. To silence Dylan's groans, Steve joked and hoisted him off the table with an extra swoop before landing Dylan onto his feet.

"He's healed well, Maren." A hand to her shoulder punctuated that proclamation. "Come here Dylan, let's go to my desk." He skipped to the oversized swivel and immediately did a 360 in both directions.

"Dylan!" Maren followed catching his hand before he made contact with Steve's MacBook. "That's not polite and it's *not* yours."

The boy eyed the framed photo on his bookcase. "Mom, look at this doctor's boat! Bet it goes fast. Vrooom." He spun the chair full circle, one more time.

"Dylan, you can call me Steve like your mom does." Steve leaned his body into the motion to stop the chair before Dylan got dizzy or he sent the loose papers flying on his desk.

Steve pulled additional photos from his drawer, and for a few moments, Maren thought she was completely forgotten, as they got caught up talking about fish and crabs and the difference in catching them.

"Maybe Mom would let me take you fishing?" Steve looked to Maren acknowledging she was the scheduler, that he hadn't forgotten her.

"Please Mom. Can we go fishing?" Dylan implored with eyes cast to both of them. "Please."

"The weather's still good on the bay. I'm off this weekend and next," Steve added to the boy's effort. "What do you think? You're invited, too, of course." He handed Dylan candy out of a jar on his desk.

"Thanks," Dylan replied. "May I have it now, Mom?"

"I suppose." Her disapproving look turned happy as Dylan earned two points on manners remembered. "I haven't been fishing since I was little."

"Well, now's the time. Or, bring a book, bathing suits. Relax. The yacht club has a pool and locker rooms, a dock bar though we can have lunch out on the water. Even better." He left out that it also had fine

51

dining but that wasn't important planning a guy's outing. "Does Saturday work?"

"Yeah, Saturday, Mom. Saturday!"

"OK, we can go." Maren smiled through her first-week-of-work fatigue. "Dylan, we've got to get home." New routines weren't easy on six-year-olds; not any easier on Maren. "Please settle down." He had been jumping since she said yes. Dylan's excitement level could perplex her.

"See if you can find *Arthur* or something on PBS out there," she said, motioning to the television in the waiting area. Steve's secretary had left shortly after they arrived, and now the PA had also, but Maren needed a few seconds for her own thoughts. "I'll be right there."

"Dr. Kramer..." He was in trouble from her first word. "Candy before dinner?"

"Sorry."

"Forgiven. Men and boys! So this ailment is wrapped up?"

"He's not in any contact sports is he?" A sideways shake confirmed that he was not. "Barring real physical contact, he can participate in gym. Fishing is a quiet sport. Take advantage of these early fall weekends while they last."

"Please tell me this isn't an early-rise fishing trip."

"Point taken. We'll make it at ten. Then we can do lunch."

"Deal," she said, slinging her handbag from a chair, over her shoulder. Steve peeked on Dylan and closed the door again. He blocked her pathway out. "He says it's boring but I think he found Arnie and the blue monster."

"Ernie and Cookie Monster. Just two of many Muppets."

"I live a sheltered life." He grinned broadly. "It'll be good seeing you again. You can tell me all about your first week dealing with us docs." He zoned in on her waist pulling her tighter. This could become a habit, he thought. "Now that this is all wrapped up, as you put it, I should get to know you better."

"What do you want to know?" Maren's voice was barely audible, intimating she had many secrets.

"Everything..." Steve stepped closer as the door burst open.

"Mom, where's the potty?"

"We better go," Maren said, grabbing Steve's hand for a tight squeeze that would have to be their goodbye. She suspected he had another one planned, but mom duty beckoned. "Saturday. Let's touch base end of the week."

"Bye, Dylan...down the hall, to your right." Steve Kramer shoved his laptop into his briefcase, turned out the light and headed to his parking spot with a stride in his step, evident of new energy in his life—an excitement that hadn't been there weeks ago. There was Maren, and in a few days, he'd see her again.

Chapter 4

With her first full week on the job nearing its end, Maren couldn't wait to get this next item off her hospital-encouraged checklist of wellness suggestions. Maren already ate healthy, fit in exercise on Mark's old elliptical trainer, but she had procrastinated on routine medical check-ups like the one today, the first Thursday in October.

Two years had elapsed since Maren had a complete physical and blood work, outside of what the hospital mandated for hiring. She'd been in twice for shorter visits following Mark's death with Claire Clements, one of the doctors on staff, board certified as an OB/GYN and as a family practice physician. Clements had put her on Zoloft to treat her low mood and anxiety before it became debilitating in those initial months of grieving.

She'd also given her a script for an occasional sleep aid. "Taking this job is a huge step forward, Maren," Clements said, bolstered by her willingness to try behavioral strategies. "Maybe in a few months, you won't need the Zoloft. This is for 25 mg, not 50. Let's see how you do. You'll get a lab report sent home. I'll flag anything that's off."

Her doctor pondered. "Lie back a second. I want to re-check something," Clements directed as Maren stretched down rustling the paper lining the table. Maren had picked this doctor as she had a reputation for thoroughness.

"I'm finding a small mass on your left breast...here, give me your hand," she said guiding Maren's own fingers to the site of her discovery. "Can you feel it?"

"Yeah, never noticed it before." Her amygdala sent another alarm through her; by now, an unmistakably scary sensation. "What is it?"

"A little hidden, a mass of some sort. Let's get films and a sonogram maybe. How do you feel about the birth control pills? Cycle better? You need them?"

Maren certainly hadn't needed them for their intended purpose after Mark passed away, but the severe stress had wreaked havoc on her cycle so they had added this to regulate things.

"Good question. No, not exactly. Yet. I mean…maybe."

Clements grinned amusingly. "Someone on the horizon?"

"One date. I don't know." Maren tried to wrap her mind around the question while processing the additional tests. "He works here actually," Maren explained as she rustled her paper gown to sit up. "Steve Kramer."

"Interesting." Clements washed her hands and leaned against the wall.

"Is there something I need to know?" Maren asked dead on.

Clements realized she had inadvertently raised her patient's antenna. "Only that he's a workaholic. Get ready to be the target of jealousy, especially if you work here. You can get dressed. Meet me at my desk when you're ready."

Maren did as directed, feeling her stomach tangle. Steve Kramer would indeed be easy on any woman's eyes. She had gotten that distinct impression over recent weeks, but Steve's popularity wasn't her primary concern.

Sitting across from Clements, Maren drew a deep breath. If she didn't regulate her breathing at times, she'd feel nauseous when extremely tense. "Should I schedule both?"

"Good benefits here if you're on the plan, and both will be covered. Start with the diagnostic mammogram. I'll give you orders for each. If the radiologist wants both, get them back to back." Clements finished typing her orders and clicked print. "Here you go. Let's reconvene when I get the results. Ordinarily, I'd have you sign a release so that I can send results for a surgical consult if it's needed, saving time. We'd talk first, of course." Clements leaned back mulling options. "Steve Kramer's on my referral list, but if you're an item…"

"I don't know what we are. I barely know what day it is any more." The large 10-03-2002 on the desk helped on that count.

"Curious, how'd you meet?"

"He operated on Dylan for appendicitis. Released him with a clean bill of health. We chatted here at the hospital, in the parking lot. Had dinner once." Maren paused. "I can't believe I'm doing this." She rested her hand on her stomach. "Any of this." She took another deep breath and wasn't embarrassed to show how hard she really tried to manage her worry.

"Maren, enjoy life a little. I'm glad you're resuming your career, and Steve's top notch. Well-liked," she said leaving out the 'sought after' part she'd intimated already. "You're allowed to have a personal life, you know." The doctor paused not wishing to lecture. "You're in charge here. I can give you this release if you'd just want him in on this, even for consultation."

Clements could see Maren's face losing some color so quickly clarified her remarks. "You're young. I'm not too concerned. That's why the tests. It feels more solid, but sometimes breast changes can even be a side effect of the birth control." Clements paused notating Maren's record. "I'm willing to leave that alone until we get the results." Clements straightened. "There are newer forms like the patch and the ring. Either eliminates a daily pill."

"My memory could use any assist," Maren said. She had come across the diaphragm she used with Mark when organizing her medicine cabinet. Intimacy hadn't been on her radar, as she watched Clements scribble notes and close the folder. Should it be? While she was here, cross birth control off the list, if nothing more than to keep regulating her periods.

"Let's try you on the ring. Lower estrogen exposure." Clements passed off another script and snatched a sample box out of her drawer. The release they spoke of sat on the desk.

Maren reached for a pen, pausing. "If I sign this, can I give you a verbal go ahead if I want him to know about this?"

"Absolutely, I'll note that. I can't send it without your permission. Don't stress about this, Maren. It could be nothing. If you feel comfortable talking to Steve, he's well connected from his years in Baltimore."

Maren didn't doubt Steve's vast knowledge or connections. Their relationship—if it was a relationship—was new, and like most other things in her life, she tried not to jump in too fast. Each day had enough in it already.

"I know…just need to collect my thoughts."

"Of course. It's your call, Maren. You've come so far. Don't let this take you back a few steps." Forcing a smile, Claire Clements left to see her last patient.

Be still inside. Maren hadn't used the mantra in nearly three weeks. Until now.

Curling into bed that evening, Maren frustrated herself. Relinquishing worry would not equate to perusing *101 Medical Questions You're*

Too Afraid To Ask. She'd quelled the temptation to browse medical websites.

Next Thursday she'd find herself truly ensnared in research attending lectures at the National Institutes of Health and a conference in Bethesda. This job forced her to learn facets of the medical world for projects she created, but if she didn't safeguard her off-duty free time from such web surfing, she'd drive herself to doubling her Zoloft, not cutting it in half. Enough, she thought.

Signing papers for Dylan's teachers, she placed everything on the night table and fluffed her pillow to turn in early. Then the phone rang.

"Hello," she answered figuring that it could be Steve trying to establish exact plans for Saturday. She hoped to keep it brief.

"What? No, I was at work, then...well...busy," Maren said almost defensively. "Preoccupied." She wasn't ready to talk about why her mind raced. "I haven't had news on all day," she said, groping the covers for the remote control.

At Steve's urging she clicked it on, but it was too early for local news, save for a repeat of Peter Jennings on cable. "Wait, I'll call you back."

Maren put the cordless phone down riveted by the top story out of Montgomery County. Only one other county separated theirs in Maryland. Local officials, the FBI, US Marshalls, and the Secret Service had been called in to investigate a shooting spree that took the lives of five people by six shots within 16 hours at local strip malls, at a bench outside a restaurant, and at a gas station as people fell to their deaths.

Maren punched the phone button again to redial the last incoming call. She hadn't known Steve long enough to commit his number to memory though she knew she had his card somewhere in her disorganized purse.

"Good Lord!" she exclaimed.

"I know. How could you not know this occurred?"

"Steve, ease up. I was busy. Besides, I've curbed current events." Ever since Mark's accident, WTOP news with its helpful traffic and weather on the eights, even fell by the wayside. Accident and injury reports raised her blood pressure just as ABC News had. "Just saw a report and I'll turn on the 10 o'clock news."

"I didn't mean to make you feel bad." It all hit home for Steve, knowing some of the shooting sites so close to where he grew up. "I'm

57

sorry...gut reaction 'cause everyone is shocked." He surmised tragedy tormented her since she was reluctant to share much about Mark's accident. "My parents said it's crazy. Cops at schools, parents left work early, no one wants to go anywhere."

Maren thought of her mother, now substitute teaching just two counties away from Montgomery. "Where do your parents live? You told me. I forgot."

"Chevy Chase...like the comedian, from *Saturday Night Live*."

"I know where it is, Steve. I grew up in Annapolis."

"Sorry." Steve was so used to describing his hometown to those totally unfamiliar. "The police said the homicide rate just increased 25% in one day."

"Oh Steve, I hope your family's not impacted. Did they know these people or go to these places?"

"My sister Liz lives across the bridge; my brother is in College Park getting a master's." They chatted about family and people's reactions. Steve's mother had lunch the day before not far from the gas station where one shooting occurred.

He and Maren solidified plans for Saturday and then hung up. Maren reached into her nightstand. Tonight, she most definitely needed a sleep aid.

The temperature Saturday afternoon peaked in the low 80s on the Chesapeake Bay providing plenty of sunshine for Dylan's boating expedition. Maren grew up in Annapolis, but if she had to think of the last time she was out on a boat, it wasn't a good sign. The summer after Mark's death meant no boating though this past July she enjoyed an hour sailing with her father.

Dylan went on a birthday party cruise, a totally different experience than today. Maren had to admit she was excited to see what he'd think. The photo in Steve's office at an angle didn't reveal much.

Maren phoned Steve as she pulled into the marina, and he showed them to the pier. Dylan's eyes widened at each vessel they walked past. Only one a sailboat, all others could be Steve's.

"Is this it?" he asked about the first three they passed.

Arriving alongside a 38-foot power cruiser, Steve declared, "This is my boat, Dylan." He turned to Maren. "It's 37-feet minus the bow platform, with a 12-foot maximum beam." The details meant nothing to Dylan but Steve smiled at Maren's satisfied grin. "Come here Dylan," he said, swooping him under the arms and depositing him inside the seating area.

"Personally, I like the navy blue hull and the white deck," she said as he took her hand leading her from the dock to the stern platform. "Sharp."

"Glad you approve." He tugged at her waist to give her a squeeze closer to him. "I think my fishing mate is already lost at sea."

"Wow Mom, come see. It even has a kitchen," Dylan exclaimed having run straight to the stairs, lowering himself the four steps to see inside.

"And a potty and shower, too. You gotta see." He came out and literally pulled Maren by the arm. Steve followed them stepping down past the bridge.

"Impressive," Maren declared, surveying the Corian counters, teak floor, and leather booth that could comfortably seat 4-6 people around a dinette table you could remove to create sleeping space. The galley featured a small cooking surface, sink, and flat screen television.

Dylan by now had crawled into the expansive forward berth, the rounded queen-sized bed, which took 85% of the cabin providing a few feet for changing clothes or gliding the drawers underneath the bed.

"Do you ever take naps in here?" Dylan asked. One would think he never experienced opening and closing doors as he maneuvered those separating the sleeping quarters. Dylan slapped them open and shut several more times.

"You will be if you don't settle down, Dylan," his mother cautioned. "Let me get some sunscreen on you." She corralled him long enough to lather his face and arms for the second time today.

"I don't think I've ever seen eyes that wide," Steve said amused "Outside of my niece and nephew this summer, he's the first little kid aboard." Maren looked concerned until the lecture began.

"Dylan, let's get a few things straight," Steve started, emphasizing such words as *always* in reference to wearing his life jacket and *never* in relation to climbing on anything—ever! When he made Dylan repeat everything, Maren breathed easier.

"I figured we'd go out on the bay, anchor to fish and have lunch." If curiosity was contagious, Maren had surely caught some from her son as she opened the small stainless refrigerator to find it stocked with water, juice, beer and wine, sandwiches and salads in labeled containers.

"Don't look in the back," Steve cautioned. "Labeled bait. Worms are above deck, on ice."

Maren slid her sunglasses down her nose just long enough to peer at Steve. The raised corners of her lips gave tentative indication. Since they were out of the sun, she removed them entirely, still collecting her thoughts.

Dylan had since discovered that under the boat's deck resided a "secret hiding place" or small sleeping area with cushioned seating and lights. He proclaimed to them that if he could stay in there, maybe he would take a nap, even though he'd outgrown the need.

"So..." Steve prompted, as she silently surveyed things. "You can stay at the yacht club if you'd be more comfortable?"

Maren's head bobbed, methodically. "Steve Kramer...you do plan ahead, don't you?" She put the tube of sunscreen into her bag, which she'd deposited onto the leather cushions in the galley. In it, she had packed the accoutrements Steve suggested such as bathing suits, towels, and a change of clothes. When she asked if she should prepare food, he was quite adamant. He really meant it that they could spend the day here. Several, she mused, pushing that thought aside as soon as it registered. Maren continued nodding as she surveyed the head with sink, commode and partition that could create a small but handy shower.

"I detect struggle here," he mocked slightly. "Like speech and language skill."

"Oh stop." She nudged him. "I had no idea when you invited us that it would be this... inviting. You bought this used?" Good consumer move, she thought.

"Gently so," he replied. "Well, let's get going. You need to change first? There's the head, and obviously those doors over there work quite well." They both laughed.

"I wore my bathing suit, but thanks," she replied, crossing her arms to hoist her polo revealing the top of a one-piece teal suit with a halter strap around her neck and a V neckline. It plunged just enough to convince Steve that between Dylan's excitement and Maren, just being Maren, today wouldn't be an ordinary Saturday afternoon.

Starting the trip, Dylan sat next to Maren, her arm around him as Steve piloted the boat precisely knowing when to slow down, throttle up, and give way to other vessels. He understood these waters, the channels, and markers. He had to be as comfortable with electronic gadgetry here as he was with the high-tech, computer-assisted surgical devices in the operating room.

When they first anchored, Maren grabbed the sunscreen again, applying some onto her face, neck and top of her chest, legs and arms, too.

"Here, give me that," Steve said taking the tube as he saw her contort herself to reach her shoulders.

Spreading some in his open hand, he rubbed it along her neck, shoulders and back. She had such smooth skin as he caressed the sunblock into it. "How's that?"

"With a little neck massage? Heaven." She tilted her head. Smiled. "Want some?"

Steve grinned. "If you're offering." He removed his collared shirt. Maren was glad she had put her sunglasses back on, as her eyes sized up his chest, tanned, muscular, with chest hair that made her wish she could apply it there. Steve had taken the tube, lathered most of himself but handed it over.

"A little tight, here," she said, kneading Steve's neck. Maren slid her hands down his back two or three times.

"Hazard of the job." His glance signaled how good it felt.

By mid-afternoon, Dylan had already learned about the Thomas Point Lighthouse, been awed by the bridge spanning 4.3 miles, and caught a few fish but no "keepers" as he learned to call them. They finished most of their lunch earlier but munched throughout their anchoring.

By four, after being in the sun on and off, Maren removed Dylan's shoes and socks, convincing him to look at some books about the bay that she brought along. Within minutes he nodded off in what he declared to be his—and only his—hideaway spot next to the stairs. It afforded enough room for possibly two adults to lie down, so for Dylan, it seemed like paradise found.

"Go on up to the bridge and relax," Steve suggested. "The hardtop shades the cushioned seats, hopefully with some breeze blowing through."

"Here, I'll carry something," she offered, reaching for her wine cooler he had poured into a plastic cup. She stepped up and positioned herself comfortably propping her feet. He followed her up the few steps with a beer. Steve's eyes soaked in every detail, including her nails, painted in delicate mauve.

"My boat has never been happier," Steve said taking the seat opposite hers, delighting in the full prospect of her bathing suit, no longer covered by her shorts. Those weren't on minutes ago as he watched her climb up the steps.

As it was October, he could see evidence of contrast, indicating Maren had been outdoors in recent months. The more she moved, the more white flesh he caught glimpses of peaking out from her suit. Dylan could stay put, he thought, but Maren could keep moving.

"How often do you do this?" she asked him.

"Not often enough. Just got this in June. My sister Liz and her husband Tim came out once or twice. She lives over there, in Stevensville. They have a boat, too." His outstretched hand pointed toward Kent Island, and as the faint breeze blew on his hair, Maren enjoyed watching him.

Steve had worn navy swim shorts that met his mid thigh. Sunglasses kept away rays from the 80-degree heat. His collared shirt, which had been off, then back on, was now in the cabin. A healthy glow revealed itself.

"Paul and I go fishing, some. Since Vicki, I see less of him, but when she teaches weekend classes we escape. She's a nurse and childbirth educator. If she's here we have to behave, but she usually brings a book and ignores us." He grinned as if a little boy who could get into mischief. "But Vicki helped decorate and outfit this. I'm indebted."

Maren had noticed the nautical accents, beautiful Ralph Lauren comforter and plush pillows so appropriately chosen with seashell motif. The galley seemed stocked with just enough gadgets one might use, but not enough to clutter it.

"Isn't he your med school friend? And, she works at the hospital…was in my orientation class."

"She does. Paul and I do go back that far. I'll have to introduce you. How was your first official week?"

"Hectic. So much to learn, but Alicia liked my suggestions for projects…and told me your department recently requested brochures."

"Told you we needed marketing." Steve beamed. "Schedule working out?"

"So far…first week's been flexible. I go to NIH Thursday and to a Bethesda meeting so I'll be out of the office."

"That's in Bethesda."

"Yeah, across from the Naval Hospital. Alicia suggested the medical library since I'm there, or another time." She had so much information to gather, and only a moderate foundation of science courses to help her form a base.

"Emphasis on another time. Not this week."

"Steve, it's my job. You know, the one you encouraged me to take and we celebrated at that lovely dinner." Maren moved her legs again adjusting the way she sat. There flashed another tan line Steve caught out of the corner of his eye. "Thanks again for dinner. It really was outstanding." She held up her wine cooler as if to make a second toast following that night's formal one.

"I'm glad you liked it. I did, too. Seriously, another person got shot yesterday in Virginia. Crazy shit's happening over there."

"Good thing you said that out of Dylan's range." She frowned at him. "I know, it's awful," she said, settling into a profoundly pained expression. Everyone tuned into news reports, even if they weren't news junkies. If you didn't hear them yourself, you heard them talked about no matter where you went. Tuning into the radio or never missing the morning or evening news now seemed a matter of survival the closer you got to the Beltway. "What do you want me to do? I have to go."

He stopped to check on Dylan, returning up the steps to his seat. "Sound asleep. OK…let's table this 'til later."

"Yes, new topic. It's so peaceful. As you said, you don't get to enjoy this often."

"Come over here," he whispered, motioning for her to sit on his lap. Though the helm seat was doublewide, Steve took enough of it that she'd have no other spot. She lifted herself off her cushioned seat and did as the captain instructed. Teal might become his favorite color starting today, Steve thought, especially as it sat on top of him.

"Why are you whispering?" Maren asked, leaning toward him. Anchored by an inlet, no one was near save for the gulls and wildlife hovering high above.

Steve skimmed his fingertips along the outline of Maren's face, following her jawline, while he moistened his lips to tell her, "Checking on your son reminded me. I never got to do this, days ago."

Steve framed her face, fondled the clip that kept her long hair off her neck, and pulled her tighter to taste the wine cooler she'd been drinking. Maren relaxed in his arms, clutching one hand around his neck. After deepening the kiss and enjoying how his mouth cruised over hers, he let her go only to feel her gentle breath against him. "I should do *this* more often," he said softly.

"Mmm, I can't believe it." Her hand had crept to the back of his head, while she realized that her other hand had found its way flat against his tanned chest. Totally unaware of gulls and the waves lapping along the boat's hull, Maren's mind fixated only on Steve.

"Can't believe what?" His breath perked her earlobe higher than his boat's radar could send a signal.

"That I'm here on this absolutely gorgeous day, blue water, clouds in the sky…warm…with you." Maren slid her free hand up his back, without having moved the one that enjoyed his chest.

"You call it warm; I call it hot." Steve fingered the strap on her halter. "Present company is very hot." As he nuzzled Maren along her neck, she breathed in the mixed scent of his cologne, the sun, and the salt all in one.

"If someone had told me a month ago that I'd be here, dating this guy…" Her words dropped off as she leaned over, creating a little wiggle room between them. The more she leaned, however, the better view she created straight down the V of her neckline. As soon as she caught on, and saw Steve's attention trail lower, her cheeks flushed, and not from the sun.

"I stand by my prior assessment," he said, realizing the situation. Steve's lips parted, releasing an appreciative sigh, as he stroked a loose hair off Maren's forehead. "Can I ask you something?"

"I guess." She hesitated. "Go ahead."

"Hot stuff and great views aside," he said looking into her face. "On a serious note, something tells me you haven't dated until now." Steve boosted his glasses above his brow, and ever so gently removed Maren's so he could see into her eyes. "Is that OK to ask?"

She nodded that it was. The slight quiver to her lip and tear forming on one eyelash told him what her words couldn't. Steve wiped her tear before it could drop with the backside of his hand, while his other rested gently on her waist. Focus on the cleavage; forget the damp eyes, she wanted to say. But she couldn't muster a sound.

Steve didn't push her to speak, leaving the gulls to fill the silence.

"Sorry, that might not have been the best response." Maren lowered her chin slightly. Steve caught it, held it.

"Non-verbal works. I didn't ask for the best answer. You gave me an honest one." His eyes, the color of the cool water, shot back compassion. He moved his other hand to her waist.

"I know it's time," Maren said, sniffling back another tear. "After 12 years being part of a couple, it seems surreal. I feel so, unprepared."

"Who is, if life or love takes a turn?"

"I guess you're right." She composed herself, able to smile past momentary sadness. "Thanks." Oddly enough, something told her he might know more than she had figured about such turns of fate. "Very understanding for someone who I guess never really was married." She looked at him sheepishly given their exchange over a week ago.

"Maren, even those of us who've been single a while don't date all the time." She cocked an eyebrow. "I guess there are some—no doubt—but most aren't in dating mode 12 months out of any given year." Steve chuckled. "And if they profess to be, they're probably lying. You're doin' great." He let the words settle between them. "But if you're not ready for this step, then just let me know where the line starts forming." He lifted her chin again. "I'll camp out."

"Well, you've been a surprise in more ways than one." Maren let a free hand drag through the back of Steve's wind-tousled hair. He laughed a little. "And I think you've jumped to the head of any line that never was or would be."

"You underrate yourself Maren Mitchell."

"A little surprised that I'm dating…a doctor and throw in that I'm working in a freaking hospital, after I swore I hated them," she said, her eyes darting in disbelief. "Shock me back to life."

"Any time you need a little wake up, just let me know." He kissed her on the forehead and shifted slightly in the seat. Sensing she'd wiggle away like a snake shedding its skin, he said, "You're fine. Stay here." Her glasses had fallen from her forehead so they shifted yet again to get them, and she put them on now that the afternoon sun shimmered off their skin. Steve did the same.

Maren's hand found its way back to his chest while her other hung onto his shoulder. "It's nice out here…relaxing."

"As they say, a captain always needs a crew, but this vessel is small. I'll make it exclusive. A crew of one." He tugged at her waist. "You seem to know a few things about boats. I've watched you today. I can teach you the rest."

"Oh really," she said. "I'm not convinced we'd focus too well on nautical lessons, with this attraction going on—that isn't totally one-sided you know."

"I'm getting that impression, but I love hearing you say it."

Maren linked her arms around Steve's neck and drew him in this time. "Maybe warm isn't the right word after all." She pulled his mouth in to lay her lips on his. Steve's mouth opened to Maren's, and when his tongue found hers to tease, it matched Maren's initiative. "Getting hotter, for sure."

"Do you know the meaning of your name?" he asked when they took a moment's retreat.

"Not…really." She wondered what he was up to. Though his sunglasses now hid his eyes, Steve seemed completely and utterly mesmerized—his one hand fondling her suit strap, the other comfortably on her lower back, inviting itself lower with each rock of the waves.

Her own breathing had quickened. Their heart-to-heart a moment ago stilled any anxiety. So it had to be the moment, Steve's hands, his words, her thoughts. Kisses. Everything.

"Maren…means 'of the sea' and if I had to rhyme it, I'd say, 'you were meant, just for me.'" He brought his mouth down to hers, harder now, testing a little more possession. She leaned into him, and she was certain that if she could feel her own heart flutter underneath the bit of teal between them, so could he. He had. His hand found its way from her waist to the bottom of her breast. It idled there like one of the gauges on the instrument panel behind him. To Steve, she brought better effects than the beer he had put aside. He could feel her registering within him.

Maren felt the faint formations of his beard as he grazed her skin along her neck again. "Doctor, captain, amateur poet, too."

"I can add to the list, 'cause if your son wasn't in there, we could…" Steve stopped. Perhaps he'd taken that too far. "See what you do to me?"

Peering anywhere but into his eyes would confirm what she had done. She gave him the look women give when they honestly realize that the myth about men having dozens of daily sexual thoughts is indeed no myth at all.

"We'll keep your roles to those. For now, Captain." She smiled, tapping his nose with the tip of her mauve fingernail. Then her chest brushed across him reaching for and handing him his beer. To distract him, she hoped. Only for several seconds that seemed like long minutes. Steve savored the feel of her breasts grazing him and wondered how he might shorten the for-now part.

"Your week ahead?" she asked.

"Surgeries, office hours, papers to push, boring, dreadful meetings. I hate sitting through so many now."

"You're like my son. Always needing to be active."

Steve swallowed the perfect comeback. She squelched that path, but now, prancing around his boat, with unmistakably contoured tan lines challenging his eyes, she surely wasn't making this easy. Steve hoped he had a few more bright October days before shrink-wrapping the boat for the season. More than that, he hoped teal would return in all its glory.

"Seriously, I don't want you traveling to NIH and Bethesda. Isn't there any way you can get out of it? You want to go to the National Medical Library, we'll plan a day, and I'll take you myself. I'll show you around, shop, we'll have dinner with my folks. Just not now, Maren."

"Steve, I appreciate your concern. Do you really think I want to drive the Beltway and go there this week? I have to. One meeting is at a hotel, and unless they call it off, I have to go." After Mark's accident, driving, especially when Dylan was in the car, made her cautious, at the very least, and left her in need of a massage or a glass of wine, in worst cases.

"No I'll bet you could…"

"No I cannot. There is a conference. It's on Thursday. I just started this job. I am required to be there." With each level of insistence, Maren's voice rose, maybe to convince him…or herself.

"Someone's mad." Both startled when a little voice joined them after the boy behind it crawled up the steps from the cabin below.

"Well look what the fishing line dragged in," Steve said as Dylan rubbed his eye with one balled fist, balancing with the other outstretched arm. Steve took another swig and put his beer aside.

Maren gave him a silence-this motion regarding their conversation.

He complied, hoisting Dylan onto his lap. It wasn't the same sensation he'd enjoyed for the better part of the last hour, but Dylan seemed to love the attention, and Maren, he knew, took notice. Dylan craved a little male contact, and Steve was happy to oblige. He genuinely liked kids, and there was something about showing off his 15,000-pound toy to another male that thrilled him, albeit one with perhaps a 15-minute attention span.

"I'm hungry," Dylan said.

"Hungry, after that lunch?" Maren seemed amazed by her son's growing appetite. "I'll see if the Captain here will let us clear out the rest of his stash."

"Go right ahead. It might go home with you anyway."

She started down the steps, such that Steve saw her backside all right. This time in teal. Turning, as if she could sense his eyes on her, she added, "Except for the bait, right?" But Steve sensed that was just a ploy to show him that she knew full well he was studying every inch of her, behind the sun specs that covered his eyes. Ray-Ban sunglasses in his car; Oakley brand on his boat. The man knew how to accessorize.

What food they hadn't consumed before, they polished off. Anchor secured, Steve drove wowing Dylan with the wake that his inboard engine created behind them. When he told Maren to hang on to Dylan, in her lap now, he meant it. Dylan had wondered how fast this boat could go from the first picture he'd seen. When his hair flew into his mom, Dylan knew this was fast. Steve throttled to full speed, skimming atop the water on their way back to the marina.

As they tied up, Steve didn't offer any direction as Maren hopped out and handled the lines, without his asking. She knew how to tie a nautical knot and crawled back on to secure other things before leaving the boat for the day.

Maren and Dylan deposited their bags on lounge chairs long enough to take a refreshing dip in the yacht club pool. Dylan and Steve sat poolside as Maren walked up after changing in the pool house.

"Steve says my name means 'son of the sea.' That means you must be the bay mom," Dylan proclaimed with vigor.

"OK...not analyzing that," she said. "And I thought my parents spoiled you." Maren noticed that Steve not only extended Dylan's vocabulary, but also gave him a beach ball and a cap with a striped bass decal. The fish looked as if it jumped from the fabric as much as Dylan kicked his feet along the pool ledge.

"Shoes. Strap these sandals on," Maren directed. They walked to her Ford Focus, which had been the subject for 20 minutes by phone

one night as they confirmed plans. She had traded in her old car for a fuel-efficient hybrid with improved safety features. Steve buckled Dylan into the back.

"Thanks for suggesting this. I had a great time, and Dylan had a blast."

"You think?" Steve laughed. "Glad it worked out. Tomorrow's off limits."

Maren pulled her head from the trunk and with two hands closed it down. "Is that so?"

"Steelers kick off at one. I try to catch the games at the bar here, if not on TV. They have several big screens."

"Well, enjoy yourself." Maren planted a quick kiss to Steve's cheek. "I'm sure I'll see you around this week." She stepped into her car, windows down with Steve leaning into hers. "Thanks for lunch, too. Sorry you don't have leftovers."

Steve's shoulders shrugged. "Would have been yours anyway." He lingered, arms resting on her window. "Dylan...dude. Be good for your mom, OK?"

"Next time can I drive? Thanks Dr. Steve!"

"Captain Steve here, I think, Dylan." Maren said turning to see him all buckled into the backseat. "I think you'll be part of the crew." There went Steve's notion of a crew consisting of one.

Enjoying the competition for the helm, Steve waved as they drove off. A crew of one—or two—had made this an especially good day.

Chapter 5

Maren had done her best to curtail herself on PubMed and WebMD the rest of the weekend, though at work, the sites helped. The research she gained could get her up to speed when she had to write and design collateral materials.

She buried the medical book on her coffee table under a stack of newspapers, not wishing to really read anything. She called first thing Monday, closing her office door, to get her tests scheduled, but radiology was booked until the following Wednesday. Ravens fans around the office talked about their victory, unfortunately with injuries on the field. Not enough of a distraction to steal Maren's mind from worrying about her own health.

Briefly, she wondered how Steve's team fared since she hadn't heard from him. Just as well. Speculating whether to tell him what she faced brought with it a trickle of tears. Maren berated herself for those, too.

A woman in her thirties was said to be at her prime, nurturing children, career underway, and sexually in her peak years. For more months than she cared to remember, Maren had missed a man's attention. She knew Steve couldn't take his eyes off of her Saturday, admiring her cleavage and trim figure that unfortunately she'd obtained by struggling to eat on any given day last year. Part of her enjoyed the tease; the other part wanted to hide under the covers and never let a guy like Steve near her—doctor or red-blooded male.

Maren planned to hide under those covers soon making this tiring day come to an end. She had just helped Dylan get his bath and settle with Cookie Monster and his books at 7:30. That character seemed juvenile for his age, but after losing his father, Dylan regressed some. A comfort creature, she figured as she heard the phone ring for the second time that evening.

"Hey, how are you?" Calling Maren suddenly restored Steve's energy. "Just pulling out of the lot. Can I stop by?"

"Well…it's been a day."

"Yeah, it's all over the news, I'm told." Steve's stressed secretary had filled him in hours ago.

"Nationwide unfortunately. Mark's mother called from Seattle...used to live in Northern Virginia. Only she's freaking out about Maryland...and Dylan." Slumped posture on her sofa framed her frustration.

"I can be there in ten. I won't stay long. Just want to see you." Maren gave Steve the go-ahead, making him swear he wouldn't disturb the Muppets—not even ring the doorbell—as Dylan was in bed with his stuffed animals.

She kept watch and let Steve in quietly. He could hear what everyone heard these days. Television news. Maren had the family room TV tuned to CNN, now standard fare, mostly out of Dylan's earshot.

His first real glimpse of her home's interior, Steve took refuge on the sofa sectional offering comfort after a long day. Eyes surveyed the large coffee table that easily became the focal point and wall unit housing her television and small stereo. After he leaned in to the plush pillows, Steve didn't notice much outside of Wolf Blitzer and the Montgomery County Police briefings.

If you didn't see the reports the first time, the clips aired repeatedly imprinting the images. Steve's mouth gaped at a repeated news segment, while Maren buried her head in her knees. She'd drawn them up protectively into her chest as they sat next to one another.

"Incredible," he said, leaning against the sectional. "Targeting kids." Today's sniper attack left a 13-year-old boy critically wounded on his way to school in Bowie, Prince George's County not even an hour from them. "You can tell even the authorities are struggling with this." The Montgomery County police chief described before cameras how shooting a child was getting far too personal.

"Yeah...it's getting personal all right." Maren would have said she couldn't imagine such pain and loss, but she had her dose, only a different kind. After 2001, everyone lived with uncertainty and terror from 9/11. Now, no one felt safe, based upon unknown assailants and random attacks in October of 2002 around Washington, Virginia, and Maryland.

Maren burrowed her head into Steve to keep from watching any more. He reached for the remote, muted the sound, and slipped his other arm around Maren, massaging tension from her neck. "What's with the call you got?" Steve asked. "It must have rattled you. I can feel it in your shoulders." He shifted so that he could massage them with both hands.

"Mark's mother, my former mother-in-law, actually asked—make that practically demanded— that I send Dylan indefinitely to Seattle." She sighed a heavy breath. "I don't need this from them. I so don't." Maren paused, closing her eyes. "That feels so good."

"People who work at desks get tight right here," he said, pressing a trigger point in her upper back. "You wouldn't do that, I'm figuring. Send Dylan out there, I mean."

"Hell no," she said, so uncharacteristic that Steve stopped momentarily, leaning his head into her to stop his chuckling at her disdain. "Their house in Fairfax had more glass than a Baccarat crystal plant. I'm sure their Seattle one does, too. Dylan would hate it." Maren shook her head. "It's their implication that they know best. Some things never change."

"Not a good relationship, I take it?" Steve had stopped plying her muscles when Maren turned, and he noticed her eyes heavier than he had seen them Saturday, with a tinge of red. Like the first night he saw her in the hospital. "You want a cup of tea?"

"Yes, I'll…."

"No, stay there," he said, walking over to her kitchen.

She got up and followed him anyway. "Mark could be determined, but his family is way over the top. If you call bullying the basis of a relationship, then I'd have one with his parents. Otherwise, I steer clear outside of holidays, sending a school photo and birthday cards. I should drop those," she muttered.

"Sounds stressful." As if in command of his surroundings, he filled the teakettle and sparked the burner on the gas range while Maren rested her elbows on the island holding her head over it. "OK, tea bags?"

"In the canister to the left." Maren's kitchen was tidy and well stocked. "Constant Comment—decaf if there is one." Steve retrieved hers and Earl Grey for himself. His attention wandered causing Maren to raise her head.

"These your labs?" he asked seeing paperwork in full view on the countertop. Hospital envelope cast aside, the report with numeric values caught his eye.

"Yeah, HR and the wellness department told us to get everything updated. I haven't even looked at them. Tell me if they're good."

She'd ventured into the pantry closet to see what they could snack on, opening a box of shortbread cookies.

"Well, you must be eating healthy with these HDL's. Looks good to me," he commented, flipping to the next page and one thereafter. Pausing, he moved closer to Maren. "What's this?"

Offering him a cookie, she saw duplicates of the orders to get a diagnostic mammogram and breast sonogram in Steve's hands. "Both?" he asked. "Diagnostic?" Not a routine screening.

"You notice everything." She seemed annoyed. No more mulling this. "I didn't realize they sent another copy, for heaven's sake." She snatched the papers from his hand and tossed them back on the counter.

"You look frustrated. Everything OK?" Steve turned off the teakettle and reached for two mugs from the cabinet above, glass door revealing what he needed. "Maren?"

Once poured, she took her teacup, and dangled the bag as she chose her words. The kitchen island separated them.

"I had a routine check up. Put that off several months." Maren held her hands like a prisoner, emphasizing, "I know, I know. Bad." Steve started to say something, but she was afraid of hearing a lecture about procrastinating on something as important as healthcare. That message—working with it day in, day out—had become abundantly clear.

"Let me finish," she said. "Have your tea." Steve eyed the trashcan to jettison his teabag. Maren could tell his ears wanted more. "She found a small…something on my left side…a mass, a lump. Claire Clements did." Steve already surmised that detail by the physician's name on the orders. They had collaborated many times. "Called to schedule, but I can't get in until next week."

"No, I can bump that up." He sipped his tea.

Maren still hadn't taken the bag out of her cup, nervously bouncing it up and down, as if to buy time.

"She said she sends cases to you. I actually signed a release so that you can get a copy of the report. I just have to verbally tell her to send it your way."

Shifting how he leaned into the counter, Steve loosened now that she leveled with him.

"She also said you had good connections, and I'd have to really consider your involvement since I knew you on a personal level."

Maren looked straight at him. "I said we knew one another, but at that point, we'd had what? One date."

Steve drew in a breath. "Yeah, boundaries a little blurry…already. Doctors don't date patients." He smirked. "They certainly don't make out with them."

Maren met his face, matched the memories formed Saturday, with knowing eyes. "I had almost an entire day of ethics in orientation. I figured as much." Maren finally tossed her tea bag into the trash and asked, "Your thoughts?"

She saw his grin grow even wider. "I'm all for kissing, necking and wanting you on my boat," he said, eyes soft on Maren. "Drop the boat part. No qualifiers. Though the boat is nice."

"About the topic at hand, silly." She shook her head at him.

"Well, I don't know what we're dealing with yet." Steve moved around the island, set his cup down and put his arms around her from behind. Just his conveying "we're dealing," in the plural, provided comfort. Maren nestled her head into him and he nuzzled her hair.

"You know I care. That's obvious I hope. I'll help whatever way I can, or that you want. But she's right. It's a little complicated on the how part."

"Can we sit down?" Maren looked weary. "I was heading to bed when you called."

Steve made room on the coffee table for their mugs, pushed aside the sniper headlines from *The Washington Post,* and found the book she'd been reading about what patients wanted to know but were too afraid to ask.

"Maren, when was your appointment?"

Embarrassed with the book jacket in full view, she responded meekly, "Thursday after work. I planned to tell you, or I wouldn't have signed that release. I just had to process all this." Constant Comment helped with every sip. "Besides, a lot happened that day if you recall. Saturday was so beautiful. I tried to cast it aside."

Perhaps she shouldn't have gone out with him, for if she hadn't he wouldn't have kissed her, fondled her, and intimated that he might like more. And her dreams might not have included visions of him with a muscled and tanned chest her hands had enjoyed, wondering where else her hands could cruise. "Steve…"

"Yes." His voice was deep as he cradled her on the sofa, his tea in one hand.

"You have a choice here, too, you know." Shifting so she could see him. "I don't want to be a burden. You don't need that, and if things...or if I have to..."

He set his mug down deliberately. "Where's this going?"

Maren fell silent. "I'm not sure. I don't want this to be all about me. We just started dating."

Steve rubbed his brow, and Maren could see his eyes harden. "There's never a good time for these things. What are you thinking?"

He heard her frustrated sigh. Steve had seen and heard it all before with women first struck by the news—sometimes because he was the one who broke it to them—news that they might face a diagnosis evoking worst-case fears.

"If..." he paused. "If this is your way of telling me I can walk away, from you, from this...that's not happening." His vehemence made her silent. "We'll deal with this. It's not scaring me away from you."

Hyper-focused on her own beliefs—faulty ones at that, Steve thought—he considered if Maren had even heard him until her questions came.

"So what should I do?" Maren tossed up her hands. "Do these things always come out or do I live with it? Best guess." She hesitated, looking up. "We need test results, I know. I'm trying to make a coherent thought, but I'm so..."

"You're worried. And, I don't make guesses. Rarely even educated ones," Steve said, one hand on hers. "These are your choices. While I appreciate Claire's referrals, and I handle these procedures, I can line you up with someone far more specialized."

Steve brushed his hand over hers just to make sure she heard him. "I can help you think things through, staying objective though." Yet Steve knew detachment was nearly impossible given that he thought of her often, planning the next time he'd see or talk with her. "Any family history? What else did Claire say?"

"I don't think so. I should check that out with Mom though. Dr. Clements also said fluctuating hormones and my medication may play a role...changing that, too." Maren proceeded to tell him that she had started Zoloft after Mark died. His eyes implied agreement. "I'd like to get off of it so she cut it to 25 mg."

"This might not be the time for that. See how you do on this dose."

"So much for my opinion." She groaned. "I don't want a lot of medicine with side effects."

"I'm being practical here, Maren. You have another stressor."

"I know." She mentioned birth control pills, but Steve cast a curious look.

"I dated the volunteer fire department!" Her elbow jabbing into his side broke the tension. "My cycle, OK." Turning to him. "I'm on something else low dose."

Steve patted her hair, softly chuckling at her, but registering the satisfying details. "You never discovered this lump before?"

Steve's skin smelled of musk, an intriguing scent after a long day, not splashed on merely to make an impression. She drew it in as she nestled closer against his shirt.

"No, I haven't," she said. "This new?" Maren's hand reached up to finger a gold chain. Who wouldn't have? The topic: Personal. His shirt: Enticing. Unbuttoned at the neck, it revealed patches of masculine dark hair. She wasn't sure what she wanted to play with more—the chain or the chest.

"Romano and Vicki gave it to me yesterday. They went to Italy last month, and he's always worn one. It's kind of a running joke," he explained.

Her fingers let the chain fall but not before she brushed his skin and plied his neck a little to ease it. "Did your team win yesterday?"

"No…good game but crushed in the Superdome."

"I'm sorry," Maren offered. She fondled his shirt. Steve saw agony in Maren's eyes again. "I hate waiting. I loathe worry."

"That's why I'm calling tomorrow to get you seen sooner. I'll need that release. Have her send it first thing."

"I will. Worst case, what am I looking at? Cancer, clearly, but the details?"

Steve heard words like chemo, disfigurement, infertility, and all the what-if's assailing her brain, now lobbed at his. She searched, but his blue eyes were as calm as ocean waters after a gentle rain. "Where is it?" He looked at her, staring down at the V formed underneath her blouse.

"Left side, lower quadrant, she says." Maren parted one button on her blouse giving him the invitation to continue.

The doctor in him wanted to reach inside to find answers they both wanted; the man in him wanted to also, only in a much different way.

Steve could offer a second opinion. Right here. Right now. She hoped he might say that Claire Clements was imagining things.

"I don't mind." She straightened, opened another button. "See what you think."

Ever so gently, Steve unfastened the remaining ones and opened the front clasp of her lacy bra, exposing only what he had to, to touch her. Trying not to be enticed, he looked up at her eyes as he blew on his hands to warm them. But his touch brought a shudder nonetheless as she arched toward him, and he decided staring past her allowed him to concentrate better.

Maren looked elsewhere, anywhere, even at startling headlines in the paper or to their tea left unattended. Only Steve's touch was ever so present. She drew in a breath, bending her neck to ease the tension, but it wasn't all anxious tension.

"Here, lie back." Steve shifted her up and fluffed a pillow so that she could lie down. He kneeled next to the sofa, where he had eased Maren onto her back, laying her flatter. He raised her arm above her head.

"Your team may not have won, but looks like you've advanced to second base at least." She grinned. "I know, totally different sport."

"Little live wire, aren't you?"

"I could say something else, but I won't."

"Good. Stop talking, will you?" He applied both light and medium touch.

Maren tried to ignore his fingers running over her left breast, in a circular motion, the right, and again the left, including under her arm and the surrounding flesh. Wincing, she stiffened.

"Relax, it'll make this easier." His fingers started circling more firmly now. "Breathe. I'm sorry. Best to do this with different pressure." Maren methodically drew in a breath. She met his eyes. "I don't see anything off in shape or color, no sores or discharge. But...

"It's your first time checking me out, is that it?" She let out a heavier breath. Indeed, he had to use his eyes, not merely his hands, at some point. "I haven't noticed anything. Neither did she." When finished, he fastened her clasp and buttoned her part way, leaving her to do the rest. Not that it mattered to Maren. "So what is it?"

"Size of a large marble, maybe. Could be a fibroadenoma, which could be ruled out with a needle biopsy...or something else. We'll want your test results."

Maren rested her hands on her partially exposed blouse, remaining flat. In exasperation, she closed her eyes, dragging a hand through her hair.

"I still wouldn't jump to conclusions," Steve said. "You're young. Did you breast feed Dylan?"

"Almost a year's worth." She sat up, and Steve rose up from the floor to sit next to her again.

"Well, that decreases your risk factors. Diet? Exercise? Much alcohol?" He snickered. "Partying with the guys at the VFD?"

"Every night, all night." She rolled her eyes. "I like wine occasionally. I thought it's good for you."

"Given your labs, a little red wine has probably helped."

"I'm so annoyed. I do eat well. I could exercise more. Everyone can."

"They're starting construction on an employee fitness club, did you hear?"

"Yeah, someone mentioned it as a benefit during orientation. So I just have to wait. Lovely." Maren's lips fell into an upside down U.

"Yes, you wait. You have to get up tomorrow. So do I." He rose from the sofa, stretching out his hand for her to grab on and do the same. "It takes some determined effort to steer your mind…from this or the craziness in and out of the Beltway…but try, OK?"

"All right," she said, following his slow strides to the front door.

"You'll hear from me, but get me the release. First thing. By 8:30. Please."

If this was Steve Kramer's typical commanding style, Maren may not need to question why his weekends were somewhat solitary. While she liked certain aspects of Steve the guy she was dating, his doctor-like directives now jabbed at her tension. Confused boundaries, again, she thought, or was it her pushing him away before he came to the same conclusion?

"Yes, I'll try not to worry. I don't want to make this your problem, Steve. Bugging you and all."

"A) You're not bugging me. B) I can help in various ways. C) It might mean stepping back to be objective. Understood?"

"Understood. Goodnight."

They hugged for what seemed an extended minute. With both hands, he brushed back hair from her shoulders. "Good idea to ask

78

about family history." He studied her. "We'll deal with this, Maren. Get some sleep. I'll talk to you."

He left and Maren just wished her anxieties would do the same.

When Steve Kramer set his mind on something, Maren learned fast that results followed not far behind. She had an appointment at the end of the workday, for not one, but both tests. He called her before 9:30 at her desk and had Suzanna, his secretary send a confirmation email.

Outside of burying Mark or worrying through Dylan's operation, this seemed the longest wait Maren had endured. She couldn't get her mind off the body she had and maybe wouldn't much longer. Spotting a mother breastfeeding her newborn in a hospital waiting room never had annoyed her before. Until now.

Maren tolerated Tuesday's tests, and commiserated with her mom that night by phone about being squeezed, flattened, and prodded.

"Why didn't you say anything last week, Maren?" Audrey asked.

"I didn't want to worry you, Mom. It was the same day that awful news hit about the DC shootings. My mind was on that and my first week at work. I didn't even tell Steve, and we had spent Saturday together with Dylan." She stopped rambling. "I'm so tired of dealing with heavy stuff." Maren let out a long, slow sigh, into the receiver. "I hate being the problem child, Mom. I'm trying to lead a normal life."

"Maren, you're never a problem to us, but we do worry about you." Yes, worry was a family affair. Audrey sensed this having watched her daughter over the past year. "And you're getting back to normal. Your dad and I are proud of you. Taking this job was big."

"Dr. Clements and Steve asked if there was any breast cancer in our family?"

"I haven't had anything besides a re-screening once." Audrey was doing the math in her own mind as to when she last did a self-exam and had been to her own doctor. "Your grandmother didn't have anything, and I don't think your grandmother Cole did either."

"I didn't think so. Family history is on the paperwork I had to fill out."

"So where do you go with this?"

"I signed a release so that Steve could consult on my case. Dr. Clements typically uses him as a surgeon if she needs one, but he also has a lot of connections with colleagues. And pull. He got me in for these tests in one day, and I wasn't able to get an appointment on my own until next week."

"Well, that's helpful." Audrey wished a telephone signal hadn't separated them. "What's going on with Steve? You said the dinner was nice and you saw him again Saturday."

"We see each other at work some, and he's been done with Dylan's case. He invited us out on the bay. It was a lot of fun." If memories carried heat, Maren's mind might sear remembering how amorous they'd gotten in their bathing suits with lingering kisses and sexual innuendo tossed about deck. "I've got some decisions to make. This adds another."

"What do you think is right?"

"I trust Steve. He really helped Dylan. He's thorough, hard working, and decisive. Exacting too and Type A," she laughed into the phone. "Someone in orientation asked what the difference was between surgeons and God."

Audrey remained silent. "I don't know."

"Surgeons accept only the best, think they are the best, and want everything now. God's OK with weakness, offers compassion, and is perfectly willing to wait." Maren replied. "Steve is compassionate, not so good on waiting and weakness."

"Full of himself?" Audrey asked with a laugh.

"A little," Maren replied. "That fits, but I like being around him. It feels comfortable. Dylan takes to him, too."

"So it's complicated."

"Way too complicated. I have a busy day Thursday in Bethesda, and I'm waiting for the test results. That's all I can focus on right now."

"Bethesda? Where some of those shootings occurred?"

"Mom, you sound like Steve. He nearly insisted I tell Alicia I can't go… couldn't believe it."

"There's the decisive part," Audrey reminded.

"Well, surgeons are used to getting their way."

"And I'll bet he hasn't with you?"

"Well, not on this. I'm going. It's my job. I told him so."

"It's another way I see you crawling out of this year-long abyss. Months ago, you would've been filled with doubt and worry. Life goes on. Just be careful."

"I will," Maren said. "Tell Dad if you want. I don't want to leave him out but it's awkward to talk about even with Steve."

"So I take it you and Steve are close, but not *that* close?" The way Audrey Cole had said "that close" left no doubt she meant intimately close.

"Mom!" Maren drawled accentuating it also before chuckling. She and her mom were fairly tight, and though the Coles raised their daughter with a religious faith and good morals, they weren't exactly Puritans either. "No, I'm not sleeping with him. But when Dr. Clements asked me if I still needed birth control for my cycle, I said I might need it for something else. It's crossed my mind," Maren said. "How's that for an answer?"

"Well honey, I don't expect you to report back when you do." Audrey laughed. "Your father might question a man's intentions more. He just worries about you, but you're 32 years old. If I didn't have your dad, let's just say, I'd go for the guy, with the looks and the attention he's paid in a heartbeat."

"OK this is definitely a little too much information—TMI, Mom." Wafts of embarrassment flushed through her. "Time to check on Dylan and get ready for work tomorrow. You're still watching him Thursday?"

"We're set. With that shooting spree…at a school, I'm so glad to be only substituting. I'll pick him up." Audrey appreciated how she could meet her vocational needs as a teacher mentoring her grandson, even on first-grade spelling words. "Don't worry. I'll start his homework, feed him, and save you some dinner."

Steve promised Maren lunch on Wednesday, and sure enough at shortly past noon, he knocked on her door carrying a paper bag and two bottles of flavored water. After their outing, he felt he could take a wild guess at what she might like. She welcomed the grilled chicken salad on mixed greens, and watched him take the seat near her desk to devour his Reuben sandwich.

"I always see you eating. How do you stay so trim?"

Glad she noticed, Steve put the sandwich down on its waxed paper. "Paul and I play racquetball, and I try to work out. Plus, I take the stairs," he said, dabbing with the napkin before picking up his last two bites. "I'm hooked on good food. What can I say?"

If he hadn't managed his weight as he did and chosen his wardrobe to match his good looks, sitting here wouldn't be as effortless, Maren thought.

"I brought this," he said reaching to the floor for a map, partially unfolded and refolded making it awkward at best. He spread it over Maren's desk, never minding the project it covered that would become her immediate priority after lunch.

"So, when you get off the Beltway, the quickest way… the NIH/Wisconsin Avenue Exit. If you see Grosvenor Metro, you know you made a wrong turn, so what I'd do is…" He snapped his head around. "Maren, pay attention."

"Turn here and make sure you're heading south on Rockville Pike or 355 because if you go north, you're going toward White Flint." Since that had been one of the shooting vicinities, Steve contorted his face into a cringe.

"Go this way, and you'll see the NIH Metro along the pike." Steve stopped to mark the map with a yellow highlighter he'd brought. "If you somehow miss that, and end up at Old Georgetown, then turn right and you can get there across the street from Suburban…another hospital on the other side of the campus. What hotel is your other meeting at?"

She had rolled her desk chair back to the wall and waited. Steve finally turned noticing that Maren wasn't the dutiful student he envisioned. Arms and legs crossed in front of her, her foot hung, tapping the air. He had to take a breath sometime, she figured.

"Steve…it's really thoughtful of you to map this out for me. Um…my father's aunt used to live off West Cedar in Bethesda." Maren put her feet to the floor. Snatching Steve's highlighter, she quickly uncapped it and edged the chair closer to point with the object in hand. "That would be between Old Georgetown and 355, otherwise known as Rockville Pike turning into Wisconsin. Correct?" Maren outlined the route with a yellow line in two seconds.

"I didn't realize." Steve nudged a small stool closer before taking it as a seat.

"The other meeting is at a nearby hotel. I have this figured out, Steve. I'll drive carefully."

"I grew up there, Maren. I know these streets like the back of my hand. Auto-pilot…even interned at the NIH." Steve cupped his hand over hers. "I didn't want you getting lost, dallying on a highway you didn't know."

"I can tell." She tugged gently on his tie bringing him closer to look straight at him. "If this wasn't so serious, we could make light of your...your little obsessive-compulsive moment here. But no one feels too safe over there." The muscle tension building up to tomorrow's drive had signaled that much. "And while you're being, kind of...persistent...I really do appreciate that you care." She let his tie drop back to his dress shirt.

"Mea culpa." He paused. "Promise me you won't go to the library. No walking around."

"Promise. What do I look like? Nuts?"

"Tanked up? They're stopping cars on the Beltway, you know. It's random."

"I'm fine. Three quarters of a tank." Plenty for her fuel-efficient vehicle to make it to Montgomery County, and back, two or three times.

Steve got up and backed himself to the door. Since her office was not nearly the size of his that didn't take but three steps. "Call me."

"I promise. Your map?" she shouted but he'd left, and she figured this was her parting gift, given out of his concern.

Maren forced herself to listen to WTOP the next day while she drove. Ordinarily, she'd choose relaxing music, but in case she needed to know something vital, she figured she had better have it on. Steve would be pleased that she was taking precautions, especially after learning of another shooting. He woke, uncharacteristically focusing on it...and Maren.

Maren's cell was a standard flip phone. After 9/11, many government officials adopted the Blackberry smartphone with more capabilities, and Steve's promotion granted him one also. Steve would have to wait, and worry, which he excelled at through early evening. Atypical he noted of his own unflappable traits, but this woman named Maren created a drug-like high in his brain.

Her day trip cast dread upon his routine as he finished surgeries and by noon at his desk turned the radio to a music station. Maybe it would distract him.

Wishful thinking, he realized as he cleared paperwork but certainly not his mind. As Avril Lavigne sang about things being complicated, Steve scrubbed his hands over his face.

He knew Maren had her hands full, still new to her job, having to juggle childcare this afternoon. She had endured tests every woman winces at. Steve had learned long ago how to shed certain emotions, but many seemed ever-present as he thought of Maren this afternoon. Complicated, for sure.

He was trained to use critical judgment based upon facts so that he could guide and deliver the best care for people. If Maren's mind had a window ledge into it, he felt as if he was perched right on the sill, awaiting her answer.

Maren complimented his handling of Dylan's case, and if she chose him for his surgical skill, it would put a serious kibosh on their budding relationship.

Romantic interactions between physicians and patients exploit the vulnerability of the patient, obscure judgment, and were ultimately construed as sexual misconduct. Hands down, if she chose him, their relationship would be stalled at least six months to a year, after the conclusion of her case, however long that would last. If things got difficult, it could take years.

That might be conservative, for there were always those who held to the absolute letter of one's code of conduct. No meant no, possibly in perpetuity. Personal involvement could jeopardize everything for which Steve had worked decades when he'd finally reached a pinnacle of his career where maybe he could call some shots and have slightly more free time for a life—any life. Hell, it might even include dinner out with a beautiful woman and a roll in bed might mean hot sex with her, not just rolling out of an on-call suite to take a case.

"Damn," Steve muttered at one point, between post-op patients thinking about Maren. "No is a viable word." All guys were taught that, just in a totally different context.

Why hadn't he just said no, he couldn't be her surgeon? The beauty of any developing relationship was the tempo of how and when each took certain steps. Used to calling the shots in the operating suite, occasionally that skill crept less desirably into Steve's personal life. The chase was something else entirely. It wasn't his style to push a woman or prod her.

The best he could do was to urge radiology to get him the films and by Thursday afternoon he called Maren's doctor to see what she thought about the results. Their conversation wasn't brief. Steve had uttered the word damn again—not to his colleague, but alone at his desk.

"I made it. Finally putting my feet up," Maren said, calling Steve around eight o'clock. "I just got Dylan to bed. Thankfully, with a shorter story."

Steve put his up, too, at his apartment. An apartment that had never appeared quite as lonely as it had suddenly with a woman in his life, for whom he longed. It had been a lengthy, miserable type of day without her in it. "Learn a lot?"

"Tons. Now retaining it will be the challenge. My neck is so stiff."

She tensed the entire ride along Rt. 50, the five lanes of the Beltway and back. She didn't want to tell him that she felt so nauseous she almost puked the minute she pulled into her garage and closed the door. A gag reflex didn't make for pleasant conversation.

"I just put on my robe. Tonight I'm taking a sleeping pill."

Steve wished he could be there to massage away the stress, some of which he had surely created with his obsessions about her safety. She would lose those quickly if he were there, untying her robe, he imagined in his mind. He'd make her safe all right—in his arms. For starters.

"Sleep tight. You have an appointment with Claire tomorrow, don't you?" Steve asked, so as not to give away what he knew.

"Yeah, hopefully she has the report."

Tonight wasn't the time to get into that. It was frankly her own doctor's task to talk to her about tests she had ordered, but Steve cleared his throat as he said goodnight and cleared his schedule late Friday afternoon so that they could talk if Maren felt the need.

Chapter 6

The weather turned brisk that Friday, and this weekend's forecast didn't call for the balmy temperatures that blessed their Saturday with sunshine the week prior.

Most leaving work embraced the TGIF mood, regardless. Steve left word that he'd be in his office after Maren's appointment. Normally working at home on a Friday, her conference threw the schedule off and she worked at the hospital.

"You had your appointment." He said it as she entered, stopping at the doorway. Steve's secretary, as well as his PA, had already left. "Come on in."

Asking how it was, posed as a question, would have been a pathetic way to greet her. Claire Clements surely told Maren that they reviewed her case.

Maren plopped on Steve's sofa, head leaned back as she waited for him to log off of his hospital computer and stuff his personal laptop into his briefcase. He came to sit next to her. Silence was a sudden commodity.

"I know you couldn't tell me. That's not why I'm quiet," she acknowledged.

He held her hand. "You want to grab some dinner?"

"Not really," Maren replied, gaze unfocused in a stare along the ceiling.

The stress of the week: Her new job, her in-laws and their pressure, his obsessing over her meetings in the supposed sniper zone—everyone in the region coming unglued about that—tragic losses compounded every other day, normal workday hassles, and now facing the need for a biopsy. Steve saw it dogging her brown eyes, tensing every fiber of her being.

"Good thing my appointment was early. When I called Mom, she insisted on taking Dylan until Sunday." Maren's stare didn't budge.

"Good that you checked in with her."

"Yeah, she asked me to touch base." Maren lowered her head from surveying the heights and looked directly at Steve. "That'll be interesting. Kids at school point out boxed trucks and ask tons of questions. No one has good answers. I sure don't." No cotton ball clouds for Dylan when kids got kept inside.

"After this terror we're living through—whatever we'll end up calling it—boxed, white trucks will forever be branded," Steve said. "Your parents seem so supportive, watching Dylan." His voice brimmed with compassion. "Just let them handle him. Your mom's a teacher. She can talk to him."

"Yeah, if you get to know them better, you'd like them." Audrey and Jack Cole had only met Steve once in Dylan's hospital room.

"I'm sure I would." Never faltering, his words fell upon Maren with a steadiness she'd grown accustomed to in Steve. He squeezed her hand.

"They dote on Dylan and said I need a break." The lump lodged inside her might not weigh much, but to Maren's parents, it carried a different heaviness. Not only did their daughter face an upsetting health report, but they had already lost their son-in-law Mark, rendering Maren a single parent. While Maren told them it could be benign, they knew it could be malignant.

"When does Claire want to hear back from you?"

"Whenever. You got me these tests in a snap. I can't snap an answer quite so quickly. It's a lot to digest. Does the damn thing even have a name?"

"Please don't look up every possible thing it could be."

"When I was in group therapy after Mark died, we learned that more information soothes anxiety."

"More info drives Maren Mitchell to her Mac...bad if you diagnose yourself. It's a neoplasm...a lump. Could well be a fibroadenoma, common in childbearing years. The tests often help with diagnosis. They didn't. So you biopsy it." Steve studied her. "Claire went over all this, right?"

"Yes," Maren said. "My brain spazzed out after the word biopsy though. Glad you can explain it...again. She said to decide when...to err on soon. Lucky me."

"Well, the weekend buys you two and a half days, at least."

"I'm gonna go home, Steve. I'm so beat." She leveled with him about her stomach having done somersaults on 495, barely making it home yesterday without having to throw up along the highway. Stopping anywhere in the DC/Maryland vicinity freaked her out and caused Steve to shudder. "I'll have more questions. Can't fathom any right now. Kinda numb."

"I can imagine," Steve said. His hand still rested on hers; they intertwined fingers. "I need to tinker some on the boat tomorrow. Not going out...too windy. But I'm around, if you need me."

"Not to play Steve here, but is that even safe given what's going on?" She pulled her hand away, propping up more on the sofa. The attacks thus far had occurred in Montgomery and Prince George's Counties, just next to theirs as well as in Virginia and in the District of Columbia.

"The marina has top security to begin with. People have million dollar yachts there, Maren, worth a lot more than my boat," Steve explained. "Let's just say, they've beefed that up triple overtime. We should be fine." He omitted the part about the high-powered rifles marina management mentioned in email. His intent was to reassure, not frighten further. He'd already gotten the sense it didn't take much to get the what-if's going in Maren's mind.

"I'll let you know," she said, finding a sudden burst of energy to spring off the sofa. She grabbed her handbag.

Steve got up and kissed her cheek. "Call me tomorrow."

When Saturday bore the prospect of being an isolated, indoor day, without the company of her boisterous son, Maren took Steve up on his offer. There was quiet and then there was way too quiet. She gathered a few things and headed over to the marina after calling ahead. Steve had to alert gate security.

October 12th was not bathing suit weather. In fact, Maren dressed in jeans with a blouse and brought along a sweater and a bag, which included the novel she was trying to get lost in. Steve putzed around on his boat fixing the wiring on his new GPS with the manual laid out in front of him, and he polished a few things on board.

"Make yourself comfortable. We can order lunch and they'll deliver it or we can walk over."

"Sounds good. I'm going to read. Can we talk later?"

"Count on it." Steve regarded Maren. "Whenever you're ready. Blankets are in the wall cabinet. It's a little crisp out there."

The interior of Steve's boat resembled the comforts of an efficiency apartment. Sleek, with muted colors of beige, light browns and blue tones to match the colors of the water. Maren opened the hatch built into the forward berth to the one side of the bed. Finding only CD's there, some toiletries in another, she opened one more to discover a blanket. Beneath it, buxom blondes broadcast their artificial enhancements gracing the pages in last February's *Sports Illustrated* swimsuit issue. *Playboy* broadcast much more. Both looked well read, creased with obvious folding that had occurred to read an article, so all men would claim, if ever questioned.

Maren couldn't resist thumbing through. When a knot formed at the base of her neck, she knew her fear led to fury, jealousy sparked sadness, even though the more perused pages seemed to indicate Steve's preference for natural beauty. If he'd been the implant type, maybe he'd have landed in plastic surgery.

He clearly had a preference for bikinis, and thong-clad models might even have rated a higher page-wear index. Next to the magazines, she spotted *Striptease,* the movie with Demi Moore, Madonna's *Erotica* music video, of the uncensored variety, as well as *Meet the Parents, A Beautiful Mind* and *Saving Private Ryan.* Maren stashed these out of sight. Some of the movies she could envision watching if they spent more time together.

She wasn't usually the type to be threatened by a few provocative images, under normal circumstances. Of course, these were anything but normal. Steve is a single guy, men are visual, and he has eyes for me, she told herself.

That was evident last week when the sun's rays rivaled their own heat for one another. But would that last, she wondered, especially if she faced losing her body image and his image of her.

"Dammit," she uttered slamming the cubby door harder than she needed to close it shut. Steve was outside so he wouldn't hear. "I hate this."

Though she left Steve's office the evening before determined to call it an early night, rest had evaded her at one and again at five until she finally made coffee. Nesting within the blanket, Maren propped the oversized pillows on the queen-sized bed, removed her hair clip, and got three chapters further, before the novel fell to her side.

Steve found her an hour later, moving the book to prevent losing her place. His presence stirred her.

"Sorry, I didn't mean to wake you," he offered in hushed tones, tip toeing out.

Maren yawned with a stretch. "All done with your stuff?"

"Yeah." He stood leaning onto the darker hardwood that paneled the boat's cabin, closest to the galley, within talking distance.

Merely rescuing her book was close enough for her subtle perfume to invade his senses and start to take over. Maren had cast aside the blanket she'd snuggled with, causing his eyes to follow every outline, every curve her tight jeans and blouse made. A navy belt drew his attention to her waist. She wore everything so well.

Standing there, he crossed his arms, sighing as inaudibly as he could. Damn, he was falling for her. If only his mind was trained to operate like his surgical skill, he would will this unwanted mass from Maren, out of their lives and choices. Seafood, steak, or pasta for dinner would seem the biggest of their decisions.

Yet honestly, he didn't want to be her doctor. He wasn't sure he could be, and now her difficult decision seemed to have evolved into his. She sat up. Seeing him, Maren figured Steve granted her the talking time she'd requested.

"I have to get clear on this. We don't know what this is exactly even with the tests, but it's solid and has to come out, right?"

"It is more solid—majority benign. The needle biopsy should tell us, and sometimes you can live with it, if it's benign."

"Live with it and worry more?" She sighed heavily. "So I see a surgeon, maybe not even at West Riverside. Biopsy. Maybe surgery. I don't do things fast, ya know."

"Then, one step at a time, Maren."

"That's gonna take weeks, right? Great...more waiting."

"Not necessarily." Steve thought he'd eradicated the New York minute from his life. Now, Maren lived by it. She wanted time to think but then she wanted answers right away. He opened the backpack lying on the leather booth, unfolding a print out before handing it to her. "The top one can see you soon."

She studied the names, all in Baltimore—two at Johns Hopkins, one at University of Maryland Medical Center. "You've done my research. When did you compile... never mind." She saw the printer generated 10/7/2002 date. "You did this the very night you found out, even though it was late."

Eyes weighted with moisture, Maren yearned for Steve. She patted the bed beckoning him to join her. Lips shifting into a frown, she bit at her bottom one.

"Safer over here." He leaned more solidly into the hardwood doorframe.

"Steve…" Maren pulled her knees up to her chest to rest her head and hide her eyes if the moisture started to tumble. "Until I decide this, is that it?"

"Pretty much." He told her this had to be her choice, he wasn't rushing it, that whomever she chose, he would go with her to the appointments, or back off, if she wanted no more help. After Thursday, sitting with his own anxieties over her safety, he was getting practiced at passing the time.

"Pouting won't help, Maren. Why don't we go outside?" Steve suggested. "Grab your sweater. Could clear your mind." The cool temperature, with some sun evident, had balanced his brain for the last two hours.

A jittery wave of impatience came over her as he stood watching. If the turning wheels in her mind symbolized gears, hers had just shifted so many times that they might have damaged her mental transmission.

If objective looked like this, she would rather lash out. She had her chance to toss the magazines or tapes overboard, by accident of course. She wouldn't have, but the fleeting passive-aggressive act would have satisfied momentary madness. Maybe she should have stayed at home, she thought. Being alone though with this mind-boggling, ping-pong process could have been even worse.

"I just asked you to sit with me. What's with that?"

"What's with that?" Steve's hands fell to his sides but now he dragged one through his hair. Crossing arms again with even more frustration, he let out a deeper, exasperated sigh. The confusion hadn't faded from her face.

"Let me spell it out." He collected his thoughts before he made a fool of himself. "I'm 39 years old. I have this babalicious woman—on my bed, no less. My focusing, without thinking about her most minutes of any given day, is a thing of the past. And, my last relationship was nine months ago." His eyes, her eyes locked in a stare. "You getting the picture?"

"I thought that was a year ago."

"Trust me on this!" She clearly had some things to realize about men, Steve thought having committed the last time he had skin-to-skin contact with a woman firmly into both short-term and long-term memory. "Maybe we should do lunch. At the dock bar."

"I'm not all that hungry right now," she said. "Well, I could be. I don't know."

"Make up your mind." He closed his eyes knowing how awful that unintentional snap had just sounded. "I need some air, even if you don't." Maren watched him start out of the cabin.

"Steve," she called after him with enough urgency that he halted mid-stride. "Please don't go."

"Maren, maybe today was…" He stopped not wanting to offend her. He had asked her here, after all. They did need to talk.

"Today was what? Finish Steve. No stonewalling."

"I am not stonewalling." The accusation struck a nerve.

"You were going to say that today was a mistake, asking me here to hang out with you. Well, sorry if I'm in the way of..."

"That's not it," he interrupted. "There are things standing in our path, but it's not you. It's circumstance, thinking logically."

"I'm so tired of logic, Steve. I'm fed up with it." A mix of emotions engulfed her system flowing from her brain, finding their way to her stomach in knots, her muscles with tension, and her hands, beseeched with wrath. "Frankly, I'm so pissed off."

"I know." Her upright body and taut muscles told him she was spoiling for a fight.

"No, you can't possibly know Dr. Cool-As-Can-Be Kramer." Maren's head whipped up to seize on his two words. "You think I *don't* know what's going on here. I'll spell out what I see."

She opened the cubby and grabbed the swimsuit issue, sailing it across the bed, into the hallway where he stood. "I'd like nothing better about now than to make you *not* need this." Steve wasn't sure what it was, but saw a flash of glossy pages and felt them snag his right shoulder. When it landed on the floor, he bent to pick up the magazine. A few pages fell out mid-air. A thong-clad, naked at the breast model crossing her arms to cover only what she had to.

"That barely passes for sale on a regular newsstand. I love how they market to men," she spit out. "And that one," she said pointing to the model spread seductively on a boat, triangles of fabric placed strategically where men's eyes would zone.

"A typical 38 bust, miserly 24-inch waist, and luscious 36 hips, I'll bet. Tantalizing when that sorry excuse of a bathing suit ends up ripped aside…"

"It does?" he interrupted. Licking his lips, his grin confirmed Maren's assumption. Steve did a guesstimate of her proportions. Maybe 34, 24, 34 give or take seemed perfect, even sexier when she showed some fire in her.

"Yes," she shot back. "So that men—the we-love-the-come-hither-look men can do what you want. A little T&A to pave the way! That was supposed to rhyme, dammit."

"You do work in marketing. Don't doubt your assessment." He took tentative steps toward Maren, straining his neck to see what else she might lob next.

"Bet this was a treat to watch," she seethed, sending *Striptease* soaring. It hit him in the gut and he flinched.

"A little higher and I'd think you aimed to take my head off. What's gotten into you?" He wasn't sure he wanted to know and positively didn't want to see or feel anything hurled at a lower trajectory. The spitfire appeal fizzled fast.

"She showed her moves on that pole in an interview." She educated him of these facts with pure disdain, her breath fuming into the space between them. "Ugh," she yelled, flinging the music video to the floor.

Fortunately, she'd just emptied the wall cabinet. Silence ranked mightily. This reminded Steve of the Monday night with the many what-if's attacking her brain. Now mere paper and cardboard pummeled him.

Fisting her hands, she crossed them in front of her, perhaps to keep from causing more destruction. She was so angry she felt sure she could rip something off the wall if she had to.

Steve let out a sigh. "Are you done? This seems like the unsafe zone still?" He leaned into the paneling again.

"I must be speaking Greek. For all your intelligence and education, I don't think you understand." She leveled him a sad stare, studying Steve's stance, his sigh, his eyes, and tension. "Don't you see," she said leaning back on her elbows. "I want you as much as you want me right now. Part of me wants to seize the moment—because Lord

93

knows and I *do* know—how precious life's moments are. Taken away, in death or disease."

Sitting up straight, she continued. "Part of me feels guilty, like it's not fair to you. You've been so good to me…to Dylan." Maren could see Steve's head snap. "I'm not done. What if the babalicious woman you described today becomes next month's regret? What then? What if what you loved about me last Saturday, and long for today, is gone? Poof. I want what I maybe shouldn't have. Maybe you shouldn't either."

"Who says we shouldn't? You just said, life's short. You're scared I'll stop caring for you…that your appearance matters more than the whole package."

"Yeah." Maybe he didn't miss the point. Her hand stroked the comforter again…nothing to brush off or rub away. Only nervous energy. Bottled up… seeping out.

"Maren, that whole package includes a wonderful personality, warmth, humor. You're such a good mom to Dylan. You're creative as all get-out. You work hard at your job and…well, until right now, at tackling your anxiety and whatever challenges have come your way."

Steve could tell his assessment caught her off guard. "What if I told you that all that T&A—your phrasing, not mine—doesn't matter as much as you do, and that we'll deal with whatever challenge presents itself." He paused, but not for long. She'd had her chance to vent. "The statistics bear out that all this emotion is just that—fear, frustration," Steve said swiping a hand behind his neck. He could feel his traps, the trapezius muscles, at the base of his neck, start to spasm. "I've seen this countless times, only now seeing it on the other side. And…I can't stand women making decisions alone, ones that ought to be discussed."

"I'm sorry. Will you do me a favor?"

"What?"

"Please close that door you were about to bolt through and sit beside me because I've decided at least two things—things I do get to decide."

Steve did as directed, stepping to close the door leading to the bridge. A chilly breeze trickled through. He returned stopping just short of the bed where she sat tall, eyes widened.

"When can I get an appointment in Baltimore? That's one decision."

"You actually have one Tuesday, if you want it. Just have to confirm it Monday." His cobalt eyes caressed her with a look of longing mixed with affection and concern. Steve sat down. She didn't have to gaze up any longer or they'd both end up with neck pain. "Look at me." He brought her chin out of her afternoon pout and into his palm. "This has to be about what you need. I didn't mean to make it about me a minute ago."

"This is very much about what I need. That's all part of decision number one. Dr. Kramer's off my surgeon list. You OK with that?"

"I'm OK with that." Very OK, in fact.

"If I have to face this, and it's my choice, then I want Steve—not Dr. Kramer—holding my hand, not holding down the surgical suite."

Hot tears welled in both her brown eyes. Emotions she'd held in check that day flooded forward as she struggled to find her voice.

"I need you. I'm scared." She dug into her jean pocket for a tissue. "Dahh! Or else I wouldn't have torn up your private little stash. I'm sorry." She sniffed out a nervous laugh.

One tear dropped, followed by another, and she sniffled to forestall a cascade of them. Dabbing her eyes she added, "The movies weren't all that bad."

Steve toed off his loafers and climbed onto the mattress to be with her as she'd asked for the last half hour. "I know your tears aren't about the stash, Maren." Reclining onto the pillows at the headboard, he pulled her in tight against his chest. "Come here...let it out." Moisture started to coat his shirt.

Maren had the silkiest of auburn hair. He loved it flowing loose and loved even more how running his own fingers through it brought the calm she needed. Steve could feel her breathing subside from frenzied to a normal rhythm. Her emotion hadn't lasted long.

"Was there something else? You mentioned two things."

Taking her head out from the curvature of his arm, Maren crooked it his way. "When I talked about being hungry, I was." Maren locked his blue eyes back into her brown, and slowly, studied Steve. "Only, it has nothing to do with food groups. Everything to do with...wanting you."

Maren found the chain around his neck, twirling it in her fingers as she leaned on him, eyes still fixed with his. Steve considered her for a moment, returning the gaze, letting this revelation sink in. His hand stroked her hair again as she knuckled away tears streaming onto her cheek, in the stillness.

"But I need you to know we can reassess this later, if..."

Steve took both of Maren's arms, rolled over top of her and pinned her down. "Enough…" His mouth seized hers rather recklessly. His needy and hungry upon hers, trembling just slightly with that messy mix of her responses stewing inside. Loosening his grip so that they could each breathe freely, he whispered, "I never meant to snap at you earlier." If she didn't quiet her brain and just move her mouth with his, he might snap again.

"You really have to stop this." Steve still held her hands imprisoning her, gently but to make a point. Everything about him made it, particularly his eyes. "I accept what you're saying, but I disagree. Clearly, I'm attracted to you and this hot body of yours currently in my hands. But trust me when I say how much I care about you, and that making love to you, with you, won't change any of that, except to maybe deepen what's already happening here between us."

He put slightly more distance between them. "Tell me that you accept that, or I'm walking out that door, I swear."

These self-assured gestures of his were going to undo her but she already had awareness that when her emotions got jacked up, it was damn difficult to tamp those feelings back down. Yet she absorbed what he said, how he said it.

"Maren…"

"I heard you. I understand. I'm not exactly rational thinking you're going to feel bad and want to bolt. I do trust you. I know you want me, and I want you, and it's been seven months for you and…"

"Nine, Maren." The saucy grin added to his eagerness for her. Ten and counting, he figured if she kept up these ridiculous notions.

"OK…nine." She rolled her eyes. "And 17 for me, and well, you saw all my labs. Healthy. Protected. Sought after by the volunteer fire department…" She sniffled saying it, half with laughter; half from stress.

"Sure, tease me with your fantasies." Steve nipped beneath her left ear.

"And I can provide shot records if you need them."

"Except for distemper." He grazed her skin under her other ear. "Want my records?" He watched her study him. "Hospital policy, Maren. We have to keep current on some; others just common sense when you're single."

She brushed hair away from his forehead. "Not this minute, that's for sure."

Steve had already eased any pressure, but with both hands, he shifted her body weight on top of his. No sooner had her breathing calmed down—that was the intent—but now it quickened once again, up against Steve's firm and sturdy thighs held beneath his jeans. Both of his hands slipped behind her head gliding through her long reddish-brown mane. Yet evidence of his firm arousal stole her focus. She couldn't ignore the sensation directly beneath her.

"Tell me what you want." He held her focus. "Tell me what you need," Steve said in a deep, raspy breath. "Right now."

"Everything. Touch me. Hold me. Don't let me go."

Steve tightened his grip. Without much warning, he flipped her slowly onto her back, pinning for another kiss, as if he'd captured her, about to plunder. The force came down hard onto her lips, parting them open with his.

They were full and strong like everything else she had noticed about him that afternoon. This kiss, unlike any of their others, was open-mouthed, unmistakably more sexual, the kind that brings warmth and abandonment and marks territory the longer it lasts.

Maren's arms clutched Steve by the waist, pressing that firmness into her even more. His weight felt wonderful, just enough to energize whatever it touched.

She tugged on his belt, pulling his shirt so she could strip him of it and feel his chest. Steve unfastened her blouse and helped her shimmy out of her jeans as if they were in a race. All items landed into a heap on the cabin floor.

When they were both down to almost nothing, Steve ran his hands across her smooth skin.

"Steve," Maren said, sliding fingers under his boxers, lowering them off.

"What?" His mouth tormented her neck and worked its way lower while his hands roamed her, having made their way down her hips, across her thighs, fingers gliding up in a straight line to her navel.

"This time, enjoy me a little more when you round the bases."

He grinned, moving in to unfasten her bra by its front closure. "With pleasure," and as he splayed it open, he ran both of his hands to fondle each breast, nuzzling and teasing her erect nipples, and finally tasting each one with the flick of his tongue across her silky skin.

Steve moved lower to slide off her panties and peeled back the comforter. The minute Maren slid beneath she shuddered, feeling the remnants of the cabin's cool air, which had chilled the smooth sheet against her naked skin.

"I'll take care of that, too." Steve pulled her closer to make her every curvature fit his and every cell of heat sear from his skin into hers. This time, Steve did with his touch what he wanted, exploring every inch of her as a woman. Yes, he was damn glad to be off her doc list, basing his discoveries purely upon lust. "Warmer now?"

"Mmm, definitely." She never felt more alive than under his steady hands. Maren arched her back, uttering his name with a slight pant. He could tell she was slowly letting her mind go, giving in to her wants as well as her needs.

As Steve's lips caressed her stomach moving lower, her temperature shot even higher. "I've wanted you so much," Steve murmured. He kept caressing, halting. Nuzzling. Stopping. Until he knew he'd found how to capture her undivided attention. She cried out softly upon that discovery.

Maren offered all of herself to him, with Steve taking every inch. If her mission for him was to enjoy her, he did just that. Feeling her hands run through his hair when he teased her delectably, he slowed a little, denying her a second finish he was determined to share with her.

Panting, pleading with him, one minute to stop and the next not to, Maren shifted out of another shudder that shook through her. All Steve saw was her magnificent body mounting his own, straddling and sliding him into her.

Tempted by urgency to take her again and again, Steve relished her tantalizing him, possessing him, with her long hair lapping at her shoulders, now on his chest. That urgency felt free and easy at first, building wave upon wave until it rammed into his senses.

"You're gorgeous," Steve whispered when she first started sending his vitals into overdrive.

"Well, I could keep you locked with me all day."

"Mmm." Kissing became abrupt and impatient with desperate attempts to take in air. The more Steve's breathing accelerated, the more Maren moved as if it turned a switch on inside her.

"Dreaming about you was one thing. Having you," Maren whispered. Her gift for visual cues, displayed in the bedroom as taunts, about sent him through the cabin skylight, and her energy level made a liar out of her supposed sleep-deprived night. If a nap could do this, he'd find a way to get her one daily.

Between her motion, his, and the gentle lap of the boat against the water outside, he lost himself deep within her that afternoon. Faces focused. Fingers intertwined. Cries muffled against neck and shoulders, their knotted muscles finally loosened as they collapsed onto one another.

It took a few minutes for Steve to catch his breath. She clutched at him, tracing her fingers on him ever so lightly.

"Will you make it?" she asked slyly. "I'll have a tough time explaining this at work if you don't."

"I'm not sure. I'm willing to make this a chronic condition." Maren giggled into his chest. "Your name has to mean goddess of the seas." He shifted, cupped her head, and pulled her in for a winded kiss with his plundering tongue. "You sure as hell took me out and back this afternoon." His chest rose and fell more naturally.

"A contented captain," she dubbed him.

"The captain surrenders. Keep me out at sea."

The gulls crooning outside indicated to Maren that it was still daylight. Steve had drawn the porthole shades in the midst of their argument, possibly to keep their slightly heated match private. He slumbered after they'd completely fell spent to one another, their limbs linked as Maren nestled her head on his chest, feeling him breathe steadily underneath her. She smiled thinking of what he'd spoken hours ago, gasping to make it.

It seemed surreal, another of those barriers she'd broken over the past year. Taking Steve as her lover. If her responses took the wind from his sails, they certainly made her heel, high into the air.

Maren closed her eyes, her mind finally still, body hidden mostly by the covers she'd pulled up keeping her warm against Steve. When she shifted to spoon against him, he moved with her though only half awake, she felt sure. His arm draped lovingly over her. His hand moved along her skin, and she eased her head back against him.

"Are you awake?"

"Mmm. Barely," he cupped her breast. "See what you did to me?"

"Sorry, I didn't mean to make it such a hard day for you," she said gingerly.

"Careful, you just might get it hard, again." He nuzzled her neck now, more alert. "Kiss me."

Maren shimmied so that their mouths could meet. Steve sealed his over hers. "Talk to me," he said.

"That was incredible." She shifted onto her side to look at him. "I love it when you hold me."

Steve stroked her hair, long and flowing, and he knew without her saying it that she loved that, too. "Then I won't let you go."

"Do you ever take naps here?" She imitated her son as she asked.

"Never. Until now. In fact..." Steve suddenly felt self-conscious, smiling.

"What?"

"I...ah, had a little fantasy going when I first considered buying this boat. Mind you, I wasn't seeing anyone at the time. But when you came along..." He cast her the most loving upturn of his lips.

She propped an elbow facing him. "Now, the truth comes out."

"Yeah." He brushed a hand along her face. "I should feed you, though. We never had lunch."

"Don't you have anything here?"

"I've got white wine, probably some cheese and crackers."

"As long as I don't have to move. It's warm." They stayed another 10 minutes until Steve realized her eyelids closed and she didn't answer whatever he asked.

He kissed her softly on the forehead and slipped from under the covers. Retrieving his boxers from the tangle of clothing, he slid into them unaware that Maren, opening one eye, soaked in the sight. She closed that eye again but fell into a smile with her hand reaching out to him. He took it, caressed it, and positioned it back under the covers.

"I'll get a shower, then I'll get us something."

Maren knew he cared for her. In small, silly ways like crumpled maps and sandwiches brought to her desk, and in bigger ones like the referrals he'd gathered and the appointments he reserved for her. And now, making sure she was content and could sleep.

Steve had said he would see her through this ordeal, with whatever lay ahead. Still, she wasn't sure what their intimacy meant, how it might change things, especially if her health didn't hold. *Stay still inside.*

Thoughts started to roll through her head, but this time, she blanked them out. Life is but a series of moments—her loss, with Mark's passing, the country's grief last year, and the region's right now.

100

Maren wasn't sure what was around the corner of her life, but she knew she had a man that cared deeply for her, and she planned to treasure this, and him, because truth be told, she'd only ever felt this close to one other man in her life.

Steve peeked out the door of the head. "You're awake. Give me a second."

Maren shimmied herself off the bed and retrieved her blouse from the floor, rushing it on. The wafting steam announced Steve's entry into the cabin where he found her, on hands and knees, searching the floor.

"What did you lose?" Steve dried his hair, standing with another towel knotted at his waist.

"My hair clip." She laughed at what must have been a strange sight of her being bent over. "Sorry..." Having found it, she rose on her knees and swept up her locks to fasten the clip with both elbows pointed at him as she secured it behind her head.

"Nothing to be sorry about." He grinned, admiring her open blouse that left all indecent ideas as plausible possibilities. "What time is it?"

"I'm hurrying. Almost five. You must be starving." They'd completely missed lunch, postponed wine and cheese, and she wanted to hustle into the shower. As she saw him standing before her, she scooted closer. Looked up. Heaved a heavy, suggestive sigh.

Steve shook his head still very amused and appreciative.

"I'm hungry again." Their eyes caught and held. "Would you be upset if...I mean, I can hurry and get ready or..." She ran her right finger the length of his leg under his towel, far above his knee, and traced it back down his thigh.

Early evening evaporated. Maren got up first after their second, saucy go-round. They were just getting out of bed when the rest of the world turned in for the night.

She found Steve sprawled lazily next to her. He had left the wine opener out and two glasses. Cheese, pre-sliced, just had to go on crackers, which Maren dutifully brought back to bed on a plate from the galley. She found fruit also, and by the looks of Steve he wasn't destined to move, though he sat up to have a bedtime snack. How many meals had they missed?

Sunday morning she found the wet towel on her way to the shower, and she remembered how she'd sent Steve over the edge, making it fall to the floor.

Maren Mitchell's life seemed to be as unpredictable as the waters this vessel moored upon, but the one thing she felt was stable lay six or seven feet from where she refreshed her body, and hopefully her mind, under a stream of warm water, to start another day.

Chapter 7

"You two never stop," Vicki Romano said, putting more food in front of Steve and her husband Paul, Sunday afternoon as the Pittsburgh Steelers traveled to Cincinnati to play the Bengals. The guys watched the action, kicking back at Paul's place.

While some friendships formed during medical school had been confined to holiday greetings, once everyone got reestablished in other cities, Steve and Paul had formed a permanent bond. Steve was as welcome in the Romano household in Pittsburgh as Paul was at the Kramer residence in Chevy Chase and their summer place in Southern Maryland along the bay.

Paul and Steve had much in common, except that Steve stood about two and a half inches taller than Paul's 5'8" height. Both had dark hair. But that Mediterranean olive-complexion, dark brown eyes with even darker brows, and under eye circles gave it away if the Roman angled nose did not. Paul was proud to be totally Italian.

Paul chose surgery and internal medicine, Steve teasing him at the time for being less decisive. When Steve moved to Maryland, Paul remained in Pittsburgh for additional years of residency. He also swore he wouldn't leave until his team brought home another Lombardi Trophy. When they lost Super Bowl XXX in 1996, and Paul shivered through that frigid winter, he called Steve with big pre-birthday news.

After hearing Steve brag about being on the bay by mid-April, Paul said, "Screw it. You win. I'm heading south." The only hitch: Steve's birthday fell on April 2. Like hell, he'd be taken as an April fool, not believing Paul until the U-Haul arrived. For once, Steve was happy to be laughed at for his persistence.

Steve joined Paul at West Riverside Hospital Center in 1999, the year Paul met Vicki, who had strong Italian looks—dark, well-sculpted eyebrows above her bright eyes, dark enough to match her hair styled into a shoulder-length bob with an S curl forming just at the shoulder. They married September 22, 2001. Vicki started her new position as the West Riverside childbirth educator in 2002 just as Maren joined the staff.

QB Tommy Maddox made Coach Cowher, Paul and Steve happy that afternoon. The Steelers lead well established, they caught up at the half.

"I see you're wearing the chain, Steve." Vicki noticed it around his neck.

Steve leaned forward scooping more of her homemade salsa onto tortilla chips. Other treats—mostly Italian lay nearby. Vicki knew Steve particularly liked cookies and biscotti that they brought from trips to see Paul's parents.

"Hasn't come off. Sweet of you to bring it back for me," Steve said.

Paul and Vicki postponed a honeymoon until 2002, with everyone's fears of flying after 9/11. In Italy they got a chain for Steve because Vicki always found Paul's incredibly sexy. Paul called it his lucky chain. Years before, Steve dubbed him "the Italian Stallion." How he got that nickname wasn't fodder for discussion in front of Vicki, but the chain made Paul feel more of one.

"My guess: It worked, Steve. You look…relaxed." Paul put that into the space between them, clearing his throat purposely.

Steve indicated he'd spent two Saturdays with someone new in his life, and Paul, always with a sharp wit, wasn't going to let that slide. "When do we meet Ms. Maren?" Paul asked eyebrow arched.

"When it's time," Steve replied succinctly. Vicki recognized Maren's name from orientation. She had only positive things to say intriguing Paul, now the only one who couldn't put a name and face together.

"Well, some rockfish in that bay need catching. For me to miss two fall weekends on that boat, someone had better gotten laid."

"Paul!" Vicki admonished. "Deck him, Steve." She hurled the accent pillow she'd leaned upon, at her husband.

Instead Steve shot Paul a guy-code grin—he might possibly have initiated that new boat of his in a satisfying way, but he wasn't dishing.

"First, fix your accent," Steve retorted. "Throw a verb into that Pittsburgese." Steve expected the whatever-roll of Paul's eyes. "Second, your standing me up for racquetball is completely innocent? No. Sorry Vicki." Steve knew them well. He'd been the best man at their wedding.

"I was busy the other morning," Paul said with an ounce of righteousness.

"Busy? At 6:30 in the morning when you aren't at the hospital spells true luck." Steve looked at Paul, who looked lovingly at his wife, and they all smiled.

"Steve, you deserve someone special," Vicki said. "We can't wait to get together with her. Honey, did you get tickets to the Raven's game?"

"Yeah, Steve. You're on next weekend, but the following one, guess what?"

Steve's eyes widened. Coming across tickets for a Pittsburgh Steelers game was damn near impossible at Heinz Field, with a decades-long season-ticket wait list. The home-field advantage was too far and forever impeded by their schedules. When the two teams met here held more promise.

"You didn't?" Steve said with honest amazement. "How many?"

Paul reached around the sofa and pulled out a drawer. Steve saw four tickets fanned in front of his eyes. "Now if you got yourself hooked up with one of those newly minted Raven's fans, I might have to hold out these Stillers tickets."

"Stop." Steve turned to Vicki. "Pittsburghese fits Paul so well."

"It does," she confessed. "This morning he told me to redd up the room."

"You don't go after her Baltimore accent, huh hon?" Paul beamed a smile.

Steve shook his head. Going after Paul: far more rewarding. "Seriously Romano, Maren doesn't live and breathe football, but I'm impressed. How much do I owe you?"

They split the cost, the Steelers won this game 34-7, and Steve made a mental note to warn Maren about Paul. He would also caution her to pack away any purple, or he might never live down the first double date they planned.

Steve blocked off his schedule Tuesday to drive Maren into Baltimore to meet with one of the top breast surgeons on the east coast. When he picked her up, Maren asked if she needed to fetch her map, and he swatted her behind playfully, knowing full well he deserved the jab. Levity started the tense day.

Last night's news hurled more stress into morning headlines. Another innocent victim out shopping was shot in Virginia, and ballistics evidence linked this with the region's other attacks. Even the Defense Department got involved with surveillance, searching databases for people with sniper marksmanship.

Maren turned off the radio once it was clear they'd make it into the city without snarls on Interstates 97 and 695. She turned to Steve, at the wheel, forcing a brighter focus after news reports, traffic, and weather.

"So much for keeping our relationship quiet," she said with the first sign of a lilt in her voice the entire ride. "You're the talk of my office. I'm not quite sure how to explain it."

"I tried to be a little discreet," he said, grinning as he focused on the highway. He had worn his sunglasses so Maren couldn't see his eyes. "Look, it's not against hospital policy to date if it doesn't get in the way, and I'm not sexually harassing you, am I?"

"Hardly." She laughed remembering how forward she'd been, and how after breakfast Sunday they stayed longer on the boat, not even making it back to the bed before she picked up Dylan and Steve went to Paul's.

"Well, I think I said thank you for them." She had—possibly a half-dozen times between yesterday and today. "They're gorgeous," she said of the dozen roses delivered Monday to her desk in a long crystal vase with a note:

Maren,
Thanks for two incredibly beautiful Saturdays on the seas!
I'm here for you always. I love you,
Steve

When she'd opened the card, it had melted her heart. Steve couldn't help but stop yesterday to catch a glimpse of them...and her. When she saw him, she'd given him a huge hug behind her closed door. Certain things they kept private. Steve's lips had slid into an exquisite fit with hers, caught up in how satisfying the weekend had become. "I've completely fallen in love with you Ms. Maren of the Seas...you know that, don't you?" Maren had nodded, tears filling her throat, whispering back the same.

A meaningful memory as Maren looked out the car window heading into Baltimore. No one at work knew of her health scare today, as typically she would work from home on Tuesdays.

They arrived. Steve greeted his surgical colleague with some banter and introduced Maren as a very special person in his life. She liked that. Steve found Maren not only a competent, but incredibly compassionate doctor who looked at the test results and examined Maren.

He took time with them that morning, knowing Maren was more anxious than most patients who might have the discussion the same day as a scheduled biopsy. If Maren had told her mind to be still five times it could have been fifty. She was glad Steve had gone with her to hear everything.

He had dinner at Maren's, earning a Dylan squeal and words like "awesome" and "way cool" when he brought a wrapped, noisy-when-you-shook-it box. Paper ripped back, Dylan opened the Skull's Eye Schooner set from what Steve called "a quick, run in/run out" of the toy store. That characterized how everyone did errands as uncertainty for safety mounted in Maryland.

" 875 LEGO pieces," Maren noted spying the box and picking up sails, an anchor, and of course, a fish from her carpet.

"It's Halloween soon, Maren. Pirates. Way cool," Steve said imitating Dylan's excitement. "Spending so much time indoors, the kid's gotta have some fun."

An understatement they both knew, and not ideal for Dylan. Maren realized she over-reacted. Seeing Steve on the floor playing with the pieces, sometimes more animated than her six-year-old son, brought contentment.

Unfortunately, the pirate ship only occupied part of Dylan's attention. He'd heard hushed tones bantering "hospital" and "surgical" and "Friday" with his mother's name mixed into their sentences.

Dylan had spent the last 17 months witnessing grief responses—from sorrow-filled sobbing to silent brooding and weeping in between. His mother was a lot of things, but she would never win an Academy Award. The pain showed on her face, as it did on his grandparents, especially through their being on the scene more than Dylan had ever experienced. It all threw him into tears. Maren and Steve stood back surveying how current events of the past weeks and now his overhearing them had taken its toll.

"I sleep in your bed," Dylan protested as Maren began his nightly routine. Bath, teeth brushing, story, prayers, unless he fell asleep during the third step.

"You're safe in your own bed," Maren told him. "There aren't bad guys outside. Really." Fears of gunmen, shootings, police searches, press briefings—they were everywhere even if you sheltered your child from the worst of it.

"I wanna be with you," Dylan implored. Maren could appreciate his concern, especially since it involved his looking out for the only parent he had now. Last year, he lost his father—a huge, traumatic event in the life of any child. Recently, he lost the freedom to play and be a carefree little boy. What next? Adults dealt with the troubling uncertainties daily, doing the best they could to make sense of senseless situations.

"Dude, what's going on?" Steve asked taking the steps two at a time when he heard the pleading downstairs. He sensed Maren's patience about to snap.

"Why do you have to go to a hospital?" Dylan asked his mom and Steve, now by his side, as Maren sat on Dylan's bed and Steve took a seat on the floor. "Why," he demanded, sniffling and pushing aside Muppets. Dylan sat up, bringing his legs up close to his chest as he rocked.

"Dylan, I have a doctor's appointment and tests. Not like you have in school, but…" She paused for the right word.

"Tests for doctors mean we look at certain problems, how we can help, or how people can live healthier," Steve interrupted. "Your mom will be here this weekend. I bet she'll even become a pro building pirate ships."

Thanks to yours truly, Maren thought, appreciating how he'd jumped in with a save, explaining what she struggled to clarify.

"Will you die like my daddy?"

Maren turned almost white. For a brief second, Steve thought he might have to thrust her head between her knees to keep her from tumbling. When he saw her bottom lip quiver, he knew she held back tears. She would let those loose in her bedroom behind its closed door.

"Sometimes people get sick, but that doesn't mean they'll die," Steve reassured him. Another verbal save. "You were sick. Look at you having a great time with new toys."

"Steve, you fixed me," Dylan said, fiddling with the spines on two books that remained on his bed. "You can make Mommy better."

There was nothing Steve couldn't do in Dylan's mind. He had grown more comfortable with him in recent weeks. Typically, Dylan would call Maren merely Mom instead of the more child-like name he'd used in preschool. Hearing it now, she felt a slight clutch inside.

"Go get ready for bed," Steve instructed Maren. "I can finish up here."

"Thanks," she said softly, leaning to kiss her son. "I love you, sleep tight." Steve stayed longer turning the conversation to other topics to distract Dylan.

He tiptoed into Maren's bedroom. Steve hadn't planned to stay this late, yet Maren needed to process today's consult in Baltimore, the plan they had created with her doctor, and now Dylan's onset of emotion that they hadn't seen coming. Maren finished brushing her teeth as Steve closed the door behind him.

"I think he's settled," he reported.

"Finally," Maren said. A quick look at the wastebasket showed half-a-dozen tissues discarded after drying Maren's eyes. She spit out the remaining toothpaste, rinsed, and rattled her cup as it slipped from her hand crashing along the bathroom counter.

Startled, Steve walked to the doorway. "Geez, Maren."

She turned, took in a deep breath. Let it go. "What did you tell him?"

"That you'll be here this weekend. He settled. It just took talking it through and distracting him. You ought to make that topic into one of your marketing pieces." Maren handed Steve a spare toothbrush from the vanity drawer. "Boys don't have gab fests like women do…you ought to know that by now."

"Thanks for poking fun at my gender. Brush your teeth and let's talk. I need to think. Some of us process out loud," she said. "But that's a good idea. I'm running that by Alicia."

"Make sure my department gets credit," he said toothbrush still in his mouth.

"It figures," she said turning down the bed. The thought of getting in, never coming out seemed appealing.

Handing Steve a toothbrush had invited him overnight. Maren would make the guest room look as if he slept there. Silly she mused, but she still wasn't comfortable sleeping together, certainly not around Dylan. Not yet.

"You OK doing this Friday?" Steve asked Maren. "It's great he can work you into that opening." A last-minute cancellation created a spot on Friday's schedule, and the doctor's office held it until her consult.

"Yes or I'll worry over another weekend." No one faces your fears except you. Maren's father taught her this long ago; living by it more difficult, for sure. "So with another sonogram to guide things, he uses these God awful needles, to remove tissue?"

"God awful?" Steve lay on her bed.

"Monstrous then," she said, one hand on her hip, the other grabbing the comforter to crawl next to him, only beneath the covers.

"A Halloween word. 'Tis the season." Never argue with an anxious patient: Steve's motto for the moment. He confirmed that a core needle biopsy uses a larger needle guided into the area to remove a small cylinder of tissue. "It eliminates an incision, but he'll go in multiple times to get the samples," Steve told her. "He'll likely use ultrasound to direct things. It'll be fine, Maren. Depends on different factors. No clear-cut answer."

"Clear cut. Surgeon-speak." Maren cringed. "I hate large needles, no matter how numb they make me."

"Beats excising it." His words fell upon a woman who failed to see any bright side. "Much less invasive."

She turned to Steve. "No offense, but layoff the fancy words for cutting. I'm nauseous already. I'm supposed to be awake, but numb? That's inhumane." She burrowed her head into his arms.

Steve held her, directed a few deep breaths, and reminded that Zofran prevents nausea. Stroking her hair and reassurance wasn't working quite as quickly.

Maren patted the empty pit in her stomach discussing Dylan and how to handle his stress, worse than her envisioned physical pain. Spending some one-on-one would help since he stayed with Maren's parents last weekend and would be there Thursday if they had to be in Baltimore early on Friday.

"By Saturday, you should feel much better. Maybe a little bruised. I'm working so just corral Dylan for a quiet weekend." Easier spoken tonight than made reality over two and a half days indoors, Steve realized. "Your parents might want to give you a hand."

Audrey and Jack would gladly help, but Dylan knew that the sudden onset of grandparents several times within one week meant crisis loomed or already had occurred.

Especially since Steve shortened his workweek, outside of a dire emergency, he couldn't take the weekend off, scheduled to be on call. "Emergency" sparked Maren to stiffen again, prompting Steve to reassure her—once again—as he'd done about a half-dozen times that this wasn't likely.

It also made him wonder if she needed to titrate up her anti-anxiety medication at the very time she was trying to get by on less. And, they had raised the issue today of birth control. Hormonal fluctuations sometimes affected breast tissue, but this was more solid.

Women lowered their risk factors overall with positive lifestyle changes—a low-fat diet favoring fruits and vegetables, moderate exercise, and by increasing their number of live births. Some birth control was better than others and protected against other cancers.

"Prevent pregnancy but get knocked up and have kids," Maren said sarcastically. "No wonder it's mind-boggling."

"It's not all your responsibility here, you know," Steve reassured her. "We can sacrifice some spontaneity if we have to."

"Why? We're both healthy, right? I hated a diaphragm...barriers... thinking you'd feel the same." Maren eyed him.

"Truthfully, you're right." He smiled back. "We were blessed with a little spontaneity this weekend," he said, sinking into the pillow, turning to face her. "Whatever else occurs on that boat—in bed, on the floor, against the counter—pales by comparison."

"Decided then. I'll use this when I switch," she said, tossing Steve the sample from her nightstand along with the pamphlet Claire Clements had given her. "Less estrogen she said. No remembering a pill."

Steve gave it a once-over and set it aside, starting to fade. With everyone's emotions, Steve had done so much talking recently that he figured it should all add up to being board-certified in psychiatry—by the end of this week.

"We'll get through this. If you really need to be sedated, ask about it." Knowing her anxious brain, Steve would make sure he alerted them though it might seem unnecessary.

"That twilight stuff. I need that."

111

Not the precise term he and his staff used for conscious sedation, but he wasn't correcting her. If there was such a thing as twilight, Steve surely wanted some now so that they could shut up, turn out the light and both sleep. "Focus ahead. Next weekend. We're going to the football game."

"I'll finally get to meet your friend Paul and see his wife again." Maren breathed deliberately and nestled her body deeper under the queen-sized comforter. She hadn't planned for Steve to be there with her, certainly not this long into the evening. She rather liked it though.

"You're doing great." He said it as much for her benefit as his own. Yet deep inside, the usually self-assured Steve Kramer was not as certain as he let on. Hearing him rustle as if he was leaving her to sleep and possibly going to use the guest room, Maren reached up to kiss him on the cheek.

"Will you stay? Please," she whispered, feeling vulnerable. Any hesitancy about him sleeping in her bed evaporated. She simply wanted him close.

Steve didn't need convincing. Shoes already off, somewhere downstairs, he shook off his shirt and slacks, hanging them in Maren's closet. He cast everything else onto the floor.

He made love to her that night, more tenderly. He had had his way with her and she with him, over the weekend, playfully spending more energy with three rounds than either of them had right now.

As a doctor he couldn't offer the woman he loved and the boy he cared about any guarantees, but he could make Maren feel special and desired, which he did effortlessly. Limbs intertwined, they whispered to one another, and Steve set his Blackberry to wake up early. Much of Maren's worry and their uncertainty he'd meet all over again the next day.

On Thursday, finishing work, Maren made two trips to her car, first with her bag in which she transported projects between home and the hospital, and next with the crystal vase still brimming with roses. She wanted to keep enjoying them, especially if she ended up physically sore and mentally out-of-sorts.

Maren picked up Dylan from after-care, started him on homework and made dinner. Audrey and Jack were taking Dylan later that evening. He would miss school, but Friday was a light day for instruction, and Audrey said she'd occupy his mind as well as hers, while Steve took Maren to Baltimore.

"Dylan balked at math, second time this week," Maren confessed.

"I can go over it with him tomorrow," Audrey reassured her.

"Thanks, Mom."

Audrey and Jack had dessert with their grandson and sat around the kitchen table as Maren stacked the leftover food in plastic refrigerator containers and wiped off the counter.

"Doesn't look as if you ate much." Audrey cast a concerned look toward Jack.

"I'm not very hungry mom," Maren said. "Dylan, show them what your teacher gave you today."

"Look…it's purple," Dylan said, pulling a foam football out of his backpack and hurling it above. Since it wasn't the kind to cause destruction, Maren sanctioned tossing it above the table. "We celebrated birthdays for the month. Grampy play catch!" Dylan waited a minute until Jack could gain some distance and threw it into the adjoining family room.

Maren's smile seemed pasted on; the distraction not enough to sway Audrey. "You're nervous, honey. I can tell when you keep busy and you're quiet."

"Maybe." She met her mom's eyes. "OK, I am."

Bringing the rest of the cookies, Audrey approached. "Have one. You probably can't eat after a while."

Begrudgingly, Maren took a chocolate chip, bit into it and closed her eyes. "Chocolate helps."

"Steve's here," Dylan yelled out, running to the door as he spotted the black convertible pull into the driveway.

He cast the ball to Jack, who took a peek out the window shade. "Nice car," he said loud enough for Maren to hear as she moved to the door. She nodded, still struggling to bend her lips into anything remotely positive. Though she wanted to see Steve now whenever she could, tonight reminded her of the inevitable. Tomorrow morning. Oblivious of Maren behind him, Dylan grabbed the knob and pulled it open first.

"Hi," Steve said, stepping inside.

"How was your day?" Maren asked, walking closer. Steve pulled her in for a hug and kissed her on the cheek.

"No major crises. How 'bout yours?"

"Over." Maren's face froze into a frazzled frown. "Dylan, please." He jumped at Steve's side like a beagle.

"He's fine, Maren." Steve tousled his hair. "What's up?"

"This one's for you," Dylan offered, handing Steve one of his prized possessions—a football trading card featuring one of Steve's Pittsburgh Steelers. "Mom told me you think the Steelers rock."

"She's right." Steve took the card, and as Maren closed the door, her parents stepped forward greeting him again.

"You remember my mom and dad, right?"

"Jack Cole, yes we met in Dylan's room last month," her father said, shaking Steve's hand. "And my wife Audrey."

Standing with the card Dylan just bestowed, Steve tried to joke. "Off to a bad start here with the locals maybe?" He waved it in the air. "Dylan, thanks dude. What a set up!"

"From Philly originally. I root for the Eagles. No worries." He gently slapped a hand on Steve's back. "One thing about Pittsburgh fans. They're loyal."

"Indeed." Steve laughed. "Took hold during my years there. My dad and brother never cease to remind me that I betrayed the Redskins."

Maren led them into the family room where they took seats. Jack learned the short story of Steve's path through three states landing back into Maryland because he loved the water. They talked about Steve's decision to get the powerboat this year.

"When can we go back out?" Dylan wanted to know. "Are there still fish?"

"A whole bay full of them, Dylan." Steve smiled. "Maybe next time, you and your grandfather can come out. We'll make it a guy's day." Steve put his arm around Maren, tugging on her shoulder. "Ladies welcome, too."

"No just us guys." Dylan was adamant, and they all laughed. Jack learned that Steve knew how to sail and extended a similar invitation, if the weather held up. He told Steve how he taught Maren to sail at about Dylan's age.

"That would be great," Steve said accepting. "I'd love to see your daughter in her element."

Maren put her head on Steve's shoulder. "Dylan, why don't you go upstairs…be sure you have everything. You're not coming back until tomorrow night," she advised her son. "Homework goes, too."

"No," he protested.

"Yes!"

If the power struggle wasn't uncomfortable enough, Maren knew her parents concealed a hint of worry in their faces—likely caught by contagion from her own anxiety—so with Steve there, staying over to get her to the early appointment, she knew the subject couldn't be forestalled. Already 7:30, Dylan needed to get to bed at his grandparents' house.

"Jack and I want to thank you for helping Maren. She says you've made quite a few calls to get her seen more quickly," Audrey said. Her eyes looked into Steve's with admiration.

"It's the least I can do," he said. "This guy's one of the best in the country. He does tons of these." Steve dug into his pocket for two of his business cards and spotting a pen on the coffee table, retrieved it to write his personal number on the back of each. "Here's my cell. I'll call you tomorrow if you'd like, and feel free to call me."

Jack took out one of his cards, taking the pen to write their contact information before handing it to Steve. "Appreciate that. We're obviously concerned."

"You've reviewed all this with them?" Steve asked Maren, still nestled next to him on the sofa.

"Best as I can," she said. "I'd rather not go into it again. I'll check on Dylan so they can get him settled tonight. I have a feeling I'll find homework stuffed in the hamper if I don't make sure he has it." Maren wiggled out of Steve's grasp and left the room. They all witnessed her tension. It wasn't on account of spelling words and backtalk.

"She takes these things in small doses," Audrey indicated. "Maren did tell you there's no family history on either side."

"Yeah she did, and that's good." Steve leveled his eyes and tone with her parents. "She's got a lot of things in her favor. We'll know a little more tomorrow and with the tissue samples and path report next week."

"Let us know if there's anything you need us for," Jack said. "Otherwise, we're bringing Dylan back tomorrow night, right?"

"Yes, and we'll bring over something quick for dinner," Audrey said. "Please join us if you can."

"Thanks," Steve said. "If all goes well, we'll be out by late morning. I'll have to see some patients, but will get her back here first then check in later. Unfortunately, I'm on call this weekend." Steve's frown indicated how much he would rather spend any free time with Maren. "She shouldn't drive tomorrow with any sedation, but by Saturday, she should be fine. Sore, but fine."

Dylan and Maren came down the stairs bearing his backpack and overnight bag. Hearing their steps, the three of them got up, walking to the door. Maren nudged against Steve again and instinctively his arm moved around her side. Hugs, handshakes and "good luck" abounded, and while it all helped, Maren just wanted the next day to be over as soon as possible.

Steve retrieved his own bag for staying the night. Maren wanted to take a sleeping pill in the worst way, but didn't. Swallowing a few gulps of water, she attempted sleep, drifting off with Steve's arm curved around her much of the night.

On Friday, his alarm woke them at five so that they could be one of the day's first cases. Neither of them joked about maps or whether he remembered his way into the city.

Prepped for the procedure in a holding room, Steve sat by Maren's side as she answered everyone's checklists. Nothing to eat or drink after midnight. Zoloft 25 mg. Daily birth control pills, at least for now. An occasional sleeping pill. None last night.

They chatted briefly with the specialist, who left as they met with an anesthesiologist. Maren's doctor had introduced Steve as a former attending.

"Can you put me in twilight?" Maren asked.

"She gets very anxious," Steve told him. The anesthesiologist saw her tension.

"Good to know," he said. "We'll relax you, Maren, along with the local anesthetic." The doctor chatted a moment with Steve.

"OK," Maren told them. "Whatever you're calling it…I don't really care as long as I don't feel it or feel like I'm in there."

"Really?" Steve grinned at her, smiled at the anesthesiologist, and steadied the clipboard as she signed the consents.

Before they wheeled her down the hall, Steve reached over the bars on her mobile bed to kiss her softly on the cheek. "I love you. See you in a while," he whispered.

Steve grabbed a bite to eat. He had dealt with his own stomach pangs, out of deference to her needing an empty stomach. Coffee in hand, he read internal news on the hospital bulletin board. A recognized name here, an accolade there all brought back memories. It had been almost four years since he had left this place to move on with the experiences gained.

Steve knew they would take their time, likely utilizing additional imagery to further evaluate if they had removed the mass and any surrounding tissue. He was trained to digest certain details and look at things clinically. A bit of objectivity went out the window now when the woman he loved and had waited for, for much of his adult life, lay in that procedure room in someone else's hands. He bided his time until Maren could be in his, once again.

Steve read emails on his smartphone, finished his java, and before long, the nurse called him into recovery where he sat as Maren became alert.

"Good morning gorgeous," Steve said, voice low but audible enough over monitors and nurses chatting. "It's all over." The surgeon briefed Steve immediately and would give Maren a report when she could listen.

"Mmm." Her eyes fluttered but landed back closed. Maren's recovery nurse hovered in and out. Another few minutes went by before Maren stirred again. "Where am I? Is it over?"

Steve smiled. He reached out to squeeze her hand. "You're sleepy…all over." Steve had a sense she still wasn't with him in a true cognitive way. But very shortly hearing the two male voices, Maren's eyes startled.

"We got it all," her doctor told Maren, outlining what he did and that a more detailed report would follow with the conclusive evidence. They had gone in at least four times removing tissue. "I'm feeling pretty optimistic, but you need to wait a little longer. I'll be in touch next week."

Though groggy, Maren thanked the surgeon. He pulled Steve outside of the curtain, stepping a few paces from it. They had known each other professionally, but not really on a personal level. Steve thanked him, especially for the expediency he'd created for Maren and managing her over-the-top anxiety.

"Serious?" Steve's colleague asked, with subtle curiosity, arching a brow.

Steve blushed and gently bobbed his head—non-committal you-better-believe-I-am guy code.

"Lucky man. I'm glad I could help, Steve." He shook his hand and braced Steve's arm with his other. "Good luck with your new position.

Chapter 8

After bringing Maren home, Steve put in a few hours seeing patients, leaving Maren to rest quietly. By early evening, Maren's parents returned Dylan, bringing pizza and salad.

As she set out plates, salad bowls and silverware, Audrey motioned for her husband. The crystal vase Maren brought home from work sat with the card still stuck between the edges of the plastic stick that held it among the red roses.

"Thanks for two incredibly beautiful Saturdays on the seas! I'm here for you always. I love you, Steve," Audrey read aloud to her husband. Maren wasn't too far from the kitchen, but Audrey said it in tones meant only for Jack. She angled her head. "This is getting serious. A gorgeous, bouquet, and this card..."

"She had a look about her last Sunday picking up Dylan." Jack smirked. "They're spending a lot of time together. Whatever's going on, I get a message here that I ought to call a florist soon myself." He gave Audrey a squeeze and planted a smooch on her cheek.

They walked into the room to sit down with Maren. "Beautiful flowers, honey." Jack caught his daughter's eyes. She spotted their affection. Blushed.

"Yeah. Talk of the office, too." She laughed. "I would have to date the hospital's most eligible bachelor. Good thing I already had friends in my department. They'd resent me otherwise."

"We got plain for me and veggie something for you guys, Mom," Dylan announced running to the boxes on the counter. "Want a piece?"

"Thanks sweetie," Maren said. "You're such a helper." Audrey gave Dylan the salad tongs to scoop and take salad to his mom, while Jack ate with Dylan in the kitchen. The rooms joined like an L-shape allowing conversation.

As promised, Steve stopped by with Dylan charging the front door again. Rounding the corner into the family room, Steve saw Audrey and Jack, now chatting on the sectional sofa. Maren lounged on the other half, in sweat pants and a loosely fitting sweatshirt, which he knew hid a small bandage.

"How ya feeling?" Steve asked as he leaned down and their mouths met for a chaste kiss. Steve shook Jack's hand and Audrey thanked him again for updating them before they left Baltimore.

"Freezing," she said, reaching under her sweatshirt to remove the small ice pack she'd been instructed to place there throughout the first day home. "How much longer do I have to keep creating the arctic tundra?"

Steve cringed knowing it was uncomfortable. He would have told her how he'd gladly warm her up, but with her parents—not to mention Dylan—and his returning to the hospital that would be an empty promise.

"If you've iced throughout the day, not much longer. Any bleeding?"

"Not really. I changed the bandage once." Maren sat to make room for him.

"I'll take a look before I leave." Steve ran his fingers through her hair, out of any clip, flowing free the way he loved it. "You're doing great. Here's your first report," he said handing her a large manila envelope. "I sent one to Claire though she'll get the final report."

"Thanks. If it's got those pictures, they can look. Not me." Maren glanced over at her parents. "He doesn't give that to all people, I hope."

"Probably for my benefit as his colleague," Steve said, extending the envelope. "They're graphic."

Audrey opened it carefully and grimaced. "Still confident it's all removed?"

"Looks that way. We'll have another report next week," Steve said. Maren looked skeptical, still a little unsure with defeat in her eyes. "I know you're feeling rough, but he's feeling positive," Steve said. "I'd prescribe a smile." She forced her lips to curve. "That's it." He ran his fingers along her face.

"You've got to be hungry," Maren said. She'd never known him not to be, unless he had an appetite for something he surely wasn't getting tonight. "There's pizza and some salad."

It was nearly eight, and Steve had called from the hospital telling them that he was running late and not to hold off eating. "Yeah, I will." Steve's phone rang. Reaching into the belt holder, he looked at the caller ID.

"Hello." Steve listened. "Hannah…my sweetheart," he said enthusiastically. "How *are* you?" He waited a minute more. "Well, I miss you, too. Very much." Maren looked at him but Steve was in his own world.

"I know, I haven't seen you in a while. What are you doing?" He kept the cell phone close to his ear. "Hannah, what are you wearing," he asked diverting his gaze, with an exaggerated tone that sent Maren into what-the-hell mode, her brown eyes burning into Steve. Her parents sitting here surely wondered who Hannah was. Maren hadn't a clue.

"OK, we'll have to get together. Soon." He waved Maren off, grinning. He caught the astonished look about Jack and Audrey. "Yes, Hannah. I did promise. My apartment. I'll check my calendar." Shifting tone, Steve kept talking. "Liz, what's up? No, I'm just havin' a little fun. Chill."

Steve got up, walking to the counter where he saw the pizza. He helped himself to a plate, placing a slice on it. "Yeah, forgot. Sounds good. Just put my name on it, and let me know how much." He took a bite, small enough to continue his conversation. "No, really, she could spend the night with me. Throw in Tyler, too. I'm up for a shift."

Steve leaned into the cabinets. "Remember Liz, I worked a 28-30 hour peds shift in my day—with no sleep, mind you. I can handle it." Steve brought a plate with another slice and sat back down. By now he was the center of attention, save for Dylan who had crawled onto his grandfather's lap with the football he'd retrieved from tossing it yesterday.

"In fact, I've got the perfect playmate for Tyler." His eyes motioned from Maren to Dylan. She adjusted her frown to a bewildered pout, shaking her head.

"Your anniversary is coming up, right? Let's pick a time and I'll take them." He took another bite, before saying, "One of you will thank me. Probably your better half."

Dylan crawled off Jack toward Steve. "Hey Liz, gotta run. Thanks for handling that. Mom'll love it. You too. Give my sweetheart a kiss for me. A big one," he said, managing a click and another pucker to Maren's forehead.

Irreverently, she studied him.

"Sorry, Hannah was here first." Steve winked and pulled her alongside him. "Hannah, my niece, wanted to say goodnight. Burns my sister Liz when she stalls and begs to talk to me." Steve didn't care that he cast a smug profile in the room. "For my mom's birthday, we went together on a gift."

"You never cease to surprise me, Steve Kramer." Maren saw Steve as confident, but he certainly was lighthearted tonight. At the mention of buying his mother a gift, however, he got a grin from Audrey. Jack laughed watching the banter between Steve and his daughter.

Steve set his plate down and took his Blackberry out of its holder again. "Here, tell me she's not adorable." He flashed her the picture of his three-year-old niece, stretching it forward and moving closer to Maren's mom, then her dad.

"That's such a good picture of the two of you," Audrey commented. The photo showed Hannah hugging Steve.

"She is really cute, but Steve, really? What's gotten into you?" Maren demanded.

"I know you're uncomfortable. My reality, though: This could be so different." Steve ran his fingers again through her hair. He knew it calmed her, and saw her neck relax with each subtle tug he had locked through his fingers. "Plus, I have to work tonight, all day Saturday and tomorrow night. That sucks."

"Steve," she admonished, poking his ribs. "Watch your language."

"Duty calls, I suppose," Jack added, chuckling at Maren's mood, trying to shift things. "One of my friends told me you removed his gallbladder." Jack told Steve the name. "Spoke highly of you."

Steve accepted the compliment but couldn't carry the conversation any further. Jack understood the bounds of that.

"How old is Hannah?" Audrey asked. "You have another niece?"

"She's three but two in that picture. Tyler, my nephew, is the same age as Dylan actually."

"Oh, no wonder," she said laughing. "Steve, Maren's always been slow to warm when she's not feeling well. I think you really had her."

"That was my plan," he said, raising a brow to Maren, smiling at her folks.

"Mom, that's not true," she shot back. "Ouch." She'd moved and the discomfort dug a little deeper. "Maybe I need to become an iceberg again." Maren got up to retrieve another fresh brick of solid cold torture, slipping it discreetly under her sweatshirt as she sat back down.

They chatted more about his niece and nephew, Steve telling them how they lived on the eastern shore and how his sister doubted he could babysit more than four hours at a stretch. They had clearly heard his offer to become uncle on call for a weekend.

Steve's pager vibrated at almost the same moment his cell rang again. "See I told you it…" Steve whispered "sucks" and pulled away to avoid being disciplined. He'd seen her poised hand ready to swat, but he evaded her. Steve looked at the caller ID and silenced the pager.

"It's the ED. Sorry," he said. "Steve Kramer, here."

He listened for a long minute, as Maren studied his reaction. Steve's eyes shifted into work mode, his brows narrowed, and she was beginning to recognize his stance of calm amid brewing storms.

"OK, listen up," he said, straightening his spine. "How far out are the EMTs? How much detail does the charge nurse have?" Another pause. "Agreed. We'll need more than a little backup and blood supply. Who is on in ortho?"

Sure enough, Maren thought, all hell was about to enter the emergency department.

"I'll take the GSW. Who is the cardiac surgeon on call? I want someone scrubbing in with me on that one." He paused. Pushed himself up and strode to the kitchen, still talking. No one else dared to, and when Dylan tried, Audrey shushed him.

"No, that's not a request. Make it happen." He took in more details. "Well, find him and get him in there with me. We're doing it right under my watch." He listened longer. "I'm about 15 minutes out. Call in the surgical residents. I can do both of those you just mentioned. Ortho can oversee that last one. I'm on my way." He clicked off his phone and put his pager back.

"Some nights busy; some deluged," he said acknowledging the truth behind Jack's earlier comment. "It's going to be a long night."

Dylan flicked on the remote and a trailer of words—the ones that started around 9/11 and news organizations still loved to use—started crawling with the words "shooting" and "car accident" at the bottom of the screen.

"Oh my," Maren said, grabbing the remote such that her ice pack landed on the floor. "GSW means gun shot wound. The DC stuff?"

Steve picked it up, handed her the ice pack, and brushed his chilly hand on his slacks. He met Maren's look of horror. "Don't think so, but I wouldn't watch the news. Trust me." His eyes shot her parents a cautionary look. "I know how these things bother her. Let's not ruin a good day."

Maren leaned back into the sofa with a sigh.

"Damn, I didn't ask about traffic." Steve reached onto his belt again. "Back-up plan," he announced, punching in a number saved into his cell.

"Hey Sarge, it's Steve Kramer. With that situation brewing, I've got to get into the ED. STAT. Not sure what the highway looks like between the hospital and ..."

Maren tried to tune this out. Her memory flooded with images of a pile-up. Steve gave the person her complete address.

"If I leave my car here, can you get me there in ten? No fanfare and lights, OK. A residential neighborhood." He stopped, listening. "I'm at my girlfriend's house." He paused, now chuckling. "Yeah, she is pretty hot, actually." Steve put his hand on Maren's thigh. "Thanks. Appreciate it."

He clicked off his phone. Maren's eyes not only rolled, they bulged at him.

"I didn't make that one up, I swear. Friday night. He feels for me," Steve said with a shoulder shrug to her parents. "If I didn't have to be there, I'd be here." He handed Maren his car keys though he'd pulled alongside her parents' car.

"I'm honored, but how will you get...your Jag?" she asked.

"I'll call you tomorrow. We'll work it out."

"If traffic is jammed, maybe we're staying here too," Jack said. "Audrey brought an overnight bag. We can get you tomorrow."

"We'd be glad to," Audrey piped in. "We'll keep her company."

Maren gauged Steve up and down with her eyes. "Everyone must do what you tell them?" Steve didn't get to be the chief of surgery without a calm command taking charge and paying attention to detail. Seeing it in action could turn heads, as it certainly had turned theirs.

"Most of the time. Except for my sister, brother, a few others. Keeps me in check." He winked. "Speaking of checking, I promised to look at that," he said, motioning Maren into the privacy of the powder room. He hoisted her sweatshirt fast, peeled open the double-width bandage, and put her shirt back down again. "Looks good, but change it before bed. Ice off and on, until then."

"Ugh," she groaned. "I'm counting down the hours."

"My ride's here," Steve said. He moved back into the family room and looked out the blinds to the squad car pulling into the driveway. No lights, no sirens. Just fast.

"Wow, a police car on our street." Dylan ran to the window to peek out. "That's wack!"

"Dylan…where do you learn this stuff?" Maren asked.

"I'll call you tomorrow." Steve kissed her on the mouth, waved off her parents and Dylan, still ogling the vehicle, and dashed out the front door.

"I've got a police car." Dylan dashed up the stairs to find it.

Maren shook her head. Steve Kramer certainly had a sense of gravitas. He was a force that others soon learned how to deal with or else they were left behind.

She knew his job brought with it high stakes and a constant fast pace. When he wasn't operating on a schedule with a carefully outlined treatment plan, he was saving lives—often on the heels of fate—such as tonight. He had studied and trained for it with long hours, years of additional education, and probably getting his ass kicked a few times learning to handle such pressure and pull it off successfully. This was his life. But could she make it even a fraction of hers, as they spent more and more time together?

"I guess we'll settle in upstairs," Audrey said, looking at the muted television where the crawl reported heavy backup along the highway they'd take home. She clicked it off.

"That's all right. Dylan won't mind," Jack said. "Maybe Maren won't either." He cast admiration at his daughter who wasn't at her best.

"Thanks for putting up with us. More active here when Steve's around."

"Well, I can tell you one thing," Jack said, meeting Maren's eyes. "That man can't keep his hands off you."

"The look of love," Audrey added. "Him and you. A little chemistry?"

"Nothing little." Jack delivered it as fact, affectionately reaching for his wife.

Maren smiled. She fell silent taking note of the tenderness between them…and at their assessment. Their daughter had a new guy in her life. A sexy, successful man, albeit one that threw her off whenever his fast-paced life allowed some levity into it. She crossed her arms against her chest.

"Ouch." Maren muffled a wince. Pulling the plastic blue brick from underneath her shirt, she declared, "I'm so done with this for today." She rinsed and popped it into the freezer, rounding back to her parents. "What do you think?"

"About what?" Jack answered.

"You know."

"Steve's right," her mother said. "We were worried, but according to what he said, you may have more reason to smile next week."

"I think Maren's asking about Steve, Audrey. If we like him."

"What about Steve?" Dylan said, coming downstairs, with a toy police car and figures. "Where is he?"

"He had to go to the hospital, Dylan. He'll be there most of the weekend," Maren told him.

"In the police car?" Dylan stood, hands on his hips. "That sucks. I wanted him to stay."

Before Maren could reprimand him, her dad stepped forward steering his grandson to bed. "Well, Maren, Dylan's approval decided it." By the hand, Jack led Dylan upstairs. Friday night: No getting up for school Saturday.

"Yeah, and Dylan, we'll talk about that mouth and better words," Maren said, her voice trailing as they climbed to the top. Maren muttered to her mother that she'd talk to Steve as well.

Audrey helped her daughter gather anything she needed for the night. "Maren, go easy on Steve. He has a stressful job." She got herself a glass of water and came in as Maren shut off the lamps. "Instead of asking us what we think, what do *you* think?"

"I miss him already and he just left five minutes ago."

They shared what only a mom and daughter could. Audrey put her hand on Maren's back, rubbing it along the base of her neck.

"You haven't done that in a while," Maren said knowing that the last time she had physically comforted Maren eased away grief and intense sorrow.

"I'm glad you're happy," Audrey said. "We are, too. Let's get some sleep."

Steve called Maren Saturday morning, having had possibly 90 minutes of sleep in an on-call room and maybe another hour this morning. He had been pressed into service by a horrific multi-car

126

pileup that landed several cases in operating rooms. Horrific seemed as fitting a description for Steve's weekend.

Jack offered to give him a reprieve picking him up. Maren's father called upon hospitalized church members granting him knowledge of the elevator, coffee shop, and usually the geriatric floor. Today Jack got better oriented as he found his way to Steve's office.

Jack sat in the small waiting area perusing magazines meant for patients. Suzanna, a woman whose age cast her as one of Jack's contemporaries, had unlocked Steve's office and was busy between her computer and files she shifted into cabinets. She chatted with Jack until Steve, still in scrubs, strode through the door at 11:30.

"Suzanna, you're here on a Saturday?"

"Same as you, Dr. Kramer. Working…catching up," she said.

He smiled knowing she would veer to the formal. "Steve," he corrected. "This is Maren's father, Suzanna."

"Ah, I got to know her in orientation." Suzanna didn't add that Maren's presence in Steve's office seemed to increase weekly ever since.

"Suzanna started when I took this job. Might look otherwise, but she runs the show here," Steve said. "And does it damn well. Come on in, Jack."

Steve motioned him in while he answered a question for his secretary. "Seriously, this stuff will be here Monday. Go home. Enjoy your family." He shut the door behind him.

The time alone in Steve's office gave Jack a few moments to survey the trappings—wooden desk, sofa and lamps. Several framed degrees and plaques graced the walls. The one above his desk came from Columbia, and the others testified to other trainings and board certification. Books and medical journals neatly standing in plastic holders filled bookcase shelves. A photo of what had to be Steve's boat sat on his desk.

"Busy night?" Jack asked, taking a seat across from Steve.

"Yes," he said, taking his own chair and rubbing his temples, elbows planted into the dark grained wood. "Amazing we didn't lose anyone either." Steve shook his head, deliberately keeping the brutal details to himself. "Thanks for retrieving me. How's Maren?"

"She's doing well. In a better mood, too." He laughed. "You know women." Jack said it amusingly, but half of him wondered how much skill with women Steve had acquired. Given the dates on degrees, Jack established about 20 years between this man courting his daughter and himself.

"You've got the learning curve." Steve smiled. "Maren's been through a lot, I know."

It made Jack speculate how much Steve knew, and being a father, made him cautious. Steve Kramer could have—and certainly did by the gossip Maren mentioned—his pick of many women. Right now, he chose Jack's daughter.

"She has. Were you here a year and a half ago?" Jack asked, gingerly broaching the subject. "When Mark passed away."

"I was, but obviously not involved on that case." Steve sat back. He started to shut down his computer but lifted his fingers off the keyboard quickly. "Maren told me…not much…hesitant to talk about it. Perfectly awful, I figure."

"Mark was hit on his way home one night," Jack shared. "May 2001, by a drunk driver, high on something else, too. Involved another vehicle as well."

"Oh my," Steve said. "She hadn't shared that part."

"He wasn't very far from home when it happened. The car flipped and rolled across the highway. Totaled. The medics were lucky to get him out; his injuries were extensive."

"They brought him here though. No air lifting him to Baltimore?"

"I don't know how they decide those things," Jack said. "I just know that the whole experience devastated Maren. Physically, she couldn't sleep, lost a lot of weight, and grew very anxious." That Steve knew all too well. "Mark's parents, and Maren to some extent, got upset at the medical community, and at the driver. Audrey and I never blamed the hospital or doctor, but the guy responsible…"

"What happened to him?" Steve asked.

"The son-of-a-bitch ended up here only to be released with a broken arm and a concussion. Don't know exactly." Jack held his head with the palm of his left hand, propped by the chair's armrest. "Settled out of court. We advised her to take that instead of facing it all over again in court." It had quieted Mark's parents in Seattle, but Jack didn't divulge that.

"That's wise. I appreciate your sharing. I won't let on, if you'd like."

"We don't keep secrets, but obviously some topics we tread lighter than others." He shifted, glancing around the office. "Maren has come this far, surprisingly about West Riverside. Obviously you've had a hand in that. Looks as if you're already calling some new shots around here given last night."

"Yes, I saw her work; she's a great addition," he said. "In this job, I hope I can make a difference. I'm a repair guy—a fixer—by nature. Love being in the OR. I better since I've given it two decades," Steve shared. "Now, with paperwork…I'd be lost without Suzanna. Wasn't easy getting her in here."

"Oh?" Jack asked. "Did you get a say?"

"Insisted on it," Steve acknowledged. "Told HR I didn't want anyone fresh from some program. I wanted experience, age, and no drama. So what did they send me in the first interview round?"

Jack's eyes looked empty, without answer.

Steve put his feet on the edge of his desk. "Twenty to thirty-year-olds. I said 'no thanks,' and HR told me I couldn't discriminate. Really. Sent me a handbook of policies, as if I hadn't already had one."

"Some men might have enjoyed the selection process." Jack contracted his face into a smile, awaiting a response.

Steve tossed his pen onto the desk blotter. "I've learned to keep things separate. The only thing I want to chase around this desk is your grandson who heads straight for this chair," Steve said, instantly retracting his stretched-out legs and letting it move at least half of the 360 degrees it was capable of when Dylan claimed it.

Jack Cole let out a hoot. Steve self-corrected. "Well, since we don't work together, I certainly don't mind chasing your daughter," Steve said. "But you figured that." He leveled soft eyes on Jack. "I hope that's OK."

"Maren doesn't need our permission for her personal life, Steve, but of course, we want to see her and Dylan happy. It hasn't been two years yet, but Audrey and I have seen Maren make many strides. As long as it stays that way."

"Well, if I don't add to her life, I'd deserve to hear about it," Steve replied. He straightened, slightly self-assured. "My intentions…are all good."

Satisfied with what he learned, Jack pushed himself up, out of the chair. "I better get you to your car," he said. "Or my daughter, wife, and grandson will tell me they're starving because they're holding lunch."

Steve checked the computer. It had shut down at first prompting. "Let's go. Won't be the first time Maren's seen me in scrubs."

As they headed out, Jack shared that he might need a new primary care physician since his retired. Steve recommended Paul in a heartbeat, adding how they'd trained together. Yet before his own heart needed a pacemaker, Steve realized he better give Paul a heads-up. This new patient would be a VIP—very important person. Paul had a heart of gold but a wicked wit bordering on the outrageous. At times sexualized, simply for effect. Oh yes, Steve would dial him on his way back to the hospital.

At Maren's, they all grabbed a sandwich before Steve took possession of his Jag and made that call. A fairly uneventful shift ahead might resurrect his body and mind by morning.

Her parents left after lunch. Jack took Dylan outside to burn off energy beforehand. Dylan played indoors the rest of the afternoon and watched a kid's movie with his mom. People still played it safe curtailing daily activities. Saturday seemed to reflect a lighter mood until another shooting that evening, this time in Ashland, Virginia. Even going to a restaurant brought terror.

"You're sure last night wasn't related to all this DC stuff?" Maren asked when Steve called Saturday night. Maren switched from frozen blue ice blocks to over-the-counter medication to deal with her soreness as well as the constant news reports that made most everyone news addicts again. A headache ensued.

"Certain of it," Steve answered. "I'd have had to turn over evidence to the police otherwise. Most cases, I'm not at liberty to say much, you realize."

"Which would be why I worry." Maren sighed. If he told her the complete and utter truth, it jacked up her nerves. Without it she wondered what might have happened that he kept inside. "I don't know how you do what you do."

"You get used to it. Some cases take more out of you than others, but that's why I get outdoors, exercise, escape with a good movie," he said. Maren told him that Dylan selected *Tarzan* tonight with a nice Phil Collins soundtrack.

"Speaking of movies, I'm having the pole installed on the boat."

"What pole?"

"The one for the galley. Not enough room in the cabin. I checked." Glad he had the phone to separate them, he explained. "Schedule some lessons, babe. Bill them to my credit card. I'll give you the number and expiration date. Even the code on the back." He tried to contain himself.

Seconds passed, not because of technology. "Maren...the movie, the interview you saw. I figured you'd want me to be really, super relaxed with all the stress I'm under."

"You're sick and hormonal," she sniffed into the receiver. She decided to leave out ego-driven for another time. "The day I dance around half-naked for you, is..."

"The day I've died and gone to heaven," he added, chuckling. "But you're smiling aren't you?"

"Smiling because you're unbelievable and there's discussion at work about what OR music ranks highest. Someone must listen to something sultry, and I'm starting to think as chief of your department you're behind it."

Steve nearly spit out the iced tea he'd nursed all evening as he laughed. "Wasn't me, but man, I wish it was. I'm much more into good Vivaldi or Mozart, a little New Age or Pop Rock. I save the sultry stuff for later." He took another swig and swabbed his scrubs of the iced tea. "I miss you. I really do."

"I'll bet." Steve detected the I-know-what-you-really-miss, but when her voice shifted lower to loneliness, they made plans for Sunday, providing he wasn't a walking, sleep-deprived zombie. "Goodnight Steve."

"Maren," he said softly. "I love you."

"I love you, too." She clicked the phone into its cradle on her nightstand.

Chapter 9

"How many times can I sort Schooner pieces and read Pirate stories," Maren asked Steve, as they cleared dinner dishes Monday at her house. "Pirates, Wolf Blitzer and Peter Jennings—isn't that normal fare for most families with young children these days?"

Surgery of one victim had removed the latest bullet and evidence in the still alarming sniper trail throughout Maryland, DC and Virginia. Unnerved residents wished they didn't have to consume news in order to stay safe.

Her weekend hadn't been nearly as eventful as Steve's, but with Dylan now consumed by LEGO building—meaning Maren didn't have to be—it was a definite step above fears of death and boxed trucks as well as biopsy reports. *Stay still inside. Only a few more days.*

"This is a sleepover you realize," Steve declared secretly whispering it to Maren, who quickly understood that the agenda had nothing whatsoever to do with sex. They both, he reminded her, had gotten a quick fix of that yesterday as Dylan played at a neighbor's house, meaning they could play in Maren's.

Monday Night Football came across ABC with the Pittsburgh Steelers lined up against the Indianapolis Colts at Heinz Field.

"Vicki feeds you and Paul, so that's my role here tonight, huh?" Maren had put veggies, hummus, and crackers out for munching. She tormented Steve as she sat crossed-legged on the floor, reviewing sections of the Sunday paper. How could she read the paper and watch football, he thought?

"Food helps with concentration," he answered, eyes to the first quarter that put his Steelers ahead. Steve's commentary at times surpassed that of Al Michaels and John Madden.

Dylan pouted when at 9:30, Maren tried to ply him from Steve's side. "You said I could watch. No fair."

"Dude, life's not always fair. Your mom and I are working on plans for next weekend. Hang tight," Steve said, eyes fixed on the quarterback's pass, but adding to the effort to get Dylan upstairs.

"What? Tell me," Dylan demanded.

"Steve, we don't have concrete plans," Maren said.

"Not yet, but…"

"Think dump trucks and construction vehicles," she interrupted putting six-year-old imagery and vocabulary into this. "If it's not cemented, it's not there." She paused. "I don't promise things I can't deliver. Do you doc?"

Watching Dylan pine for more details, Steve apologized. Maren listened to Dylan's complaints for the next 10 minutes, but she got him upstairs without too much stall.

"Settled?" Steve asked when she returned beside him.

"You'll pay for this," Maren said baring her teeth before softening. "Feed me…"

He leaned forward stabbing the hummus with carrots and a piece of cauliflower, handing it to her on a small plate. "Next Sunday," he said, nudging Maren closer to him during the half-time report. "Better know a little football trivia. How many Super Bowls have we won?"

"I've no clue. Three." Maren chomped on a carrot, not caring how loudly it crunched into his ear.

"Four," Steve corrected. "1975, '76, '79, and '80." Steve's eyes would have added a non-verbal exclamation point, if they could. "Next: Must-have item for any Steelers fan?"

"Food. Plenty of it." She extended her plate. "Two more please and we're putting this stuff away." Steve obliged. Probably true, it wasn't the answer as he grabbed his gold towel with embossed black lettering.

"The Terrible Towel, Steve. Is this really necessary?"

"It's more like 'tear-ble tahl' with a drawl. And yes, Paul may come across all professional at work, but in private, and with me, I'm warning you."

"He knows all your dirt then? This'll be even more fun."

Steve's head whipped around before he smirked. "I wouldn't put it quite that way. Just take him in stride."

"Well, I may not know all the intricacies of your team, but the Baltimore fan base is still miffed at losing their Colts in the middle of the night," Maren revealed watching that team now don Indianapolis jerseys. "Wear black and gold to work Friday. Find out where you stand. They won't give a crap you're the chief of surgery."

"We'll see about that," he said. Maren decided she'd definitely keep her thoughts about his ego in her pocket at all times. She hung around for another quarter tolerating football analysis and more tips on deciphering dialect. She wouldn't be caught dead using "yinz" when she met Paul, as Steve dared her to do. God help her, if she did. During the breaks, she cleared the coffee table.

"Keep your commentary down please," she warned, kissing his cheek. Steve stopped long enough to place hands on her legs, as she leaned over. Any other night, he'd worm his way upstairs, but as the ball snapped, he gently pushed her body aside as he sat up into the play. Action upstairs: another night. "Sleep tight," he said, patting her behind. He set his smartphone alarm. Steve never finished watching the 28-10 victory, having fallen asleep on Maren's couch.

Officials confirmed the tenth fatality in the Beltway sniper attacks as a bus driver was shot and police shared a chilling statement from the assailant: Children were not safe anywhere, any time. Half the region had to be turning to pharmaceuticals, Maren figured. Headlines drove up a normal blood pressure reading, set off muscle spasms, or caused a few temples to pound.

Too frightened to send Dylan to school that Wednesday, Maren had received another frustrating phone call from Mark's parents declaring that she must come to her senses and ship Dylan off to safety in Seattle. Appreciating their concern, that wasn't happening.

Without the complete pathology report, her stomach felt knotted as she woke at six a.m. to begin Thursday, until Maren flicked on the television. Every newscast carried the footage of police capturing two suspects found with the New Jersey tag numbers on the Chevy Caprice everyone looked for the prior evening. Fortunately, a truck driver called authorities and blocked the gunmen from Interstate 70 in Frederick County.

Maren rang Steve's cell. "They caught the people doing this. It's on CNN."

"Thank God," he replied. She told him more details, that there were two snipers—one underage. They were as shocked as the rest of the region.

That day, children like Dylan enjoyed outdoor recess. Most people—save a few anxious holdouts unconvinced the terrorizing ordeal had completely ended—no longer dashed from parking lots into their offices, and gas stations tore down huge tarps erected to protect patrons. Random searches causing snarled traffic—in a region that needed no more gridlock—ceased immediately. Schools went off lockdown, white trucks were exonerated, and Halloween would occur this year like any other.

The next day, Maren received a call from her doctor in Baltimore, asking if it would be OK for him to phone Steve also. Her report came back clear late Wednesday, but he was out of the office until today.

When Steve strode to her desk later that afternoon his eyes looked victorious, melting into hers. She rounded the corner of her desk where Steve kicked her door shut as he snatched her into his arms. Maren's breath felt warm on his neck. "I'm so done with these past few weeks," she said, with a martyred sigh.

"Me too." Steve dragged his fingers through her hair and held her face in his hands. "Me too, babe."

"Were you worried, Dr. Kramer?"

Steve looked into her eyes. "I knew we'd deal with whatever it was. Worst case, it would've been caught early, but I didn't want you to have to face cancer, chemo or radiation…so, maybe a little." He'd tried hard not to let it show.

His soft-spoken confession landed in Maren's heart and tugged at it. "I wouldn't have made it without you. From my heart, and Dylan's, thank you for making these weeks easier, with appointments, connections, your time…even your map." She chuckled, pulling him in for a tangled kiss. "I love you so much."

"You don't give yourself enough credit, Maren. You're stronger than you think." Steve shifted to a whisper. "I love you, too… want you, alone, in the worst way…to celebrate."

"Good luck with that one. Dylan's with us this weekend, and we're out Sunday." Maren hadn't explained to Dylan that they'd be going to an NFL game while he watched it on television with a sitter.

Steve groaned. Dating a woman with an always present, mildly rambunctious child was new territory, never a consideration in past relationships. "Well, we've got to get outside Saturday with Dylan. It'll be 60 degrees or better. We don't have too much good weather left."

"OK, Dylan won't pass up spending time on the bay."

"How 'bout we go out early? As I recall, your son rivals my Blackberry some mornings." Steve laughed remembering Tuesday when Dylan bound down the stairs asking, "Who won?" Steve had set his alarm for 5:15. He couldn't believe Dylan would be up so early.

135

"My parents also mentioned dinner to celebrate Mom's birthday. My brother's home; Liz and her crew will be there, too."

"I'll finally get to meet Hannah, your little sweetheart?"

"She'll be jealous. Be prepared." He ran the back of his finger along her face and smiled. "Women fighting over me. I love it! We can head to Chevy Chase mid-afternoon if we go out in the boat early."

"That will work," Maren said, turning cautious. "What should I wear? What about Dylan? I'm meeting your family for the first time." Visions flooded of Mark's judgmental parents.

"How do I say this? Their oldest son pushes 40 with no woman to tame him in their sight." Steve held her hands in his, as he shook his head admitting this. "And she's hinted—subtly but with tact—how my sister's the one with kids and how it'd be great to give them cousins."

"So I have a few points in my favor already."

"Yes, and they're business casual, Maren. You'll be fine. Relax or I'll have to find ways of making you relax." He raised his eye.

"Dream on." Maren laughed as they turned out the light and left her office. They could linger, walking the parking lot, no fears of hiding snipers. No more dashing, keys in hand. Stopping alongside her car, Steve shared one of his musings. It involved the pole he vowed to install. That only stirred yet another erotically intriguing idea as they taunted each other before they left work.

Maren and Dylan huddled together across from Steve as he piloted out on the bay Saturday morning. Oyster season coincided with crabbing, still active on the waters. With outstretched arm, Maren pointed out the different kinds of vessels to Dylan from the wooden V-hulled workboats, that used to be hand-made, dead-rise boats, to the commercial ones seen sometimes with a hardtop to protect the crabbers from the sun and to hold the marine electronics into the air.

"You really love it out here, don't you?" Steve asked Maren as Dylan tried desperately to find skipjacks he saw in his books.

"I do," Maren said. "Life takes over. We forget to appreciate just where we live." She smiled at Steve who made these recent outings possible. "It's fun discovering this again through Dylan's eyes."

"I know. But we can't stay out searching for one of only a few dozen—not in this century." Fewer than 50 skipjacks remained by most estimates.

"In the spring we can book a skipjack sail or a tour at one of the museums."

"Dylan, come over here," Steve said. Dylan felt bulky with his blue-zippered life vest, but Steve hoisted him into the captain's chair as they headed back to the marina. Dylan beamed as he handled the steering. Steve sat vigilantly behind him, his own hands on top Dylan's at the ready. Throttle it up today, Steve thought.

"You're so good to him," Maren shouted over the engine, the wind, and the sound of cutting through the open water. Dylan loved it when he and Steve steered smack into a wave with the crash, thud and spray they made, before the boat seized the calm water path created by another boater's wake. She pulled out the camera she had brought and snapped a priceless shot of Dylan piloting on Steve's lap. They cruised the water for more than an hour total, chatted on the boat, and closed it down.

Steve snagged her for a squeeze. "I've waited many years for a first mate like you," he said. "I can get used to this." He skimmed her hair with his lips.

From the looks of it, so could Dylan as he climbed in and out of the cabin, chatting about crabs and oysters, which he'd never eat at his age. He spotted high-flying Canadian geese with child-size binoculars. They had begun their winter migration to grace the Chesapeake shorelines for several months. Dylan announced that he could play all afternoon in the boat's cabin, never leaving.

"Ah dude," Steve said, shooting a glint of lust at Maren. "Big kids can have fun, too." Their eyes had to communicate what their words could not. Forget fish and tackle, the word pole would now forever steer their thoughts to the sexual, eliciting a snicker between Maren and him.

By early afternoon, they changed for the drive to the Kramer home in Chevy Chase. "We do need to spend a night on the boat again," Steve said from the driver's seat.

"Unless you want a full crew, we'd best not talk about it right now." Too late; Dylan asked when they could go back to the marina. They stalled that answer. "So tell me about your family," she said. "You told me about Liz, but not about your brother and parents."

"Eric is 25. The Mr. Rogers' generation, if you recall. Being 14 years apart, we get along well though Liz and I are probably closer."

"He must have felt like an only child if the two of you were away at school."

"He did," Steve acknowledged. "I should spend more time with him, too. Next spring, I'll have him out on the boat more. In grad school, cruisin' for hotties far more important than cruisin' the bay. When not hitting the books."

"What's he studying?"

"Now, environmental sciences, but got his undergrad in architecture. I have no idea what he wants to do with all of this, mind you. I'm not sure he does either."

"Save the Bay?"

"He's the type," Steve replied. "Free-spirited. He sings in a band, plays guitar."

"Really? Sounds fun," Maren said. "We should go see him."

"If he's any good," Steve said.

Maren chided him with a disapproving look. "Your ego strains the edges of this vehicle, you know that?"

"I'm kidding," Steve corrected. "I don't even know where his gigs are."

Dylan nodded off along Route 50, strapped into the back seat.

With a better understanding of the family dynamics, Maren felt relieved as they pulled into the driveway of the Chevy Chase home where Steve had told her he had studied religiously, earning a scholarship that netted him nearly a full ride for his undergrad years. Monies saved then went to medical school resulting in way less debt than peers, who were easily on the hook for paying back $200,000, if not more. His loans, thankfully, got retired years ago.

Elegantly set back from the street, the Kramer house was a three-level classic brick colonial. Mature trees shaded the lawn, and a small pond sat to the side. Around back, a patio set the stage for casual cookouts and childhood fun, and now to moments like tonight when their adult children gathered. Inside, the home boasted four bedrooms, a separate study and an oversized eat-in kitchen where Steve acquired his interest in cooking….and his appetite.

Dolores Kramer, looking terrific in hair that had added more white highlights this year, turned 63 this month. Steve pitched in, making mushroom risotto in the kitchen as part of her birthday meal. His father Bill prepared lamb, and Liz handled another side dish. Maren took a seat on a barstool at the counter, rolled up her sleeves, and helped dice mushrooms. More sips of chardonnay than chopping, but she had fun.

138

Maren saw Steve, managing his mother's kitchen with the confidence she expected in the OR, save for his younger sister Liz who pushed him aside a time or two.

"Steve, come on… searching your whole life for low-sodium chicken broth is ridiculous when there's regular right here," she told him. "Eight ounces won't kill you." Steve brought the porcini mushrooms, Arborio rice, and Parmesan cheese, figuring his mother's pantry provided the rest.

"Look, I left out the peas with three kids who will refuse to eat this otherwise," he countered.

"Watch out…coming through," Eric said, nudging Liz as he made room on the counter for the beer and wine he brought in. "Wassup, bro?" He cast a hand into the air to high five his older brother. "And you must be…"

"Maren," Steve introduced. "My brother Eric."

"Pleased to meet you," Maren said, shaking Eric's outstretched hand. Eric strode in from College Park around six p.m.

"That should really go in the garage fridge, not here," Liz rebuked. "Sorry, Eric thinks alcohol is another food group."

"Isn't it?" Steve asked wryly. "Sweet… that's the good stuff." A six-pack and two wine bottles remained on the counter.

"Some role model. And you want to watch my two impressionable kids?" Hands on hips, Liz surveyed the kitchen. "Eric, in the garage."

"Since when are you Ms. Organized?" Eric asked, fetching the six-pack by its handle and the white wine needing a chill. The look he cast his sister said she needed the same.

Maren chuckled at Liz who used a you-think-you-know-everything tone on Steve. When Eric walked in, Liz playfully tugged on his ponytail as he passed. The Kramer kids greeted one another with cheek pecks or flattened palms. Steve called Eric's excuse for being late rather sketchy considering he might not have left parties until three a.m., unless otherwise occupied—a straight-up innuendo.

"Stop drillin' me," Eric insisted. "Like I was shitfaced or randomly hooking up." He shot Steve a sly smile. "Wonder what you did at my age? If you can remember back then?"

"You'll pay for that." Steve tossed aside the risotto spoon locking his arm around Eric's neck for a headlocked tug.

Ignoring the male one-upping, Liz focused on Maren, since her brother wasn't. "Tyler's in heaven with another boy. Usually he doesn't have anyone his own age to play with," Liz said. She asked Maren about Dylan, and they began talking about an outing they could all do since they weren't confined indoors, snipers safely jailed behind bars.

"I can't imagine what families lived through over here," Maren commented, knowing the fear was more intense where Liz and Steve had grown up.

"This is my first visit home in months," Liz said. "We planned to come weeks ago. Mom and Dad came to the shore instead."

Maren got the distinct idea that family mattered to the Kramer brood, especially after Hannah's nap when she toddled downstairs shocked to find Uncle Steve with his arm around another girl. He even fed that girl cheese and crackers, after taking a break at the stove. How dare him!

"Hannah, I want you to meet someone else very special. Her name is Maren." Steve reached down and jiggled his niece up onto his hip. "Maren this is Hannah." He turned the little girl to face her directly.

"Nice to meet you Hannah. I love your name," Maren said.

Hannah, at three, seemed to understand the relational skill of glaring at another female in her midst. She was Uncle Steve's sweetheart, and every woman in his life would understand that.

"Hannah," Liz said walking up to Steve and guiding her daughter by the wrist. "Shake her hand. That's what we do when we meet someone." Hannah obliged, not of her own choice. Better any resistance should come from a pint-sized member of Steve's family than from an adult, Maren thought, making note of how she might warm Hannah to her in the future.

Tim, Liz's husband finished playing outside with his son Tyler and Dylan. Steve introduced them, and they all launched into a conversation about the real estate market. Steve owned his apartment-sized unit—a condo in real estate parlance—and Tim told Steve that his firm now offered rental and property management. "Live aboard your boat," Tim teased. "Think of the added income."

Steve paused. He barely used his apartment except to sleep. "Until the next hurricane, and I have to haul out," he said. "Hmm…maybe."

It was a low-key, delectable dinner followed by Smith Island cake that Liz brought from the shore. Eight white, thin layers with a raspberry filling between each. Topped with buttercream frosting. Each time Liz made the trip, she brought a different batter and filling combination. Eric shot hoops with Dylan and Tyler, giving Maren and Steve time to linger over coffee with Steve's parents.

"It's so nice to see kids afoot in this house," Dolores Kramer told Maren after opening a cloth bag unveiling the bottle of dessert wine Maren brought as a hostess gift. "Dylan's a great little boy."

"Thank you," Maren acknowledged. "And, for inviting us to share your special day. Steve beams talking about his family. Fun to be here."

"Well, we're just glad to see him take a little time for a personal life," Bill added. Steve's father had the stature of a seasoned man, but with an unlined face showing few signs of age. He sat back next to Dolores with shoulders pressing his chair, chin high, and a bit of gray on the temples of his otherwise dark hair. Maren thought he looked distinguished sitting next to Steve's mother, hands held. They exchanged smiles that had to connect shared memories. Maren didn't detect any desire to wave high their own accomplishments or those of their children, though Dolores and Bill Kramer showed pride in their three children nonetheless. Maren had seen all the self-aggrandizing she needed to see during her years in the Mitchell clan.

"How do you like the boat?" his father asked, eyes indicating Maren in the question as well.

"Love the boat, Dad, and making the time for it," Steve reported. "It's got everything you'd need to live aboard." They discussed winterizing.

"Ours does fine on the lift," Tim said. "Unless it's a harsh winter. Does Dylan like boating, Maren? We took Tyler out tubing. He fell off only once."

"We were out today," Maren mentioned. "He'll go into mourning if the boat gets stored. Hasn't been tubing." She said it with a wary laugh.

"Maren knows a few things about boats. Makes it way more fun." Steve's gaze shifted to Liz. "Looks like you're ready to head out," he said as Liz came alongside her husband. "Where's the…" As soon as he spoke, the three little ones came into the room. Tyler carried a long box atop both outstretched arms.

"He won't share, Mommy," Hannah complained.

"I'm bigger," Tyler insisted.

Fortunately, Dylan kept out of their squabble. Maren quickly summoned him to bring over another bag she'd walked in with, this one containing a beautiful scarf. Dylan had drawn Mrs. Kramer a card to go along with the gift enclosure tucked into the bag.

Liz presented their mom with the birthday gift from Steve, Eric and herself. It baffled Dolores by its size. She peeled off the wrapping of one larger box containing a beautiful robe—the kind any woman just knew would bring comfort after a long day. Then, she discovered coffee and tea, in a smaller box, noticing yet another enticing her further. In it, Liz had planted the gift certificate to a day spa with a card from the three of them. Her two children, Hannah and Tyler, had each made pictures that Dolores promised to frame next week, right alongside Dylan's drawing.

Dolores Kramer took time to thank them all, hauling Hannah onto her lap to sneak a last bite of cake. Hannah knew how to get what she wanted. Until her parents had car keys in hand. "I stay with Grandma," she tried to assert.

"Bye Liz...we'll talk about next weekend." Steve kissed his sister on the cheek, brushed hair from Tyler's forehead, and helped Hannah accept her departure with a final smooch. She kissed him back.

"You're slobbering on him, Hannah. Yuck," Tyler said. Steve loved it, handing slobber sister, as Tyler had dubbed her, over to his parents.

"Maren, it was great meeting you. Here's my number. Glad we're getting the boys together."

"I am, too. Thanks, Liz." Maren tucked the number into her purse, handing Steve's sister one of her cards with numbers scrawled on it. She and Steve returned to the table while his parents continued goodbyes.

Maren appreciated how at ease she had become. The Kramers lived well, but seemed sensible, open, and welcoming. Bill Kramer had put in nearly 40 years as an attorney before taking a post as a foundation executive. He had no immediate plans to retire although he was 65. Dolores had worked as a legal secretary, part-time once babies came along. With two self-sustaining adult children, and Eric living away, they spent more time in Southern Maryland where they had a bayside house, as they called it, on the water. Maren could picture the sailboat Steve told her about, the swimming pool in which they had all horsed around, and the countless family meals they shared. She finally had a minute to peruse the family photo album Steve's mom had placed on the table.

"Hey Steve," Eric asked, motioning for him. "Let's shock Mom with a clean kitchen."

"Sure, be right back," he told Maren.

Steve's parents sat back down, explaining the photographs. None had captions, but all had stories. Other photos Maren sized up on her own, especially the one with the blonde in a form fitting one-piece snuggled against Steve on a pool lounge chair. It had to be one of his former girlfriends, maybe in college, not that it mattered.

Twenty minutes passed and Maren made a mental note of how thoughtful sons could put the kitchen back in perfect order before they left. Eric said goodbye and high-fived Dylan before heading to the door with Steve.

"No, we'll win. Certain of it," Steve said in the distance. Fingers jabbed to make a point about football. Eric used the word "traitor" and in a hushed tone she heard Steve tell his brother he had no hard feelings. The game they obsessed over, Maren figured. Tomorrow, she'd get another dose.

"Thanks for everything," Steve said to his mom. "We better get Dylan home."

"Say hi to Paul and Vicki," she said. "Have fun at the game." Dolores studied Steve for a minute. He rolled his eyes, uttering "whatever" convincing Maren that Dolores kept the sibling taunts in check.

"Don't start, Dad," Steve said as they hugged. "Playing the 'Skins in pre-season doesn't count." If his team had won, he might have counted it differently.

"Happy Birthday, again." Maren reached into Dolores's outstretched arms. "Everything was lovely. Thanks for the great dinner." She prodded Dylan.

"Thank you," Dylan said on cue. "I love birthday parties."

"I had good help with this one," Dolores said of her brood pitching in to make it a fun night. "I heard talk about getting together. Feel free to stop if you're over here next weekend."

"We will, Mom. I've learned not to mention certain words without a locked-down, squared-up plan." He smirked at Maren and hugged his mother whispering "the zoo" in her ear. "Love you."

"Maren's teaching you well, Steve." Dolores's casual touch to Maren's shoulders seemed like a seal of genuine approval.

Sunday morning, Maren insisted on going to church. She hadn't been faithful in attendance recently, but wanted to give thanks for her good health and offer prayers for the victims of the region's horrible attacks. They went to the early service where Steve finally got to meet her minister Luke and hear why they all commended his sermons. That he made a football reference sealed it for Steve.

Dylan took a liking to the sitter when she appeared, and Steve and Maren headed to the game, the topic all week, either with Steve or co-workers putting purple on display.

"I love Dylan, Maren. But we have to use sitters more often," Steve announced from behind the wheel. "Maybe I should hang on to my apartment. Yeah…there's a thought." A smile crept up his face, better than the frown last night when Steve complained about returning there, lonely.

"I know, a little hard to be spontaneous."

"Pun intended, I presume. Very hard."

Maren blushed. "Sorry."

"It's just the effect you have on me, babe."

"Well, I heard your brother and his girlfriend babysit in College Park?"

Steve quieted. "What did you hear?"

"Something about a new lady in his life," she said. "Your parents didn't say much except that they've known each other."

"Yeah, it's kind of complicated." Steve kept his eyes on the highway.

"If your family spends weekends at their place near us, it might work. Eric hit it off with Dylan. Maybe his girlfriend can help."

"I'll talk to him," Steve replied. "Better with just Eric."

"Why?" Maren had noticed a reaction last night. Not much talk about it focusing on Dolores's birthday, the grandchildren, Dylan, and their meeting Maren for the first time. "Begrudging your brother a love life?"

"Not at his age," Steve snorted. "As long as he doesn't need penicillin."

"Steve!"

"It was a joke. Let's concentrate on the game." Almost at the exit for PSINet Stadium, they needed to find a parking spot amid the crowd.

144

Temperatures got to the upper fifties by noon in Baltimore. Quite the duo, Maren chose a white turtleneck under a black sweatshirt; Steve a yellow-collared polo underneath his sweatshirt adorned with Steelers logo.

"Our pleasure," Paul greeted Maren, kissing her on the cheek as he shook her hand. Any woman in Steve's life would be bound to theirs.

They chatted about Maren's new job and the football rivalry, Maren assuring Steve's friend that while she had lived in the area all her life, she was certifiably not won over by purple.

"Yoose all agree with renaming the stadium?" Paul joked. Yinz; yoose all. It mattered not as it all meant the same in two different cities.

"I agree with those recent letters to the editor," Maren answered. "Makes sense from a marketing standpoint."

Vicki asked about Dylan mentioning to Maren their wish to start a family. That spawned banter between Paul and Steve about why their scheduled court time vanished. Maren saw that they had an easy relationship, perhaps more brotherly because they shared similar age and interests.

"We'd love to meet Dylan. Come for one of the games," Vicki said.

"Want practice with childcare, we've got the perfect specimen," Steve told them.

"Steve has a sudden interest in aligning the sitters," Maren said, cozying into the arm he'd stretched around her. "Such a take-charge kinda guy."

"Cramping your style, Steve?" Paul asked. "Maren looks happy so I guess it's all good n'at."

"And that, can you manage?" Steve shook his head, looked at his wristwatch. "We're here 15 minutes, Romano. Easy." He turned to Maren. "See. He can't behave, nor speak correctly." Driving four hours southeast, Pittsburghers painted part of the stadium in black and gold with fan attire, banners, and Terrible Towels like the one she'd seen Steve cart around. Their vernacular made Paul feel right at home.

He and Steve sat on the ends with Vicki and Maren between them.

"Once I dated Paul, my hometown football enthusiasm fizzled," Vicki reported.

"Paul saw to that, I'll bet," Steve added. He leaned back to chat with Vicki, who not only culled culinary catalogs but also knew of great galley recipes for the boat.

Maren leaned closer to Paul, still enjoying Steve's attentive hands on her. "We're getting quite the sitter pool established. Steve's brother Eric and his girlfriend Shelly babysit for a family in College Park."

"That's an interesting way to get some action on a Saturday night. Steve's brother...how old is he?" Paul asked running the math in his head. "Mid-20s. I remember him just starting high school."

"Yeah, I take it he's known this girl, but they just started dating actually," Maren offered. "Her parents know Steve's parents. They must have some connection." Maren paused realizing Paul knew Steve's family much better than she did. "I think I got that right."

"Shelly Morgan?" Paul asked, causing Steve's conversation with Vicki to merge into his with Maren.

"What?" This jolted Steve from accessorizing his floating apartment.

"Your brother is dating Shelly Morgan?"

"It would appear," Steve answered flatly.

"How'd that happen?"

"Small world. Look, they're coming onto the field." Steve said, literally pivoting Maren's shoulders, meeting Paul with a don't-go-there glance.

The game excited Pittsburgh fans having driven the distance. By the end of the first quarter, Pittsburgh was ahead by 14 and Baltimore had failed to score. Explaining game minutia gave Steve more reason to lean closer to Maren, who caught on to key players. By the half, Pittsburgh was up 28-3. Everyone took a break and the guys went to the concession line while the women headed to, where else? The ladies' room line.

"OK, so what's with your brother? I was shocked, that's all," Paul admitted, sensing he'd put Steve in a tough spot.

"Not much to tell. They recognized each other. At a school that large, you seek out familiar faces. He told me yesterday."

"Was she there with your brother last night?"

"Of course not. My mother has a little more sense than that," Steve pointed out to Paul. "They just met Maren yesterday. You should have seen the are-you-alright-with-this look she gave me."

"Right, your mom wouldn't have invited Shelly, but who wouldn't be curious about your reaction." He paused. "What are you going to do if they get serious?"

"Punt," Steve answered as they inched to the counter. "How the hell do I know? I love my brother, always wanted the best for him."

"Except now."

"That's not it. It's just weird." Steve stopped, getting annoyed. "Let's talk about something else."

"Well since you and Maren haven't taken your hands off one another, I'm getting the sense here that…"

"You would be correct!" Steve interrupted, cutting Paul off with a tone that only got brighter. "She's fabulous."

"Agreed. Gorgeous. Smart. Easy going. I take it she likes the water?"

"She grew up around boats. A definite plus." The two were going to have to put in their orders.

"Nice tan. From all that time on that boat!" Paul licked his lips.

"Even better contrast." Steve licked his, too, and they chuckled. "I want this to go well, Paul. She's had some struggles—lost her husband, single mom, stressed like everyone recently and had a cancer scare this month—so maybe I'm being a little protective, but…"

"I'd no idea," Paul said. "Is she all right?"

"Yeah, had a biopsy, over a week ago, here in town. Her anxiety was through the roof." He paused. "All this other stuff, not important. Outside of work, I want to focus on her and Dylan."

Paul put his hand on Steve's shoulder. "Go for it. It's time, Steve." He leveled his friend a satisfied look. "Most of the planet's wondering what's taken you so damn long."

"Easy then." Steve's expression indicated even with a plea, he knew he would get only partial compliance. "Oh, her father is looking for a new doc. Jack Cole, and I swear Paul…"

"Say no more. I got your message." By this time, the cashiers called them ahead and the game was about to resume.

The Ravens started to rally but not nearly enough with one TD and conversion in the third quarter. By the end of the game, Pittsburgh had put three more points on the board trouncing the Ravens 31-18.

Steve and Paul were elated and allowed the opposing team's fans to exit as they remained in their seats. The foursome grabbed a quick bite in Baltimore where Vicki invited Maren and Steve, along with Dylan, to come to their house for the next televised game. A mutual friendship formed fast.

Chapter 10

After several intense weeks and with a new job, Maren looked forward to trick or treat, saying goodbye to October. She'd slowly become more self-assured at work and certainly less anxious about life.

Dylan slept better, no trouble being alone. He didn't worry about Maren. Steve saw Dylan as a prime recruit to teach about his football team since fishing season had nearly ended. He peppered Dylan with questions just as he had Maren.

"He's sleeping better, but I'm not," Steve complained to her sharing coffee in the cafeteria, a place that took on significance after they had first gotten to know one another there.

"I'm sorry, honey. At least we got an extra hour last weekend."

"Not about setting clocks back. I know what can make me sleep better, Maren." Steve deadpanned. "Not pharmaceutical either."

She did her best to ignore him pulling out photos of what Dylan would dress as for Halloween. He insisted on becoming a pirate.

"That's cute. Maybe he'll share some of his loot with me since I'm working late tonight, unless his mom freaks out over too much candy."

"I ration it, and for you, I bet he'll share. With the rain lately, we might just focus on the community party tonight at the VFD." Maren studied his diverted disposition. "Steve, I don't feel like you're listening."

He pressed his back into the chair. "VFD hanging out with the guys and Dylan in a costume. Make me jealous."

"Well, I wish you could come with us. I know you hate paperwork," she said. "But the lonely look is pitiful."

"Let me spell this out, Ms. Mitchell," Steve said. "I'm 39 years old, I have this babalicious woman, who is *not* in my bed and…"

"Stop already." Maren shushed him, before breaking into a hearty laugh. "People will hear you."

"I don't care. I have a point to make."

"Point registered," she answered with empathic, longing eyes. "We already have plans for the National Zoo with Liz and her kids. And Sunday, at Paul's."

Steve respected Maren for setting some limits. Soon, it would be two months since they met, and with all of the loss Dylan had faced, Maren was adamant that she didn't want a failed relationship to be a replay of Dylan's losing his father last year. Steve made it his mission to assure that wouldn't happen.

"I want all of those things. It'll be great to get Dylan together with my niece and nephew. But I want you." While he could invite himself to Maren's on occasion, she kept a firm boundary. "If my secretary didn't get in early and work late, I'd suggest my office. I'm about to regardless."

"Like hell you'll have me on your office sofa." Her tone was soft as they sat in the cafeteria, but her eyes hard on him.

"Who said anything about the sofa. Desk, against the wall." He paused with a wicked eye, leaning closer. "I could press that exam room into service real easy."

"Here, you need my ice water more than me," she said, making ice cubes jiggle as she pushed the glass in his direction.

Steve checked the calendar on his phone and dumped it back into the pocket of his white lab coat. He got up briefly to refill his coffee and returned to their table.

"Maren Mitchell." He extended his hand. "My name's Dr. Kramer, chief of surgery. But you...you can call me Steve."

Maren shook his hand and shook her head.

"I hear from inner circles you have extensive knowledge regarding that *other* computer where people think differently," he said referencing the Apple ad campaign. He sat down. Focused amusingly on her brown eyes. "My laptop is a complete mess, and I can't tell you how much attention it needs, from expert hands like yours."

Maren planted both elbows into the table between them. "My office is in the east wing of the building. I'd be happy to help later today," she said. "Oops, it's Halloween. Can't. Next week...maybe."

"No, Mondays, Wednesdays and Thursdays absolutely do not fit into my schedule. I hear you have another office, and you'd be doing a great service for this facility, and my work here, if we can schedule something...there."

Steve brought his smartphone up, shielding Maren from the raised arc of his lips. "So, tomorrow is Friday, November 1st. As I see it, I can be at your home office, by 11:45, and I estimate this might take, ah…let's block off until 1:30." Steve struggled to be matter of fact. "I have to be back by two at the latest."

Is he delusional, Maren thought? Within 20 minutes of this scheme, she'd be relaxing in his arms.

"Dr. Kramer, I realize you might have many…problems needing my resolution, but there are other members of this staff who need me also."

"Not like I do," he shot back. "Do I sense resistance to authority?" Steve planted his elbows on the table. "I *am* the chief of surgery, let me remind you."

Maren leaned closer across the table to Steve. "You really don't have to work this hard," she whispered leaving the warmth of her breath on him. It only stirred several more provocative thoughts.

She cleared her throat. "Let me restate that. Keep it…that way. I'll meet you tomorrow, 11:45. Bring that laptop."

"Ms. Mitchell," Steve said, locking her eyes as he took her hand. "I'm a business, very casual kinda guy. A minimalist."

Maren gave a loving nod as she rose from the table. Steve slid his chair in, his hand onto Maren's waist, walking out. He headed to his office, and she to hers, to finish a project in time for trick or treat.

At precisely 11:50 the next day, Steve pulled into Maren's driveway in his convertible, not bothering to secure the top before trotting up the few steps to her door. When she opened it, he stood grinning, hand behind his back, and stepped immediately inside. The shades were down and the stereo greeted him with Peter Gabriel's progressive rock streaming out of two speakers.

"For you," he offered, handing over a long stemmed rose. He removed his blazer and neatly draped it over a bench in the foyer. When he stepped closer, Maren began playing with the collar of his dress shirt, still holding the long stem. She sniffed the rose.

"Smells good." On Steve, she detected fresh soap and aftershave, likely from a recent shower after morning surgeries. "You do, too. Where's your laptop, Dr. Kramer?"

151

Maren stood in a simple black, waist-tied wrap dress with matching black semi-high heels and her long, auburn locks held by a clip that looked like a spider the way it bent.

"I brought other hardware, Ms. Mitchell."

"Well, as your computer consultant, I sure hope I have the right software?"

"I am absolutely certain that you do." As he delivered the words, he scooped up Maren, carrying her with one arm supporting her back, and the other having gathered her under the knees. Maren let out a "whoa" that traveled through the foyer into the family room.

Steve took her straight there where he'd spent several evenings already, but never alone like this, in the middle of the day. Dylan's pirate costume lay scattered across the coffee table, some pieces left on the cushions they were about to claim. Maren tossed the rose onto the table.

He lowered her onto the sectional. Maren quickly raised herself, poking at his chest with her finger. "Don't be in such a hurry." She kneeled on the sofa her hands on his shirt deliberate with each button she pried apart.

"Why not?" Steve picked up a pirate bandana, lying in their way, and cast it aside. Both hands urgent, he reached under her dress. As they traveled the backs of each leg, his eyes, which had never left focus on hers, widened.

"Maren Mitchell, you little vixen." He breathed onto her neck as he kissed her on it. "Nice ass." He moved to her mouth commanding it with a kiss as his hands hiked her dress higher.

Maren enjoyed the firm squeezes she felt on her backside. With each one her breathing quickened. She cast off his shirt and started unbuckling his belt.

"I know better than to *resist* authority, Steve Kramer," Maren revealed. "Minimal enough?"

"Just about." He shifted onto the sofa. "Talk about costumes, the day after Halloween. I like yours much better."

"Yeah, that's what the guys at the fire department said, too." She plied his pants lower, standing in front of him. "Great pole they have at that place."

"I hope you're getting sufficient practice then," he said, a husky hum in his throat.

"They invited me back," she teased, helping him to discard everything else. "That's more like it." She ran her hands over him, stopping where it mattered most. Flirting there. Steve forgot and remembered why he was there as lust lunged through him.

Maren's eyes nearly burning into his, she untied her dress letting it fall to the floor. Her mid-high heels were all that remained. She watched his eyes overtake her, while she reached behind her head to let her hair fall loose.

Seeing it flow down her shoulders and tease his view, Steve stretched out his arms, pulling her in tight. His lips overtook hers, strong, hard, making them his, until he let go.

"If I didn't know any better, you'd have me convinced that you're the goddess of sex, and of the seas."

"Whoever you want me to be," she said saucily. "Maybe this will help you decide." As much as she wanted him to enjoy the tryst he'd so creatively planned, she seized the moment to enjoy him just a little more, lowering herself on her knees.

He groaned. "Damn, definitely goddess of both." Maren enthralled him, watching his eyes close. He might have had a plan, but she could prove herself skillful with one as well.

When he thought she might transport him, he touched her hair signaling a shift. With her apart from him, he could hear the music once again. Peter Gabriel sang about steam. As Steve saw it, something hot, wet awaited him.

If pirates were the rage this Halloween, Steve might have proven himself to be one as he pilfered every inch of Maren and plunged uncontrollably into that heat.

"Make sure you get enough," Maren whispered as they moved together tearing up the blanket beneath them and crushing the pillows to their sides. Steve had tossed one overboard already, greedily grasping Maren, wanting nothing in his way.

"Oh don't you worry. I'm here for the take." But when her body stiffened and went limp minutes later in his arms, and Maren gulped in a breath of air, he knew without a doubt that he gave her the pleasure she craved, the love she deserved equal to any desire he seized.

When gasps went shallow, Steve laced his fingers through her long hair. He eased a shot at his watch while he held her. "12:30. Not bad."

"I made you a sandwich," she said, fingering the gold chain around his neck. "Hungry? I'll get it."

"Sure, why not." Steve eased over so that she could get up. "You kept a high heel on through all that," he noticed with a sigh. "Christ, you're sexy." He grabbed her ass. Squeezed it. "Red hot."

He watched her slip on the other shoe and slink away nude, with a gentle sway in her hips. She came back with a plate in one hand with small, cut-up sandwiches and an open bottle of iced tea to share. Setting the drink down, she took one off the plate to feed Steve who nibbled a bite before finishing it.

"I hope I've satisfied whatever hardware issues you had." She chewed a sandwich seductively while he watched.

"Sorry, we have to test the system again." He met her wide-eyed. Her hand covered her mouth afraid she might choke out a piece of roasted turkey and whole wheat.

"Are you insatiable? You have to get dressed and go back where you came from." A hand on her naked stomach didn't suppress her giggling.

"Maren, it's now 12:45. I have time for one more of these." He took a sandwich. She handed him the iced tea, and he chugged two swigs, setting it back down. "As I was saying…"

Steve reached out to cup her breasts in his hands. "Pirates never seize only one bounty. If I leave in 30 minutes, I'm way ahead of schedule."

Dylan had wanted to go to the National Zoo ever since the Giant Pandas Tian Tian and Mei Xiang made their first public appearance in January 2001. Maren had actually planned an outing that summer, but May had dealt them a terrible blow with Mark's death. After the terrorist attacks and as she nursed her own grief as well as Dylan's, that day trip simply slipped away.

Few ventured out earlier this fall feeling unsafe. Now in November, with the leaves in a dramatic array of autumn colors, people planned to enjoy what they could before the holiday season approached.

"Tell me more about your sister Liz," Maren said with Dylan in the backseat of her Ford Focus. Steve drove as they headed along Route 50 merging onto the Beltway. The National Zoo wasn't far from where Maren first met the Kramer family.

"Liz is four years younger, so 35. When we were kids, she was annoying."

154

"Maybe you were annoying," Maren posited adding the playful lilt for effect. "I think the way the two of you put that meal together was hysterical."

"Normal sibling stuff, I guess. I let her win a few rounds."

"Ah no. She looked like she could very well hold her own with you," Maren corrected.

"After high school, she went to UNC, North Carolina while I headed to New York for med school."

"At least you had siblings. I missed that. What did she major in?"

"Social work. Went straight through for her master's in two years. She moved home to Chevy Chase, worked with kids in some special ed school, and by the time I moved to Baltimore, she took a job at one of the hospitals," he said.

"Look, Disney," Dylan exclaimed from the back. Maren and Steve both laughed because as they approached the Mormon Temple the view from the Beltway would look like a castle to a child. Maren corrected him.

"Tyler and Hannah call it that, and my sister had one hell of a time– oops– convincing them that Mickey Mouse didn't live near Grandma."

"Did you work at the same hospital?"

"No, she was at the competition. She stayed with me at my apartment. A blast and a half," Steve added sarcastically.

"That's not very nice."

"But accurate. Didn't last long. I'd tell her to clean up and she'd preach how the first two children in a family are often very different."

"Well, that's the prevailing notion."

"I told her I didn't care what her social theories were, she needed to adhere to a little order in her life, and in my apartment." He snickered. "That got her butt geared to leave."

Maren gasped. Steve seemed nonplussed. "Seriously, she hated casework, so when she met Tim, her husband, they moved across the bridge and she started a private practice. I had my apartment back. The way I wanted it. Triple win."

Steve concentrated on getting over to the right lane. "You probably heard us talking real estate last week. They lucked into great waterfront property. We can go by boat."

"When on the boat again?" Dylan asked.

"I'm not sure you'd like it," Steve answered. "You'll freeze your butt off."

"My butt?" Dylan giggled. "I want to see that." Maren did not.

"I hope Hannah has warmed a little over the past week." Maren deliberately changed focus.

"Warned you, didn't I? She was here first, so in her eyes she's my sweetheart." Steve took one hand off the wheel to touch Maren's chin acknowledging that she held a special place in his heart, and if his eyes could add words, they would have said "especially after yesterday."

At the zoo, Steve deposited a kiss on Liz and watched Dylan take right up where he left off a week ago with Tyler. Hannah reached from her stroller with outstretched arms, yelling, "Uncle Steve!"

Steve bent down to unbuckle and lift the little girl under her arms into his. "Hannah, I've missed you so much." Maren chuckled at Steve's greeting. They had just seen each other the week before.

As long as Steve confined his charm and affection to women bound by blood, decades younger, Maren would approve. He planted a kiss on Hannah's cheek, then immediately eased closer to Maren. Hannah returned a brief "hi" before Steve fastened her back in and they strolled through the zoo.

The two women Steve felt closest to shared details of their lives. Tyler needed braces soon. Dylan did well in first grade, but his attention could wane. Lagged a little socially, but with all he had been through in a year and a half, he had become more introverted, shy, entering school. Hannah, a real girly girl by Liz's report, held her own with an older brother. Dylan too. They wouldn't have to worry about Hannah standing up for herself on any playground.

Maren appreciated getting to know Liz. Mark's sister, still living in Virginia, extended a hello on holidays. The dismissive kind, she remembered. Maren, born of an innately creative sense that settled well on her in adulthood, felt like the plain Jane of the Mitchell family. Spring break for Mark's sister meant Rodeo Drive on daddy's dime.

They sat on a bench between animal exhibits while Steve took the kids to see the monkeys. Liz leaned over saying, "Steve offered to watch the kids for our wedding anniversary. Do you think he's up to it?"

Maren met her mischievous eyes. "I haven't seen the bachelor pad yet." Liz looked a little stunned, but realized a boat and Maren's house must have supplied the space for her brother's attentive hands on his new girlfriend. The two times now that she had seen Steve, the way he cast his eyes upon Maren broadcast a mix of worshipping and lusting after her. "I do think he really wants to watch them though. I was there when he came up with the idea." Conspiratorially, Maren whispered, "Don't worry, I'll be on call." The two women shared a laugh at Steve's expense.

Liz Kramer Phillips dressed in a cotton long-sleeved blouse, slim bluejeans, and ankle boots with a practical heel. The short, layered look of her brunette hair probably took a few combs each morning with the toss of the blow dryer before she had to get her children off to school and herself to work.

While the kids were happy to eat at zoo food stands, being locals, Steve and Liz had their own ideas, within walking distance along Connecticut and Wisconsin Avenues. Steve voted to eat at Maggiano's.

"Delicious and a date for you and Maren, but Steve…simple with three kids," Liz insisted.

"What about over by the Cathedral?"

"No," she said standing her ground. "Pick a place and get your deli fix while the kids eat burgers or pizza."

"What do you think, Maren?" he asked.

"You two grew up here." Maren shook her head. "I'm not touching this with a ten-foot…pole." A sly grin erupted. She looked to the pavement hiding it.

Steve laid a hand on her waistline as if it might suppress any giggles. "You win…deli, kid fare." He smiled at Liz, could finally look at Maren without laughing himself. "This time."

"It looks like Dylan's found a new friend in Tyler," she told Maren, once they ordered their food, seated in a circle for six. "Tyler couldn't stop asking about him until Tuesday, and it started up again Thursday."

"Not sure how you have the energy, Liz. Two kids, with all you do."

"Tim helps out. He works a flexible schedule. I don't fret the spilled milk and toys all over the floor; try to take things in stride."

"Oh she's got stride," Steve piped in, offering his assessment. He had already told Maren how far apart he and his sister were on the neatness spectrum. "Operates on Caribbean time."

"Not true," Liz defended. She turned to Maren. "Steve is definitely more the neat freak, his book shelves more organized than the Library of Congress, and his kitchen drawers might make it into the Williams-Sonoma catalog." Liz lived to give him a rough time when they got going on one another. "He got so much bossier when he chose surgery."

"Quiet, little sister." Steve enjoyed giving her the run-around as he sat across the table. "You got your restaurant."

"And you got three dozen or so sandwiches to pick from." She crinkled her nose at him, and Steve held his head higher, making sure she noticed. Tyler and Dylan sat next to Steve with coloring books discussing animals.

"This elephant's peeing like the one we saw," Dylan whispered to Tyler. Tried as they could to mask it, immense giggling gave way to Steve erupting himself.

"Mine is farting," Tyler added. "Uncle Steve says farting's a good thing."

"Yeah, he told me that in the hospital," Dylan added.

Collective eyes that would make any zoo animal run for cover made their way to Steve. Liz and Maren both glared.

"What?" he asked. "In my line of work, it's necessary."

"What's so funny Uncle Steve?" Hannah leaned upon him, granting him the most adorable gaze. If it weren't so heart-warming, Maren thought she might need to counter Steve's burgeoning ego.

"Maturity sits at this end of the table," Liz said.

"Hannah, what are you drawing?" Maren asked. The three-year-old sat in her booster between her and Uncle Steve. Hannah wouldn't let him out of her sight.

She extended a crayon. Maren reached for it to join in Hannah's creativity. "No," Hannah said pulling the crayon back, motioning to Steve.

Liz started to mitigate the embarrassment Maren must have felt, but with his hand out, Steve indicated he had this one. "Hannah, I think Maren's really nice, isn't she?"

"Yeah," Hannah managed slowly to the leading question. Pivoting jostled her pigtails.

"Glad you agree. She's a lot of fun."

Hannah looked at her uncle. "No," she said, curving her bottom lip toward the table.

"No," Steve bristled back at little Hannah. "Why not?"

"*My* Uncle Steve."

Maren smiled at Steve being overruled by a three-year-old.

"Well, Hannah, I told Maren before she even met you, that *you* were my number one sweetheart." Steve turned her little face into his. "That won't change. Promise."

"OK!" Hannah beamed. They all laughed.

"Dylan is such a happy kid," Liz assessed.

"Becoming all boy. Hearing more, seeing more this year." Maren sighed. "After-care keeps him from seeing school-bus mischief most days."

"Hey Liz...you're gonna be at the house for awhile, right?" Steve asked.

"Yeah why?"

"Favor." Steve came around to her side of the table, crouching to talk to her. "You think you could watch Dylan for about an hour and a half so that we might take a stroll down Wisconsin to a few shops? Make it two hours." He raised his brow as if to beg a little of his younger sister.

"OK...on one count," she said having cultivated a way to work with her older brother long ago.

"Name it," Steve replied, exasperated that she made this into a quid pro quo.

"You really need to talk to Eric. He thinks you're upset with him."

"Liz, I'm not. He pulled me aside last week. He told me, OK."

"Exactly. But he looks up to you, and it's just my sense that he feels judged over Shelly. You might have called him this past week or sent him an email."

"I'm not judging him. It's not like I have a ton of disposable time," Steve said in hushed tones.

"An email takes a minute. You've been your usual quiet Steve self."

"Whatever! The whole situation makes things a bit awkward." He shot his sister a look that said if she continued down this path he'd be pissed so she'd better drop it.

"Awkward isn't half the word for it." She lowered her voice. "But your issues with..."

"Liz," Steve interrupted with the authority she accused him of copping when he wasn't even at work.

159

"OK." She followed Steve's glance to Maren and tugged on her brother's arm. "You two look really cute all head over heels. Don't mess this up."

"Well, if you'd stop lecturing me, it would sure help."

"Won't say another word. Let's get going. I'll keep the kids busy. Mom'll like seeing them. Hannah needs a nap anyway. I can put her down in my old room."

"Thanks. I owe you one." He kissed his sister on the cheek.

Maren and Steve put Dylan's seat into Liz's SUV for the short ride to the Kramer house. Luckily, Dylan had no trouble separating from them. He liked Tyler. Steve's parents had some toys left from the week before and enjoyed seeing the kids play.

That afternoon, Steve and Maren strolled through a few stores in Friendship Heights and Chevy Chase. Steve wanted to pop into Brooks Brothers and look at his favorite footwear store, convincing Maren to buy a pair of sneakers because if you don't take care of your feet, the rest of your orthopedics go to hell, and you'll pay the price in 10 years. Or sooner.

Maren peeked into a few women's clothing shops. They fed each other samples at the culinary store and when Maren noticed Tiffany & Co. Steve suggested they go inside.

"The holidays approach," he said, opening the door for her. "I find out new, exciting, things about you every day. One more opportunity."

"You should know when it comes to jewelry, I'm minimal, if you haven't noticed already."

"Like yesterday," Steve whispered, grazing the Saturday beard he'd purposely not shaved on her neck. "I love minimal."

"You're incorrigible," she said, clasping one of his hands into hers. "Scruffy."

"Look, I love your subtle elegance and sophistication." His hands on her waist glided over her as they moved from counter to counter. When the sales clerk answered another customer's question, Steve captured her ear again, with both hands hoisting her closer and up toward him. "I cannot stop thinking about you in those high heels and nothing else."

Steve kissed her full on the mouth, in the middle of the store. An older couple, picking out multiple items, zoned in. Steve put Maren down, and she leaned her head into him. The woman watching blushed;

her husband took his wife's hand. A store clerk smiled, and a younger couple shimmied closer to one another.

Steve took note of Maren's sense of style as she commented on pieces. Design mattered. She preferred platinum, silver not so much, and occasionally wore yellow gold but not as often as simple costume jewelry, which she knew he'd never buy here. Steve liked being surprised by what she wore at work, often occasional beads or large pieces set off around her neck.

"Another thing I love," he told her. "You always look so put together. Anything here just adds to it." Maren slipped her free arm around his waist since she'd slung her handbag on her opposite shoulder. "If you want to go further down Wisconsin, we can. Or we can start back."

"Let's head out," Maren agreed. "Enough shopping for one afternoon. Could use a coffee, though." He led her out, finding a Starbucks. They each took a cappuccino with them. "Steve, seriously. You don't have to fuss with fancy things. We can joke about minimal, but I'm not a fashion plate."

"You mean I get off easy?" He chuckled immediately. "Like yesterday. Very easy."

"Honestly…"

"Maybe this holiday season, I'll get you and Dylan matching life vests so we can go 'awesomely fast' for your son." Steve did a double take to see if she thought he was serious. "Could wear them in your dad's sailboat. Double duty."

"The ones you have are plenty fine, blue not bright orange. Come on, before we wear out everyone with three kids."

The next day, Steve piled Dylan and a LEGO set, just in case, into his backseat peppering him one last time with Steelers trivia. The Cleveland Browns, a long-time rival, came on the TV screen shortly after Vicki opened the front door to Maren and the guys.

"Man, trick question," Dylan told Paul, when he asked who the Steelers quarterback was. Maren started to correct Dylan for speaking to an adult like that. No shyness showed in her son now.

Time-out, Steve signaled. "Let him finish."

"Stewart is the QB, and so is Maddox." Dylan's body met his voice escalating into an up and down jump.

161

"Good one," Paul granted him. "Now Dylan, those action figures...my mom sent us a box this week from the 'burgh." He crouched down to Dylan's level, eyeing Steve. "Don't let him steal them. They're for you."

"OK," Dylan replied conspiratorially. "Thanks."

"That was very nice of you," Maren added. "Steve, these are great." Mrs. Romano had sent Vicki and Paul a box of Pittsburgh favorites. A Terrible Towel for Dylan; some biscotti for Steve.

He took a bite as Maren held one for the taking. "Did she get these in the Strip?" he asked Paul.

"You bet. Steelers central down there." Paul stood back studying Steve and Maren. Her cheeks were warm and red as he smiled wryly. "What?"

"Maren didn't believe me about the Strip," Steve told him. "Sounded too suspect." He laughed.

"Nah, no strippers. Well, in *Flashdance* maybe," Paul said.

"Keep it clean guys," Vicki interrupted. "First movie we ever watched together on a VCR was the one with Jennifer Beals," Vicki whispered to Maren. "No complaints 'cause the actor in that was easy on the eyes."

Maren agreed. She could tell Vicki was only marginally into football. Dylan, however, hung on the guys who went out of their way to incorporate him into their banter, curbing language even when a ref called a bad play.

During half time, Vicki and Paul muted the commentary while Dylan played. They went into the kitchen to get food, and Maren climbed onto a stool around the island, while Vicki hiked up onto one also. Paul put veggies and dip on the island between them not a minute before Steve speared a carrot to crunch on.

"It was so good getting over to DC for the day," Maren told Vicki, who appreciated the stories of Hannah's crush on Uncle Steve.

"What a cutie," Vicki dubbed Hannah seeing the pictures on Steve's phone.

"Yeah, I'm making this one my screen saver," Steve declared of the one with Hannah hanging on him.

"Steve, Mr. Ultimate Planner," Paul started. "Any plans for mid-May?"

"Romano that's a little far ahead right now even for me."

"Well, you are covering for me later this month right?"

"Yes, but May? Where are you flying off to now?"

"No place special, just labor and delivery," Vicki said.

"What they call a staycation?" Steve asked. "He gets more days than you as a new hire?" Maren was silent but elbowed Steve.

"Steve, sometimes you are dead-on perceptive; other times, slow on the uptake," Paul razzed. "I'll need coverage. We're having a baby."

"I knew it," Maren said nudging Steve once more. He left her side and drew Vicki into a hug.

"Congratulations!" Steve added with a kiss. "OK, I wasn't great on the uptake. Right, on racquetball." Eyes to Paul suggested at least he'd been having fun. "I'll mark my calendar."

"How are you feeling?" Maren asked.

"Tired…more than usual." Vicki informed Maren that she'd been diagnosed with lupus years ago. While she managed it well, the condition complicated her life. Vicki, at 36, was a year older than his sister Liz, and four years younger than Paul.

She showed off the nursery she'd just had painted in yellow because they didn't wish to know the baby's gender until birth.

"She wouldn't go with black and gold," Paul lamented.

Steve laughed. "How long will you work, Vicki?" Privy to the miscarriage his friends had already endured, Steve understood how much was riding on a healthy, successful pregnancy.

"As long as possible, but I'm training someone if I have to take leave early."

The game continued and Dylan met both guys' hands in high fives when the Steelers won with three points. Waving his fan towel, Dylan thanked Paul and Vicki for the loot and tried to wrangle another biscotti before they left.

"Let's stop at the plaza and get them something for the baby, Steve," Maren suggested as they backed out of the driveway. As stores closed at six, they had better get there soon.

"If it's quick," Steve consented. "Otherwise, not two days in a row."

"It'll be quick. Dylan's with us."

In the ten minutes it took to pull into Target, Maren conceived a baby basket idea, and she planned to order some baby football fan gear, shopping online if she had to. Once inside, they followed Maren.

"What do you think?" she asked holding two hangers, one in each hand.

"This one," Dylan chimed in pulling a baby sweatsuit from the steel bar securing all the hangers at the top. As he did, two other items fell to the floor, and Maren stooped to pick them up.

"OK, we'll choose from these three," she said. "Steve…"

While Steve physically stood beside Maren in the infant department, his eyes had drifted across to children's clothing soaking in the sight of a little girl about seven or eight, with blonde hair, parted to the side and cut shorter above one ear.

"She's cute, isn't she?" Maren said, acknowledging the child who followed someone, disappearing behind the shelves. "Do you know her?"

Steve didn't answer, his eyes still fixed. Startled actually. "Yeah, she's cute," he said finally.

Maren sensed his preoccupation stemmed from something he couldn't talk about, like a former patient. He had taken on recent pediatric cases. She grew accustomed to information that couldn't be pieced together for reasons of privacy, privilege, or plain prudence because the details would be too awful to comprehend once, let alone twice.

In the zone of her brain, that if labeled she'd call "favorite things I love about Steve," Maren tucked a nugget away this weekend—his definite soft spot for children. He'd already formed a satisfying bond with Dylan over the past two months. He teased his nephew Tyler, nuzzled little Hannah until giggles overcame her and quickly passed to him. Today, she saw Steve light up as Paul broke their baby news.

For the first time, in as long as she could remember, Maren wondered what it might be like to have another child. Only now, this would mean conceiving Steve's baby. Another nugget she tucked away.

Chapter 11

Tuesday's election brought a new Republican governor and a clear Democratic majority for Maryland in the 108th Congress. Daily, the investigation unfolded regarding the two snipers who terrorized the region as officials debated whether Virginia or Maryland would first prosecute them.

"Are we going to Steve's?" Dylan asked when Maren met the school bus.

"Yes Dylan." Maren walked; he skipped. "Any homework?"

"On Friday? That's wack." He turned around mid-stride. Walked backwards. "Really. Can we eat dinner with him?" Influences of older kids flashed through Maren's mind.

"The sooner you get ready, the sooner we meet Steve for dinner," Maren told him. "Grammy, Grampy, too. We're all staying over." If they wanted to go sailing, they had to seize the chance while the season allowed it.

Not the procrastinator he could be, Dylan straightened his room the first time Maren asked, evident when she got on hands and knees checking under the bed. Nothing stashed there. For that, Dylan got to choose his favorite local burger joint.

"I used to love sailing," Maren told Steve later as she deposited her handbag onto his sofa. "Brings back memories." Ones she wanted to pass along to Dylan and so did her father.

"It'll be fun." Steve stashed items in a duffle as he talked. Boat shoes, sweatshirt, and layers since the air had started to chill. "Make yourself at home."

Steve stopped, watching Maren stretch out on his sofa having already studied his small place. Dylan had run off feeling like a king and jumping on the bed, that very size.

"Mom said how much she likes watching Dylan with you."

"Glad they approve," Steve replied. "They've noticed how much I like their daughter, I'll bet."

"She wasn't subtle about sleeping arrangements." Maren angled her head to read the cover of *Esquire* on the coffee table. "They get the picture." She looked at Steve, wrinkling her face. "Speaking of pictures...a little suggestive." The cover featured a woman in high heels, bare legs and a well-sculpted yet clothed derrière as Pierce Brosnan looked through the space created by her stance. "The kids visit soon." Hers tonight, but she bit that back.

Steve walked over, taking the magazine. "How your heart ages...that's why it's here," Steve countered. "I'll move them before they start sailing through the air. Interesting how that happens." He stashed the magazines in a basket on the bookshelf. "Back to sleeping arrangments."

"The old 'great articles' defense." Maren surveyed his shelves. "I quote, 'We'll put Dylan in the guest bedroom, if you and Steve would be comfortable in your old room?'" Maren could tell Steve swallowed that morsel easily enough. "Dylan, back in here," she shouted. "What are you still doing in Steve's room?"

"No...Dylan, it's OK. You can open that LEGO set."

"You got him another one?"

"A cottage to build with the kids," Steve explained. "Stays here. What'd you say to her?"

"What could I? It's obvious we're a couple," she replied. His eyes bulged forward to get a definitive answer. "I said 'fine.'"

"Mmm...don't even have to fantasize...having you, under your parents' roof, in your teenage hottie bed." Steve pulled her tight. "Still hot, but all woman."

"Really...can you handle it?" She ran her hands up the front of his dress shirt feeling his chest underneath. She'd have to ease him out of it later. "No complaining about deprivation," she said, turning serious. "They might put the house up for sale, moving closer to me. Can't believe it."

"Childcare," Steve said. "Convenient."

"Is that all you think about? Getting me alone? I grew up there."

"No." He swatted her behind. "Six times a week, I allow other thoughts into my hormonal brain. Want a decaf cappuccino? In a half hour, traffic will ease."

"Please." He had a sense of humor, she thought. "So this is a single guy's place?"

"Look, it's functional," he said from the kitchen. "I'm hardly ever here, usually at the hospital, on the boat, or with you."

Maren let her eyes rove. You could learn a lot by the spines on a person's bookshelf. *Men Are from Mars, Women Are from Venus; Tuesdays with Morrie; The Healthy Kitchen; Leadership* by Guilliani; and *Seven Habits of Highly Effective People.* His sister Liz had sized him up well. Steve organized by height and category. Some showed nautical interest. The book with stunning bay photos you could indeed judge by its cover.

"Ah, Steve…" He couldn't hear for the noise made by frothing the milk. She shelved her remarks, turning to his walls. The Manhattan skyline—before September 11th—made anyone take pause. A dramatic sunset with a sailboat bore initials. Along the top left an "S" and in the lower right hand corner "Love, P." A gift, no doubt.

Steve handed her a cappuccino topped with a nice rise of foam.

"Thanks. Nice books," she complimented first. "They say several in one genre spell a fascination." With her free hand, she reached for *The Joy of Sex* shelved next to simply *Sex* by Madonna. "Liz will love your bedtime stories for her kids. Me, too." She fluttered her lashes. Smiled. "Coffee hits the spot."

"Look, Paul gave me that Madonna book," he defended. "I knew I'd get crap over it someday." That time had become this evening.

"Might want to remove them before your uncle extraordinaire weekend."

"Good point. If not you, then Liz will be up my bu…back about them."

Maren had caught the stumble. "Speaking of language. Dylan has taken to using 'sucks' as in 'I have to be on call. That sucks.'"

"What happened to freedom of speech," Steve muttered as he meandered back to the kitchen.

"I heard that, Steven." Maren hoisted herself onto a tall barstool.

"Steven?" He reconsidered. "My freedom fades fast."

"Showing considerable restraint," Maren huffed. "I like your kitchen. A little worried you're short on appliances." A Krups cappuccino machine, he'd just used along with the hefty coffee grinder. These kept the juicer, blender, toaster, and waffle iron plenty of counter top company. By no means large, the apartment's eat-in bar separated the kitchen and living room.

167

"Dylan got lost in the bachelor bedroom, oh no." Lord knows what her son could discover. Maren came back out with Dylan by the hand.

"Ah, I wanna watch something."

"Watch it out here."

Steve picked up the remote to his living room television. "No parental controls." He found a suitable channel, handing it to Maren before she found the *Playboy* channel on the menu selections. Its days were surely numbered.

"I'll bet not," she said, climbing back onto the stool. "Wouldn't have pegged you the culinary type."

"Yeah, that was another boyfriend of yours cooking at his mother's," Steve declared setting down his own beverage to open the cabinets. His hands turned like a model on *The Price Is Right* displaying stacked cookware and a drawer full of utensils and professional looking knives.

"All-Clad no less."

"In Pittsburgh, Mrs. Romano would buy us cookware at Christmas or for birthdays," Steve explained. "Some people get ties they'll never wear. We got the good stuff."

"Make us dinner then, only it'll have to be kid-friendly cuisine."

Steve leaned over the bar separating them. "I'm p-a-i-n-f-u-l-l-y aware." He planted a kiss on her lips, the quick I'd-like-more-but-can't kind.

"Count your blessings for tonight," she reminded him.

"Trust me." He'd best tamp down his libidinous thoughts. "Next weekend, we should have dinner someplace nicer since Vicki & Paul offered to keep Dylan."

"If you're sure it's not too much for them...or for Vicki."

"They want to. I'll work out the details." Placing their empty cups into the dishwasher, and grabbing a bottle of water for Dylan, Steve shouted, "Ready to see your grandparents?"

"Yeah," Dylan exclaimed darting his attention from the TV.

Steve grabbed his duffle and jacket, perfect for a chilly sail. "Let's move it. Your stuff in your car, right?" They were leaving his and taking hers.

"We're prepared Captain."

"I like the sound of that," he said, tugging her hips.

"You would, but Dad is Captain tomorrow."

"Tonight, you've got me."

Steve settled into the start of a friendship with Audrey and Jack. They still appreciated how he hovered over Maren weeks ago. That had been a bigger scare possibly for them than for their daughter. Steve's office chat with Jack helped him better understand the memories Maren and Dylan both held of Mark.

Maren mused that she breathed more easily and slept better, especially on nights with Steve nestled against her. Still, the more time she spent around him, the more Maren saw Steve close off facets of life—his and everyone else's—so that he could focus on other things, like surgery and hospital bureaucracy, most recently. Not a terribly bad trait but she noticed it, nonetheless.

"Keep the volume down," Steve whispered to Dylan as they both got up early Saturday in Annapolis. Dylan watched a half-hour of a PBS kids program before Steve commandeered the remote for ESPN.

"Thanks for starting the coffee," Audrey said as she came downstairs, dressed in jeans and a sweatshirt, grateful for the aroma.

"Without at least one cup my cognitive faculties wane," Steve told her, coming over to the counter to pour more in his mug. "Your daughter's, too."

"Takes Jack and me two cups each to hold a meaningful conversation most mornings." Audrey had prepared a quiche to bake for breakfast, which they ate after Jack and Maren meandered down. Audrey stayed cleaning up the dishes and putting together lunch when the four of them returned. The Coles moored their sailboat at a community dock, a short walk away.

"I'll walk with Grampy," Dylan proclaimed, reaching for Jack's hand. The boy sensed that his mom wasn't budging from Steve's side. Dylan jumped less, not seeking as much attention as in weeks past.

"Happy?" Maren whispered though she and Steve had fallen back far enough that their voices wouldn't carry. She looked up as his arm encased her.

"Fantasy fulfilled." He kissed her hair pulled into a ponytail. Nothing like handling the rigging of a boat and having hair all over your face. "There's something even sexier quietly covering up the obvious. I'll be sure to thank your parents when we leave."

"You won't," she forewarned, with a naughty smile, hand slapped to his chest.

"Hey, I might need that rib." He uttered it quietly as she hadn't really inflicted damage. She'd given him enough of a push to forestall his chuckle, however. "How did two mild-mannered people manage to raise such an aggressive daughter? Confine it between the sheets. Seriously."

Maren stopped in front of him. "I'll give you aggressive." She kissed him quickly. "Always in charge, always on top." They chuckled. He had been, and she'd enjoyed it considerably. "You do like calling the shots, and today, Steve's part of the crew. Not the captain. My heart bleeds for you."

"I'll do just fine, you watch," he said, tugging her tightly to keep her out of mischief. Getting to the dock, Steve offered his hand to steady Maren, but she politely pulled away, stepping down into the boat. He followed. "Jack, I read that these got inducted into the Hall of Fame last year. A great weekender."

Maren's father broke into a broad smile. "You've done your homework."

Jack had traded the 18-ft. sailboat he'd taught Maren to sail on, delighting in this newer, sloop-rigged model with a fixed keel, 10-ft. beam and draft of more than five feet. While it wasn't designed for offshore sailing, the Catalina sailed well for the bay or wider-water passages.

"A little more weather helm than I'd like especially in a good gust," Jack noted. "But she does fine." A slight amount was desirable, but if the boat pulled toward the source of the wind too much, it could create an unbalanced helm, requiring the captain to fight it steering the tiller to counteract the effect.

Dylan made a beeline to his lifejacket, remembering where these were stowed and how Steve had taught him to fasten one.

"Steve, you can take naps here, too," Dylan announced running up to his side. Steve shot Maren a glance. Surely the child wasn't astute enough to catch their private jokes. Steve searched his temporal lobe. No, he was damn sure he hadn't uttered the word "pole" nor the phrase "getting some" while in Dylan's company. Maren would have taken out part of his chest if he had.

"Dylan, put my bag in the cabin please and grab the sunscreen out of it," Maren said diverting him. Dylan did as she directed.

The forward cabin featured a V-berth, a spacious salon with comfortable seating, a full-sized galley with sink and stove, and a double berth aft, where no doubt Dylan had staked out his spot.

Steve helped Jack get the boat ready to head out.

"Maren, stash this somewhere," her father told her. "Not aiming for speed with Dylan aboard."

"What Dad?" Maren wasn't turned in his direction.

"The whisker pole," Steve said, grinning. He took it from Jack, handing it to Maren. "No speed or performance necessary. Not today anyway."

Maren clutched herself trying to stifle her amusement. Not hard enough. She'd caught Steve's wicked eye seconds before she burst into a huge laugh.

"What's so funny?" Jack asked.

"Women," Steve said, emitting a hoot himself. Saving her ass, he thought, mindful that if he'd said it, he'd be wincing again. "One minute they complain about going too fast. The next they're speed demons. That daughter of yours!"

"Sure, throw me overboard," she muttered under her breath as she grabbed the pole from Steve and stowed it.

There was a slight chop on the water, but after a few instructions to Dylan about remembering to watch the boom and keep his lifejacket on, they headed out, first under motor power.

When they faced into the wind, Jack gave Maren the cue. She hoisted the sail and smiled at the sound of the canvas rippling, until it snapped full with the wind. Quickly taking her seat, one elbow on the edge of the boat behind her, she motioned for Dylan to sit. Her arm entwined him just as they caught a gust. The boat took off as if in flight.

"Wow," Dylan exclaimed. "I don't remember it going this fast."

"That's because last time you didn't seem so interested," she told him, dragging her slender fingers through his child-sized mop. "Look, we're flying like the gulls out there."

"This would be why weekends matter." Steve threw his head into the wind.

"I second that," Jack added. Nothing ahead of them except deep blue, postcard perfect water, as they skimmed the surface. It was hard to hold on to problems when you surrounded yourself with Dylan's cotton ball clouds, salt air, and the sea beneath you.

"We're tilting," Dylan squealed as the wind screamed.

"Heeling, Dylan." Maren positioned herself with her feet apart just enough to balance the sway so that her butt wouldn't hit the boat's bottom.

They stayed on course for quite a ways until Jack shouted, "Coming about," as they tacked from one side of the wind to the other, moving themselves accordingly, and in unison, as a crew.

Dylan asked about the channel markers and learned their purpose. "Where does Tyler live?" he asked Steve, pointing aimlessly.

"Other direction, Dylan," Steve said, snagging his arm to point at Kent Island. "You can't see but over on the other side. That's where Hannah and Tyler hang out."

"Aren't you uncle on call soon?" Maren asked Steve. "Which weekend?"

"It's approaching," he said, dragging his phone from a secured pocket in his boating trousers. He certainly knew how to dress for a sail. He often wore the new sneakers he'd purchased in Chevy Chase. Not today. Sperry Top-Siders worn for their on-deck traction. "Next Saturday. Liz is bringing them by three."

"I'm invited, too, right?" Dylan piped into their discussion. It had started as his conversation, after all. As the boat rose and fell, kicking a misty spray, Dylan swatted at the water spitting up over the sides.

"Are you kidding," Steve answered. "Tyler will be a mess if you're not there, bud. I have to figure out logistics. I have them that afternoon through Sunday morning."

"Better take your vitamins, doc," Maren teased.

"You and Liz. You just don't think I can do this without calling in back up. We'll have loads of fun."

"Well, if I'm your back-up, I can't commit the whole time. I can leave Dylan overnight if he wants." Unless bedlam breaks loose, she mused.

"Nobody sleeps at sleepovers," Dylan informed them. "You just don't."

"No, sometimes you don't," Steve concurred, wise enough to avoid eye contact with Maren. He let the remark sit. "You're in charge of movies, Dylan."

"Make sure you set some controls on that TV, Steve. Six-year-old boys and a three-year-old little girl." Maren rolled her eyes to Jack. "This will be rich!"

172

"Give him a chance, Maren," her father said. "You're tough."

Steve nodded, glad someone else noticed.

"Dylan, take the wheel." Jack created space for Dylan as captain. Until they tacked; then Dylan decided he'd had enough, predictably taking refuge in the aft berth. Steve took over while Maren repositioned herself, admiring how he maneuvered her dad's boat.

Steve had powerful hands, fluid motions setting their course, propelling them through the open waters. Maren drank in the sight of his wind-blown hair, eyes behind sunglasses secured today with a black holder that could rest upon his chest if not shielding him from the rays. Bright on the bay, temperatures hit only 60 degrees.

Maren rubbed her arms. Steve relinquished the helm to Jack, wedging himself next to her, an arm protecting against the chill. They tacked a time or two and as they began their final one, Dylan stepped up, out of the cabin. He hadn't heard the "come about."

"Ouch," he yelled as the boom clunked his forehead. Fortunately, it wasn't a forceful hit. To Dylan, it ended his fun. For the rest, it terminated tranquility. Even the gulls noticed the competition for the loudest squawk.

"Come here, honey," Maren motioned, getting up from Steve's grasp to take Dylan's hand and lead him in between them. His wails became loud and forceful. Steve pushed his hair aside to check him over. No bleeding. Looked in his eyes. Fine, at first glance. Steve held two fingers out for Dylan to follow. He tracked well and seemed to have his coordination in tact.

"He's not seeing stars," Steve assessed. "If lung capacity was an indicator…"

"Maren walked into the boom a time or two when she was young," Jack recollected. "She learned fast. Never did it again."

"Is *that* what happened to her?" Steve joked.

"Not funny, Dr. Kramer." Maren's eyes flickered; her hand ran along Dylan's back.

Steve had already banded his fingers through shocks of Dylan's hair, several times. The crying lowered from sobs to sniffles. Calmed him. Like mother, like son, Steve thought.

"Maren, relax," he said cozying up to her as Dylan moved away. "We're almost back, and you can warm up."

"Wait 'til you have an apartment full of kids and someone ends up in tears." She stared at him, alarmed and amused. "You'll need me, you wait."

"Babe, I need you all the time," Steve said pulling her for a smooch. "Now come on, we've got to get this in and put away." Dylan decided the best place for him would be down below. Of course. Remaining in the same spot for more than 10 minutes challenged a boy his age.

Soon they let down the sails, Steve taking on that task. They would motor back into the pier.

"Maren, take her in," Jack suggested.

"Me?"

"You're the only Maren on board." He winked at her. "You can do it."

She sighed, cautiously taking position at the wheel. Jack leaned over. "That's it. Ease her in slowly. Turn," he directed. "That's it." He surveyed their position. "Nice." Steve had already grabbed the line and hoisted himself out to secure the boat. Jack patted Maren's back. "How's that?"

"You're the best," she whispered, leaning her head into him. "I needed this."

"Me, too," he said. "Next summer, we'll take Dylan out more often." Jack hugged Maren. "Good crew today." He said it within earshot of Steve, who took in the father-daughter moment, but didn't want to intrude on it.

They had lunch with her parents and made a few shopping stops to stock up on mac and cheese, cereal, snacks, healthy juice, not sugared water Maren insisted, when Dylan put a popular brand in the cart. Returning to Steve's apartment, Dylan helped Steve prepare tacos while Maren set out cheese and crackers to munch on first.

"It's fun watching you in your element," Maren said. "Since it's not likely I'd watch you operate."

"We all had a great time…seeing you in your element, too," Steve replied. "And if you ever wander into the observation theater, an intern *will* no doubt pick you up off the floor from fainting." Maren knew he was right.

"Do I get a double dessert?" Dylan asked. Vanilla ice cream atop brownies already smacked of two.

"Dude." Steve looked up from the skillet as Dylan carried taco fixings to the table. Maren put out silverware and plates.

"Well, I hit my head." Dylan looked entitled. "I got coloring stuff and toys for my appendix."

"Nice try," Maren told him. Privately, turning to Steve she whispered, "He is OK, right?"

"The concussion that wasn't. Dylan, it's a bump. You're fine," Steve reassured. "No football if you're not feeling well. Rest tomorrow...in your room."

"No, the Steelers play," Dylan said. "Can I watch with you?"

"Paul and I made plans," Steve told him. "Beer and kids don't mix."

Having had two, maybe three weekends of football, and with a few things to catch up on, Maren needed a quiet Sunday at home to herself.

Dylan was disappointed, but happy that his mom had brought along board games. They played Mouse Trap with him before he took to reading and fell asleep on Steve's sofa where they fixed him a spot with blankets, a pillow, and two of his Muppets.

Relaxing with a glass of wine each, they read lounging in their jeans and street clothes on Steve's bed—Maren catching up on a week's worth of *The Washington Post* and Steve a medical journal.

"Is your brother watching Dylan over Thanksgiving?" Maren asked. "Your mom said they might be at their place. What do you call it again?"

"The bay house," Steve said.

"It would give us a night to go out."

"We talked. He's got one gig lined up that weekend."

"Eric can have his girlfriend over, but ah...not for an overnight."

"Honestly, let's revisit that later." Steve closed his journal and pulled her closer, making her lose the grip on her pages. "End of the semester approaching; a lot going on."

Maren turned and faced him on one elbow. "I get the sense you and Eric have a lot in common." Steve looked at her quizzically. "You're both distracted by women...you've admitted as much."

"Yes, we are." He leaned in smiling. "You know, Paul and Vicki said they'd be happy to keep Dylan. I can make those reservations at a classier restaurant Friday. Saturday's my night with the three kids."

"Paul told me he already got a stash of toys out," Maren said. "We have coffee dates."

"Glad you're getting to know him…even better they're getting away before their lives get busier."

"Another thing: we should go hear your brother's band."

"We will." Steve got up, locked the door, and returned to steal her once again from the news she tried to glean from the paper. He unbuttoned her blouse, moving his hands across her. "I have another distraction right now."

Chapter 12

On Monday, Eric gave Steve the low-down on his band bookings through the holidays. Five friends comprised Eric's band, most from his undergrad and grad school days, with one girl he knew from high school singing vocals. Eric sang in addition to strumming the rhythm guitar. The rest played keyboard, drums and bass guitar.

"Am I going to like this or make excuses to Maren?" Steve asked.

"She'll be impressed that you know me," Eric countered. "Just bring earplugs…then you won't have an old person headache."

"Smart shit." Steve chuckled. "Thanksgiving weekend. It's closer."

"Hey…your team only tied it yesterday," Eric reminded.

"And the Skins couldn't even pull off a win." Thus Steve considered the conversation a victory between him and his brother, at least from his perspective. "About watching Dylan. You mentioned this, and if it works great, but if not I completely understand."

As he suspected, Eric wasn't into the childcare scene quite like Shelly, but it was good money, free food, and other benefits, Steve surmised.

"It's having Shelly around that's the problem, isn't it?" Eric asked.

"No, not really. I've always liked her." Steve was matter-of-fact. "Maren doesn't want you two shacking up in the guestroom nor anywhere else with Dylan around. Read between the lines." The brothers laughed. "Giving you an out, bro."

"Oh, just you enjoy *that* privilege?" Eric could lob innuendo as well as his older brother.

"Occasionally." Steve chuckled. "She's not running a frat house though."

"You really are into her, aren't you?" Eric asked. "I haven't seen you this in love for a long time."

"Thanks for reminding me."

"That didn't exactly answer the question." Eric sat in his apartment in College Park, attempting a term paper, but the muse wasn't striking so he picked up when his cell rang. If he missed one of Steve's calls, Eric never quite knew when he'd catch his brother on the phone again.

"Serious potential," Steve said. "Sharing with you. News shouldn't travel through any grapevines, however."

"Safe with me, but tell that to Mom." Eric heard Steve acknowledge that. "While confidential…did you ever try pot?"

Steve sat back in his office chair. "Full of questions today. We're asking this because…"

"Cause it's hell living in your shadow as the stellar student, perfect one, your highnass." Eric had accentuated the last word pronouncing "ass" to make his point. Steve howled finishing his sandwich before afternoon patients.

"I'm too old to get busted by Mom and Dad," Steve said. "Though you're not if they're paying your freight through a master's program. Tried it once or twice, after the prom. Memory fades," Steve said, echoing Eric's claim that he was out of touch. Not likely, if Eric confided in him. "What's this really about?"

"One of the band members swears it's not harmful. I've tried it a couple of times. It's not really addictive, is it?"

"Eric, maybe not as addictive as other things you could be doing, which I hope you aren't, but it is addictive." Steve opened a browser, pulling up a good site. "Do a search on cannabis dependence."

Eric listened, trying to interrupt unsuccessfully with Steve on the other end. "Not to mention, pot's often laced with other harmful compounds, increases heart rate and appetite, affects BP…"

"That's a gas station, right?"

"Blood pressure…you really are a smart ass today. Impairs memory and coordination. Studies underway on its affects on adolescent brain development."

"I'm not an adolescent."

"The age for adolescence keeps rising." Steve wanted to tell Eric that if he kept smoking the stuff he'd definitely fit into the category a lot longer, but he stifled that reply. Older siblings could come across as a third parent. Steve knew that wouldn't help their sibling relationship. "Look, you get enough lectures where you are. Chalk it up to experimentation. And if God forbid you're ever given a tox screen, it stays in your system."

"It makes sex better doesn't it?"

178

Steve leaned his head into a hand, elbow planted on his desk. "I knew this had to be good." He closed his eyes. When his hormones came on board, Eric wasn't even playing with Matchbox cars.

"Not sure any study that claims that is reliable and valid. If you need a joint to enhance things at your age, loaded with testosterone, with a hot blonde, you've got bigger problems."

Steve heard a knock. "Hold on, Eric. Come in." It was Suzanna alerting him. In five minutes he had to begin office hours.

"Thanks," Steve mouthed to her. "Look Eric, I have to run. Hope I answered your question. Probably not what you wanted to hear."

Eric had certainly provoked Steve's thoughts, including how suited he might be as a sitter for Dylan. Or not.

"It's all good. Sorry 'bout your Steelers. Better luck next week!"

"Not worried…'cause ah, the Rooney family keeps coaches."

Eric fell silent. One for the big brother, Steve thought as he got back to seeing patients.

Maren's Wednesday got off to a rocky start with a project that had to be redesigned and with the hospital's ad agency adjourning a meeting later than expected. She left Steve a message that lunch wasn't happening.

Mid-morning one of Steve's residents paged him. With a case headed for surgery, he checked on it since it was Paul's patient, and Steve covered Paul's surgical caseload as well as his own this week.

Reassuring those who entered the OR, and dealing with the worried expressions on the faces of their family members, didn't normally daunt Steve who kept a respectful distance. This posed a dilemma. The patient: Bradley Morgan.

Steve knew the family and ordinarily would have referred him to another surgeon. They were short-handed today; every other surgeon had a case.

Steve found his brother Eric in the waiting room comforting Bradley's younger daughter, Shelly, seated alongside her mother, Hilary Morgan.

The three of them stood as Steve walked in. Steve acknowledged Eric with a slight punch on the forearm. He hugged Shelly and put his hand on Hilary's back. As the younger couple walked back to seats by the TV, Hilary stayed with Steve searching for something positive to say.

"If Paul had to be away this week, I'm glad you're covering for him," Hilary told Steve. She gripped his arm so tight that Steve could feel her fingers dig in.

"Thanks. I'll brief you as soon as I finish." Steve touched Hilary's shoulder and motioned to his brother and her daughter. "I've got to run. We'll hopefully know what's causing this, and I'll try to send someone out, if it gets to be too long. I'm glad they're here with you."

Hilary Morgan hesitated. "I did call her, Steve, and she's cutting her day short, but doesn't know that Paul's away." Steve studied Hilary Morgan, who held back, still trying to put something into words. "If I told her, I was afraid she wouldn't come. She hardly ever comes back. I need her."

Steve lowered his head. "Wise move then. You have enough on your mind. I'll talk to her."

Hilary nodded. "Thanks. Good luck." She watched him pace away quickly.

Hilary Morgan had great faith in Steve Kramer's training. She understood it well. She held much respect for him, even though he and Pam, Hilary's other daughter, never made a life together. She and Brad along with Dolores and Bill Kramer never fully understood why. Some answers naturally fell into place.

As Steve scrubbed to begin her husband's surgery, Hilary turned her thoughts back to the medical emergency Brad faced. The better part of an hour elapsed. Eric and Shelly had gone down to the cafeteria, bringing Hilary some coffee. This was the first crisis of their dating relationship, with Eric trying to ease the strain. "Steve will pull him through," he told them offering reassurance.

"I sure hope so," said Shelly, a bundle of tension that Eric could feel as he held her hand. At 26, she was a year older than Eric, who like most young men gave one sidelong glance to that tall, slim body, strung out blonde hair flowing down her back, and dark brown eyes resting below perfectly shaped eyebrows, when he recognized her. And like any other guy, he had one hell of a fantasy going on that night.

Cut shorter around her face, Shelly's hair needed a frequent tuck behind one ear, where you'd find three studs in each lobe. A tattoo of hearts hidden beneath her sleeve had been her most recent display of self-expression.

Hilary moved her eyes from the clock that displayed 4:40 and spotted someone darting off the elevator. The determined walk of authority gave her away.

"Mom," Pam called, stopping short of the waiting room. Hilary got up and hugged her older daughter. "Thanks for coming. So good to see you." Hilary's arms lingered on her. "This will mean a lot to your dad, too."

Shelly, her only sister, got up to embrace her, and Pam caught sight of Eric.

"You sure have changed since I last saw you."

"Hi Pam." Their hug: the perfunctory kind.

Eric had remembered Pam from his first meeting about 15 years ago. He remembered her short blonde hair and somewhat petite build, but it looked that she'd gained a few pounds, possibly making her look more attractive by most men's eyes. Of course, Eric didn't look at Pam that way. Another set of Kramer eyes had, but not Eric's.

Eric couldn't remember really when he'd seen Pamela Morgan last, and by now she had added another last name. A name one wouldn't address her by because, as Eric recalled, she was staunchly independent and more career-minded than his own brother…if that was even possible.

Now that he dated Shelly, Pam's sister, their chance encounters increased, especially since the Morgans prepared to retire to a condominium they had purchased on the bay.

"How long's he been in?" Pam asked her mother.

"Over an hour. All we can do is wait."

"Yeah, it's been a while since I've been on this side of things. Your thyroid surgery, I think. What on earth happened?"

"I don't know. I had dinner out last night. Bridge club. Your dad didn't feel like going with me," Hilary said, wishing she'd done something regarding her husband's ailments. "He got up awfully early. Stomach cramps. Had the same thing days ago." Hilary stopped her ramble. "Not his appendix. That came out in '89. The pain was excruciating."

"Any nausea, vomiting, diarrhea? Bowel sounds? Fever?"

"All that. The resident called it 'acute abdomen' with diminished bowel sounds. They did a CT, x-rays, ultrasound…wanted him in surgery right away."

Hilary knew her daughter demanded more detail. She felt frazzled, not the best reporter but added, "I'm not sure if they have a precise handle on this."

Pam looked annoyed. "He shouldn't have let it go."

"I should have persuaded him, but you know your dad."

"It's not your fault." Pam knew her father was cut from the same cloth as she, tightly woven with no ability to stretch. "If he'd have called me, I'd have told him to call Paul. Stat!"

Hilary let that slide. "Pam, you look exhausted."

"Two deliveries last night; surgery this morning. I cancelled the rest of the day, caught the first train out of Philly and rented a car when I got off at BWI."

"I'm really glad you came. Haven't seen you since summer when we visited. How's my granddaughter? It was so good seeing her this month." Hilary's eyes teared up. "I miss her."

"Well, she misses you, too. I might have some pictures." Pam dug into her handbag to retrieve them.

"I love this one," Hilary said. "She looks so much like you. And, this is a nice one of you and Jerry."

"Which one?" Pam asked looking over Hilary's shoulder. "I'll get you copies. Chloé really enjoyed spending time here. Spoiling her with shopping sprees again!"

"A grandmother's perogative, Pam." Hilary doted on her only grandchild. "Nice of Jerry to bring her; wish he had more trips to DC." Hilary took another sip of coffee. "We do miss living near you, but we're settling in down here."

Pam had urged them not to sell their home—the one she had grown up in—because she knew their retirement plans just one state south would cause distance and discomfort. For her, that is. "You can stay anytime. Good thing we built the guest suite the way we did."

"Your dad will probably need to stay put through the holidays."

Pam looked up at the ceiling. She didn't want to spend holidays here. She shifted seating so that she could be closer to her mother.

"When did this little love match occur?" she whispered, motioning to her sister and Eric Kramer watching TV.

"Pam, they recognized each other. What can I say?"

"Whatever." The obvious replay of a Morgan/Kramer match was just too damn odd to even process the scenario further. Pam took time to find the women's restroom, and returned two calls from her office. She came back, resumed her seat, and thumbed through a news magazine.

"It'll be good to catch up with Paul. Haven't seen him in ages." Pam mused on a private memory. There had been plenty involving Paul. "Daddy's in good hands." Her voice echoed a trace of worry, but like others in her profession, she hid behind the initials after her name.

"Pam, Paul Romano is out with his wife. Back tomorrow," Hilary informed.

"Her name's Vicki. We've not met," Pam admitted. "Who's doing the surgery?"

Pam noticed her mother's eyes avoiding hers, apprehensive now. Silence penetrated. A visceral reaction rose within Pam.

"You're kidding me," she said, voice escalated and eyes flickered, diverting Eric's attention and her sister's from the television. Drama brewed right here.

Pam hoped at least one of them would erase her assumption, but it was her mother who bore the depths of her wrath. "You knew this and you didn't tell me?"

"Please understand, Pam. I wanted you here," Hilary confessed.

"You *don't* understand," Pam voiced back sternly. Every curse word Pamela Morgan had ever learned raced over her tongue to exit, but Pam held those words back.

"He just got promoted," Eric said, in Steve's defense watching Pam pace the room, hands gripping her arms, crossed in front of her, as if she wanted to strangle each one of them. "It was an emergency."

"I know that!" There was a sharp edge to Pam's words, an edge that cut through most people except for family and those who knew her well. And Eric had practically grown up with Pam hanging around.

"Pam, Mom's under enough strain," Shelly added to Eric's failed attempt to sway the situation. "Times like these aren't easy, you know."

Shelly figured Pam ought to know with what she did for a living, and with their family history. It hadn't always been just the two of them. A brother nestled between their ages, died of childhood leukemia at the age of 11. He hadn't made it to his teen years. Generally, it had brought their family closer, and maybe even served as a catalyst for Pam's medical career.

"Sorry. I need some coffee myself." Pam sighed, left her jacket and an obstetrics journal, but grabbed her handbag in search of a coffee stand. That she'd find the nearest one in the lobby bought breathing room.

Pam never questioned Steve's medical prowess even if her grade point average was half a point higher than his leaving Columbia. She had heard about his promotion. If anyone could pull her father through this ordeal, Steve could. That was professional; her concerns anything but.

Pam took 20 minutes to simmer. Slightly more collected, she returned nursing a cup of tea that she decided might calm her nerves better than coffee.

There, as she strode closer to the waiting room, Pam took in his unmistakable presence, sorry that Steve still looked good in scrubs after 10 years, give or take a few months. If dread was staged like cancer this would be at least stage four.

Steve briefed the others with his back to the doorway. Maybe if no one looked up, Pam could slip away and get a report later, avoiding Steve altogether. That wasn't Steve's style, and it was a stupid, cowardly thought on her part. Hilary wouldn't give her the detail she demanded, and after making this trip, Pam couldn't alter what she had to face now.

Seeing Steve stopped her cold. Her mind froze with memories that for now Pam had to push aside, yet the emotion wasn't as easily moved. She swallowed hard, placing one hand on her stomach as if it would keep the intensity buried. Pam moved forward in baby steps until her voice carried into the waiting room.

"How is he?" Pam questioned softly, clutching the reality of this meeting. Close proximity brought back another flood of feelings she'd forced away. To the others, it looked as if every ounce of color in Pam's face had fled.

Steve turned around at the question. He looked at Pam, whose green eyes looked troubled, darting down, around, anywhere but near his. Pam felt the moisture start to collect and blinked hoping it would stop.

"Stabilizing. Come sit down," Steve said, standing up to offer her his chair, shoving his own thoughts aside. "Ischemic bowel. I removed 14 cm of the small intestines; it was strangulating."

Steve removed what had become knotted and rejoined the intestines at the severed ends. The obstruction was turning gangrenous and would have killed him. His white count shot terribly high, and Steve knew as soon as he'd seen Bradley in the emergency department that they had to operate quickly.

Even after years apart, Pam could read him like a book. Steve held back as he pulled another chair to claim. He looked drained. Eyes exhausted and pained. "Give it to me straight, Steve."

He looked at Hilary, next to Pam. "He arrested, shortly before closing."

Hilary gasped.

"I'm glad we got the English version," Eric said. "Why can't doctors say heart attack?" he whispered to Shelly, tension in the small room already palpable.

"He coded?" Pam's voice broke. She took her mother's hand in hers.

"Twice." Now, Pam saw some of the color escape Steve as well. Bradley's heart had stopped as Steve described. He and his team worked frantically, shocking her father back each time. Steve gave Pam a fairly complete rundown, medications used, surgical details she alone comprehended. What should have been a shorter surgery became painstakingly complicated. An extremely close call, and they still weren't sure what had gone wrong with his heart.

Hearing this, understanding half of it, Hilary had no more energy to listen. "I need to get some air," she said, standing to grab her things. Steve stood, taking Hilary's hand. "Thanks, Steve. I know this has been quite a night."

"I'm not leaving for a while so I'll talk to you again."

Hilary Morgan looked into his eyes and squeezed his hand. Steve was certain that meant gratitude and it might have meant more.

Eric and Shelly followed Hilary Morgan with their jackets slung over arms and shoulders. They left the room, leaving behind only two people, but probably more of a strained space than with all of them being anxious in it.

She couldn't hide behind her medical degree now, not with Steve, who sat back down in the chair next to her nudging it so he could face her. Spotting her jacket she'd tossed into a chair, Pam gathered it and put it on. A kind of feminine armor, needed more now than in any professional setting.

Hearing it outlined as she had asked for, left her immobilized, her voice quivering. "You must have gone through...through hell in there. You come so much closer to the edge, than I usually do in surgery."

"Maybe so." He tried to hide it, but he felt close to the edge himself. Muscles tense, tightened from the strain of knowing he almost lost a patient—Pam's father—and the thought of breaking that news to her. Still, Bradley had a new lease on life. They both knew it could have been worse. Far worse.

"That's a lot more than I normally give a patient's wife," Steve said. "You'll interpret, if I'm not around?" An unnecessary question, he knew. Pam Morgan was nothing less than thorough herself. Only Pam would bide time with professional reading with a loved one rushed into the OR.

"Of course," she assured him. "I asked for the details."

"Long day?"

"Tiring. Surgery—the planned kind. Two deliveries—one a C section, the other was most of the night."

"A good pusher, huh?" Steve glanced at her.

"Yeah, still like that kind." She laughed. That had broken the ice.

"Congrats on your new job."

"Thanks. Word travels, I guess."

"Thanks to our siblings."

"Yeah." He wouldn't go down that path. "How long are you in town?"

"You tell me. I don't know." If it were up to her, Pamela Morgan Carlton would run like hell, straight out of this waiting room and hospital, but she loved her father and wouldn't abandon her mother. Not with his condition tenuous.

"If you're staying a few days, maybe...maybe we need to clear the air a little."

"Really?" Pam sprang from her seat as if she was about to bolt. Pam wanted to agree, but her recollections made it so utterly painful to be near him right now.

Steve rose looking at her squarely. "Would you really not have come here if you knew Paul wasn't in there and I was?"

"I can't answer that. But you were exceedingly clear last time we spoke."

"That was almost 10 years ago."

"Like yesterday." She looked at him with moist eyes. "I think the 'get the fuck out of here,' laced with other choice expletives, my name, and 'I don't want to see you again'…with the word 'ever' tacked on…that's painfully clear, Steve."

"All the more reason we need to talk."

"Don't make this about us right now. I'm so not up for it."

"Me neither, but…if I recall…one of your peeves with me was avoidance."

"Compartmentalizing." She met his eyes again. "You certainly are persistent and determined, Steve Kramer."

"I learned at the feet of the master." As Steve said the words, Pam's chin dropped. Some of her had rubbed off on him long ago.

"One o'clock. My office. We'll make it Chinese around the corner." He knew the menu would guarantee she'd show. "Recovery's this way…" Pam strode in that direction.

Steve left to shower and change, thinking about the differences he noticed in Pam. More brown streaks through her blonde hair, stylishly swept to the side, cut above her ear. A crease or two around those green eyes and her jaw. She had probably turned 40 last year, he figured.

Today, they had a chance meeting neither would have ever anticipated, and as fate put them in each other's midst, it was best that they bury old grievances.

If they could.

Chapter 13

The next morning, Maren grabbed a cup of coffee and spotted Paul adding half & half to his. She walked up to him needing to stir some into hers.

"How was your trip?" she asked.

"Wonderful," he said handing over the pitcher. "Hilton Head before it gets too cold."

"How's Vicki feeling?"

"Rested. Glad to get away," Paul conceded. "Looking forward to watching Dylan."

Maren laughed. "He's a riot Paul. Promise you won't teach any more potty words than he learns on the school bus. I don't know our exact plans though."

"No worries. First day back...gotta run." But as Paul turned to exit, that wasn't happening.

"Paul Romano." A blonde in dark slacks, a turtleneck sweater and blazer bound over, flinging arms around him to plant a kiss on his cheek.

"Am I seeing things?"

"No, my father was brought in yesterday by ambo. He's in ICU," she said. "Of all times for you to be away." This woman's pouting face and softly delivered grunt spoke a strange mix—complimenting Paul, yet registering displeasure and regret for his absence.

Pam immediately stuck forth her hand. "I'm sorry, I didn't mean to intrude. I'm Pam, a friend of Paul's."

"Pam...Maren Mitchell," Paul offered leaving it at that. "Dr. Morgan is a former classmate of mine."

"Nice to meet you," Maren said shaking Pam's hand. "That's quite all right. I need to get back. Paul, one of us will let you know about Friday."

Maren stopped at the ledge built into the wall to add just a smidge more coffee and cream to her cup to take with her. She wasn't completely out of earshot when she overheard Paul's friend, obviously a close one, light into him.

"Wouldn't there be anyone else in this hospital to cover your cases besides Steve?"

The two of them had their backs to the coffee supplies though Maren could tell Paul nudged his friend farther away. Steve's name piqued her curiosity.

"Not this week," Paul said. "How's your father?"

"I guess I'll find out more at lunch, 'cause now I'm railroaded into that with his attending physician—the chief of surgery." She stood back. "I'm sorry, this is so unexpected. I'm not mentally prepared."

Neither was Paul, curious as hell, realizing the quagmire this could become if he didn't divert Pam's little rant.

"I'll head up there. How's your mom handling it?"

"Shelly's upstairs with her now. Mom didn't sleep well."

Maren sensed, like a lot of conversations one might overhear in a hospital, that this was an emotion-filled one. She thought nothing more of it as she left the room with more people gathering at this early hour.

Pam and Paul agreed that they, too, would grab a bite and catch up. Pam got something for breakfast before venturing up the elevator to be by her father's side. Paul immediately punched numbers into his cell phone holding it to his ear as he left the cafeteria.

"Welcome back. Did you get my message?" Steve saw the caller-ID. He had left voice mail about yesterday's surgery and other cases, expecting Paul's call.

"Haven't listened to it yet," Paul admitted. "Already getting bits and pieces. Our former apartment-mate just ripped me a new one because apparently her father, my patient, has become yours. I'm heading upstairs, but ah…I was having coffee with Maren during this bombardment."

"Shit!" Steve entered the building after pulling into his parking space. "What happened?"

"Pam paced across the cafeteria, straight at me, oblivious to Maren. I introduced them. I had to, but…"

"How much damage control are we talking about?"

"I didn't exactly spell out who was who, Steve. I don't know what Maren overheard after she stepped away. You gravitate to intelligent women. The wheels may be turning if she overheard Miss

189

Congeniality's numerous complaints with your name brandished in there."

Steve sighed. "Thanks for the heads up." Without description, he could picture Pam in action.

"I tried, obviously surprised when she approached. Just add this to your list of Thursday problems."

"Thanks. Listen to the message. I'm here except for lunch."

"I heard about that, too."

"It's the right thing to do. Not to put you in the middle, but a conversation needs to happen."

"Good luck."

"Later…" They hung up. It was going to be a long day.

Pam and Steve hadn't just given their hearts to each other years ago. They lost them. The two met in 1983 when Pam was getting her master's in public health, meeting Steve on his first trip to Columbia to check it out. Smitten, Pam joked that Steve was there to check her out.

Not far into medical school, studying merged with seeing one another socially, in the library, often in a lab, and frequently in each other's arms where textbooks fell to the floor if they weren't careful. Everyone needed study breaks.

They moved in together as it seemed senseless to spend money for double the space. Steve and Paul had signed a lease and the two-bedroom apartment worked out well for three of them. Four if you included Paul's girlfriends that Pam would relentlessly tease him about.

Their schedules grew worse. Living together, Pam and Steve knew they'd have near daily contact. The three of them supported one another. When one got discouraged, the other two came through with the right amount of encouragement or a swift kick in the ass.

The Kramers and the Morgans grew close until Pam left Steve, and the subject closed permanently. Surgical residencies lasted five years, and Pam being a champion of women's health, passed her boards and began working at the women's hospital in Pittsburgh. While Paul knew career mattered more to Pam than most, he also knew the hurt she had inflicted on his best friend. Steve, who had settled into a fellowship at Hopkins after returning to Maryland, always evaded that discussion.

Pam probably insisted on plotting the course of their love, as she did everything else, Paul assumed. Only Steve couldn't take the

190

detours. That relationship had its tension before Steve's final year. Then, they broke it off altogether. Within months Pam had Jerry Carlton in her life, and she'd given him everything that perhaps Steve yearned to have. The experience may have colored Steve's view of women from that day forward.

Not even 24 hours after surgery, Bradley Morgan remained in intensive, cardiac care. Visiting had to be kept brief.

Pam knocked on Steve's office door, left open as Suzanna wasn't back from lunch. "I'm here." Steve could tell by the tone, Pam was perturbed. "Wouldn't grabbing a bite downstairs be easier?"

"No," he answered getting up, grabbing his jacket. "Hell no" raced through his mind. All Steve needed was Maren to stumble upon them, and he'd have an even bigger headache.

"This place is just around the corner, quick, and private." He motioned her out with his hand. "We can walk there."

Steve updated her on her father's progress, but as they sat down to a corner table, they both knew they weren't here to discuss Bradley Morgan's surgery. A quick catch-up on their work lives didn't last long either.

"You insisted we have lunch, so..." Pam sat back, arms crossed, studying Steve. She took out reading glasses to ponder the menu, giving the waiter her order. Steve quickly asked for General Tso's Chicken, just to get his over with.

Walking the sidewalk and with a jacket over her, Steve hadn't noticed Pam as he did now, still petite, pervading more strength. Steve guessed she'd jumped at least one clothing size. She filled out her turtleneck more than he had remembered. Noticing this annoyed him.

"Having years to reflect, I'm sorry if I was a complete ass when I found out." Steve put his elbows on the table and rubbed his forehead. "Having said that, I stand by some of what I said, even to this day." If she had felt cornered back then, he only granted her a small swath of space to navigate now.

"Your tricking me into seeing you the way you did, over stuff you had of mine, I can't even remember how you did that, getting me to come to Maryland...that was a complete set up."

"How would you have liked me to confront you? By phone?" Steve sniffed out disgust. "No. Needed to be in person." He tried as he faced her to keep his anger tucked away. Ten years, he reminded himself.

"I still don't know how you got my medical record."

"I told you, it came over with other charts that doctor you used sent for surgical consults. Obviously it wasn't intended for the stack. Saw your name only after I'd opened it."

A quick glance of the first-page history spoke volumes with everything Steve never really wanted to know. He had sunk into his chair absorbing its contents that night so many years ago. Clearly sent by mistake, nothing related to surgery but a lot interested him. Information, that in his mind, he had a right to know after a nearly 10-year relationship. But Pamela Morgan had made unilateral decisions.

"You were awfully pissy about it. I couldn't get a word in edgewise, Steve. I'd never seen you so...ramped."

"Agreed." Steve drew in a long breath. "Do you remember what you said?"

"I'm sure you remember."

"Something like 'Trust me, you wouldn't be where you are if I hadn't handled it.'"

It, a word so impersonal and hearing Pam use it back then felt like she had knifed him twice and twisted it at least once. When she aborted it, she aborted their future.

The waiter at the Peking Palace set down their food in the stillness of their painful memories of that confrontation. Steve had found out the facts in 1993, just before June. Moving to Maryland that summer seemed even more fitting. He had made a copy of the one page, pondering his next steps, which took time to effect.

"Earth to Steve," Pam interjected into the silence. "If things had played out differently, do you know where we'd be right now? We'd have a nine-year-old, we'd be divorced, in different cities, absolutely miserable, and make other people miserable along with us. Factor in legal expense. Add stall to our personal lives and careers."

"You're always so certain of the outcome. I thought I planned things."

"Not to mention, I'd have been the one to give up my goals to follow yours."

"I didn't have all the facts, either." Of course, he figured out one of them. Jerry Carlton, whom she met and married the following year. They approached their 10th anniversary working and living in Philadelphia with their daughter.

"You ended up moving, right?"

"I did, but..." Pam couldn't finish.

"But you left to be with Jerry," Steve interrupted. "Maryland, with me, wasn't in your plan."

"No it wasn't," she admitted. Steve knew too much, as if he'd obsessed over it.

"Well...back on topic. I'm sorry I was..."

"Forcibly confrontational."

Steve looked at her, not remembering.

"You grabbed my arm, practically pushed me into a chair with 'Sit down, you're not going anywhere!' I'd never seen you like that. If you could have stoned me with your eyes, I'd be flattened to this day."

Steve closed those eyes, momentarily. This brought it all back.

"I guess... I could have handled it differently, at least telling you," Pam said.

"You treated the news as if you got knocked up during a one-night stand." He let those words settle in. "Nine years. Almost ten if you count the year we first met. *That* was the worst part." Their conversation snapped off.

Steve stared across to another table, remembering how she kept the secret from him. Her swift action rendered him powerless to propose any alternatives, and she had to know what he would have proposed. They were a couple. He thought they were in love. Clearly, he hadn't gotten the memo that they weren't.

"It was the hardest thing I ever had to do." Tears formed on her eyelashes smudging her mascara, as Pam picked at her Sichuan shrimp. "I never wanted to hurt you. I thought I was doing you a favor."

Was she for real? Steve searched her eyes—eyes that realized he didn't buy her explanations, even today. "We had two different worldviews starting our careers. I thought...maybe you wouldn't be so opposed to ending it."

It again. "Maybe not. You know where I stand, supporting reasoned choice."

"I guess I was afraid you'd pressure me, and that was about my fears, and you're right. Maybe we could have made the choices together and, Steve, it would have been a huge loss either way." Pam jabbed her fork into another bite of food, swallowed it, and put her fork down, before leaning on their table and reaching for his wrist. "Does this somehow help? I do respect you Steve, and I know it was a terrible way to display that. Can we put this behind us?"

Steve didn't say a word. He couldn't help but consider the contrasts between the two women he'd ever loved so completely. Pam so driven, so intense, and so set in her ways, and Maren, restrained, giving…so very warm and playful. While Maren had struggles, like everyone, he'd never seen a sly or selfish side.

Pam dug back into her food. This whole era was tough, more so for Steve. Even she knew when not to push, giving him a few minutes to think. "I guess not," Pam said finally, letting her fork fall to her plate. She backed into the chair. Arms crossed. "What is it?"

Steve looked at her. "I don't have the best answer, Pam. The way it all came about, the secrecy. Unless …" Steve paused, biting back what might exit his tongue without forethought.

"What?"

"Unless, there was a question about paternity."

Pam's eyes, turning darker, looked as if they could pierce him from across the table. "Make me out to be a slut, why don't you?"

"An honest question, after I've had sufficient years to think about this."

"An honest answer then. It was ours. Yours, mine. Need more detail?" Her voice sounded incredulous. "Remember December '92. I'd taken my own apartment, the lease starting in January. I came by to get some things."

"Paul was at his parents house that weekend for the holidays."

"Yeah." Pam was sorry she'd conjured up images too personal, wondering now which ones flashed through Steve's mind. She and Steve had argued that day but landed in bed for the rest of it, through the night, in what she had come to realize was flat-out goodbye sex. She had just gotten over illness with a seven-day course of antibiotics, which must have knocked the effectiveness of her birth control pills to hell and back. "Anything else?" she asked.

"When did you meet Jerry?"

"I met him in February, alright. Let's put this in the past. What else?"

"The swift nature of it. You described it: A loss. One I had no say in." He leaned back as well. "Christ, I saw a kid in a store recently… a little Pam."

"When?"

"I don't know, one day out shopping. What difference does it make?"

Pam stiffened. It might actually have been Chloé, her daughter. Chloé Carlton had spent a long weekend with her grandparents while Jerry came to Washington on business. Her parents owned a condo nearby. Rendering her father at West Riverside. Had he seen Chloé out with her mom?

"Steve, I was six weeks along when I realized." So many skimmed edges of their time together brushed their lives again today.

"And eight weeks for the procedure." Steve would never forget her chart's obstetric history: gravida 1, para 0, abortus 1. Meaning, she had one pregnancy, no viable children, and one abortion. The date of the procedure came on the heels of their break-up.

Pam motioned the waiter to bring more tea. Gin would get her through this lunch even better. Pouring oolong bought her a few seconds as she struggled with the turmoil then—turmoil unleashed, stashed away. Until this visit.

"You always liked kids," Pam said. "I was scared you wouldn't listen to me."

"And you wouldn't get what you wanted? Right?" What he wanted got tossed into Pittsburgh's three rivers. Steve's eyes might have bored holes like a drill going through bone. "Who else knows about the abortion?"

"Only a few people," Pam conceded. "A friend of mine. My own doctor. As you know all too well, it's a part of one's medical history. And Jerry. I didn't tell my parents. Didn't want to be hassled by them, either." She wondered if she should continue, but figured what the hell. "They expected us to keep it going, but they don't blame you. They know I ended the relationship. I lied when they asked me why." Pam wondered if she should come clean.

"So you saved your reputation neatly tucking that nugget aside." Lovely, Steve thought.

Pam straightened in her chair. She really didn't want to have to defend her actions. "And you shared the details with...?"

"No one."

"Oh come on," she said. "You had to tell Paul."

"No."

"You compartmentalized this, too?" she asked, hotly annoyed. "No one. Not one person?"

"I guess, since that's what you love to call it. You did it with part of the story, but it's OK when you do it." Different people, different rules. Steve looked more rattled. "I think it was harder to get over that than your falling for Jerry."

"Steve, the cracks in our relationship started well before I moved out. I met Jerry in Philly, but we weren't really involved until the spring."

"Convenient." Steve threw that out there, still questioning the timeline. Steve remembered the day she moved out. She couldn't explore a new relationship living with him, sleeping in his bed, as they'd done for the better part of a decade. "It's over," he responded in a calmer voice. "We've both moved on."

"Do you hate me?"

"Hate is a strong word, Pam." Steve leaned closer over his now finished food. "I can't hate someone I shared so much with, even though it came to an ugly, unplanned ending. I stopped loving you long ago."

"I'll always care about you, Steve. I hope you can say that someday about me."

"Pam, I can already. We should have talked this through years ago. But I know I cut you out abruptly. I could have done that all differently, as well."

"You're forgiven. Someone is going to be thrilled with you. In fact, I heard there's someone special in your life these days."

"You heard correctly," Steve took a sip of his ice water. The chill helped shift things. "You even met her, I understand."

"What?" The revelation startled her, he could tell.

"In the cafeteria. With Paul, over coffee."

Pam thought for a moment and cringed. "Ah…I wasn't too happy this morning." Her face confessed that she'd bitched up a little storm and now regretted it. "I'd no idea."

Steve loved seeing awareness stir her senses. He laughed.

"Well Pam, sometimes not entering a situation like you're speeding along the Beltway or the proverbial bull in the china shop pays off." Steve paused. "Slow it down. I was hell bent one time and look how that lasted. Just feedback."

"You're not the first to tell me that, and you won't be the last. I'm glad if you're happy, Steve. You deserve it."

"Happy is the word. I'll leave it at that."

"I understand. She's lucky to have you. It wasn't our time, but it was good while it lasted. I don't have regrets there. I really don't." Her gaze captured Steve's attention. "We had some good times. And you appear to have mellowed."

Steve nodded in agreement. "We did have a few." Shifting from sentiment, he added, "I was that bad?"

"Not entirely." Her lips curved. "I liked beating the other women to you, back then." Pam laughed at how outrageous that sounded regarding her competitive spirit. She knew then, that Steve could turn a blind woman's head.

Last night seeing him in scrubs captured her, and today in business attire, but without a tie, Steve Kramer still would appeal to her in a strictly physical sense. Pam pushed that aside. He was someone else's catch now.

"I sure hope the new woman in your life—sorry her name escapes me—likes the water. That was another major difference in choice and lifestyle, you realize. I like cities. You like small towns."

"She does." Steve laughed. "She grew up around boats. It's end of the season so we haven't had much time to share that."

"Doesn't get seasick?"

He sat back into another memory. "Wow, I forgot that one."

"Yeah, don't tell her 'get over it and pop a damn Dramamine.' Not if you want this one to last, Steve." Her eyes watched for his reaction while hers conveyed that she meant those words entirely. Pam reached into the tray holding their check. "This one's on me." She gave her credit card to the waiter.

"I do want this relationship to last, and it will."

"So go for it. It's time." Pam forced open one of the two fortune cookies left for them. "Conquer your fears or they will conquer you," she read from the tiny paper. "Fitting." She stashed it in her purse.

"I'll say." Steve put his napkin on the table. "Thanks for lunch." He left his cookie unwrapped on its tray. Chinese was more her favorite, down to the dessert. Not his.

"I'm sorry I put up a fuss about coming here. We needed to air this out, regardless of whether we're forced into the same room again by fate or by virtue of Eric and Shelly." She shifted her chair, signed the receipt, and put her card back into her wallet. "Were you as mortified as I was to learn of their dating?"

"Oh yeah," he admitted. "And ah, given the nature of this conversation, I hope you've counseled your sister on preventing such a dilemma."

"It's always up to the woman, isn't it, to prevent these things?"

"That's *not* how it started out with us, but as I recall, it was your specialty. You insisted on controlling that also."

"That didn't come out quite right," Pam said. "Yes... had that discussion and warned about antibiotics."

Years ago, Steve had asked how the hell a woman trained in gynecology could find herself in this situation, but they didn't need to go down this road again.

"I like your sister, Pam. I'm just not sure how I'd feel if they do get serious."

"It certainly would make a few things awkward. Time will tell. I guess we'll have to deal with it...like grown ups." Pam looked at her watch. "I have to get going. I appreciate your help with my dad. He always admired you, Steve."

"I'm glad." Steve stood up and so did she. "I've always liked him, too. "

Having said what they came to lunch to say, they returned to the hospital, and once inside the front door, went their separate ways.

Still preoccupied with the project that had waylaid her this week, Maren skipped lunch. Her intense concentration got jarred as her desk phone rang.

"Maren Mitchell," she answered.

"Missing you." It was Steve's voice on the other end. "I've hardly seen you since Sunday."

"I know. I'm slaving over this project," she said. "How's your day? Did you grab lunch?"

"Yes, I did, with a colleague." Steve knew he would have to disclose that his ex was in town, but the last 24 hours hadn't given him too much chance to think about that conversation. He could avoid Maren, which he decided was foolish. Or, he could hope she hadn't overheard too much. "I'll be late tonight. Again. You have time for dinner here?"

"I've got to pick up Dylan, and besides, I have a headache and want to go home. I'm not feeling that well."

"Oh," Steve said. "What's wrong?"

"Let's just say our back up plan worked or I wouldn't feel bloated. Cramps yesterday." Maren had stopped her birth control pills. While on them, her periods were usually pain free.

"I'm sorry. Feel better," he said. "I'll call you about Friday."

"Second thoughts about that, Steve. I'm exhausted and we've got a bunch of kids on Saturday. Let's take a raincheck sending Dylan...go out another time."

Extra work and emergencies had sped the week away for Steve. "I'll talk to Paul and postpone it."

"Thanks."

"But Friday, come over with Dylan. We can have dinner. Watch a movie."

"Let me see, Steve. I need to get this blasted project done first."

"I'll talk to you soon. I love you."

"Love you, too," Maren said, putting down the phone.

A half-hour later when her energy waned, Maren decided skipping lunch wasn't such a smart choice. She ventured to the cafeteria for coffee and a snack to bring to her desk.

"Maren, hi. How are you?" When she turned to the voice in line, the ponytail confirmed who stood beside her.

"Hey Eric, didn't expect to see you here."

"Yeah, I'm visiting a patient."

"I'm sorry. Does Steve know you're around?"

"He does," Eric replied. "It's actually my girlfriend's father. He had emergency surgery. Steve operated on him."

"I hope everything's OK." Maren knew Steve had been lost in cases—his own and Paul's. She grew accustomed to days without contact.

"We do, too. He was very sick." Eric looked over at the table with Shelly, almost ready to ask Maren to meet her, until he realized that Pam was sitting right across from her. Dolores and Bill Kramer had taught their sons polite behavior, yet how to deflect attention from an embarrassing situation such as this wasn't one of their lessons. "I better run. Take care, Maren."

"You, too, Eric. My project calls."

As Maren strode back with her coffee and container of veggies and dip, she saw Paul Romano's friend from this morning sitting at the table that Eric returned to. If she was Paul's classmate that made her Steve's as well. For a split second, Maren scanned her memory for the colleague's last name. Morgan, Maren remembered.

"Wow," she said out loud. No one was near as it left her lips. Maren stopped in her tracks for another look where Eric had walked.

Leaving the cafeteria, she pieced together the conversation she'd overheard when retrieving her first coffee—something about Steve covering for Paul and being railroaded. The other details seemed sketchy as she got to her office. But as she set down her snack by the phone from which she'd talked with Steve, she figured out who ate lunch with whom. And, it damn well wasn't merely two colleagues.

By 4:30, Maren finished the project, almost ready to leave work. Before she did, she had to obtain another doctor's approval. One benefit of this job, she'd surmised, was the exercise walking back and forth to get coffee and now to obtain required signatures. Alicia instructed marketing staff to obtain these on proofs and carefully document exactly who had seen them.

Folder in hand, Maren stepped off the elevator at the ICU hoping she'd not capture a glimpse of trauma unfolding or raw emotion of struggling families. Having been one of those not all that long ago, Maren tried to keep such work jaunts brief. Emotional replays still felt rather raw.

There were six seats around the nurse's station. Maren stood while the doctor she needed to see finished a phone call. When the doctor hung up, she took out her pen and signed the memo recording her approval.

"We'll get this going tonight," Maren said glad she wouldn't have to chase this doc down tomorrow on her work-at-home day.

"Hey there," Steve said, rounding the corner to sit, chart in hand. Seeing Maren, he stood right hand on her waist, tugging to say hello. A kiss would have been inappropriate in the middle of such a busy unit.

"Hi. I was just leaving," Maren said. "I have to get this to my office, and then get out of here to pick up you know who."

"If you give me a second, I'll walk with you. Is this a hard-fast five p.m. pick up or he turns into a pumpkin?"

"Very funny. After 5:45, I have to rush."

Maren stepped back so that Steve could enter data into the computer and return the patient's chart. She fingered her hospital badge as the cord strands had twisted dangling from her neck. She took the badge over her head, straightening the strands. Returning it, she tossed her hair worn loose that day. She wore a brown skirt and a tan sweater, brown tights and matching pumps. Simple earrings and a standout necklace accented the sweater's bodice.

"All done," Steve said landing his hand back on her waist and motioning her toward the elevator where they waited. "I wish I didn't have to stay here."

"People warned me you worked long hours. I'm turning in early anyway."

Steve nudged closer to whisper into Maren's ear when his brother and Shelly came up. While they stood, Steve punched the elevator button again. It lit up.

"You remember Eric, and this is Shelly," Steve introduced. "Maren Mitchell."

"I'm Shelly Morgan. I've heard so many good things about you." Shelly extended her hand and they shook.

"Likewise. I'm sorry to hear about your father."

Steve stood. Patient confidentiality trumped conversation, and there had been a lot of those around West Riverside in the last day and a half.

"Thanks, we were just going to go to my mother's for dinner." As she said it, her sister Pam strode up fast-paced, stopping in her tracks. A pattern. Hurry up and wait. Rush to the traffic light to slam on the brakes. Only now, with Steve standing in his white coat, hand on another woman's waist, nestled comfortably close, Pam couldn't pull her feet back now.

Steve contained his grin before it completely erupted. He'd given her feedback to slow it down just hours ago, amused that she'd, as usual, not integrated that suggestion.

"Pam Morgan…Maren Mitchell," Steve said, disbelieving that he introduced the only two women who had ever meant as much to him. "Pam was…a classmate at Columbia." Steve's hand never left Maren's side.

Really, Maren thought, extending her hand which Pam took in hers. Steve had left so very much out of his description as classmate clearly didn't cover the depth of their relationship.

"Yes, we met this morning," Maren said. "Paul introduced us." She bit back asking Pam how their lunch had been. That might surely be a conversation she'd have with Steve, and if he didn't initiate it, then she might find herself spewing, not biting back. "Sorry for the circumstances," Maren added.

"Thank you. It was an unexpected trip."

"I can imagine. I hope your father's on the mend."

Pam looked to Steve for that answer.

"He'll probably go to the floor tomorrow. A good sign."

"Well, I'm heading out after breakfast with Paul. I have a planned C-section I pushed off to late tomorrow afternoon."

"You coming for Thanksgiving?" Shelly asked. "I missed Chloé weeks ago."

"We'll try. I hope you're giving Mom a hand. Order a take out."

Steve held his laugh. If Paul Romano or he hadn't cooked at their apartment, Pam would have wasted away, lucky if she could boil pasta. Once when she served sauce from a jar, Paul claimed his Italian relatives turned in their graves.

By now, Eric caught the shared recollections and looked to the floor. He felt responsible for the sensed tension by virtue of his dating Shelly. All of them boarded the elevator for what had to be the most silent ride down four floors that ever existed. When they got to the second floor, home to Maren's office and many others, the door opened. Paul Romano stood ready to board. He took one look inside as Maren stepped off, followed by Steve.

"Well," Paul said. He held the door back with his right hand. "On second thought, you go ahead," he said to the rest. "I have to talk with Steve. Pam, tomorrow at 7:30." He let go of the door.

"Can you do 7:45?" Pam shouted out.

"Fine. 7:45." Paul rolled his eyes when the doors closed. Just like Pam to still tweak what they'd already agreed upon. If Paul had to choose to board or stay behind, he'd much rather review cases Steve covered. "The AED is over in the corner," Paul quipped. "Need it?"

"Shut up." Steve spit out the response. It wasn't personal, not directed at Paul. It was the problem, and he knew Paul understood. "Can we do this in half an hour? I'll come to your office."

"Sure. Goodnight Maren," Paul said. They waved him off.

Maren nudged Steve. "That wasn't nice." She heaved a sigh. "Steve, I need to go. I'll be late for Dylan."

"I know." Exasperated, he ran fingers through his hair. "That was awkward."

"What part?"

"My entire day, from my first steps into the building when Paul called me. Make it my last two days." He edged closer. "I just don't know where to start."

"The truth about your brother, his girlfriend, and the link to yours might have been helpful. For starters, anyway." Maren was matter of fact, but temples still pounding, and now even further behind and having to rush, she, too, felt pushed.

"Can we please get together tomorrow? I'll call you in the morning." Steve tugged her waist and gave her a quick kiss. To hell with who saw them.

"I'll think about it." As she headed to her office, Maren realized that she likely would think about it. Most of the evening.

Chapter 14

At 7:50, Pam Morgan rolled into the cafeteria as Paul scoured the bulletin board. "How's my father this morning?"

"Improving. We may spring him from ICU. Home by early next week."

"Good. I'll see him when we're done." They took trays walking through the line. Pam got an omelette with wheat toast, and Paul one egg plus a waffle, admitting to Pam that though she couldn't cook worth a damn, he appreciated when she left him and Steve breakfast years ago.

Once seated, he considered her. Still vivacious and self-assured, more strained because of circumstance. "Catch me up on life in the big city?"

"Busy as usual. Added an associate in my practice and another nurse practitioner. That makes two. Jerry has risen in the ranks, in advertising. He and a partner opened their own firm years ago. We built a house. Our daughter is eight, quickly approaching 18." She pulled out the same photos she showed her mom. "How 'bout you and Vicki?"

"She's great…works here in childbirth education. You two would hit it off, I'm sure. She might stop by."

"Sorry I didn't come to your wedding, but I hope you understand." That big Italian wedding, with food that didn't stop followed by trays of Italian cookies, seemed tempting last year. With Steve as best man, Pam stayed clear not wishing to inflict their strife on such a happy day. So she had sent warm wishes and a thoughtful gift.

"I do. Things still tense…or better after lunch?" Paul paused to eat a bite. "Whatever happened back then I could tell it wasn't good."

"Tense…but better. I think. Go easy on him, Paul."

"That bad?" Paul looked at her. Pam, knowing Steve had kept everything to himself, figured that he wouldn't divulge things, even now. If Paul, the third of the three amigos, as they were dubbed, would understand, she'd have to spill.

"I broke his heart, never intending to. I wanted another path. And things got complicated."

"Surprised me when you moved out. I heard the *Love to Love You Baby* part, Pam. You perfected the moaning. Just didn't hear *War of the Roses*."

"Paul, really." Pam put her fork down, hands on the table. "Grow up!"

"What? Deny it," he said. The walls had ears his eyebrows told her. "Vicki doesn't know you. When she arrives, I have to behave."

Pam leaned closer. "Watch it. Steve and I likely remember… Elizabeth, New York, right? Bethany. Suzy, Francesca, and damn… what was her name? Vanessa. In Pittsburgh, if I recall…and her friend." Pam's grin could have reached her father upstairs on the fourth floor. "To name *only* a few."

"Steve's too polite to bring that up."

"I'm no Steve." Pamela Morgan could always hold her own with Paul, or anyone else trying to outsmart her. Moving in her seat signified more than a postural shift. It was a power play. "What would Vicki think of you having two women that night?"

As the memory returned, Pam remembered being woken, pissed beyond belief because she studied late for an exam. If she had nudged Steve, it would have incited him. With Steve's good fortune—not hers—he woke from the antics, also. Hence no one in that apartment slept. A night etched in Pam's brain. One she wasn't about to let Paul Romano forget. Ever.

"Steve didn't give me the Italian Stallion title for nothing," he said, boasting in laughter. "Sorry…it was your story."

"Paul, if I tell you this, it's because I learned yesterday that Steve kept it to himself. I thought he'd have confided in you, at least." She took a sip of her coffee mulling her soon-to-be confession.

"At the end of our relationship, I got pregnant. I never told him. I terminated it. I'm not getting into how he found out. He was furious. Threw me out of his life, practically out of the state. So I stayed away." She took another sip. "It was ugly."

Paul's easy-going exterior sobered. He drew back. "That explains a few things."

"What things?"

"He was very jaded, isolated himself. Focused on work. Buried himself in it. Just fits."

"I was a real bitch. I regret how it played out, but it was time for us to move on." So Pam had decided. Paul knew that part.

"This got settled yesterday?" Paul asked. "A lot of synchronicity these days."

"Damn straight on that. I hope it's cleared up. He said you introduced me to Maren. Her name, right?"

"Yes indeed. That made me squirm." Paul rolled his eyes at how Pam had lit into him. "Maren's really great for him."

"I'm glad. He's got his issues, but who doesn't? Overall, Steve's a great guy. I just think we ran our course. I never wanted to hurt him."

"If you're civil, that's all I care about." Paul spotted Vicki, waving his hand to come over. "He's my friend and I consider myself yours, too."

"Not an easy spot, I'm sure."

"Exactly. Now, you behave," he warned cautiously. Vicki brought her tea to their table. As she approached, Paul moved another chair near them. He kissed his wife on the cheek, introducing her. An OB/GYN and a childbirth educator had much in common. They chatted, the three of them. Before Paul left to see patients, he let their baby news intentionally slip to Pam.

"Congratulations…when are you due?" she asked.

"Mid-May," Vicki reported. "Hoping the nausea lets up. It's so random."

Pam shared a few ideas, as perhaps the only other person Vicki knew who saw pregnant women more than she did.

Paul leaned closer to Pam, "Come May, Steve's covering," Paul said. "I don't want to hear about it if you're in town."

"Not a word. Listen, I'll walk upstairs if you're heading out. Vicki, take care, and keep me posted."

"Thank you. I hope your dad is on the mend."

"He's getting there. During the holidays, I'll give you a call."

By Friday, Maren's headache subsided. Good sleep helped after she and Dylan read some books, documenting them on his first-grade reading log. Maren always enjoyed that time of snuggling and just being silly.

Shortly before nine o'clock, Maren, at her home-office desk, discussed projects with Alicia who called about the important one Maren shepherded.

"Thanks for being diligent, leaving it for me. Hopefully I'll get it to the agency. Otherwise, I'll call you right back."

"Off my desk and onto yours." Maren chuckled. "I'm starting on the annual report unless I need to do anything more with that."

"Great. Every winter there's a ball thrown by the West Riverside Hospital Foundation. Look at photos of last year's event." Maren rummaged to find that report in the stack brought from the hospital.

"Here it is," Maren said. "Looks upscale to me."

"Raises a pretty penny. If I'm not mistaken, Steve Kramer's late grandfather had some involvement, and I'm almost certain Steve's parents bought a table last year," Alicia said. "We finish the report after that to get it into the publication. Quite the night...possibly a ticket in your future."

"Haven't heard about it. I've hardly seen Steve this week."

"How are things?" Alicia spoke with curiosity females understood to mean do-tell. "You took those flowers out of here fast."

"Things are sailing along." Maren sighed. "I really do have feelings for him, though it's weird. I never set out to date this year. This Christmas, second one since Mark died, I don't feel the dread I thought I might, that's for sure."

"Because you're in love, silly. Does Dylan like him?"

"Adores him. That's scary too. If this doesn't work out...I mean, you read about not introducing kids into your love life, but Dylan was how we met."

"I hear ya...things are progressing, right?"

"They are. I met his family and friends; my parents like him, but..."

"But...but what?"

"There are things I just don't know about Steve, and I swear if he doesn't open up like Mark did, I don't know if that's a red-flag."

"It wasn't always nirvana for you and Mark," her friend reminded. They never argued about spending or sex. At times: in-law's and Mitchell money.

"We worked at it but the communication was there. That's so important."

"Tell me about it. My ex blamed me for everything that went wrong in his life." Alicia stopped, realizing she had to make another call. "If you want Steve to talk, ask the questions."

"I just might have to. He's had a busy few days. Have a good weekend if I don't talk to you again."

"You too, Maren."

They hung up and within minutes her phone rang once more. Tempted to answer, "Hi Alicia," she reconsidered, receiver in hand. "Maren Mitchell."

"How you feeling?" Steve finally had a few minutes.

"Better. And you?"

"Just got out of surgery. Didn't leave until 8:30 last night. I have rounds, patients, a meeting at four. Then, done."

"Busy." Maren wasn't sure what else to say. "You put in long days." Her skepticism mounted, but she was determined to give him space to talk about the week, wanting to see if he would on his own. "Dylan says hello."

"High five him for me. Hey, what are you doing this evening? I need to get the hell out of here."

"I don't know. I just started my day."

"Why don't we have pizza and salad at my place. Bring Dylan. I'll rent movies for him, for us if he falls asleep. Any preference?"

"*E.T. the Extra-Terrestrial* may be too scary for him. I never saw *Ocean's Eleven.*"

"*E.T.* is PG, but you're the boss. Thank God it's Friday."

"Steve, on a scale of 1–10 with 10 terribly pressured, rate the week."

Steve paused. Was this a test or mere conversation? "An eight, maybe higher. I just want it to be over."

"OK."

Steve knew Maren's anxiety most recently over snipers and biopsies had faded, lost somewhere in the fall foliage. She'd never sounded as terse with unmistakable tone.

"I know you heard bits and pieces. I'm not at liberty to talk about everything."

"Steve, I work at a hospital. I understand that you can't reveal your cases, but you're quiet. Too quiet, if you ask me."

Steve started to regret phoning her, lapsing into damage control.

"You know Maren, when people date in mid-life, there's bound to be baggage. I haven't exactly wanted to wear everything on my sleeve."

"Baggage gets weighed at the airport. Reminds us to consider whether we're dealing with a carry-on case, a Pullman on wheels, or a trunk load."

"OK, Maren. Let's try to have a fun evening. Plain cheese for Dylan and something more eventful for us?"

"I'll trust your judgment.

"Since I was in here late, back at 6:30, come by any time after six. Bring a bag if you want to crash here."

"Steve, I told you that…"

"Maren, I know. I can sleep on the couch. You and Dylan can have my bed. I have an air mattress. Or, you can drive home. Whatever you want."

They said goodbye. Women! About now, Steve wondered if spending a solo night on his boat might be a hell of a lot easier.

At 9:30, Steve knocked on Brad Morgan's door as Pam sat on the edge of her father's bed. "Sorry to interrupt," Steve said. "How are you feeling?"

It was a question to Steve's patient, but the startled reaction in his daughter, made Brad wonder who needed to take care of whom.

"Better today," Brad told Steve.

"How's he look to you?" Steve asked turning to Pam.

"Much improved." Her father's color was back, and the numbers she gleaned from the monitors looked good. From his self-report and chatting with nurses, Pam could leave town breathing easier. "Mind if I see Dad's chart?"

Steve looked at his patient. "That'd be up to your father."

"I'll never hear the end of it if I say no," Brad said as Steve held back the smirk forming. He knew exactly what Pam's father meant. He had raised one tough cookie. "Give it to her, Steve."

Steve handed it over. Pam met his eyes and her father's, annoyed at both of them. She took the silver chart and laid it on the tray table to flip through. Pam tuned them both out for the few minutes it took her to review things and Steve to examine her father.

"Thanks," she said, sliding the chart toward Steve on the tray table. "Your intern and resident have issues…I didn't get much out of either. Cardiology wasn't much better."

"Boundaries," Steve replied, biting back a different response. His intern and resident likely didn't bend, perhaps not knowing she was a physician. Pam would have no trouble demanding more than they would ordinarily give a family member. He could picture it, in fact.

"If there's anything you want to chat about before you leave, meet me at the desk, if that's OK with your father."

"Steve, it's fine," Brad told them both.

"Let's get a release because if I call in here, I don't have time for the grand inquisition," Pam insisted.

"We wouldn't want to put them through that would we?" Steve winked at her father. "We'll get you one," he said reconsidering. It was indeed time for her to find her way back home to her patients, Steve thought.

He scribbled notes onto Brad's chart. "We're moving you to the floor today. From my perspective, I'm pleased with your progress two days post-op."

"I'm nowhere near getting sprung yet, however," Brad said.

"You got that right. Maybe Monday/Tuesday. No promises yet." Steve replied. "I'll consult with cardiology, and Paul will look over things since you're his patient. We're erring on the conservative here." He would have played it this safe with any patient, but Pam's hovering couldn't be ignored. Steve didn't begrudge her a certain amount of that. A certain amount.

"Thanks, Steve." Brad shifted in his hospital bed.

"No problem. I'll check with you later."

"I'll be back in a few minutes to say goodbye," Pam told her father.

She followed Steve to the desk where he rounded the corner, holding the chart above the counter. "We need this any longer?" he asked Pam.

"Not exactly," she replied. Hesitation held between them. Steve set the chart down. "I know you're in the middle of rounds, but do you have a second?"

210

"Do we have a release here for Dr. Morgan to fill out regarding her father," Steve asked one of the nurses who handed him a form from the file drawer. Pam reviewed the release and signed where the nurse pointed. "Let's go in here," Steve suggested. He led Pam into a small room off the nurse's station, enclosed by glass and a door he pulled closed behind them.

Steve leaned into the counter, crossing his arms in front of him. Pam looked more rested than she had yesterday at lunch, and certainly the day prior when she'd made the quick trip down from Philly, yet Steve could see traces of worry linger in her eyes.

Blazer on, a blouse tucked into neatly pressed, belted slacks with dress shoes making her an inch taller, Pam looked ready to ride in her rental back to BWI and catch the next Amtrak.

"You wanted to talk?" Steve started. Pam straightened. It had always leveled the playing field with Steve who stood at 5'10"—four inches taller than she. Only two inches, today, on account of heels.

She pinched at the fabric of his white lab coat, at about his elbow. "How is it I still feel like the pariah? Is it some unfinished business or is it me?" Pam rolled the release in her hands, pointed it at Steve.

Steve took in a breath, looked to the tiles beneath his feet, and back up at Pam. "Neither one of us was quite prepared for this encounter, agreed?"

"You can say that again."

"OK. We got some things out. It takes time." Steve's blue eyes took on the appearance of stony marbles. "It's also been one hell of a week, Pam."

"We should have done this before," she said, thrusting her hand onto her hip, parting her jacket. "I wanted to call you years ago."

"Like, 10 years ago."

"Shit…there you go again." She glared at him. "Cut the snarky comments."

Steve started to speak, but she continued, wagging the release at him. It had been a longer week for her, she figured.

"If we never had to encounter one another again, I frankly wouldn't give a crap what you thought of me, Steve. I'm trying…don't you be so self-righteous. My family's all but officially moved here. Our parents are mutual friends. Your brother and my sister are living it up like we used to, for chrissake. Have you ever thought what you and I do if they end up where we didn't? Married?"

"It's crossed my mind."

"Exactly. Guaranteed if she'd ask me to be her honor attendant…if I had to walk up an aisle with you as best man, someone would be a GSW in that mix."

Steve let out a hoot. He rubbed his forehead. "Gunshots probably would fly, Pam. You're jumping way ahead of things, though."

"So help me out here, Steve. Ease up on the tone." She looked at the time ticking. Almost 10 o'clock.

"I presume you have patients today because I surely do here."

"See that's what I mean. Tone. You know, this morning I told Paul we were getting along better, and I gave him the low-down."

"Why?"

"What difference does it make between good friends? You never told anyone. Anyone."

"Let me decide what's good for me, Pam. Not you. You got what you wanted, free of our relationship, lifestyle, apartment … any plans so that you could run wild, go find yourself. It made you happy. Great! We covered that."

"Hardly wild. The comment about Paul, you mean? You'll never let me live it down. I had way too much to drink that night."

Steve thought. Laughed. It took a flash through his memory. "Now there's something. Rather than be quiet—since you hate that in me—I should just let Paul know you wanted to knock on his door too, back then." He smirked at Pam. "His one-night with Vanessa and whoever she was got *your* mind turning."

"I was inebriated." Both hands on her hips, finger in his face, and complexion flushing, Pam was losing control of this. No jacket she wore nor heels could be high enough to help her out. "If either one of you thinks I wanted to…with both of you…in your moist dreams!"

"It's pretty pathetic when you can't even lob that 'screw you, Steve' you're saving inside." Steve laughed out loud. Pam's favorite expression.

"You sound just like Paul, and it doesn't become you. Trust me," she said. "Shelly's the wild child. Outside of Carlos in college—my father never took to him—then you, then Jerry in '92, I had a love affair with a stack of textbooks. The studious one."

Steve eased his eyes to the wall clock again. They'd spent another five minutes arguing senselessly.

"I've got to get going, Steve," Pam said. "This discussion went no place."

Steve slanted his head toward her. "I thought you started seeing Jerry in February? February of 1992?"

"I..." Pam had to analyze the dates before she spoke. "No, February of 1993."

"You made it awfully clear that you didn't want me to go to your parent's house that Christmas, even though your mom personally invited me." Being around Hilary Morgan these few days brought this back. "Again, when did you start up with Jerry, and more precisely, when did you sleep with him?" The tone—a disgusted one this time—stuck out. He didn't care.

Steve thought he had tucked any lingering hurt away years ago, and whatever remained got shelved yesterday. Knowing he stood in a room glass enclosed on two sides should have helped him to keep his cool, but suddenly he wasn't sure which one of them felt more hemmed in.

"This is pointless. You're bullying me. I told you that I got pregnant the end of December that year. I wasn't sleeping with Jerry then." Pam didn't look at Steve, instead eyeing her exit. "I'm going to say goodbye to my father, get him to sign this," she said wagging the rolled-up release. "Then I'm leaving."

Pam turned on her heels, grabbed the doorknob, and thrust it open with such force that it rattled the blinds attached to the window. Two nurses snapped their heads. So as not to make a scene, Steve watched as Pamela Morgan Carlton stormed away. A slight throb formed in his temples.

"Is everything alright, Dr. Kramer?" one of the nurses asked.

"Everything's fine. I need a few minutes with this chart."

Rather than leave the desk to see his last patient, Steve reviewed that patient's chart, eyes darting up frequently. She wouldn't be long. He had a feeling she'd high-tail it out of West Riverside, and in less than four minutes flat, he saw her slap the button for the down elevator. As the door opened, he walked determinedly without breaking stride.

"Oh no, you don't," Pam said seeing him about to invade her space. She tried to force the door closed faster.

"We're *not* finished," Steve told her, jutting his arm to catch the door. His last stride landed one foot firmly planted into the elevator, pivoting his body around to shove "close" quickly. "Answer me:

When?" Steve's voice carried more authority now, and when the two doors met, the rest of their conversation got boxed into a 5x6 container.

It wouldn't have been audible unless you paid attention. At the desk, medication had to be dispensed, rounds needed to be finished, and the marketing department still had to meet its requirements. That meant an updated signature because of a last minute change.

After she hung up with Steve, Maren heard from Alicia, who apologized for an error she hadn't spotted, and for the inconvenient extra trip Maren had to make to the hospital. All in a morning's work, as Maren saw it.

She made the change, hopped in her car, and went straight to the ICU where she reviewed this new, now final draft with the doctor who needed to sign it. She found her promptly. Unfortunately, Maren discovered two more doctors, enclosed by glass that day, looking in at them when she waited for a signature.

"It started in September, after you and I spent a few days at your parent's place over Labor Day. Then I went to Philadelphia." Pam could see the white stand out in Steve's eyes. He remembered that year. He ended his residency. Pam ended their relationship.

She leaned against the steel bar as it stuck out from the silver wall, grasping it with both hands behind her. "And yes, it was physical, only a few times, in the fall. I was confused. I knew it wasn't right." Steve had already shifted both fingers into his belt loops, hands on his hips as she owned up to the truth. "We took added precautions, Steve, if that's what you're wondering, and I wasn't with Jerry in December." Pam paused. "I couldn't spend holidays with either of you. Not vacillating. It didn't start back up until February, and by that time..."

"Apartment shopping. One of your more thoughtful gifts to me that year." Two others: safe sex with a paramour and an abortion. "This only confirms what I thought all along, Pam. Why you couldn't have been honest, even yesterday, is beyond me!"

"I left. Who cares about a timeline?" Obviously, Steve did. "Bad judgment calls. I'm sorry."

Pam's vision darted to the ceiling lights. Their elevator was just about to hit the lobby. With half a haunted look, Pam panicked. She grabbed the stop button on the panel, causing Steve to grab hold of the railing.

"What the hell are you doing?"

214

"We shouldn't leave things like this, Steve. I can't."

"This isn't a confessional, Pam. It's an elevator in the middle of a busy workday. What's wrong with you?"

"We've come this far and likely have to interact again. Yesterday, we reminisced about good times. You had the last say 10 years ago. I get it now."

"Then hurry up." An alarm sounded that the elevator was stuck. If he had boxed her into this space, her presence drawing closer cornered him in return.

"This is to seal the good memories, Steve...a lot of them. Please...let's leave on that note." Pam toed herself off the floor to reach Steve's face where she angled hers, planting a soft kiss on Steve's lips. It lasted but four, maybe five seconds, and she drew away the hand she'd placed on the back of Steve's head.

She tapped the button springing the elevator back into action, and her eyes met his startled ones. "I have a husband to get back to, and you have a hot new girlfriend you better seal the deal with, Steve. Soon."

The door opened. Maintenance workers approached. Pam hesitated with her hand keeping the door from closing this time. "It's working fine guys," she said, halting them in their steps. Turning to face Steve, Pam said, "Thanks for your help with my father. I really appreciate it." She turned and walked out the doors of West Riverside Hospital Center, and in Steve's mind, he hoped out of his life. Again.

Steve had one more patient. He abruptly left the ICU to confront Pam, and rode the elevator back up. As the door opened, Maren stood waiting to board.

"It's working now," she said, wide-eyed at Steve. "The alarm went off."

"Maren, what are you doing here on a Friday?"

Resisting the urge to counter with "what are you doing, period?" she paused. Steve stepped off, motioning her around the corner to a waiting area.

"I had to come back and get this squared away with last-minute changes. I'll drop it off for the printer and head out." Maren kept her comments factual. Nothing added. Tone steady. Impersonal.

"How long have you been here?" Steve's breath had quickened.

"Long enough...over there." Maren pointed to the portion of the ICU station that curved to a small corner, where she and the doctor reviewed the changes and Maren obtained the required signature, out of view from the conference room Steve had commandeered with Pam. "Eventful morning?"

Steve leaned into the waiting room wall and scrubbed his right hand over his face. "Told you I wanted this week to end." He sighed heavily. "Assume you saw the two of us having it out."

"As did most of the ICU. Looked intense, but they probably see her as a patient's daughter. Rather unhappy with you, but..."

"Well, obviously we weren't discussing his case," Steve interrupted.

"No, not obvious. You seem flustered." Maren looked perplexed. "Tonight's not a good night. I'll watch movies with Dylan at home."

"No, really." Afraid the evening was about to tank, he pulled her toward him. "I'd like to pretend the last few days never happened. I want to be with you." Disappointment refused to settle on him. "Make that need to be with you."

"Steve, it's always about your needs." Impatience mounting, she wiggled away, stepped past him, until Steve gently tugged her back.

"If I don't see you tonight, then tomorrow's with all the kids. Please."

"Why?" Maren lowered her voice, and with no hesitation said, "Something other than what you need." The eyes he loved looked like brown boulders.

Steve drew in a defeated breath. "Because I owe you some explanations. You have to be wondering."

"Wondering how much I'll have to pull out of you. This is the first day I've felt well, and I'm not in the mood."

"Maren," he whispered. She didn't know any puppies with blue eyes before today. "I'm behind already with stuff to pick up. The timing of all this su..."

She stopped him mid-sentence. "Don't say it. Give me a list and I'll pick up what you need. We'll get the movies, too. Anything else?"

He watched her reaction fade from a rather concerned stare. He took a pen from the pocket of his white coat. At least he had one, Maren thought.

"Only that I adore you. I'll pay you later. Paper here?" he asked of the tablet with her clipboard. She pulled out a piece, upon which Steve wrote: Milk, French and focaccia bread, red peppers and a pound of fresh mozzarella. "Can you pick up pizza and salad?" He fingered Maren's ponytail. "Please. This place is getting to me."

"I can tell."

He wielded the puppy eyes even more. "Just got confirmation of facts I'd pieced together. Insert awkward—my standard expression—I know. That's how I feel dredging it all back up when I wanted the weekend to be fun, childlike."

"Three kids and LEGO creations will reclaim your inner child in no time, Steve." Maren looked at her watch. "I really have to go. You do, too."

"Geez…Mom is dropping off stuff later. I do have to run." Behind a large plant, he kissed her on the cheek. "I'm so lucky to have you."

"I'll see you tonight, Steve." Maren pressed for the elevator while he quickly paced away. She got out of marketing, went back home, and spoke briefly to her mother about plans to go shopping with Dylan Sunday afternoon.

At about 3:30, Suzanna buzzed Steve serving as the gatekeeper between him and his mother.

"Very nice," Dolores said, with a satisfied smile. It had been her first time seeing Steve's office since his promotion. He closed the door behind her.

"Good to see you, Mom. Let me get that stuff." He pecked her cheek before setting down two large shopping bags by the door. Steve plopped himself on the sofa, defeated.

"I know…it's been a week." Dolores took the chair he'd positioned for her. Steve had become a couch grazer when he was upset as a little boy. "I just had lunch with Hilary Morgan downstairs and visited with Brad briefly."

"He's moved out of ICU. At least he's supposed to be."

"He is. I heard his surgery got harrowing for him and you." Dolores looked concerned. "Did you have any lunch?"

"No, mom." Steve seemed amused. "I'll eat a good dinner. Salad." He left out about the pizza. Steve stretched out, crossed his ankles. "I have a meeting in 20 minutes, and then I'm outta here." Having stared up at the ceiling, he turned his body toward his mother.

"The kids are excited. Liz and Tim made reservations along the Annapolis harbor…dinner and a room. Sweet of you to do this for their anniversary."

"I try," he said. "She's skeptical I can pull it off with her two, plus Dylan."

"How's Maren? Your dad and I are so happy to get to know her." Dolores studied her son.

"A breath of fresh air in my life," he replied.

"Steve…" Dolores's tone shifted down an octave, reminding him of when he left the family car with little gas or forgot to call home in college or at Columbia. "Hilary told me that Pam was in town, that they had some heart-to-heart talks." Dolores captured her son's full attention. "I owe you an apology."

"For what?"

"All those times I chided, half-teasing, about you not settling down, providing us grandchildren." Dolores looked at Steve, and he could see her vision begin to cloud with moisture. "I had no idea. Pam disclosed she was pregnant with your baby and terminated it without telling you, after she moved out."

"This week, just gets longer by the hour. It's nice of Pam to tell the world. I'm surprised she hasn't sent out a mass email."

"Why didn't you tell us? You came back from Pittsburgh that summer so annoyed at life, and we knew you were hurt that she'd moved on, but you have to know you can talk to your dad and me about anything. You're nearly 40 years old. Do I have to say that?" Dolores dug a tissue from her handbag sitting on the floor. She dabbed her eyes.

"For this very reason, for one thing. I had a hard enough time processing it myself. I was pissed, disillusioned, all while starting a fellowship. I needed to focus, and how could I inject any of this shit—sorry, but it's a word—into your lives. I knew you'd be upset. I was furious."

"Well, it's certainly lowered my opinion of Pamela Morgan. From the looks of it, Hilary's also. I don't think she's going to tell Brad right away with whatever's going on with his heart."

"Someone in that family has an ounce of restraint." Steve seemed disgusted and pressured as he eased his wristwatch to check the time. "I've got this meeting, Mom." He pulled his feet from sofa to floor. "Do me a favor. Please don't broadcast this outside of telling Dad."

"I have a feeling Shelly knows, and if so, then she's had to mention it to Eric…which begs the question about Liz. Would you like me to mention it so you don't have to?"

"As long as Liz doesn't go all social worker on me. It's over. In hindsight, Pam looked months into the future. I didn't." He paused, noticing air constrict his chest. "Today, she confirmed—I had to press the issue—that she started up with Jerry before ending our relationship."

"If she cheated on you, was the baby yours?"

"She swears it was; the timing matches precisely. I've asked more than once."

"That's what she told Hilary. I'm sorry, Steve. Don't let this affect you any longer." She rose from her chair; he followed her lead. "You've got most women in this hospital eyeing you. I understand now why you threw yourself into your work, but…"

"Oh here it comes again," Steve said, chuckling at his mother.

"Well, a mother gets curious, especially with Maren in the picture."

Steve brightened for the first time since Dolores Kramer walked through his office door. "I think she's the one, you know."

Dolores beamed. "Then don't take forever."

"Well, I don't want to push her either. She lost her husband, and there's a child involved. It gets complicated."

"Life's complicated. You've always charted a course, met challenges. You'll see to this." She leaned to retrieve her handbag. "I went into the attic. Matchbox cars, science stuff, assorted toys."

Steve peeked into the two bags. "You saved the Etch A Sketch and Bayliner boat?" He grinned. "You're the best."

Dolores had packed away select toys for each of her three children. Liz had already taken hers from the family home. When Dolores learned that Steve cast himself as uncle on call, she couldn't resist giving him his favorites, especially when he had no toys in his apartment, not even for Dylan.

Dolores hugged her son. "Have fun. Get some sleep."

"Sunday, I'll make you a cappuccino," Steve said. She gave him a thumbs-up as she left. Steve grabbed his notes to attend his four o'clock meeting and call it a week.

Chapter 15

"He's settled, under your covers, with his movie," Maren said, taking a seat next to Steve on his sofa as he handed her a glass of white wine. "Thanks."

"I'd rather be under the covers, too." Steve took another sip, set down his glass. He nixed the idea of coffee. If they drank a whole bottle of chardonnay between them it might impede sleep also. Pick your poison, he thought. "What a week!" Turning toward her, he tossed Maren's hair behind her shoulder.

"This morning you rated the week an eight on 1–10 for stress."

"Never imagined Pam would be in town. Not now, though her parents are retiring here from Delaware." More frustrated, he continued, "It's the first time I wished you didn't work at the hospital."

Maren took another sip, fiddling with the glass. "I'm supposed to respond…how? You encouraged me to apply."

"Having you in the same building means I get to see you," he explained, stranding her hair. Calmed him, too. "But having you witness her burst in to bitch at Paul, light into me…it's awkward."

"Awkward, as I told you, is having you ignore four or five opportunities to tell me about the Eric/Shelly relationship and how it affected you." She paused to sip again. "You didn't want me to know. That's what it looks like."

"I'm not hiding anything. Today, my mom found out details that got to her. I haven't talked about any of this. Mom wasn't thrilled with me either, even less with Pam."

"She's upset because clearly Pam hurt you. To cause such a reaction, you must still have feelings for her." Maren settled back, disappointed. Sadness crept into her face.

"Wait…that's not fair." Steve pulled her against him, hands framing her face. "Pam and I don't bring out the best in one another. I didn't want you to have a skewed impression…of me."

"Skewed impression?" Maren's thoughts skidded to a halt. "Steve…talk to me." Seconds turned into a minute. Longer.

Maren pulled away, slipped the shoes she'd toed off onto her feet and got up. "Tonight just didn't seem right. When you're ready to level with me, let me know." She gathered her purse, the jacket slung over a barstool, and headed to the bedroom toward Dylan.

Steve came after her, slipping his arm around her waist. "Stop."

Maren did a 180 to face him, lowering her voice and walking him away from Dylan. "Steve, this feels hugely uncomfortable between us. Talk to me. At this point, from the beginning."

"OK, then sit back down." He tossed her handbag and jacket on a chair and handed back her wine. He took a sip from his glass. "I met Pam at a mixer/social thing before med school. She completed a master's. We became…involved. Paul and I had the apartment; Pam moved in. I told you all that."

"Real estate. Sex. When did you fall in love with her?"

"I don't know. Wasn't thinking love. Sounds shallow, but you're studying your ass off with years ahead of you."

"I'm not judging you, Steve. How did she feel?"

"About sex, love or both?"

"Both," Maren said, rolling her eyes.

"We were exclusive. HIV/AIDS cast everything in a new perspective, with protocols and precautions. Neither of us slept around," Steve said. "After that first year, when our families treated us like a couple, it was definitely more than lust. We'll call it love. Certainly by graduation when we headed to Pittsburgh."

Maren remembered the Kramer album, the bathing suit-clad blonde lying all over Steve, his hand on her ass. "Why didn't you get married?"

"I don't know that either." Steve could tell that looked like a cop-out. "I had all the benefits, I'll admit. I was self-focused working 100-hour weeks. I wasn't thinking ahead. When I saw us grow apart, I thought about ring shopping… but she was already checked out."

"She broke it off…why?"

"Wanted different things that last year. I don't know if she panicked, wanted to play the field?" That she fell out of love tugged too hard on Steve's ego. "Maybe I wasn't in her field of dreams."

He got up to bring the bottle closer to where they sat and poured more for each of them. Dylan laughed in the next room, and Maren noticed that Steve chose to look in on him, on that remark. When he returned, she persisted. "What about that field…of dreams?"

221

"High school dating wasn't serious. A steady girlfriend in college. My first. That's what you're asking, isn't it?" He arched his brow.

"OK, I'll own it. The list you gave on our first date is growing… hmm." Her second glass relaxed her mind and body. She leaned closer to Steve. "You didn't get this good without experience."

"Notice, I'm not demanding a run-down of your partners, before the VFD, that is."

"Steve!" He promptly grabbed a sofa cushion to shield his rib cage. "I went out in groups in high school, had a boyfriend my senior year, into college, then Mark, my first. In a true technical sense."

Steve nearly spit out his last sip. "A technical virgin. I love it." His smile shot wicked. "To think how you make towels drop and fix hardware all in a lunch hour, now." He shifted the cushion behind him, opening his posture to Maren.

"Stop making this about me. No more wine," she said, swirling some. "I have to drive home."

"We both need it." Steve didn't dare confess that plying her with another glass might indeed keep her next to him all night long. "The point is, Pam hadn't dated much. The Morgans were conservative back then. She was too."

"So you know something about deflowering, technically speaking?"

Steve smirked. "Are you drinking on an empty stomach?"

"I only had one piece of pizza, now two glasses of wine."

"Doesn't take much." He cleared his throat intentionally. "I was saying, she chose a specialty largely about sex. Raised conservatively, I think she regretted not running a little wilder…honestly. Couple it with a fierce drive to get ahead, panic that she might not get to call the shots if we got married."

"Her loss," Maren said, burrowed deeper into the cushions, hearing Alicia's advice in her head to ask more. "Why did you shout at her in the elevator?"

"I wasn't shouting," he insisted.

"Steve…you were shouting." It was as if Steve had lost any true awareness.

"Conflicting stories about Jerry. They got married after we broke up. I called her out on the timeline. Caught her in a cheating lie…my hunch years ago."

"Ouch." Maren stroked Steve's face. "That had to hurt."

It had. Maren could see it etched on him. He pushed his shoulders into the sofa, his legs resting on the ottoman. Maren stretched her legs on top of his. "But there's more…right?"

"When Pam came to get the last of her things we had the place to ourselves. Ended up more in bed than out of it, and she must have gotten pregnant."

"Must have as in question mark behind that?"

"Did. Was. Only she never informed me."

Maren's mouth gaped open. "Was there a love child? I remember that little girl when we were shopping. A blonde."

"No…we would've had a baby that September, only she never consulted me when she decided to have an abortion in February. After a nine-year relationship." He breathed in and let out a mouthful of air. "Hell, some marriages don't even last that long. That's the part Mom learned today."

"That's awful. Cruel." Venom forcibly flooded her veins so she could only imagine the rage Steve must have felt, the disappointment, broken trust. "You're so good with kids. When did you find out?"

"Right before I moved back to Maryland." Steve looked sad, raising the last of his wine to his lips, downing it. "Want more?" He poured for himself, offering Maren the rest.

"Sure…what the hell." She extended her glass. "What a story." Treading lightly, she added. "I saw Pam make points, grabbing your sleeves. What didn't she like about your relationship…or in you?"

"Maybe I wasn't good enough in bed," he said. Sarcasm dripped.

"Surely you jest."

"Since I accompanied her to a Masters & Johnson course, I doubt that, too." Something lingering in his bruised self-image triggered his clarifying that.

"Name three things that annoyed Pam most about you."

"You will offer the same list from Mark's perspective?"

She smiled. "Fair's fair. But I asked first."

"Pam said I compartmentalized things. I was uptight since she claimed I mellowed some. And once she dragged us to counseling about communication."

"Really?" This intrigued Maren. "How did that turn out?"

"Argued less; had better sex." Steve shrugged. "You asked."

He could tell he wasn't winning points. "Communication is imperative, Steve. I can maybe see why...I feel as if I drag things out of you."

"What?" His eyes seemed to fall back and then pounce.

"Yeah...I sense you hold back."

"When we met? Hell, I wanted you to go out with me, and you were very tentative." Steve frowned. "Three things Mark didn't like."

"Off the top of my head, getting anxious and procrastinating—sometimes." She thought. "I wasn't tough enough on Dylan, but he was little." Steve could tell she wanted dispensation.

Just as she ended, Dylan came padding out in his black pants and Steelers sweatshirt Steve had gotten him at the Ravens-Steelers match-up. Steve hoisted him onto the sofa. "How's your movie?"

"I paused it. Can I have dessert?" Fortunately, Steve had quite the snack supply, which he showed Dylan, informing him to pick one thing—cookies Dylan made it—with milk Steve poured. "Can I eat it in there?"

"As long as you don't make a mess." Steve took the milk in for him and sat back down.

"What?" he said to Maren in a zone of her own. It was 10 o'clock.

"One thing Mark and I had was good communication, which meant fair fighting, more problem solving." Maren absorbed him. "I miss that. I hate guessing, Steve. It brings on all those—what do therapists call them—automatic thoughts. Then, my anxiety ratchets."

"I second Mark's frustration with your anxiety." He cornered a look. "Red flags would go up if you weren't working on it."

"No, I can't see you with an anxious mess," she said, disparaging herself. "However, I notice that you complain about the way Pam communicated, but you do the very same thing." Her observation wafted over Steve. "You're upset with her for not divulging details years ago. Only when you had chances—plural with me—to leverage details, you avoided them. That doesn't build trust, Steve. It builds worry. The same worry that concerns you."

"I'm talking now," he said.

"Yes...because you had to," she continued. "Remember our argument on the boat. You hated women making choices instead of discussing things. It fits. She cut you out of a crucial decision. Now, it's a trigger for you." Maren looked at Steve squarely.

"Communication can't always be on your terms, when *you* want to talk. The Golden Rule, Steve."

"I suppose I would have told you someday about the abortion, the break-up."

Maren looked annoyed, then shifted. "The way you take to Dylan, and what you're doing this weekend…I wouldn't be with you if you didn't love kids." She brushed lint left by a blanket from her pants. "Something so important to you…and you didn't feel you could share it with me."

With no response, Maren started to stand up. "It's getting late…wow." Two and a half glasses of wine instantly shot to her head.

"Let's finish this another time." Steve said, reaching for her. He held her snugly. "You're not going home. We needed to talk— communication after a long week. When have we ever polished off a bottle?"

She handed Steve her car keys. "I forgot to bring my bag up. Would you mind getting it for me?" Maren couldn't fathom talking more though this conversation definitely had to continue.

"Not at all. Let me get Dylan and he can sleep out here on the sofa." Maren followed him into his room, where they found Dylan fast asleep. "There's another pillow and blankets in the closet. Grab those and I'll carry him out."

"But he didn't brush his teeth."

"Maren," Steve said, picking up Dylan. "He'll live."

While Steve went to her car, Maren turned down the bed and got undressed. Dylan's teeth still bothered her as she brushed hers with the travel-sized toothbrush from her purse. She found a shirt of Steve's to sleep in.

He set down the bag in the bedroom, closed the door, and watched her brush her hair. Maren stood with bare feet, in his shirt, buttoned only by the bottom buttons. Steve stepped toward the sink where the view got even better.

"You know how many people have asked me if I'm serious about you?"

She smiled as he picked up toothpaste and his toothbrush. "Hold that thought. I need to give something to Dylan. A Muppet." She dug it from her bag, padded out and back, hand holding the fabric from displaying cleavage. Steve was under the covers as she crawled in next to him.

"Who asked?" As she nestled in, the shirt splayed.

"Your doctor in Baltimore pried me a little." He smiled. "Paul, and while he didn't actually ask, your father. Today Pam. I take that back. She didn't ask, she just told me what to do." He chuckled. "Said I better seal the deal with my hot new girlfriend." Steve ran his finger in the space his, now her, shirt revealed.

"Interesting. How did this come up?"

Steve thought fast, suddenly wishing he hadn't brought up what he had intended to be a tender topic, a prelude getting into bed and into her. "If I tell you this next part, I'm in trouble. If I leave it out, I'm in trouble, too."

"Out with it," she said, propping her head next to him, hand on his bare chest.

"She kissed me in the elevator."

"Was that her stopping it?" Maren's eyes widened such that Steve saw more white around the edges than the beautiful brown he always loved. "She stopped the elevator to kiss you?"

Steve smirked. "She stopped the elevator because she said she didn't want to leave on a bad note since at lunch we aired out a lot of crap. She said something like 'this is to seal the good times,' kissed me—quickly—and then told me she had Jerry and I needed to seal the deal with you." The reminder that she had Jerry had perturbed him. "What d'ya think about that?"

Maren pondered. "Show me how she kissed you."

Steve laughed out loud. "Seriously, I'm supposed to re-enact my ex-girlfriend kissing me."

"Damn right. Was it a social peck?"

"No, but…"

"Kiss me. I wanna know." She elbowed up, suddenly energized. Steve sighed, leaned, with a hand behind her head, and for a few seconds kissed her on the mouth.

"Satisfied?"

"For now." Did he make it tame on purpose? She fluffed her pillow with a punch. "Wine takes the edge off." Snuggling to Steve she said, "It's stirring other things." Maren undid the bottom buttons on the shirt.

"Definitely my good fortune." Steve grazed his mouth over hers, grazed lower still then launched into a deep, delicious kiss, darting his tongue to her throat. His wine plan had worked.

Sure enough in the middle of the night, the wine woke them in a rebound effect. Neither minded, however, as they reveled in another round tearing up Steve's sheets.

"She didn't leave you because you weren't good in bed," Maren said, panting to catch her breath as he did the same.

"I guess the sex seminar paid off." Pillow talk. "Learned a few things about women's health, which she would say is all because of her, of course."

"Didn't quite drag you to that like the counseling, I'll bet?"

His embarrassed eyes answered. "Amorous tonight. What's gotten into you?"

Maren let out a devilish groan. "Mmm, you have. Staking out my claim." She definitely recognized a little more sex on her brain recently. "Maybe it's changing my meds. Maybe I just feel more subdued."

"Whatever it is," Steve said. "I love it." He kissed her full on the mouth. They nestled together for another three hours of sleep.

Maren got out of bed after Steve, showered, and changed the linens while he made Dylan breakfast and found something suitable on TV. The boys were bringing sleeping bags for the night.

"I put sheets on the air mattress you set up and tidied your room." Maren looked like a woman on a mission, snatching items belonging to Dylan as duffle bag deposits. "Finish, Dylan. We have to get out of here if you're coming back this afternoon. Steve has rounds."

"I only have a few patients. Here, have some," Steve said, offering her a small plate of French toast. Maren briefly took a seat at the counter. He handed her coffee. "Dylan's staying over tonight, right?"

"He is. I'm not." She saw Steve glower. "Frown, but you've had enough." She wasn't sleeping in his bed again with three kids around. "We'll have dinner. Then it's me, and my novel. You, and three kids." She smiled. Dylan got his duffle, and they left Steve's apartment.

"You're certain you're up to this?" Liz asked her brother as she refrigerated medicine for Hannah's ear infection. "She has two more doses left." Tim and Maren sat at the counter chatting with Steve as Liz hovered. She had just shown Tyler and Hannah for the second time where all their stuff was in Steve's bedroom. "Hannah's on the air mattress? You're not leaving her with two rambunctious boys."

227

"Good assumption. The wilder ones out here." Since Tyler and Dylan couldn't keep their hands still since entering his apartment, Steve adopted cautious optimism about being uncle on call. "Going to show me how to measure her antibiotic?"

"Oh shut up, Steve." Liz shot him the Kramer-woman look—one Liz had perfected only after years of studying Dolores level it upon all three children, and sometimes Bill. Usually, enough to effect silence.

"What's for dinner? We had pizza last night," Maren said. After helping him with groceries she had no clue what menu Steve created.

"I'm surprised Liz didn't raid the fridge." Steve tugged on the door pulling out three containers. He opened the lid of the longest displaying bamboo skewers assembled with focaccia bread, cherry tomatoes, Canadian bacon, and fresh mozzarella. In the second, wild rice ready to heat. The third revealed pan seared chicken, zucchini and red bell peppers, all pre-cut. "We warm these, the kids add them to the skewers, and there's dinner."

Liz's chin dropped as she turned to the others at the counter.

"The pink cheeks match the accents in your sweater, Liz," Steve said. "Now Tim, please take her out of here. Go enjoy your wife." He shot his brother-in-law a rather roguish if-you-waste-one-more-minute-here, you're-a-fool grin.

Tim snickered. The loving bond between Steve and Liz went deep, but you wouldn't know it from surface interaction.

"I'm here for a while," Maren told Liz, following her to the door.

Liz kissed her kids goodbye. "He's got all three of them alone overnight?"

"Go," Steve shouted, still planted in the kitchen.

"He'll be fine," Maren said. "See you tomorrow. Mom and I pick up Dylan."

"Great, I'll get to meet her. Mom will, too. We're going to the bayside house while Tim shows properties tomorrow afternoon."

"Goodbye Liz," her brother emphasized from a distance.

"Have fun, Uncle Steve."

The kids already found cartoons on TV. Steve pulled plates out of the cabinet as Maren came alongside him. "You could be more understanding."

"Annoyance in action," he said. "You got to see it first hand."

"She's a concerned mother. Are you going to be this impatient when the rose petals fall off our relationship?"

"I highly doubt it." Steve tugged on her now that she joined him in the kitchen. He lowered his voice though the kids giggled watching TV. "This little domestic scene makes my mind conjure all kinds of images."

"Always…"

"Like little Kramer kids we make together, feed, and have fun with." He paused, glowing. "If I decide to seal the deal, as I've been directed to do."

"More talking needs to happen." Her finger jabbed his stomach. "Then…and only then…do we take next steps."

Her anxiety could really kill joy, Steve miffed inwardly. He handed Maren silverware as she set the table that separated the small living space from the kitchen. He motioned her closer when she finished.

"OK, you win. Here's a surprise." He whispered the next part. "I have a conference next month in Orlando. Disney's BoardWalk Inn. Conference center has access to the parks. They booked me a suite because I was on the planning committee." His revelation definitely intrigued Maren, who visually showed appreciation for his discretion whispering the Disney part. "You and your little sidekick over there should join me. That is, if I'm communicating this properly, since that skill seems to be highly desired among most females I bed."

"Sure you don't want to redo that last part?"

"You know what I mean," he insisted. "I've felt this strongly about two women, dammit, and you're one of the two." Steve saw the credits roll on the kids' program. "Think about it. It's a two-day conference the weekend before Christmas. That's the only hitch, but some wanted to extend their trips over the holidays. I have a reservation Friday the 20th with check-out on Monday, December 23rd."

"I have to ask Alicia. I get ten days within the first year." Maren pondered. "My parents asked me last month if I wanted to visit my aunt and cousin in Orlando for Christmas. It's the second year without Mark so…last year we went away locally. I couldn't bear to be home, and I was too afraid to fly last winter." Most of America had been.

"See. Think of the fun Dylan would have. And us," he said. The suite he once thought would go to waste for just him suddenly brought salacious thoughts. "I was going to take the rest of that week off and just hang around here, but…"

"Let me think about it later and check with my mom." She put her arms around Steve's waist, smiling. "We haven't done a trip together. Another first."

"Firsts are always special." Steve nuzzled her neck at a tender spot. Maren ribbed him playfully.

"Show's over. Evening's on…Uncle Steve."

Who would think that Dylan trying and actually swallowing marinated zucchini, sharing another skewer with Tyler, would end up as dinner's highlight. Hannah ate well, and the kids took their plates to the dishwasher. All three seemed fascinated with the toys Dolores had rescued.

After brownies and ice cream, and Hannah's nighttime medicine, Steve oversaw teeth brushing, pointing this out to Maren, while she got each one into their jammies. All three piled onto Steve's king-sized bed in anticipation of *The Little Red Lighthouse and the Great Gray Bridge,* the story he promised.

"I haven't seen this book," she said, picking it up from his dresser.

"It's a classic," Steve told her. "About a small red lighthouse on the Hudson River that feels his lights are no longer needed when the bridge is built. It's got boats, good graphics—you'd like that part—and the message that everyone has a special, important job. Even the lighthouse."

"Makes me want to stay," Maren said, setting it on the comforter by the kids.

"I wanna read it," Tyler said, picking it up.

"No…Uncle Steve's gonna." Hannah grabbed it from her brother.

Steve started to speak, but Hannah held her position. A lot like Liz, Steve thought.

"Graceful exit here. Dylan, be good for Steve, OK? Goodnight Tyler and Hannah." She kissed her son on the forehead, planted a smooch on the other two then moved quickly before further book squabbles broke out. Hand on the knob, she said, "My phone is by my bed if you need me."

"Hmm," he raised his wrist to tell the time. "Give it an hour or two."

"You may want me, but you don't need me. You got enough for the weekend. I remain firm about that."

"In a few hours, it could be," he hushed.

"You, Paul and double meanings! Not coming back here unless there's an emergency."

"Well, there won't be, and…it's only Saturday night. A weekend includes a Friday, Saturday, and Sunday." He nuzzled her behind her ear whispering "into the night."

Maren kissed him quickly. On the forehead, like the other three children she'd just wished goodnight.

"It's a small apartment," Maren said, walking out of the elevator onto Steve's floor with her mother. "Don't be surprised." It was 10:30 Sunday morning.

"Forget the apartment, I wanna see his boat." As Maren rang the doorbell, Audrey looked at her. "You sure spend a lot of time on it."

"The boat is quite nice," Maren said, somewhat sheepishly. Her mother angled a wry smile. "Mom, stop." Maren looked away, memories starting to sear. Tyler opened the door before Audrey could say another word.

"Hi," he greeted. The ladies could hear Dylan's boisterous laugh across the room as he watched television with Hannah.

"You're on door patrol I see." Maren stepped in and hung her mother's jacket in the coat closet with her own. "This is Tyler."

"Audrey, how are you?" Steve said as he rounded out of the kitchen, greeting both Maren and her mother.

"I'm fine, Steve. Nice apartment," she replied, smiling at Tyler. "How was the sleepover?" Audrey heard bits on the drive over. Maren and Steve chatted by phone that morning, the kids peacefully coexisting around waffles.

"Hannah got rice cereal up her nose, Grammy," Dylan reported before Steve could answer Audrey. "Tyler dared her when Steve was in the shower."

"He did," Steve said, shaking his head. "The plot thickens. Audrey, this is Hannah."

"Hi," Hannah said, turning to her brother. "He picks on me, but I'm Uncle Steve's…ouch, favorite." Tyler elbowed her for the remote; she elbowed him right back.

"Cause you're a girl." Tyler looked annoyed. "He kissed her to get it out. Gross!"

"Come have a seat. I'll make you some cappuccino." In the kitchen, he talked while brewing and steaming. "She's adorable…what can I say." Steve looked at the ladies sheepishly.

"We know…the nose dare is new info?" Maren cast a how-could-you-not-know grin. "Was it the mushy kind?"

"Nah, crispy. I held her one nostril and blew through her mouth." Steve held up his finger to momentarily silence Maren while he frothed the milk.

"How was Dylan? Behaved I hope." Maren wouldn't wager money if Dylan was ever egged on or showing off.

"To my knowledge, he was fine. They were only out of sight when asleep and during a quick shower. Enough time to inhale cereal."

"Well, if that's the worst of it," Audrey said. "Thanks, Steve…this looks great. Something smells good."

"You're welcome. Bruschetta in the oven." He handed Maren her cup. "Hannah tried to take a chunk out of Tyler's wrist over the Etch A Sketch—aggressive little sweetheart. Not far behind my other one." Steve leveled his vision on Maren.

"Hey…" She smiled, foam on her mouth, which Steve leaned over the counter to kiss off. He stepped back, pulled on a mitt, and took the bruschetta out, moving it to a plate when the doorbell rang again.

"Must be Liz and Mom. Maren, will you get that please?"

"Sure." She jumped off her stool to open Steve's door. Dolores and Liz stepped in. Dolores kissed Maren on the cheek. Maren managed their coats as Hannah ran over.

"Mommy, Uncle Steve made chetta to eat." Liz crouched down to hug Hannah, straightened and sniffed.

"Bruschetta…that's your Uncle Steve." She tousled Hannah's hair and walked to the counter, extending her hand. "Hi, I'm Liz…Steve's sister."

"I'm Dolores…so nice to meet you. We think the world of Maren and Dylan." Audrey introduced herself also.

"Here, you sit down Dolores," Maren said, moving her coffee across the counter. "I can help Steve in here." He'd already put the bruschetta out and Maren reached into the cabinet for small plates and napkins. Liz stood and nodded to his invitation for coffee.

"This is good, Steve," she said, munching on the toasted bread. "Homemade?"

"Of course. How was your get-away? Relaxing?"

"Very nice. You win big brother points. Can the kids eat this over there?" Liz knew from her apartment-sharing days how anal her brother could become over crumbs and strewn clothes.

"That's fine," he said. "I've got clean up to do, but overall it's not bad." Liz deposited slices with napkins on the coffee table, coming back to the counter. Dolores and Audrey exchanged small talk. Steve handed them cappuccino.

"So how was it?" Liz studied Steve. She'd stare him down if he tried to minimize what she knew her two kids were capable of. "Did you finish Hannah's last dose?"

"Her medicine?" He slapped a hand to his forehead. "Damn."

Liz rounded, opened the refrigerator door, and bent to see no sign of the bottle. She pulled out the trash and saw it discarded. "OK, I figured you'd be on top of that. There's play dough through your leather sofa cushions, you realize."

"Oh no...you didn't think I could handle it. Apologize anytime, little sister," he said back. "Play dough. Who brought that?"

"I did," Tyler shouted over the dalmatians movie. "Here." He tossed his uncle the container of bright orange. Steve opened it. Empty. Stored now in the creases of his sofa.

"Anyway, they did fine. Ask Maren. They ate dinner, played...we read stories." He put the leftovers out in front of his mother and Audrey. "Finish these if you're hungry." He was pleased when they looked duly impressed. Steve set out some silverware by the small plates.

"Mommy, Tyler told me to put rice cereal up my nose," Hannah whined. Liz set down her mug and jiggled Hannah onto her hip. "Uncle Steve blew it out."

Liz leveled a look that asked what-did-you-do-to-my-daughter?

Steve rolled his eyes. "Easier than foreceps or suction. Not like I had either."

"Is it all out?" she asked, alarmed.

"Liz, really. He's a surgeon," Dolores said, coming to his defense.

"When the dog belonging to Tommy next door got its paw mangled with pinecones, they pried it out with screwdrivers...in his kitchen." Liz's hand turned palms up conveying the same kind of room as right now.

233

"Never mind that your brother was 11," Dolores added. Maren glanced at Audrey as they held back chuckling.

"I looked with a flashlight, Liz. Next time I host kids I'm bringing home supply drawers from the ER. Better yet, I'll just take them in, and you can fork over the $50 co-pay."

"It's $75 now, under our plan."

"Then, shut up already." Steve laughed though. "I've had one hell of a week."

"Steven!" The Kramer-woman look came at him, shot by Dolores.

"Mom filled me in," Liz said. "Glad Brad's coming along. Shelly said Pam's coming back for Thanksgiving."

"I'm skipping town," Steve said abruptly. Looking at Audrey, realizing his sarcasm didn't put forth perhaps the best impression, he continued. "My former girlfriend was in town. Her father had emergency surgery, and my brother's dating her sister. It's complicated."

Liz's eyes moved from him to Maren. "It's cool," he assured her. "Maren knows. Met her as she burst into the cafeteria berating Paul."

"Well, Steve." Liz whispered, checking the kids were across the room. "With what Mom told me, she's more of a blonde bitch than I thought she was 15 years ago. You could just have Avril Lavigne's new song as soundtrack for the last decade…and a half."

"The two of you," Dolores chided. "Audrey, I apologize. It's like high school again. I'm none too happy with Pamela but you needn't call her that, Liz."

"Yeah Liz, there are preschool age children here. Yours." Steve said it knowing full well that when he ran Pam out of his life a few far-worse F-bombs had slipped from his lips.

Audrey laughed. "It's quite all right."

Liz softened to Steve. "Seriously, if you ever want to talk. It's not good to keep it all inside."

Steve scrubbed hands over his face. "It's Sunday: A new week. Please don't go all therapist on me, Liz." Cell phone ringing, Steve looked at the caller ID. "Hey, not leaving until 12:30." He covered the receiver mouthing it was Paul. "Thanks for doing rounds. Everything fine…with our mutual patient?" Steve listened a few minutes. "Great. No, no problem. I'm just drowning in too much estrogen this week. You wanna drive, that's fine with me."

At that, Liz acted aghast. "Hand me the phone. I want to say hi to Paul."

"Oh, Paul, here's a prime specimen. Estrogen with attitude: Liz."

"Paul Romano, how are you?" she asked taking the phone. Steve paid no more attention.

"Are we keeping you from Paul? There's probably a football game involved," Dolores told Audrey. Turning back she said, "We wouldn't want you to drown in the wrong pool of hormones."

"I'm sorry, Mom." Steve laughed. "I think I've earned the afternoon off."

"With the week you had, Hilary was thankful for everything you did. Said you looked drained on Wednesday." Steve thought to himself "and Thursday, and Friday, and…"

"What? Oh, that," Liz said, handing back Steve's phone. "Shelly said everyone fled you and Pam. Like lightning." Liz leveled a bet-that-was-rich leer. "She said her dad's heart stopped. In the middle of your surgery?"

"I can't really go into detail, but yes. Ordinarily, I wouldn't even take his case. We were short-handed." He stopped. "Can we table this? More bruschetta, Liz." Annoying as an adjective didn't do his sister justice.

"Sorry…just how awful if you had to go out and tell them…if, he didn't make it, to Shelly and Hilary…and Pam."

"He does have a stressful job," Dolores commented.

"Imparting something like that never gets easier. Never." Steve rolled his wrist to check the time. Noon. The estrogen surge surely would end soon, with his sister, at least. "How's Paul, Liz? You always had the hots for him."

"Steve…" Liz looked at the other women. "He dishes it, but he doesn't like it coming at him. You're the one who told me 'no way, he's my best friend…and too randy,' which I'm not sure what that warned me about. We're both married, but I can say hello. He's picking you up at 12:30, he said."

"Good, I'll have an extra beer for you." A six-pack sounded better with the week he had, especially since he wasn't driving. "You might want to talk with Tyler about egging on his little sister," Steve said. "No comments, Mom."

"Like your telling yours to fly out the first-floor window when she was four or five." Dolores got off her stool. "No broken bones, but I think he was grounded for a week."

Audrey got off her stool as well. "Steve, thanks for the coffee and impromptu lunch. I enjoyed meeting you all, truly."

"It's never dull," Steve added, walking with them to the door. "Come on kids. Let's convince your mom you both made it without advanced life support." He kissed his mother as she left.

"Steve, thank you." Liz hugged him tight. "You know I'm kidding. You did a great job." Hannah had outstretched arms demanding to be held. Steve hoisted her up high into the air bringing her down for a smooch. "Goodbye sweetheart. Don't do everything a big brother tells you."

"And you 'member the Muppet names," Hannah said.

"You gonna quiz me by phone?"

"Yeah." Hannah lit up.

Shouldn't have planted that seed, Steve mused. When he put her down, he waved them away. Steve's arms landed comfortably on Maren. "I'll call you after the game. Remember what we talked about for December. I'll see you tonight." She met his eyes. Didn't say a word. Didn't have to. "The weekend's not over," he reminded.

"You get an A for being uncle on call, Steve. An A+ for persistence."

"Always." He kissed her. "Bye Audrey. Bye Dylan."

Chapter 16

"You need a Yuengling," Paul said as they took seats near the bar with the one big screen illuminating their team, on the road in Tennessee. "We haven't had a chance to really talk."

"Liz didn't tell you to play therapist, did she?" The Steelers and Titans hadn't kicked off. The waitress brought them beers—a Rolling Rock for Paul—along with crab dip. To hell with cholesterol.

"Stop on Liz." Paul could relate to Steve's sister, having met her when he was 24, Liz 20…and hot. "She's cool," he said instead today.

"Oh please, first time she saw my king-size bed she claimed it fit my doctor-sized ego," Steve told him. "The only reason I took her in, in Baltimore, was Dad's offer to pay off $15K in student loans if I housed her in the big city for a year." A who-wouldn't look shot across to Paul.

"Even with a two-bedroom she probably intruded into the, ah…bachelor pad."

Steve swigged his beer and daggered his darkened eyes. "When I dated the nurse, we were at her place most of the time."

"Speaking of apartment mates…we had breakfast Friday."

"So I heard." Steve downed another swig before kickoff. "Impressions?"

"Same old Pam. Life, practice in order. More direct, certainly about the bombshell." Paul observed his friend the way one did the year before hearing stories of loss that required comfort. "Blew me away she did that."

"You and me both. Couldn't wrap my head around it then, Paul. I didn't have any business putting it out there for you, or others. Apparently, she told her mom, who told mine." The estrogen pool during the week, actively discussing what Steve had held as private.

"Made sense, remembering how silent you were," Paul said. "We were both preoccupied back then."

"One reason I shelved it," Steve said, lathering a chunk of bread with the lump crab and cheese concoction. "Maren mixed into this week made it oh so much fun. Thursday. Friday. Yesterday."

"What's her impression of Pam?"

Steve jerked his head back. "You know…that's a damn good question. She hasn't said, nor did I ask." Steve felt like an idiot suddenly. "So much back story to fill in…we had to talk hurts and feelings, and the proverbial need to communicate. Better and faster."

Paul's gaze communicated how hard Steve must have tread in that estrogen pool. "Just the way most women like it." They exchanged guy smirks.

"I forgot how much women like words…honestly."

"Ah geez," Paul snorted. "I taught Vicki long ago. I give her a certain cue now. She knows not to go there with 15 or even five questions."

"What's the cue?"

"R & R," Paul told him. "*Not* rest and relaxation. Raw and real. Many meanings. Some better than others."

"OK," he chuckled. Paul likely meant the lewd ones.

"Speaking of a little raw, Pam terrorized me into good behavior reminding me about my one-nighter with the girls." They both knew what night he meant. "It wasn't exactly what the two of you think."

"Do not *even* try to downplay that." Steve snickered, silencing the temptation to throw Pam's mind under the bus with her one-time suggestion they invite Paul down the hall.

"What?"

"Nothing." Steve knew Pam had downed a six-pack in New York, plus a mixed drink, he recollected, diverting his attention to the 7-7 score in the first quarter. "From what I've seen, Pam's family seems to have eased up."

"Morphed into contemporary. Shelly had a tattoo, hearts hidden under her sleeve," Paul said. "Pam had to hide Steve under the sheets. Shelly broadcasts Eric-sex with art. Bet that burns Pam."

"They always held her to higher standards." Steve shook his head. "Pam's relationship with her mom was tense, maybe still," Steve added. "Shelly gets freedom." He wondered just how much, if she experimented with pot like Eric. "Brad and Hilary weren't thrilled when we 'shacked up' but they got over it."

238

"You won them over. *We* won them over."

"I can only imagine their reaction over an abortion." Had he joined in that decision, their image of Steve may have tumbled, too.

"In all honesty, the secrecy stung the most, right?"

"Secrecy," Steve said with eyes as chilly as his second beer the waitress just brought from the tap. "Hands down." Steve dug at crab dip, averting Paul until their eyes purposefully met. "She concealed that…and Jerry."

"I had a hunch she had someone else. At the same time?" Paul speared his own appetizer. Steve nodded affirmatively. "I'd be pissed, too," Paul said. "She owed you more than that. Has figured that out, I think."

"Well, our Dr. Morgan seems all about communication…now," Steve said sarcastically. The Titans put another seven points on the board, and neither Steve nor Paul felt too upbeat. "Told me to lose the tone, drop the attitude. Kissed me to shut me up. Imagine."

Steve saw some slack in Paul's mouth. "Kissed you?"

"She stopped the elevator…to communicate."

"Hopefully with no one else on it?" Paul asked, laughing.

"We were alone," Steve said. "Get this….tells me to 'seal the deal' with Maren, calling her hot. The kiss ostensibly to restore good memories."

"He'll take another one," Paul told the waitress who cleared bottles. "Look, Maren *is* hot, and Pam but… she's like oil spilled outside your boat. You think you're drowning now."

"Yeah." Steve sat back. "Gonna have to remember R&R."

"Raw and real. Sums up so much some days."

Turning to his life, Paul shared how fatigued Vicki was with her pregnancy and her lupus. With Paul's concern about her and the Steelers trailing, life felt raw. Their fourth quarter rally wasn't enough as the Titans won by eight points.

Pounded by projects, Maren had hardly seen Steve until Thursday. Tomorrow she worked from home, and Steve started a weekend on-call.

"Remember when you calmed Dylan about my tests?" Maren asked him as she savored pumpkin soup purchased along with salad. His came with a BLT.

"Vaguely. I told you to run that idea by Alicia."

"Well, I did." She leaned over clandestinely. "She told me to develop it on my own."

Steve turned his head. "Because..."

"Alicia said 'we're not having this conversation, but...think concepts like work-for-hire or copyright." Maren sat back. "Pays to have a boss who has been your friend first."

"If you develop it on hospital time, it's not yours."

"Exactly," Maren said, sipping her soup again. "So thank you. Your idea, but you'll have to live with an acknowledgement if I publish it. Your department won't get credit."

"You can pay me back...creatively," Steve said lifting a brow and crumbling wax paper from his sandwich. He reached to Maren's wrist. "I'll miss you this weekend. Haven't seen Dylan."

"Hinting about this evening?"

Steve smiled. "Whenever I stay over, you benefit. Often, multiple times."

He won. Hardly created a hardship. Maren had acquiesced to Steve following Sunday's football game, certainly enjoying several of his skill sets.

While shopping, Maren broached the Florida topic with Audrey, who checked with both Jack and the extended family in Orlando. Maren's aunt invited all of them, including Steve, to spend Christmas there.

Hearing this, he began scheming how he might whisk Maren to the Gulf Coast for an overnight. Jack and Audrey said they'd watch Dylan. The trip one month away, everyone scoured airline websites booking flights. Steve rearranged his, paying a minor fee, to fly with Maren and Dylan. As she pushed her bowl aside, Steve lowered his voice. "You'll love our getaway."

"I will, will I?"

"Time off to escape. Too much on my mind."

"Like what?"

The following Thursday was Thanksgiving. Steve's parents invited Maren, Dylan, Jack and Audrey to join them at their bay house where the Kramers would spend the long weekend, and Steve would help cook.

"Decisions…if I'm going to lease my condo," Steve said. "Might live aboard the boat."

"What about snow?" Steve witnessed the first frigid look he'd ever seen on Maren's face. "Not to mention counter space for your appliance collection."

"Seriously," Steve said. "That's what storage is for, and the boat has heat and A/C." He stacked his soup bowl atop hers. "Reality is, I'll have the boat one year in June. Do I need double the expense?"

"But to give up your apartment?"

"Worst case, I'd be homeless. You'd have to take me in." He feigned pity.

"I…I could make room for your All-Clad," Maren suggested. She brightened. "And cappuccino machine."

"I get it. Cabinets and counters can accommodate my stuff. I have to cajole my way upstairs." Steve had thought about stashing things at her place—things they both enjoyed, but he was glad she initiated the idea.

"I have my priorities." Nonchalant, Maren confined amusement. She knew Steve needed the chase. An overfed ego might only grow hungrier. Satisfy his stomach and sex drive; stave off too much self-regard.

Steve had opened up more this week. High walls he'd built to keep people out because they'd hurt him. Burned the better word, Maren thought. Lower now, but walls nonetheless. With Mark, there had been an open landscape.

"Liz is on me to see Eric play at a club."

"What night?" Maren asked. "We could ask Alicia and Drew to join us."

"Fine with me. Saturday the 30th," Steve said thumb scrolling his smartphone. "Hanukkah starts the night before though."

"Her kids might be with her ex. I'll ask Alicia and call Liz since you're busy."

"Good idea." Steve rose from the table, leaned down to cup her chin. He kissed her goodbye. "I'll see you tonight. I'll help with dinner if I can get out by six." Such maneuvers, she thought, jockeying herself out of her chair.

Steve working the weekend, Maren tackled Christmas shopping before the mad rush. Dylan played with his grandfather while she and Audrey caught lunch at the mall and talked about Florida. They had agreed to delay sharing the surprise with Dylan.

"Your cousin Courtney is thrilled we're all coming," Audrey told Maren as they sipped tea and each had a salad. "Can't believe...almost four years since she married Josh. Wasn't that the last time you saw her?"

"Mom, she and Aunt Nora came for Mark's funeral."

"Oh, that's right," Audrey said. Concern that her memory lapse steered Maren to sadder times showed on Audrey's face.

"I'm going to still think of Mark, even with Steve in my life." Maren told Audrey that Mark's parents—Mildred and Walter Mitchell—were coming to Washington to see their daughter Janice. They wanted to take Dylan overnight. Saturday would be perfect. The night she and Steve wanted to go out. "Between plans for Dylan and Steve's old girlfriend, I've thought a lot more about Mark."

"Oh, how do you mean?"

Maren locked visually with her mom. "I love Steve. A lot," Maren told her. "But I miss Mark. Not painful missing like last year...in little ways."

"And big. Your anniversary would be Friday." November 29th.

"I haven't forgotten. That's why there's no way I want Mildred and Walter around that day. I'll rope Alicia into a Hanukkah invite if they insist," she said. Dylan knew Alicia's children and would have fun spinning the dreidel.

"Kids I taught got jealous when friends celebrated eight days." Audrey straightened her spine and took another sip of tea, easing her cup down. "They may react poorly to your dating."

"Not something I plan to advertise. Let's face it, if they pepper Dylan with questions, you honestly think he won't mention Steve?"

"Yeah, they'll be out for details." Their eyes made circles. "You have a right to a life, honey. Mark's been gone a year and a half. Don't allow Mildred Mitchell to guilt you. I mean that." Audrey emphasized the last part, because she'd seen her daughter keep the peace in that family far too often. "Have Steve spend Friday night. Tell him it would be your anniversary." Audrey took another sip while Maren thought how Steve would be sensitive, savoring another reason to stay at her house versus his lonely apartment.

Audrey's mug hit the table as if it signaled her next thought. "He can be there Saturday morning when they pick Dylan up, with his car in your driveway. Steve can open the door." Audrey directed a wicked gleam to Maren. "He looks good in the morning, with just a bit of a beard on him."

"Mother...why don't we put him in a bathrobe parted at the chest?" That her mom would love that scene began to register. "I'll figure it out. Meeting him might make sense. Not in a bathrobe."

Audrey enjoyed flustering Maren only momentarily. "You started to mention why you missed Mark. I interrupted."

"It's OK. Steve and I have a lot of fun, but Mark and I had long talks. I felt close, like I really knew him. Entire chapters of Steve's life remain a mystery." Maren wanted the Cliff Notes version at the very least.

"What's the chapter with the girlfriend like?"

"I think that's why he's guarded," Maren said. "Or the left logical brain always in gear. Either case, he closes off in ways Mark didn't."

"They're two different men, Maren. You know that. Steve seems fairly laid back. Now, this girlfriend?"

"Pam," Maren said. "She reminds me of Mildred Mitchell, at least in how she enters a room."

"Heads turn. She has a presence about her."

"You got it. She and Steve were together most of a decade, and at the end, she started secretly with another guy, took back up with Steve, only to cast him off. Not before she got pregnant discarding that also." Surprise swept over Audrey. "Please Mom, don't let this go any further than you and Dad. It's sensitive because she never told Steve. He found out, after the abortion. Complicated."

"That's an understatement," Audrey said, still dumbfounded. "Explains Liz using the B word Sunday."

"Apparently, Steve confronted Pam, but never told anyone. Their parents remained friends. Steve's brother Eric dates Pam's sister Shelly. Now, Pam's told several people."

"I might need a playbill here but I think I have the cast of characters. So how do Steve and his ex get along now?"

"It's tense," Maren stated factually. "Her father's illness brought her back. They hashed things out over lunch." She wasn't about to add detail. "Pam was polite to me. She told Steve he should make things more permanent."

"I don't think Steve needs any long lost love to tell him that. Your father thinks the way his eyes and hands move on you shows awfully clear intent."

"He does?" Maren's cheeks looked as if they'd been touched up in a mall makeover.

"Sounds like Steve's not completely over the incident," Audrey said. She drank more tea. "Nice of his parents to invite us for Thanksgiving. Any dress code?"

"No Mitchell-like formal. Bill and Dolores can certainly do the town. I've seen the family photo album, but they're easy. Nice slacks, sweater. Blazer and button down shirt; skip the tie for Dad." Maren ran her fingers through her hair, down today as she inserted her credit card into the billfold. "Thanks for listening. My treat, Mom."

As Dylan watched the Macy's Thanksgiving Day Parade, Maren and Steve got their morning jolts, chatting in her bedroom while she folded laundry.

"Thanks for the Starbucks," she said.

"You're welcome. We have an hour before your parents arrive." Steve studied her steady movements. "You've been quiet this week."

"I've been working on that 'how to talk to your kids' project, which on my own time, takes plenty. Hence, laundry on a holiday," she said. Steve set down his cardboard cup and lent a hand. "Plus, a lot on my mind." Eye contact remained off.

Steve stopped her before she could reach another towel from the basket. "Maren…what?"

"Tomorrow would be my 10th wedding anniversary." Her voice flat, face downturned. She stepped toward her coffee cup on her dresser. A few swigs of the still steamy brew helped her focus.

"I'd no idea," Steve said, reaching for his own. "I don't know what to say."

"You don't have to say anything. This whole week brought back memories—planning my wedding, a rehearsal 10 years ago tonight. If that isn't enough, the Mitchells arrive on my doorstep Saturday morning. That's who's watching Dylan, at their hotel in DC." Maren set down her cup. More movement with this chore might push away difficult thoughts. "You're not the only one with a past."

"You still miss Mark." The circumstances of their relationship losses had been entirely different. "And his parents aren't easy people, you said."

"No," Maren sniffed. "Mildred reminds me of Pam. All force. When she finds out I'm dating, I'm sure to catch hell. That's what Mom thinks." Maren continued folding, filling Steve in on her mother's remarks. She left out the parted bathrobe, chest hair, and sexy stubble.

"I'm happy to camp out with you this weekend." After working the last one, Steve wanted to. "That doesn't mean what you think." He reached for one of Dylan's T-shirts, eyeing Maren. "Quote: I'm not deprived."

Maren smiled. "Liz wanted to get the kids together Friday. Mildred and Walter are pushing for two nights, so this all came into the conversation." She gathered the stack of their progress and wedged it into the basket. "Liz had a good point."

"Occasionally, she makes a few," Steve said, chuckling since Maren hardly ever heard him compliment his sister.

"She said if I'm to cement new memories to build another brain pathway. Not that you totally forget but the past won't be so painful."

"Good advice." Those years at UNC paid off. Liz had earned her keep in Steve's mind, comforting Maren and maybe him. Pam's kiss now seemed symbolic, making their history less tortured. Two women he considered difficult made damn good sense, at least today.

"Steve…"

"Sorry…I zoned." He reached for his cardboard cup downing the rest. "How can I help? Even if it means… space." Steve's voice trailed off at that word.

"I want to spend the weekend with you," Maren said. "I need you." She brushed his face, with just that bit of beard he'd purposely left on his day off. "I need a few hours tomorrow though. I'm locking my rings in the safe deposit box when the bank opens." Maren got up and moved around the other side of her bed from where Steve sat against her pillows.

Reaching into a drawer, she pulled out a jewelry box with slits, confining rings that held hope 10 years ago. Steve shifted so that she could sit comfortably.

"May I?" Steve asked. Her nod gave the go-ahead.

He removed the larger band first. Heavier, in white gold or platinum. Engraved inside "All my love, Maren 11-29-92." Mark's band to Maren showed similar sentiment. Then, Steve gently lifted the remaining ring from its groove. "It's beautiful. What's this one?" He pointed to the prominent light blue stone flanked by two half-carat diamonds. "Put it on." She did as directed.

"Aquamarine. My birthstone." Steve looked as if he grasped new information. "The modern March stone." She handed it back and watched as Steve carefully closed the box over her rings.

"You're locking them away?" He regarded her.

"Only stopped wearing them in May. I wore the aquamarine and the diamonds this past summer. My cousin—the one you'll meet—told me no one would see it as an engagement ring." Maren shook her head. "Those that did would see it as a sign to keep away."

Maren strolled back to the dresser drawer, burying them. "When Mark and I went to the jewelry store, I wasn't the traditionalist I am now. I suppose I might wear it again someday. If not, I'll save it for Dylan." Steve's eyes appeared soft. Though he'd finished his coffee, he fingered the cardboard heat band. "I hope Hannah likes aquamarine," she said. A puzzled expression flashed over him. "Dylan's in love after last weekend."

"We'll have a man-to-man talk." Steve smiled, pulled Maren closer. "So you need a few hours. In the morning?"

"Yeah…if it's late, my parents may spend the night here." She looked up at Steve. "You can, too." Smooth eyes moved in as his hand edged her lips to his. They parted.

"And I'll kiss you." Steve's hands brushed Maren's hair to both sides of her forehead, his thumb ending up under her chin. Their heads moved together.

"For new memories," Maren whispered, voice husky. She angled so that he'd pull away, returning his lips on hers.

"We'll make some new ones." Steve's beard crawled across her neck, moving behind her ear, to the sensitive spot he knew. Maren pulled back, searched Steve's eyes and reclaimed his lips. Tighter. Hungrier.

"Mom, it's for you," Dylan said, arm outstretched. "Yuck, I'm not kissing Hannah like that." He handed her the cordless phone. Maren quickly remembered she'd left it near Dylan.

"Hello," she said, thankful whoever was on the other end couldn't see her flushed in rosy red. "Walter, hello..." Mortified, she motioned Dylan out.

"Yes, I'm glad you had a chance to chat with him." She listened a few seconds. "Sure, I decided Friday's fine. If you'd like to pick him up around noon, then you can take him to lunch. Sunday same time sounds great." Maren hoped Walter Mitchell, Mark's father, couldn't hear the breathlessness in her voice. First from the effects of Steve, followed by fear.

"We have a suite at The Hay-Adams," Walter said. "Mildred wanted to see how they renovated it." She would, Maren silently figured. It was minutes from the National Mall where they planned to museum hop with Dylan, when they weren't in Virginia with Mark's sister Janice. "Maren, how are you?"

"I...I'm fine, Walter. It's kind of you to ask. My job's going well, and everything's going...well. Really...well." Steve slouched into the pillows. She needed to be rescued, but he already played enough of a role.

"Tomorrow at noon then." Walter Mitchell spoke with the authority he often used as president and chief executive officer of his nationally known advertising conglomerate. "Ah, Maren...who are Steve and Hannah?"

"They're...friends. Good friends." Maren had to get off the phone, had to find out what happened when Walter spent but a few minutes with his grandson. "Listen, I need to get ready. We're leaving soon."

"With friends, I'm sure," he said dryly.

The doorbell rang. Dylan, in the distance yelled, "I'll get it."

"Yes...and my parents. They just arrived. Good chatting with you Walter. Happy Thanksgiving." She felt relief putting the phone into its corded cradle.

"I'd kiss you again if it would force more air into you," Steve said. "I hear your parents. I'll hold that thought." He looked empathic as she propelled herself off the bed, extending him a hand to go greet Audrey and Jack.

They took two cars to Southern Maryland. Jack had been curious about Steve's Jaguar convertible when he first laid eyes on it. Dylan rode in the back, strapped into his booster. "With the guys," he told Maren only after he told Audrey and Jack that "Mom and Steve were

247

kissing when Grandpa Mitchell called." Steve tried to minimize that when Dylan surfaced it a second time. From the passenger seat, Jack left his daughter's lip locking alone, struck more by the car's performance.

Audrey, on the other hand, pressed Maren for details. What business did Walter Mitchell have asking about her personal life? Why had she given in to their request for an extra day?

"They see so little of him. I decided to be nice…to them and to myself with the extra time," Maren defended as she pulled into the rural driveway after following Steve along Maryland Route 2. She cut the engine, reached for her handbag behind her seat, and looked squarely at Audrey. "Answering your last question: Yes, good kisser. I'm sure Mildred Mitchell wonders the same."

Maren would deal with Mildred's inquiries within 24 hours. "Let's feast. Steve's probably helping, so park yourself in their kitchen and you can ogle him all you want." Maren knew the tone she took with her mother remained curt. Nerves raw, Steve mentioned the phrase Paul had taught him. This whole week seemed beyond real right now.

"OK, let's enjoy ourselves," Audrey said.

They did. The Kramers' bayside home dated decades, but had been totally renovated. The main level, the home's original footprint, held a large master suite for Dolores and Bill, along with a family room blended into a small kitchen to the side. Three other rooms—a study and two bedrooms remained on the ground floor with a separate bath, easily accessible from the pool outside.

One flight up—unless you took the recently installed elevator—a pub-style bar seated four people underneath three ceiling-extended lights. The kitchen opened to an equally generous living area with big screen TV and a rounded sectional. On the side, the expanded table was set with a rust tablecloth for 11 people. Liz, Tim and her kids would arrive momentarily. The men immediately took to the pier, one of the few private docks, since the nearby condominiums shared docking privileges.

The water view got better on the second floor. "Enjoying yourself?" Maren whispered to Audrey. They sat at the counter talking with Steve who took charge of the root vegetables and hovered over simmering cranberry sauce.

Maren's parents brought a housewarming basket filled with two bottles of wine, cheese and crackers, which Dolores served, along with another appetizer she placed on the coffee table.

"Notice he doesn't park in front of football?" Audrey hushed.

"Trust me, he can. Wrong team." Steve turned to them unsure how he was being talked about, but with Audrey, he felt he had a fan in his corner.

"The Skins play at four. That's why dinner was planned for three," he said, stirring. "More like 3:30 at least." He smiled to his mother, looked at Maren and her mom. "If Eric was here, I could be passive-aggressive and carve slowly."

The Kramer-woman look came his way. "You're starting on your siblings, Steve." Dolores patted his back and mouthed half-audibly, "He wouldn't really do that."

"Don't be so sure," Steve interrupted. "I'm for the Cowboys." Eric and Bill backed the Ravens during important match-ups. Retaliation today.

"Steve always carves the turkey with the utmost precision," Dolores told them as they'd taken the bird out to sit in its juices.

Besides turkey, the menu included wild rice stuffing with pine nuts, butternut squash, mashed potatoes for the kids, along with cranberry and pumpkin pies Liz brought.

She had kept the kids downstairs taking turns between Candy Land and Battleship for the boys. At 3:20, they sat down to eat. Liz offered the prayer after Hannah finally left Steve's lap for her own chair. Everyone enjoyed the food, conversation, and at least two bottles of wine. Maren carried her second glass back to the table after putting food away.

"Your son is flirting with my niece over there," Steve said as he sat around the table with his own second glass. Dylan taught Hannah how to play Uno. "His eyes rove on her."

"Who's hitting on Hannah?" Eric asked as he came in with Shelly, hugging his mother. Steve introduced his brother and Shelly Morgan to Audrey and to Jack who took seats, having had enough football.

"Dylan's winning her over," Steve said. "I'm jealous."

"That's so cute," Shelly added. She thrust herself into an available chair next to Steve. Eric had two things on his mind: the couch and the Redskins.

"How's your father, Shelly?" Steve asked.

Shelly pursed her lips. "Physically…fine." She paused, pulled her long blonde hair behind her as if she had a ponytail clip, which she did not. Arms stretched, she revealed the two-hearted tattoo.

Shelly let her hair go. "Fortunately, my mom made the dinner. I helped. That left someone else to prosecute on the health-care and dietary front." Shelly's eyes met Steve's. "She argues like a lawyer." Dolores handed her a glass of wine and brought the pies out while Shelly vented. "And…she cannot cook," she continued. "Hysterical when Dad just let her have it."

"A sign he is feeling better, I guess." Steve wasn't quite sure what else to say though fairly certain everyone understood that "her" meant his ex. "All that supposed to be new information about your sister?" Steve's sarcasm revealed it as ancient history.

Shelly sensed she'd put Steve in a tight spot. She liked him. Maybe he'd become her brother-in-law, only in this decade, in a different way. "Jerry told her after living with you and Paul, she must have an attention problem not to have learned some culinary skills."

"Hanging out with Mrs. Romano, you learn to cook." Steve beamed at the olfactory memory alone. "Like a semester in culinary school."

"So my sister had her chance?" Shelly asked. "Probably had her nose in her books instead."

Steve quieted. Dolores and Liz smirked, dissing Pam and feeling Shelly fit right in.

"Dad said you guys not only kept her safe in New York, you likely kept her alive."

"Good one," Liz added.

Steve tilted his eyes in what could become a Kramer- man look. "So, how's grad school?" Steve took a much-needed sip of wine. This would be why a Kramer-Morgan matchup could become tenser than football rivalry. Steve steered clear of that, too. "Eric says you're concentrating in a facet of neuroscience and exercise physiology."

"Sorry, Steve. It's just that she's so…but, I get the point."

Steve reached to Shelly's wrist. "It's OK. Tell us about life at College Park." He took a deep breath. Helped him 10-15 years ago with the same stressor.

Shelly Morgan explained about cognitive motor neuroscience, movement disorders, and working with young kids. When she finished, her babysitting for a college advisor with a special-needs child made more sense to Steve.

"Come on kids," Liz yelled. Tim put coats on them. It was seven o'clock.

"Liz, thanks for the other day," Maren whispered.

"You did the right thing. We'll get these three together some other time. We'll see you Saturday hearing Eric's band."

Dylan whined at Hannah's departure. Tyler nodded "what-about-me?" Everyone exchanged goodbyes outside of Eric and Shelly as they remained at the bayside house for the weekend.

Chapter 17

Maren got up early, took the rings to the bank box, and finished errands. By 11:30, she grabbed a sandwich Audrey prepared from leftover turkey Dolores sent. Steve took Jack and Dylan to see his boat. Having turned her ankle stumbling on the stairs the night before, Audrey propped and iced it as Steve advised. She counted on his promise to take her to the marina another time.

Walter and Mildred rang the doorbell at 11:45. Maren darted her eyes at Audrey. "They aren't back yet." She had no choice but to ask her former in-laws to sit down while they waited for the guys. Maren could have kicked herself for not giving Dylan his first Hanukkah experience at Alicia's for the evening…or the entire day.

"Mildred, Walter…hello," Maren said, opening the front door. "Come on in. Mom's here and Dylan is off with my father…back any moment."

"Hello, Audrey," Walter said extending his hand. Mildred did the same. He removed his blazer, smoothing out his dress slacks. Gray prominent on his temples, Maren realized Mark would have been a handsome man if they had aged together.

"You both had a good holiday?" Audrey asked. She felt more at ease with Walter, who had social grace coupled with business acumen that his wife could have used long ago. "Please sit down."

"We did. It's nice being back in town," Mildred said, laying her fur stole on the back before sitting on a chair. She wore a dress, black hosiery, and a string of pearls that nearly matched the color her hair had become. "Maren, bring us up to date on Dylan. I'm so glad those snipers were caught. Janice said it was dreadful." Janice was Mark's sister.

Mildred's eyes darted the room. The last time she'd been here, she asked Maren what had happened to her draperies. Nothing had. Mildred merely eschewed Maren's muted color scheme. Massive, burgundy draperies had hung dramatically in the Mitchells' Fairfax home. What wasn't heavy and brown had been glass and fragile.

Mildred never lobbed remarks in front of Mark. She boxed them up, saved especially for Maren, whom she would never consider creative. Mildred was that force in the family. Back in her day Mildred dabbled in design and decorating. Mark had told Maren that his mother had a B.A. in art history, calling herself an interior home couturier—whatever the hell that was, they both had wondered—without any certification or formal training.

To Maren, Mildred felt more the interior destructor designing to diminish. Facing her today, Audrey's eyes reminded Maren "only if you let her."

"Dylan's great. Loves school. Good grades, making friends…a happy, healthy little boy."

"Dylan said he was in the hospital this fall."

"A brief stay," Maren admitted. "I meant to tell you. Same time I was approached for this job. I apologize."

"I'm not sure why you felt the need to take a job at this phase in Dylan's life. In the future I do hope that you could consult us…even you and Jack, Audrey. We still want to be very much a part of Dylan's life."

"Her taking this job, Mildred, has been a positive step in many ways," Audrey replied, suppressing more.

"You realize, Maren, that if you wanted to work in marketing, I could set you up in the company," Walter added. "Full salary, benefits, flexibility. With a much better title." Likely boring assignments, too, and constant reminders of all they'd done for her, Maren thought.

"That's kind of you Walter, but I negotiated flexibility with my boss, who is a friend from art school. It's close to home, and I only work at the hospital three days each week."

"The hospital where Mark died?" Mildred interrupted. "You must be joking?"

"At first, that bothered me also, but..."

"I certainly hope Dylan got better care," she said with vitriol.

"Excellent care. I stayed with him. Oh, look who's here?" Dylan bounded through the front door. Jack and Steve trailed, chatting about the boat.

"Dylan, come here," Mildred said. Rather tentatively, Dylan let her envelope him. Walter's hug seemed slightly more genuine.

"Hi," Dylan said sheepishly. Maren breathed better seeing that he hadn't stained his dressy khakis nor gotten anything on his Sperry shoes, which he insisted on getting after spotting Steve with a pair. Lunch, by reservation, followed shortly.

"Walter, Mildred...how are you both?" Jack greeted, stepping closer. "Let me introduce Steve, a friend of Maren's." Walter got up to shake hands, his curious eyes extended to Steve.

"Good to meet you," Steve said. "Dylan's a great boy. I see the resemblance."

"You should see Steve's boat Grandpa. It can go really fast." Dylan's excitement rose. "We rided in it weeks ago."

"Rode in it, Dylan," his grandmother Mitchell corrected. "School *is* going well, I can see." Head moving like a basketball, Dylan didn't catch the dig.

"We were asking how you felt after being in the hospital," Walter added.

"You poor dear. You had surgery then got bounced on a boat," Mildred said. "Really? Maren, next time, call us if he's hospitalized."

"Grandma, it's a *smooth* ride." Dylan's six-year-old voice elongated the word "smooth" for effect, causing Jack to snort out a laugh. That turned Mildred's head. "Steve fixed me...yanked a bad part out. I had to stay in the hospital 'til I pooped," Dylan informed.

Mildred Mitchell looked as if she could never do lunch within the hour after that remark. She and Walter each bristled.

"Steve is the surgeon who operated on Dylan," Maren said. She turned to him sitting next to her, by habit nudging close. "Feel free to add anything." Her eyes indicated "please" and "get them out of here."

"Dylan presented late one night with acute pain, vomiting, onset of diarrhea...and tachycardia," Steve told them. "Sorry, rapid heart beat," he clarified. "His workup: urinalysis, blood counts, CRP, scans. Clearly wasn't his active self. Got in there before his appendix ruptured."

"Wish I could have saved it," Dylan said, eyes wide.

"We don't put parts in jars for show and tell, dude."

Mildred cringed. Audrey bent to rub her ankle, truly to stifle amusement.

Turning to the Mitchells, Steve finished. "His incisions healed quite well post-op. Boating, fishing...several weeks after. Rather quiet."

"Incisions?" Mildred asked, undeterred. "Two operations?" If her nose froze that high on her face, Mildred Mitchell would require 12 hours of corrective surgery, Steve assessed.

"Laparoscopic appendectomy." The benefits he explained halted their concerns, thankfully.

"Wanna see?" Dylan hiked his sweater, pulled at his khakis.

"Dylan, no." Maren reached for his hands. "That's not polite and no one needs to see your tiny scars." This visit was long enough. She stood to signal them. "Thank you again for taking him. I'm sure he'll have a great time. There's a bathing suit in his bag for the hotel pool."

Mildred ran her eyes the length of Maren from her ponytail to her low heels. She dressed informally in crisp jeans, blouse belted at the waist. Steve stood also as Maren's cue hadn't effected their rising. His did. Dylan hugged Audrey, Jack, and Maren. He gave Steve a high-five smack in the air. "Game day Sunday. Steelers rock."

"Dylan doesn't root for the Ravens anymore?" Walter asked. Maren resisted the urge to answer that he never did. Mark followed the Ravens initially; Dylan hadn't acquired a team preference.

"We could call it a side effect of anesthesia." Steve's joke landed with a thud. "I did my residency in Pittsburgh. Dylan's caught on."

"They won four Super Bowls," Dylan boasted. "Other teams suck."

"Dylan," Maren objected, face flushing. "I've talked to you about that word."

"Steve says it."

"And, your mom reprimands me, too," Steve said uneasily. The Mitchells remained stuck in two sets of icy frowns, moving through the door without a handshake. If peacocks, their feathers would have surely shown acute ruffling.

"Dylan, be good. I love you," Maren said. "You both have my cell number?" Dylan had his bag. "Do you need an extra booster seat?"

"Yes, we have your number," Walter replied. "No, Janice had an extra."

"Dylan will be fine. You mustn't worry." If looks could kill, Maren would lie on the front stoop frozen from cold, lingering eyes Mildred Mitchell cast. "Happy Anniversary, Maren. Please tell me *you* put those flowers at the cemetery."

Frustration mounting at the tone and unkind implications, Maren's voice weakened. "I did." She closed the door, resting her head against it. With Dylan by the hand, the Mitchells moved quickly into their rented Lincoln Town Car.

Maren drew a deep breath. She remained in place, fearing Audrey might reprimand that she went too easy on Mildred or that Steve would see fresh tears welling. He came to her side and pulled her into his chest, stroking her back. "I see what you mean." His lips braised the top of her head. Jack and Audrey watched the exit from the window.

"Mom, please...don't say anything." Maren sniffled.

"You did fine, but I'm glad we were here," Jack said. He focused appreciative eyes on Steve. "That may have been tame."

"Yeah, I saved Dylan from peritonitis, but ruined his language and Sunday afternoons. Horror."

Jack laid a hand on Steve's shoulder. "Once they pump Dylan for details, expect worse on Sunday."

"You'll be here, Steve?" Audrey asked.

He laughed. "If the boss here allows me to crash on her couch, watching my awful team...and mouth."

"All of you stop. Mom and Dad, it's been a great Thanksgiving. I enjoyed having you, but today is difficult. I'm sure you have things to do." It wasn't like Maren to give them the push off, but they were about to leave regardless. Steve assessed that Audrey's ankle benefited from rest suggesting more of it. Seemed the appropriate prescription all the way around.

"Pack a bag," he told Maren later. "Want to cement new memories, let's spend the night on the boat. Unless today's not the day." Steve left the choice ultimately to her. "I can try out the heating system. A preview of living aboard."

"Give me 20 minutes, and we're outta here."

They stopped at Steve's long enough to check mail and gather some things. Steering clear of malls or most restaurants this Black Friday, Steve suggested a booth at the marina bar for an early, quiet dinner.

"You didn't order much," he noticed. Some, but not all, of the tension had eased out of Maren. "You visited Mark's grave today?"

"Yeah." Maren looked out at the boat slips. Water usually seemed so peaceful. Another minute—or six—went by. Steve wondered how often Maren made that journey, where it was, and how she felt. Given the silence, he didn't ask. "Steve…" She hesitated, torn by conflicting emotion. "I didn't mean to drag you into all this today."

"Do I look dragged?"

"No." Steve looked casual to her, with an ease she wished she could steal from across the table. He sat against the leather booth with a long-sleeved, button down shirt belted into khakis, lighter than Dylan had worn to lunch with the Mitchells. She wondered how that was going. "I'll die if they're giving Dylan the once over."

"You know they are." Steve wouldn't mind resuscitating her. They had the night to themselves. It wasn't his style to exploit the situation if Maren's mind traveled a million miles or simply 10 years away. "Hard to know if I help here."

"You do." She glanced at the clock. "Our wedding was at two. We'd be heading to the reception now." Maren told Steve how they'd planned the ceremony in their college town, but with Mildred's huffing, they acquiesced to a reception in a large Washington hotel. Guests traveled an hour plus following pictures, drawing out the day. The Mitchells underwrote much of it and brought that up often. Not to their son; only to Maren. Privately. No witnesses.

"Weddings are fraught with friction," Steve said. "Liz and my mom had a few rounds years ago."

Maren smiled. At least hers wasn't the only experience marred by pre-nuptial discord. "Mark and I earned those ten days in Hawaii."

Their food arrived. Maren ate a salad. Steve opted for crab cakes and having already had soup and salad, shared his entrée with Maren.

"I stashed a bottle of wine in the fridge. Do you want dessert to take back?" Maren picked chocolate cake to share. Steve put the tab on his marina account, and they left hand in hand, walking back to the docks at dusk, lit by lights along the pier.

"You know, I'm here to listen," Steve said. She told him Jack felt wistful as father of the bride, how overall the day became a positive memory. "But soon the part where you leave the reception," Steve said. They made it to the swim platform, stepping aboard. "If we're supposed to form new memories, what pressure." Steve goosed her playfully. Shivering, they quickly stepped down into the cabin and closed the door.

Maren removed her pant-length coat, and Steve put it with his jacket in Dylan's hiding space. "Now there's one space we haven't initiated." Steve smirked. "Should we before Dylan steals a kiss with Hannah in there?"

"Steve...our memories. How 'bout a movie? You brought more."

"Perfect, go pick one."

Maren turned on the light in the forward berth and opened the wall compartment. Not in the mood for pole jokes with *Striptease*. *Bridges of Madison County* with infidelity? *Sleepless in Seattle* where the Mitchells lived?

"We could watch two." Steve poured them each wine. "I'm in no rush to top your wedding night. Performance anxiety on board." His lips curved.

"Experience and your book collection make a liar out of you."

"You want communication, vulnerability?" Steve started to hand over her glass, but set it down. Hands went to hips. "That book *Light Her Fire*," he said. "Bought that in '92." Steve handed her a button-down shirt. She took it into the head to change.

"I'm listening," she shouted from inside.

"You think after presumably satisfying someone for nine years, being replaced, I might start to wonder?" He toed off his shoes, undressing.

"I'm sure," Maren said, putting her clothes in her overnight bag now.

She wore his shirt so well, he thought. Buttoned unfortunately, but that wouldn't last. Maren grabbed her glass and crawled under the covers.

"Put the pressure on tomorrow night. Technically speaking," Maren coughed conjuring images of another discussion. "First times are never as good. Second...so much better." She took an alluring sip of wine.

"Good, buys another 24 hours." In opened shirt and boxers he got beside her.

"I am impressed. Chick flicks." She pressed a kiss on his cheek.

"Thanks for noticing. *When Harry Met Sally*?" he asked. Maren nodded. They nestled together while Harry adamantly revealed to Sally that men and women couldn't be friends without sex interfering. They too ended up in bed, later married.

"Friends with any ex's?" Maren asked, contemplating dessert.

Stabbing his fork into their chocolate cake bought extra thinking time. "The one in medical sales I've worked with," he said. "No friendship with Pam."

"Would you like it to be…friendly?"

"With our siblings dating, Paul as a mutual friend, it would help. Time will tell." Losing love through death or desertion each brought challenges, dealing with sorrow and memories.

Chocolate, wine, and a romantic comedy paved the way for their tender lovemaking that night, and when the sunlight streamed through the hatches, neither Steve nor Maren felt motivated to do anything except enjoy one another. They took a mid-morning breakfast break. Steve read journals. Maren fell back asleep.

"Last night, you didn't add much about Ms. Medical Sales."

Women…their need for words. Steve sighed. "I never was the type to go out for the sole purpose of getting laid," he said. "Except…"

"…with her?" Maren gave Steve a you-can't-stop-there stare.

"Met Samantha on the heels of being jilted, disillusioned, and yeah… sex on the first date." Steve nodded. "Later… every one after. Surprised?"

She considered him. "No one-night stand?"

"No," he answered honestly. "Let's say…it wasn't based on friendship." He caressed Maren's face. She lounged under the comforter wearing his shirt, loosely buttoned, baring her breasts when she moved looking gorgeous. "Like the phrase Paul coined, sometimes, there's a dark side."

"And she fulfilled those raw and real needs?"

"Yeah, she did." Steve hoped that would satisfy her, but just in case, he got out of bed. "That's all in the past. I want more now," he said, kissing her on the lips, thumbing her face. "I'm getting a shower."

Between Maren and the memories, he needed cold water before his boxers couldn't hide how hard he might become.

Samantha was sexy, Steve remembered. An asset she used to turn a sale. The last time he'd been intimate with a woman before Maren came along was with Samantha, he mused. Cold water washed those thoughts away.

Snarled traffic wasn't Maren's idea of spending time with Steve yet she drew up a shopping list from the passenger's seat. They ate lunch and ducked into a bakery for morning croissants. They'd have those in bed they joked.

Dressing for the evening, Maren chose a sequined black camisole with a matching jacket and shimmied into a brand new pair of jeans and dressier shoes with slight heels. When she opened the cabin doors to Steve, sitting at the table, he looked up from his journal and whistled.

"We'll just eat at this club?" Maren asked.

"Yes, it's close." He had already changed into jeans, a button down shirt and Docksiders. "So close we can walk."

"At the marina bar?"

"How do you think Eric lined this up?" Steve grinned. "I gave the manager his name weeks ago. There was a sign yesterday." Maren had been preoccupied; tonight, far more relaxed.

"You're full of surprises," she said. Steve helped her on with her coat while she picked up her hair, worn down this evening. He grabbed his leather jacket.

Nearing eight o'clock, they spotted Alicia and her boyfriend Drew. Steve knew Alicia from work. "Purple and black, love it Alicia," he noted while pecking her cheek.

He fell into conversation with Drew, who worked in IT and had met Maren around the office.

"I tolerate PCs from nine to five, but I'm an Apple man," Drew told her and Steve when computers came into conversation. "The Think Different ad campaign...brilliant."

"Drew's sorry they didn't pick him for the Switch ads," Alicia said, as they each told about their favorite celebrities touting moves to the Mac.

"How was the first night of Hanukkah?" Maren asked. They each nursed a mixed drink and ordered several appetizers. "I almost called you."

"That bad with Mark's mom?"

"With others there, she dialed it back. Still snarky. She can't help herself."

"There's Dr. Romano and his wife." Alicia focused on Maren. "Steve's friend?"

"Steve." Maren tapped his wrist. "We should say hi." Once she stole his attention, they looked over. "On second thought…"

Their eyes met. Steve's best friend had just sat down with Pam and a man whose arm enveloped her. Jerry. She'd once introduced him as a family friend, not a lover designing to steal her out of Steve's bed. Visceral jealousy coursed.

Steve saw his brownish-blond hair, thick and wavy enough to catch anyone's attention first. The faint beard made Jerry look younger, but Steve knew he was a few years ahead of them, probably 42 by now. He dressed well, with a crisp shirt and jacket parted atop casual slacks.

Pam wore a red shirt for the holidays as Steve's eyes lowered to the neckline scoop. Liz never brought as much relief as when she and Tim slid chairs to sit down.

"Eric's pumped. Liz, a drink?" Tim asked, shaking hands with those he hadn't met.

"Seven and seven," she replied. "So great having Mom and Dad babysit."

"Two weekends in a row," Steve said. "You social butterfly."

"Stop looking over there," Liz chided him. "That's Jerry?"

"Unless she's two-timing him, too," he whispered sarcastically. "This band better play soon." Steve started to the bar, sat back down as the lights dimmed and Eric's group took to the small stage. The All Nighters: musicians in between hitting the books offering steady alternative rock. Steve recognized the lead singer, a girl Eric had known from Bethesda. She had a good voice and a body that looked just as smooth, Tim announced.

Across the room, five people around another table swayed and spoke.

"She cooked a side dish?" Paul repeated as Shelly told Thanksgiving stories. "Anyone in the ER?"

"That's rude," Pam interjected. "You told him that comment?"

"I said it," Jerry confessed. "Honestly Paul, beyond boiling water for pasta, maybe pancakes, she's lost in a kitchen." He rubbed his hands over Pam's back soothingly, as if that would ease the verbal jab. Jerry pulled Pam in for a kiss.

"She did bake and left us cinnamon rolls. Redeemed herself," Paul replied. "Pasta. No. Sauce. ER trip there, too."

"Waffles," Pam defended. "Omelettes. How quickly you forget."

"Paul says you can't make sauce unless your ancestors came from Italy. I can warm it. Can't generate it," Vicki replied, getting group amusement.

Steve finally got up for drinks. Maren found the ladies room. With the crowd, she had to scoot past Pam's table. No one noticed until her return.

"Maren, thanks for coming," Shelly said. "Eric's excited you could be here."

"We wouldn't miss it. He sounds great," she replied. "Hello Pam, Vicki." Paul got up to greet Maren kissing her cheek.

"Maren, this is my husband Jerry Carlton…Maren Mitchell, a friend of Steve's." Pam's report that Steve Kramer had someone, possibly serious, in his life would assuage Jerry's guilt—if any existed in the first place.

"Any relation to Mitchell Enterprises?"

Maren smiled uncomfortably. "I don't work for that company," she said. Wouldn't if her life depended upon it, but she left that out. "I'm a marketing associate and graphic designer at West Riverside."

Heading back with drinks, Steve saw the scene play out at Pam's table. Maren and Jerry chatting it up, Paul obviously one-upping Pam. He decided to deliver Maren's drink where she stood.

"Pam, Jerry," Steve acknowledged, alongside Maren. It was the first time he'd seen Pam since the elevator incident, and he wondered what Jerry knew.

"Hello, Steve." Jerry took his hand resting on Pam's thigh to shake. "How was your Thanksgiving?"

"Uneventful," Steve said. "The best kind." Doubtful she shared, he thought.

"This one actually attempted a side dish." Paul instigated as usual. "The salmonella hasn't hit yet."

"Get over it," Pam complained, looking for rescue. Jerry nodded.

"Notice: I didn't say a word," Steve said. Pam sensed a double meaning. She knew he wasn't pleased she had shared what he'd kept silent between them for 10 years. "How's your father?" Steve redirected.

"On my case, so clearly fine. You referred him to cardiology? No post-op appointment yet?"

"Not yet. I'll discuss it when he comes in," Steve told her.

"You need to tell him about cardiac rehab, Steve," Pam insisted. "He's not listening to me."

Steve sipped his seven and seven, needing it. "I'll leave that to cardiology. Not sure how you discharge patients, Dr. Morgan," he said. "Doctors don't hound. Though I guess daughters do."

"Not a happy scene when she starts on him." Jerry put his arm around Pam. "Though I know she cares." He changed course. "Paul says you have a boat here in one of the slips."

"Yeah, we're staying the weekend on it. A change of pace." Steve looked at Maren lovingly. Though she made small talk with the women here, Maren looked as if they could move on.

"If you'll excuse us...have a good rest of the weekend, Jerry." Steve extended his hand again. "Pam," he said, shaking hers. She looked into his eyes. Their last parting: hands hadn't met, lips had. A natural thought standing with a birds-eye view down her blouse, open to the swell of her breasts.

"That had to be interesting," Liz whispered as they returned.

"Leave it alone, Liz," Steve told her. "We're here for Eric."

They turned their attention once again to the All Nighters. Eric took to the microphone for several songs.

"He really sounds good," Drew said.

"I'll call Eric this week," Steve told Liz. "Since we're walking back, you want one last round, Maren?"

"Why not? Rum and coke...weak." She admired him walking away.

"You're so in love," Alicia told her.

"I am," she admitted. They fell back into conversation though she couldn't take her eyes off Steve. He really helped her through this weekend.

"Two rum and cokes," Steve told the bartender. "One light, one double."

"Of all places to meet, Steve Kramer," a smooth voice said as the woman speaking sidled up to him uncomfortably close, pushing into his body.

"Samantha." Steve eyed the length of her. Samantha indeed. "Never seen you here. What brings you tonight?"

"Don't be silly, Steve," she said tossing her black hair past her shoulder. She slithered against him. "It's been too long. Your brother's in the band. I knew you'd be here."

If how she dressed in leather skirt and jacket with her breasts tautly banded in white, and with the red Corvette Steve knew she probably drove to get here were any indication, Samantha may have had a master's degree in slick moves.

Tonight she honed in, selling something he felt sure. Samantha turned her back to the bar, jutted her chest out and cozied along Steve. Eyes bore into his. She bent her leg, one stiletto touching the bar behind them. Steve knew that black stocking ended at a garter…and a lot more.

"How are you?" Her voice husky, she reached over as if to ply lint from Steve's shirt. Only there was nothing that needed to be removed from it.

Except for her hand, Maren thought. Her mouth fell open. "What the hell?" she mumbled. Alicia caught Maren's glare.

"She's hitting on him," Tim said. "Another former girlfriend?"

"He never brought her home," Liz said, equally as taken aback. Mystery woman's hand had run up Steve's shirt toying with the top button as she leaned into him. Their table wasn't the only one noticing the barfly activity.

"Paul…who's that with Steve?" Pam's voice carried unusual urgency.

"Marone," Paul let slip in Italian. Really drowning in estrogen he thought. Steve the Stud Muffin would be his new name.

Pam hadn't heard that slang in years. Jerry pivoted his head, needing no translation. Vicki sat up. That woman's dark eyes, long, black hair, and a lanky, leather-clad body made them all take notice.

"Ah…a medical sales rep," Paul said, biting back anything else in either language.

"Does she call on your office?" Vicki asked.

"You better hope not." Pam looked across. Liz Kramer stared at her brother, along with Maren, with a he-sure-as-hell-gets-around gaze. Two different tables. Similar sentiments. Until, the tension ended.

"No, we're not leaving together, Samantha." Steve took her hand effectively, removing it from his body. "We're done. We've been done."

"Really?" Samantha breathed the words onto him, pitching harder. "That's what you said before." She took her drink's cherry, teasing

264

with it on her lips before savoring it on her tongue. Swallowing. "And every time, you come back for more."

"Have a good night," Steve said staring her down one last time. He strode toward his table, depositing Maren's drink on it and downing half of his the moment he took his seat.

"Your entertainment?" Jerry asked Pam, noticing she followed Steve with her eyes like a cat trailing two mice as Steve met the laser beam of women's eyes.

"If Maren doesn't know about her, she sure as hell does tonight," Paul added. Vicki and Pam pounced on Paul demanding do-tell-us.

"OK, he got more than medical equipment." Paul knew damn well that when Samantha slithered along nine years ago, Steve's post-Pamela drought had ended. On. Off. On. As of last year: Off.

"Sparks have to be flying," Pam said. Maren's problem so why did she care?

Jerry Carlton studied his wife. "I'm getting you a drink," he said. "I can only hope to be as lucky at the bar." Pam shot her husband her favored screw-you sneer, realizing how it lacked the "screw-you, Steve" alliteration. Steve had usually returned a hearty chortle to it.

Moving closer, Jerry asked, "Should I invite her to join us?" He had heard the Paul story, wondering if his wife embellished it. He hadn't hushed his question.

"Every man's fantasy, I'll tell ya," Vicki Romano said innocently.

"No fantasy for some." Pam's face radiated delight.

For once, Paul Romano wanted to take a life rather than save one. Fortunately, Pam said nothing more. Fortunately for Steve, Maren kept the carnage down at their table.

"That was awkward," he said, eyes pleading forgiveness for a sin he hadn't committed but felt the heat over nonetheless.

"This month's word." Maren reached for her drink and took one full swig.

"Who the hell was that?" Liz prompted. Drew and Tim grinned, glad it wasn't them, half wishing it was as the woman had stolen their long looks.

"Samantha." Steve sighed. "We used to go out. Of all weeks to be blessed with more estrogen…she saw that Eric was playing. Showed up. Happy?"

Looking at Maren, Steve took a long hard gulp of his double-dosed rum and coke, diminishing it. Maren said nothing. Maybe it was the heady atmosphere or the alcohol. She plied Steve's thigh under the table.

Already aroused, that stirred him more, and with way more women in his midst than his mind could handle, one thought reigned supreme. His hand moved to Maren's hair. He kissed her gently.

"Let's get out of here," he whispered as he nuzzled her neck, her ear.

How could they leave without offending anyone, Maren wondered. "Liz, you never told me your brother was so popular?" Maren took another sip. Casually.

"Both brothers," she answered seeing Eric off stage, chatting with band fans, especially a dozen young women. "You're taking it in good stride. My brother's madly in love with you, Maren. You have to know that."

"Observant sister," Steve said, offering his hand to Maren, eyes to Liz and his brother-in-law. "Tell Eric he did great. We're calling it a night. Alicia, Drew, great seeing you. Happy Hanukkah."

"Six more nights." Alicia put her head on Drew's shoulder. "We won't be staying much longer. Have a good one."

Steve brushed Maren sliding his hand down her back the farther away they got. "I'm stopping in here," he said, pointing to the men's room. "Once we're out that door, I have serious plans."

She took the hint ducking into the women's restroom, stopping to apply a fresh red streak of lipstick. As if he needed any help finding her mouth. They met in minutes, Steve placing his hand where he last left it, pulling her in for a lust-filled kiss. They walked out hurriedly locking lips one other time before the pier. Maren made a chase of it on the home stretch, losing her one high heel along the gangplank. Getting to the swim platform she caught her breath.

Steve stopped to retrieve her shoe. "You won that one," he said. "You're mine now." When they got into the cabin he tossed her shoe down, his jacket and her coat aside. Maren wanted new memories. Steve would deliver.

"Pick a spot because in five seconds, I'm taking you where and how I want." Steve's voice was thick, eyes dark. He looked at her with a kind of raw need and heady desire that to Maren looked so tangled it could snap.

She moved from the galley into the cabin… slowly, almost still. Her heart throbbed against her chest, stirring excitement. She couldn't speak. Turned to him. Filled her eyes and mind with him.

"If anything's off limits, tell me."

Maren leaned up. Whispered. Licked her very red lips.

"Perfectly reasonable." He pulled her tight, grabbing a fistful of hair in one hand, feeling her up with the other. "There's nothing under here." His thumb brushed her nipples, standing at attention.

"Minimal," she managed.

Remembering how he liked it couldn't have been more of a straight-up turn on. Using both hands he raised the sequined garment over her head and threw it to the cabin floor. "I've wanted to strip these clothes off of you all night."

"Well, here I am." Their mouths met, tongues tangling, lipstick rubbing off onto him.

He unbuttoned her tight jeans and drove both hands down, seizing her glutes. Steve's eyes went wild. "Holy hell, I didn't know you even owned one of these." He pushed her back onto the bed. "Unzip those…now."

Maren complied and with a two-handed, forceful tug he yanked off the jeans that had hugged her long legs. She elbowed up on the bed. Steve stood back, appreciating the sight. No bra, only a thong. Maren got up, grabbed at his buckle, undoing it, sliding off his clothes. She unbuttoned his shirt, growing more desperate. She stripped him as he'd done her.

"Now, put those heels back on."

Maren slipped into them. Her own raw need starting to swamp her, she fell back onto the bed. He straddled her, fingering the thong. "This thing can't be too comfortable, right?"

"Not in the least," she said. "Make it worth my wearing it?"

His mouth moved over the silky triangle, biting it, grazing it until with both hands he tore it off, startling her. Maren jumped. Steve's appetite tore into her, parting limbs, finding flesh. Hands landing on her hips he tugged her closer as she gasped, throwing her head back, to the sides, into the pillow. She couldn't take in enough air. Her breathing felt blocked. Her only outlet deep moans of pleasure. Steve had never—ever—been this rough, this demanding, but she didn't care. Loved it. Wanted it. Needed it.

Maren burst violently right in his hands—hands still affixed to her hips. He let her go, slowly, as he heard whimpers mixed with aftershocks proving just how thoroughly he'd satisfied her. With a broad smile, his eyes narrowed into hers.

"Look at me," he said, running his hands subtly over her, teasing her nipples, caressing her stomach that had just hardened and become soft again.

"Don't leave me here waiting." She breathed it out. "I need you."

"Can you take more?"

"Steve…"

No sooner had she said it, but he whipped her around onto her stomach. "This way for a change." His hands seized each breast reaching underneath to slide her closer. Steve's mouth made it to her throat, vulnerable as he held her.

He bit it ever so gently, scraped his teeth against the nape of her neck as he brought her up and into her heels again with one arm holding her tight against him. His other one reached possessively, plunging fingers, coursing through her until she felt enough pressure that shot through every muscle, every nerve ending, even some she hadn't known she had.

Maren went lightheaded, glad that he held her with one arm. She'd lost total control as if she was the vessel and he seized the helm. Within seconds, he took more. Commanded more. Plunged into her and buried himself deep.

She loved every bit of him. Close and tight. As she lost her breath, once again, all she could offer were firm squeezes telling him how good he felt inside.

Her hands dug into the comforter, loving how he moved against her skin. Her hair fell into tangles in front of him. Steve loved the scent of it as he veered closer with each thrust. Maren cried out.

"Want me to stop?" he asked.

"Don't you dare." Minutes passed. She shuddered, he groaned, and with his weight pinned her to the bed. She caught her breath a final time, consuming air more freely. "I don't think I've ever had sex quite like that," she said.

Steve laughed, his own breath warm on her. "I lit your fire?"

"I'd say it would need the fire department, but…"

He buried his head into her, laughing harder. "Mmm...fueling more fantasy."

"Oh shut up." Maren squared herself to him on her elbows. "Plunging neckline Pam and sudden rush Samantha, not to mention several mixed drinks, got *you* going."

"Only one crucial factor you left out?" She eyed him suspiciously. "Maren—my goddess in and out of my bed." He squeezed her into him so that he could feel every ounce of female flesh pressed against his skin.

"One factor you forgot," Maren added. "In the movie, Harry says you pretty much want to nail every woman you see...and we know you saw a few tonight."

"Nine or 90 women...I only want to nail this one," he said, positioning her at the ready.

"Will we ever be here alone without rocking this boat more than the waves?"

Steve held her beneath him, one wrist to the side. Kissed her. Passionately. "I sure as hell hope not."

Chapter 18

The beginning of December meant a busy week at work. For Alicia: Hanukkah each night. For Maren: getting her vacation request and comp time.

"In two weeks, you're outta here," Alicia said, having lunch Thursday, the first day they'd connected in any personal way. They sat with Vicki, whom Alicia got to know Saturday, with so many others.

"Don't remind me...I'm overwhelmed with my to-do list," Maren said.

"Tell me about it," Alicia added. "I'm interviewing. We're that busy."

"Wow...anyone I know?" Maren asked.

"Remember Gabe, from art school? Alumni office recommended him." Alicia paused for more of her morning jolt. "Plus outside candidates. Gabe's stopping by today."

"If it's who I think he is, he was talented, and we got along really well." Maren considered. "Alicia, this trip isn't putting you in a bind?"

"Not at all. Steve stopped me yesterday as we both grabbed coffee." Alicia lifted her head. "He thanked me. Twice. Never minded my purple, either. Must mean *a lot* to get away."

"Why not? He's had a long year, a lot of changes—boat, promotion—and you Maren." Vicki smiled. "To resist teasing you during football season...hmm, must need a break."

"I haven't seen him since Sunday after we got rid of the Mitchells," Maren said. "Sorry. They pumped Dylan with questions. Threatened I think by Steve becoming part of his life. Glowering alone indicated that."

"At least you weren't glaring at Steve Saturday," Alicia said. "After you left, we all moved over with Vicki and Paul."

"And Pam and Jerry?" Maren smiled. "I saw how Pam looked at me when Samantha appeared."

"I don't know Pam that well, but she quizzed Paul," Vicki revealed. "Jerry noticed her. We all watched to see if you killed him." Vicki laughed.

"Instinct told me dating Steve could be interesting." Maren remembered Alicia's advice. "I did ask questions."

"Any answers?" Alicia asked.

"Some, not all." Maren peered into her coffee.

"He definitely is into you." Alicia lowered her voice. "Steve whisking you out of there spoke volumes." She winked at Vicki. "He's so hot for you."

Unless there was heat in other places, Maren thought. Any doubts coupled with pulling information out of him still bothered her.

"Blazing," Vicki added. "Of course, my husband pointed that out. Liz overheard, Pam caught on."

"Paul is…descriptive," Maren acknowledged. "Liz uses some charged words describing Pam. How was that?"

"Nothing too personal," Vicki said. "Especially around Shelly and Eric."

"Gabe's waiting. Good talking to you, Vicki. Maren, see you upstairs."

"Nice chatting with you, too," Vicki told Alicia. She waited a moment, turning to Maren. "You seem down. Everything OK?"

"Busy…worse, working and packing for our trip. Saturday, Steve's at his parent's. I'll catch up. His parents gradually moving; mine might also. So much change," she said, pushing back into the chair. "Steve hasn't talked about it, but I know he lost two patients. Not sure what I'm supposed to do when that happens." Maren looked perplexed.

"Women always feel overwhelmed this time of year. Scale down." Vicki reached to Maren's wrist. "I know from being married to Paul when a case gets really involved, you have to give them space to figure it out."

"I know they can't talk about it," Maren said, truly glad she had someone who understood. "Beyond patient privacy, Steve has this independent, I-don't-talk-about-things approach that drives me freaking crazy."

She laughed. Vicki could picture it. "Steve's a perfectionist pushing 40." She locked eyes with Maren. "Antsy being alone, unlike when I first met him."

"I forgot the 40 part," Maren said. "Would Paul ever be serious long enough to give me sound advice on Steve?"

"I'll plant that seed," Vicki said. "We need to get going, but look…though this is all new, when I see him with Dylan, it's like he's the child Steve never had in his life. We all know he loves kids…we both see he loves you."

"Sometimes Steve acts like a kid," Maren acknowledged. "I know what you mean. Dylan adores him." She paused. "He's a good kid despite stomping and stalling over homework. More back talk this week. I think he picked up on his grandparents and feels caught between liking Steve and their snarky attitude."

"Kids are smart. Running the older sibling class, I have some books for parents. One called *The Angry Child* says it's sometimes OK to be angry, never to be mean."

"I could use that book for sure." Maren had a low tolerance for Dylan's behavior especially with a frantic schedule and holiday approaching. "How you feeling these days?" The two rose from the table walking out.

"Morning sickness has been a bear," Vicki said. "Hoping it gets better. As this week will for you."

"When are we telling Dylan about Florida?" Steve asked when they had dinner at Maren's Friday, the first December weekend. Quick and easy take-out pizza and salad had become their habit.

"Don't come up here, Steve," Dylan shouted from the banister on the second floor. "Darn it."

"I'm talking to your mom." Steve expressed puzzlement turning to Maren.

"Let's wait until next weekend."

"Really?" He sighed. "I'm on call. Sucks." Steve ducked behind the kitchen island.

"You did that on purpose," she said. "If we tell him now, I'm the one dealing with his questions. I haven't even looked over the Disney book."

"Read it tomorrow when I'm at my parents. We tell him Sunday." He was decisive, used to the instant gratification he received in the operating room.

"But…fine," she relented. She'd seen Steve resign himself too easily to defeat this week, so let the directive roll.

"Hey…who was that I saw you having coffee with the other day?"

"I dunno, Paul?" One day ran into the next. "We have coffee a lot."

"No…he had blonde hair. Italians do *not* have blonde hair."

"Oh," she remembered. "A guy from art school Alicia's interviewing. Gabe."

"Hmm," Steve murmured. "Seems like you know him well."

"How so?"

"Just…looked that way." He mulled it: Maren chatty; Gabe guy, grinning. Lots of grinning. With a Ravens tie around his neck, but he let that image alone.

"What way?"

"Friendly," Steve said. "He touched your shoulder. Back. Hand. Three times."

"Oh, Steve…he did not. We're friends." She studied him.

"No, three times," he insisted. "Another thing: Next year, we're having a big tree. Big, you understand?"

We, she considered. Roll again, she reminded herself, having put up only a small artificial tree. Sunday during football, frustrating Steve even further.

Maren stood in the kitchen, hands on the counter. "*We* are going to church this weekend. And next since I missed taking Dylan the first Sunday in Advent."

"I can't commit to next weekend," he said. "But I'll go with you Sunday."

"I'd like that." She shut out the kitchen light. "Dylan…we're coming."

"No, this is stupid…not yet."

"I could do without the men in my life telling me my every move," she said, now moving faster up the steps with Steve trailing.

"Hey, I just said I'd go to church. Ends by noon, right? Game starts at one."

Maren stopped, spun around and glared. Steve froze. It remotely resembled a Kramer-woman look. Good thing he committed to a worship service. God help him, he thought.

273

"Why don't you want us up here," Maren asked, impatient with him and Steve. "Dylan…"

He'd gotten out of the bathtub and was supposed to towel off. At six he could, but the puddle on the bathroom floor not to mention water streaks along the carpet, triggered Maren's chagrin.

Dylan stood, damp hair and wet body underneath pajamas that looked pulled on in a hurry. Something else stole their eyes underneath his bed. Maren got down on her hands and knees.

"What is this?" She tugged on the evidence, mildly soaked but stashed out of sight. She unfolded it.

"He's lost it…totally. Call in psych."

"Steve…" A shut-up glance and explain-this-now one made it to her guys.

"Don't be mad," Dylan said. "Grandma Mitchell gave it to me. Said I'd be ungrateful if I didn't use it, but I don't like it."

Maren's eyes relented. "Good that you accepted it. You said 'thank you'?"

"Yeah, like you taught me, but I hate it."

"Hate is a strong word." Maren looked at Steve then burst out laughing. "That's so my mother-in-law. Just like her to buy a Ravens towel for a Steelers fan. And guilt her grandson." Maren shook her head. "Pull another towel out of the closet, Dylan. Get dried off and into other PJs. Put it in the donation pile."

"Paul and I could have some fun with it. Bonfire!"

"Steve…"

"Has to dry off first." Three looks from her in one night—his limit. "OK, chill. I'll get Dylan changed." Steve was staying and wanted to change her mood fast. She smiled. He raised his eyebrow. "I'll bring you another smile. As soon as I'm done with Dylan."

Maren kissed her son goodnight, angled her head to Steve as she left the room. "Little boys," she muttered on her way out.

Steve seemed impressed by Luke's sermon, even more that he kept it to 23 minutes. Maren couldn't believe he'd clocked it, but chose to focus that he went to church and read the bulletin in detail. She chuckled when Steve remembered to grab the newly laundered Ravens towel reminding Maren to donate it to the holiday mission. "Sure to find a loving home," he told her.

That afternoon, Dylan became the entertainment since the Steelers lost 24-6 to Houston. Orlando became Dylan's laser-beam focus.

"Can I go on Test Track?" "When do we leave?" "How do we get there?" and Maren's favorite "Steve doesn't have to work. There's no hospital at Disney World."

"That was a good one," Steve said. "Your son cracks me up."

They told Dylan after the football game as Maren made dinner. Excited to tell his friend, Dylan ran next door.

"At least he's pumping them with questions," Maren said clearing the counter as Steve loaded the dishwasher. "They spent a week there this summer. Dylan will persist until he gets every detail."

"So they'll ship him home in an hour." Steve cornered a look at the microwave clock, clinching his arms around Maren. "Ah...how 'bout if we go..."

Maren leaned into him. Stopped. "Steve," she said, splaying fingers on his chest as she reached for her cell on the kitchen island. "Hello," she answered. Steve tried to nuzzle her, and Maren held him back. "Gabe, how are you?"

Steve rolled his eyes and pointed to his watch, then to the upstairs. Ignoring him, Maren moved to the family room, phone in hand.

"You're kidding. When did Alicia decide?" She listened. "That's fantastic. Welcome to the department." Maren sat down on the sofa, leaning her elbows on her knees. "Don't worry...I'll bring you up to speed if you need me to."

Steve had followed her and plopped himself on the sectional, eavesdropping.

"Can't wait. It'll be great. Stop by this week...for coffee." Maren looked over at Steve. Perturbed. "You too. Hopefully I'll see you before Christmas."

She flipped her Nokia after saying goodbye. "Steve...what *is* the problem?"

"Problem? I don't have a problem."

"Sure looks like you do." Maren stood, hand on one hip. "I know Steve. We have an hour with Dylan next door..."

"No, 45 minutes now," he corrected.

"And you...want me. No, you want sex," she said. "Forget that we have work tomorrow. We're leaving next Friday, not only for vacation, but for a major holiday. Not to mention, your professional meeting."

275

"Oh stop, Maren." Steve got up. "Note, I'm walking to the kitchen. Sex is upstairs." He stopped. Smirked. "Well, and over there too, I guess." He pointed to the sectional. Puppy eyes again peered at her.

Maren followed Steve into the kitchen where he opened the refrigerator and crouched peering into it. "You're letting the cold air out. Honestly, if it's not sex…it's food. We just put away lunch."

"Basic needs," he replied, still searching. "Look, I don't see why you answer every phone call when we hardly have time alone together, that's all. Besides…who is this guy Gabe?"

"Close that door." Was he even listening to her? "I told you a friend from art school Alicia just hired."

"Oh, fantastic," Steve said mocking tone she used over the phone. "Doesn't he watch football on Sundays?"

"If it's not sex or food…it's freaking football. You're anyone to talk about being preoccupied."

"What's that supposed to mean?" Hunger got shut into the fridge.

"It means you're just full of yourself and what you want, Steve." Maren fumed now. "Listen to your questions. Meanwhile, I've put up with your stonewalling mine about your brother, your past, why you never leveled with me, and…"

"I did level with you."

"No, I had to drag it out of you. Stop interrupting. Let me finish, dammit." Maren slammed her hands on the island.

"You swore. You just swore." Steve half laughed but quickly snapped back to serious.

"See…always the last word. You're full of yourself. You need a fan club."

Steve scowled at Maren. "Looks like you're forming a fan club for blondie in the marketing department."

"Blondie," she said coolly. "Did you just call him blondie?"

"Yeah…so?" Steve smirked again.

"You're anyone to talk." Different rules for him, of course. Vicki and Alicia wondered if she would kill Steve at the club. How 'bout if she did it right now?

"I put up with Pam making you patently miserable… and then, sleazy Samantha in front of all our friends…and family." Maren's voice crept louder with each complaint.

Steve walked closer. "I never meant for you to deal with them. I didn't want to myself."

"Deal with them...knowing would've helped. But you'd have to share. Talk. You wouldn't have told me unless you had to." Maren was on a roll not even managing a breath. "Do you have any idea how humiliating it was to sit there and watch that...that little ho of yours with her hands all over you?"

Steve laughed now. "Let's get one thing clear. I never paid her." He paused trying not to erupt a second time. "The hospital might have when she sent them an invoice, though."

"Very funny," Maren said. She saw him approach her, reach out a hand. "No, don't even think you're gonna sweet talk me."

"Maren...really. I'm sorry. You've been tremendous." Steve strode up to her and nuzzled his beard against her. "You really are sexy when you're pissed off.

"That's exactly what I mean. Sweet talk." Maren turned, considered his demeanor. Considered the time. "You need to leave."

"Now? Dylan's not even back."

"Too damn bad," she said. "I want some time to myself, in my house, preparing for a holiday, plus vacation and another week on the job."

Maren handed him the jacket he'd hung on the banister. "Go home," she said guiding him by the elbow to the door. "I have plenty to occupy my time. So much, Steve."

"Maren, be reasonable." But as he said it, he stepped onto her front porch putting on his jacket in the chill. "What a way to spend a free evening?"

"How 'bout you go to your boat and curl up with Demi and her pole or the chick that struts her stuff in that Pittsburgh movie...or Madonna." She drew in a breath. Looked him in the eyes. "I'm guessing you have even worse. A secret, really secret stash." Reaction alone confirmed she might be right. "I'll see you tomorrow. Maybe. Goodbye."

Suddenly, Steve got a very good view of the wreath attached to her front door. Only a pinecone fell off when she closed it harshly.

Maren flung the door open again. "By the way, I *can* swear."

The wreath only jostled this time. Nothing dropped to join the sorry looking pinecone, lonely on her porch. Steve bent down and set it aside. If pinecones had feelings, Steve understood how this one felt.

"I tried to warn him," Maren told Audrey as they talked about springing the news on Dylan. She and her parents had dinner Wednesday. "He's not the one dealing with the barrage of questions. And trying to get homework done."

"Homework sucks," Dylan said.

In her firmest tone—which Steve would probably say was the auditory equivalent of a Kramer-woman look—she pointed her finger and announced: "If I hear that word come out of your mouth again, you'll be grounded from TV one entire week. Make it month. Get ready for bed." She heaved a sigh. Dylan fumed as he left.

"You seem unusually tense tonight," Jack said. It was unlike her to mete out discipline unmatched to the misdeed. "You survived Thanksgiving. We had a great time at the Kramers. What is it?" Even as a child, Maren's anger masked worry.

Maren retrieved a manilla envelope from underneath a stack of mail and sat back down. "This came Saturday. Express mailed for effect." The return address read "Mitchell Enterprises, Seattle." She handed it to Jack. "A job offer, along with a letter. Go ahead... read it out loud."

Dear Maren,

We had such a lovely visit with Dylan. He's indeed a delight. We look forward to watching him grow into a confident young man just like his father.

While Mildred and I realize you attempt your best as a single mother, we're gravely concerned. It's so important that you work from home that I've drafted an offer with the firm. You could conference in by phone and come to the DC office once or twice a month. Please review this and respond by early January. Also, while you may be lonely, Dylan is quite impressionable.

Consider, Maren, what your actions broadcast about your character when you invite men to sleep in Mark's home, and when you take Dylan to stay at another man's apartment. We're astounded at your lack of judgment and poor behavior. Mildred and I only want what's best. Our sincerest wishes for a happy holiday season.

Warm Regards,

Walter & Mildred

As Jack concluded, Maren held her head at the table while Audrey nearly jumped from it, looking as if the blood had rushed to her face.

"The words I'd use to describe this would get me scolded far worse than Dylan and Steve. The nerve," Jack said. "Check on Dylan and let's talk."

"I promise not to scold you," Maren said realizing how she'd lost it.

She went upstairs, watched Dylan brush his teeth, and settled him into bed explaining he could read himself a book tonight. The kid's book about Florida got Dylan to stay put. She closed his door and trotted down the steps.

"I'm back." Her parents reviewed the job offer.

"Maren, how many men do you invite into...*your* house?"

"Dad...Steve," she answered, catching on.

"How often does he stay when Dylan's around?" Audrey asked.

"Once a week. Maybe twice," Maren answered. "Though Mom wanted Steve to answer the door half naked for Mildred and Walter."

"Maybe they'd have keeled over in a coronary," Jack said with disgust. "I know that's awful, but I'm livid with them. You don't need this stress when you've come so far."

"How are you going to respond?" Audrey asked, having changed her facial expression from boil to simmer.

"I'm putting it out of mind. Not sharing with Steve," she said. "Not after I kicked him to the curb Sunday."

"You did what?"

"I didn't literally kick him mother," Maren said defensively. "This arrived when he was off doing whatever." She breathed in, let air out slowly. "We had an argument, that's all. I've put up with a lot, and I needed time to myself."

"Women and holidays," Jack said, slanting his eyes. Women had taught him to steer clear in December. "So you took it out on Steve?"

"Not totally. You know he's not perfect."

"Maren, you shouldn't be so hard on him," Audrey implored. "Didn't you say a patient died this week?"

The tutorial tone again, Maren thought. "Two. I feel bad, but I can't make everything right." She brushed a hand through her long mane. "Back to the letter. It's another busy week, and Steve's on call this weekend. The following Friday, we leave for Florida where he's on the conference committee and presents. Walter can wait."

"That's my girl," Jack agreed. "Maren, people with true class— make that truly happy people— don't put other people down. They're too damn happy to make someone else miserable. Period."

"I know, Dad." Maren breathed out a deep sigh. "The job offer gives me a little more than I'm making now, but so what? I like getting out of these walls even with crazy mornings and getting to after-care on time."

"Imagine Walter Mitchell as your ultimate boss. This sweet offer could sour," Audrey said. "I think they just want you away from the hospital. Away from Steve."

"One ulterior motive." Jack realized he spewed sarcasm. "We're so proud of you, honey." He relaxed.

"We like Steve," Audrey said.

"We know," Jack and Maren said, simultaneously.

"Does Dylan?" Jack asked Maren.

"Are we *really* having this conversation?"

"Then you get my point. Their calling your character into question is patently ridiculous and out of line." He hugged his daughter. "If it's anyone's place to speak, it might be ours, but you've done nothing wrong. Not in our minds. Not at 32 years old."

"Get some sleep," Audrey said, kissing her cheek. "Ten days 'til Florida." They got their jackets and left. As Maren plunked her head into her pillow, escape was all she could think about as focused breathing eased her to sleep.

Maren physically and mentally shoved the Mitchell matter into her desk drawer. She would have loved to share it with Alicia, but couldn't. Not when she was hiring more staff. Showing her a job offer would look bad.

Maren hadn't seen Steve until after his hospital shifts. Given both weekends, they were excited to be together Sunday night. Maren, even more, for it would surely tick off Mildred and Walter, if they knew. She almost wished they did, she thought, waiting for Paul to fix his coffee on Tuesday. Maren smiled, remembering her refusal to cave to their complaints.

"Ms. Maren of the Seas," Paul said as he sat down. "You're floating my friend's boat this holiday season. What's your secret? Bright colorful lights or elegant white ones?"

"Both, I hope." Her grin faded. "I don't have it as together as you think."

"Don't underestimate yourself," he said, turning serious. "Vicki said you wanted advice. What's going on?"

"Trying to figure him out," she said. "Steve seems like an island, all to himself sometimes." Maren peered over at Paul. "I've called him on that a time or two," she said. "You heard he had to curl up on his boat with a beer, I'll bet."

Paul sneered, reached for her hand. "Maren, curling up—a girl phrase."

"Whatever, Paul. I have feelings, too."

"You know, Steve and I trained where they toughened us up on our feet, exhausting us. Made us self-reliant, and we learned to cast some things in nice tidy boxes. Without bows or package tags. No Martha Stewart or Dr. Phil. Of all surgeons, Steve connects with people, in his own way."

"More social than some." Maren agreed. She hung her head.

"He can be full of himself. We all can, but..." Paul's tone: a surgeon's command. "I've known Steve 18 years. I've not seen him this mystified by any woman, including Pam. Una bella Donna." Paul smiled. "You're a lovely lady."

She blushed. "Maren...you're smart, talented, giving. Have a career, house, cute kid. Love the water." Paul finally sipped his coffee. "I'd think you were after that boat, but he invited you on it, which I bet captivates Captain Steve in...oh *so* many ways."

"You can guess which ways, too," she said egging him on. "How do I help when the pressure here builds? I know R&R. Don't go there." Maren already had a sense how raw, real needs got satisfied.

"Time. Affection. A little distance to recharge," Paul said. "Don't take that one personally." He paused. "Play...in and out of bed."

"Paul, I knew it." Her touch to his shoulder evidenced that affection. "I blew it last weekend on time and affection. He got his distance, though." They both laughed. "I appreciate your thoughts."

"Oh, very important." He slid his chair underneath the table. "December 23rd, in Florida right?

"Yeah, we leave in three days for the conference, then go to my cousin's house."

"Well, you better invite *Monday Night Football* 'cause we play the Buccaneers—your cousin's team I bet."

"Paul, it's a game. Not nearly as intense as this place." Maren made a mental note, however.

"He calls you the goddess of a few things. Clearly not of sports."

"Oh he does?" Steve wasn't exactly the type to dish in the surgical locker room. Or was he? "Merry Christmas Paul." She smiled. "You still need serious help."

"I wasn't the one looking for advice, my dear." He hugged her at the shoulders. "We'll continue these coffees next year."

Since first graders celebrated holiday parties Thursday, Maren allowed Dylan to miss Friday's nothing-but-movies half-day. First time Steve and Maren sat down, Dylan's cotton ball clouds started to form as they flew in the morning sky.

Nestled into the boardwalk, their hotel provided easy access to the Epcot theme park, restaurants, and a giant waterslide that Dylan splashed into two dozen times by late afternoon. Maren fed him lunch by the pool while Steve attended his two-day meeting. Saturday afternoon would spring Steve for fun. Maren lounged in a chaise, large towel beneath her, ultra-relaxed.

"Nice," Steve said, nudging her thighs over, with a full hand on one, as he sat. Steve looked over his Ray-Ban sunglasses. Maren knew he wasn't commenting on the resort. "Teal used to be my favorite color...you held out on me."

"Are you kidding? I wasn't wearing a bikini when we first met." Maren yawned. Her nap felt good.

"Didn't keep me from dreaming of you in a lot less," he said nuzzling her.

"Stop. Where's Dylan? I dozed." Her eyes opened wide.

"Playing Marco Polo by the lifeguard." Steve wore a pink polo and navy dress slacks, name badge still around his neck. "Have you picked a place for dinner?"

"Seafood buffet across the lagoon at seven. Boat or short walk."

"I vote walk after sitting inside...and lounging," Steve said. "Ah..."

"What?" Maren studied his hesitation.

"They advertised this heavily to Columbia grads." He paused. "Pam's here." He edged his glasses lower, no point skirting the obvious. "With her daughter, who is with some fairy or nanny." Maren shot him a Liz-like look.

"You know…Disney child care."

"Well Steve, it's a big place," Maren said. "Be cordial. No elevators."

"Ha, ha. Jerry's joining them…staying over the holiday." Steve already felt claustrophobic. One of their mutual classmates all but assumed he and Pam married and talked to them at the break as if they had. "Hey…Dylan dude."

Dylan dripped beside them. "Steve, come on the slide."

"We're done for today. I'll go change."

"Watch me first." Dylan dashed as Maren called after him to walk, which he did with sprints. A minute later he stood atop the slide waving as they awaited a very large splash. Steve removed his glasses to wipe off the droplets.

Maren leaned up and smiled. She ran her hand through Steve's hair. "Thanks for bringing us. He's having a blast."

"So will we." Steve inched his hand up her thigh. Dylan still in the water, Steve pulled her face toward him, locking lips. One hand moved to her hip, fingertips sliding on the blue bikini.

"Restrain yourself."

"Why?" He raised himself off the lounge, leaning to plant a tamer kiss. Every inch of her filled his attentive eyes. "I won't be long."

Across the pool, Pam and Chloé surveyed where to park their towels. The younger blonde ran to the edge and jumped right in. The older one stood back. The look, the gestures—ones she hadn't seen in over a decade. Both broadcast what Steve Kramer wanted. Pam still read him better than a well-highlighted textbook. She had read plenty of both.

Maren dragged a T-shirt over her bikini and took the long slippery plunge as well. Steve joined them 15 minutes later, watched as Dylan and Maren did the slide, before getting hounded by Dylan to try it also. Maren leaned against the tiles of the pool deck to watch him.

"Wakes you up, doesn't it?" As she swam to the ladder, Steve grabbed at her T-shirt.

"This ruins the look, ya know." He smiled. "Let the sun dry you."

Dylan bobbed near them, got out, jumped back in. "Look mom, over there."

Dylan ran up to high five Water Goofy, putting in his character appearance. Maren used the opportunity to grab her camera with Steve's sidelong glances as she climbed the ladder. With outstretched arms, Maren shimmied out of the T-shirt, wrapped a towel around her, and followed Dylan, camera in hand.

"Ah...natural Vitamin D," Steve said as she returned. Drop the towel was what Steve really meant.

"Five minutes. Then, I'm getting ready ahead of you guys," Maren announced. Steve pouted. "Hazard of long hair...and one shower. We should leave by 6:30."

"You're the boss."

"I like the sound of that." Maren enjoyed his improved mood after tense weeks. "It's good to see you relax."

"It's good to see you...period," Steve said. "Great to get away." Steve put his head back, closing his eyes. "Which park tomorrow?"

"Magic Kingdom then we'll meet you at Epcot. Dylan so wants you to ride Test Track after you're done."

"I present mid-morning. We adjourn around three." They held hands and savored the sunshine in relative silence except for shouts of Marco Polo, splashes, and the lifeguard whistle once.

"As wonderful as this is, I have to get ready." Maren leaned to grab her bag beneath her chair. "Stop staring at me," she whispered. "The earlier we eat, the earlier we call it a night."

"Mmm, now you're talkin'." Steve enjoyed the peck she planted on him and watched her walk away.

Maren and Dylan started at Frontierland and in amazingly good time had hurled down both Big Thunder Mountain and Splash Mountain. She coaxed him through The Hall of Presidents, and wanted to at least walk through Cinderella's Castle before heading to others.

"This is for girls," Dylan muttered as she led him through the castle.

"Well, I am one, but you can like it, too." At least the weather was mild, making it comfortable, especially at a fast pace. "Smile. You chose lunch." Quick from a food stand and not timed immediately before a thrill ride.

As they took their place in another line, Maren glanced at her watch, reminding Dylan that they had to catch the monorail later.

"Mom, you can do this," a little girl encouraged behind them.

"What I do for you, child," the mother replied.

Maren turned around slowly, thinking she had recognized the voice. "Pam..." Maren removed her sun specs in the now shaded line. "Steve mentioned you were here. This must be your daughter."

"Yes, it's a small world after all, as they say." Pam nudged the girl forward. "Chloé this is Maren, a friend of ...a friend," she added awkwardly. "And this must be..."

"Dylan, my son." Maren shook her daughter's hand, vaguely recognizing her with light blonde hair, parted with long bangs pushed behind an ear. Brilliant blue eyes, too.

"See Mom, they're not scared," Chloé said, peering up.

Embarrassed now, Pam looked at Maren and barely whispered. "Jerry can't get here tomorrow fast enough." Pam rolled her green eyes—same color she feared turning next. "Sensitive to motion." They had just passed a sign bearing those precautions making Pam wonder if she should be standing here at all.

"If she doesn't want to ride alone," Maren said finishing Pam's thought, "she could ride with us."

Pam's eyes brightened, less fear-filled. "That's a thought, but I'll try this one."

"That's the spirit, Mom. Maybe you grew out of it."

Pam laughed. "Chloé repeats what we tell her. Only it's not so easy when we cajole you to ballet, is it?" Pam ran a hand over her daughter's back.

Inching in line, Chloé and Dylan chatted while Pam told Maren how well Steve presented on laparoscopic surgery before she decided to scoot out, after lunch. The childcare was great, but she'd promised Chloé a look at the castle.

"Mom had to see it, too," Dylan chimed in. "It's for girls. Test Track for us guys."

"Chloé wants to do that this evening," Pam said. "If I survive."

"You'll do fine, I'm sure," Maren said. The cast member attending the ride guided her and Dylan to board the train in the Space Port. After the flashing lights, tunnel, slopes, and turns Dylan bounded off at the unload station, and Maren glimpsed Pam.

285

"Air will help," Pam said, one hand clutching Chloé.

"Wait 'til I tell Dad you did this," her daughter exclaimed, pulling away to walk with Dylan.

In the sunlight, Pam took the nearest bench, digging into her purse for her sunglasses. Maren stood next to the kids as Dylan crinkled a map out of his pocket.

"Pam, you look a little pale." Maren hesitated. Pam was the physician. "We're headed to the monorail, meeting Steve at Epcot."

"I'll be fine," she said, honestly not so sure. "That's on our list. Only, if we tag along, I won't give Steve the satisfaction of this." She sniffed. "Well, maybe I should." As they walked to the monorail station, Pam realized Maren hadn't a clue. "You like boats, don't you?" Pam asked. "So motion doesn't bother you?"

"Well…I guess if the sea was rough enough it could."

"Not to sound awful but Steve can be…" Pam looked to see that the kids still chatted among themselves. "A real ass about this." She hushed that. "Macho about motion."

Data, Maren reminded herself, unsure how to respond. "Maybe he'll have empathy now."

Pam suppressed that she'd fall over if she saw that. As they got to the monorail entrance, the kids jumped at the prospect of sitting in the vehicle's nose, which by their position in the queue, looked quite possible.

"Will this be too much?" Maren asked Pam.

"I'll close my eyes if I have to." Tempted to, at least twice, she didn't want to miss seeing the kids so excited. With her hectic job, Pam tried to give Chloé as much fun as possible on this trip.

"You did great," Maren remarked as they got off. "This way guys." Blindly, Pam and Chloé followed as if Maren played tour guide. Pam had already heard Dylan pleading for Test Track. "Dylan insists he rides it with Steve."

"It's a guy thing, Mom."

"Macho," Pam said again.

"Seriously, I can ride with Chloé, Pam." Maren sensed Pam's reluctance with every inch forward. "Steve can…be nice," she added sure hoping he was. Within sight of the ride, Maren spotted him waiting. She would have loved a window into his thoughts as they strode closer. Instead, she saw Steve sniggering.

"It's a small world," Pam repeated, her voice brimming with discomfort. "Steve, meet my daughter Chloé. Chloé this is Dr. Kramer."

"Steve, please." He paused. Chloé looked familiar though Steve was sure they had never met. "She looks just like you, Pam." Except for the blue eyes, but he didn't say more.

Turning to Maren, he kissed her on the cheek. "It is a big place here," Steve said. Maren immediately recognized the phrase she'd told him yesterday and sensed seeing Pam at a medical meeting was one thing. Pursuing the parks another matter entirely.

"How was your day?" Maren asked.

"Interesting," he replied. Getting more so, he thought.

"We were in line with Pam and Chloé." Maren shuffled ahead next to Steve.

Dylan left Chloé's side, pulling at Steve to tell him how Maren screamed on a few rides. She rolled her eyes at Dylan's dramatic take.

"Mom, you can do this one, too. Take one for the team," Pam's daughter implored her. Maren smiled.

"We teach her too much, I swear," Pam said.

"Mom, really…just take that medicine Dad told you about."

Steve jerked his head around. Predictably, Pam thought. "What medicine would that be, Dr. Morgan?"

Maren cozied up to Steve's ear. "Be nice, she looked white before." Undeterred, Steve pulled the cord holding his sunglasses, landing them onto his chest. Eyes now on Pam, the corners of his lips curved to the blue sky.

"Fine…all of you. You, Jerry and my daughter," Pam muttered. "Chloé hand me that water bottle." Pam dug into her purse, pulling out a generic antiemetic box, downing two tablets. She chugged a mouthful of water, twisting the cap back on before handing it to Chloé. "Happy? Lose the smirk, Steve."

"You carry it with you, but it took three people to get to this moment?" As they made the turns in line, he lowered his voice. "Takes time to take effect. Unless it's not your first dose."

"Three words, Steve." He puzzled a look at her. "Grade point average."

He smiled. Looked down. The words had usually bought Pam Morgan a few extra moments in any given argument, certainly after graduation.

"Get over yourself already," Steve replied. "Probably the same formulation as 15 years ago." He tried to keep a straight face. "Now, avoid alcohol and…driving…oh, they do it for you here…careful you don't become tachy." Uttering the excuses she'd once given him for avoiding the medicine, he couldn't hold in his laughter.

If Maren's eyes had been daggers, Steve would have been bleeding, people stepping over him in line. At the looks of his getting into trouble for being a clear-cut ass, more than a decade after he'd already been one, Pam suddenly beamed. "*Who's* gonna need the drink at the end of *this* day?" Her long look was wasted on Steve.

They moved through the interior welcome center with the kids talking about how fast they'd zoom. As they got to another queue to be loaded into test cars, Pam shook her head. "Oh no…not in the same one." Each seated a group of people.

"Oh, get in," Steve said. "You might need medical attention." Pam glared at his mocking.

Dylan nestled into the front row between Steve and Maren, who had stepped in first. "Steve, sit," Maren ordered, turning toward him to fasten her seat belt and check Dylan's.

Chloé and Pam climbed in behind them. Steve did as directed, focusing on the thrill at least four of them would have. Exhilarating it was. Dylan screamed several times.

"Awesome dude," Steve said, stepping from their car at the unload platform. He turned to the seat behind him. "Gee, 65 miles per hour. I don't think I've ever sailed that fast." His choice of verb didn't escape Pam, who knew she annoyed Steve sailing only once with him, citing motion as to why she couldn't from that day forward.

"Mom, you're not a wimp after all."

Figuring he'd said enough, Steve kept silent before Maren or Pam hit his mute button for him. "Where next, Dylan?"

"Mom promised me Test Track Goofy."

"We're doing maybe two more attractions here, then the countries," Pam said.

"Which ones?" Maren asked, directing Dylan into the store as they followed.

"I'm not sure. We'll figure that out." Antarctica, far away from your boyfriend, Pam thought, but she didn't wish to cop an attitude with Maren, and there was no such country in World Showcase. "Thank you for offering to ride with Chloé. That was very kind of you,

Maren," she said. "Steve's right. You really are incredible." Pam turned to Dylan, who had latched onto his promised purchase. "I'm glad Chloé had someone her own age today. Now, you'll just have Steve. Kinda the same."

"You had that coming, honey." Maren laughed at Pam's derision. "Enjoy the park. Have fun Chloé."

"Bye Mrs…Mrs. Maren," Chloé said, waving as Pam clutched her other hand and led her off.

"Yeah…Mrs," Steve said, tugging at Maren. "We'll have to work on that."

"Not if you keep that up." Maren gave him a perturbed scowl from the check-out counter. "I told her you might have empathy."

"Empathy. With the crap she gave me about sailing. She didn't even try something I liked. Unlike you," he said, cozying Maren again for a kiss. "Better just the three of us," he whispered.

"You're still very full of yourself, you know that." For a moment, Maren didn't budge. "Dylan, you have the map. Where to?"

Chapter 19

Sunday morning at World Showcase, Maren and Steve enjoyed strolling, watching a few films, amid Dylan's remarks. When Steve suggested the two guys visit the huge LEGO store at Downtown Disney that bought good behavior through lunch. It helped that the Japanese chef chopped and entertained as he grilled along the large cooktop.

"Sure you're OK by the pool?" Steve asked Maren. "Come with us."

"I'll sit this one out," she said. "Besides, we're headed back for the light show. Go do guy stuff. I made a reservation for 6:30 at France, and I'm seeing the film."

"Not another movie," Dylan moaned.

"You'll learn something. Your mom gets to order…in French," Steve said. "Not making that mistake on another date." He caressed Maren's cheek. "Come on, Champ. Back in a few hours."

Dylan loved the giant LEGO sculptures. Only after they built creations at tables mounded with plastic bricks did Dylan and Steve peel themselves away, stopping for ice cream, and dashing into a clothing store.

Steve found Maren sitting with iced tea, reading on their balcony after he stashed items in his suitcase. Dylan beat him to the doorway.

"Mom, we built the coolest stuff," he told her. "Steve went shopping, too." By now, Steve had taken the second chair inviting Dylan onto his lap. Without asking, Steve stole sips out of Maren's glass but she didn't mind.

"Last minute Christmas shopping?"

"It's the 22nd," Steve reminded her. "I'm ahead of the game."

"With one tomorrow night, I'm betting there'll be no mad dash to the mall."

"I'm impressed." He took another sip. "You know the football schedule." Maren smiled, not giving away that she had a coach.

"Steve got you something…like PJs," Dylan added. "Won't stay on long, he said."

"Dylan…" Thankful he hadn't repeated the word "sexy," Steve merely groaned. "It's getting close to six. Shouldn't we head over?"

"Let's take the boat," Dylan said, jumping off Steve's lap, running inside.

Steve steered Maren with one hand. "What *did* Mickey get Minnie?" she whispered.

"You'll see…he's gotta keep Minnie happy or his dreams won't come true."

"Is this how your dreams work?" Maren asked the next morning when Steve brought croissants and coffee from downstairs. She sat up in bed, hugging the sheet.

"If your son wasn't watching cartoons, having cereal, I'd yank that and go another round," Steve said. "I think we've all enjoyed our stay." He sat on the bed. "Your parents are picking us up when?"

"Around 10:30. Mom's message indicated the flight is on time, barring back up at the rental counter. We can grab lunch before we head to my cousin's."

"I'll take Dylan down to the pool while you get showered. He said he has to say goodbye to the water slide." Steve rolled his blue eyes.

"He has to have his dreams, too."

Steve swigged the last gulp, leaning to snuggle. "Good to see you so happy."

"I am happy. Dylan's had a great time. Seeing him with you…" She stopped.

"Finish. What were you going to say?"

She collected her thoughts. "It's as if he's smitten or has fallen in love with you. Like I have."

Steve tugged more, inhaling the scent of her. "You have, have you?" He pulled away to glimpse all of her. "I love you, babe. In three days, you and I will get away. Just us."

"You haven't told me what we're doing?"

"It's a surprise," Steve said. "Now, you better get a move on. It's 9:50. We'll be at the pool."

The late checkout Steve arranged allowed Dylan to show off his waterslide speed to his grandparents then quickly change for lunch.

"Stay here with your folks," Steve said. "I'll oversee him, leave the bags at the desk, and we'll grab lunch at the Flying Fish."

Jack shared an iced tea with Audrey while Maren opted for water under the umbrella, sitting not far from the poolside bar.

"You see the couple across the way, with the little blonde," Maren said to her parents. "They just sat down."

"The one getting lathered with sunscreen?"

"Yeah. The one lathering her is Steve's former girlfriend with her husband Jerry. She attended the same meeting."

"The one who can't cook and had the…" Audrey trailed off as others were around she realized.

"Yes. Shelly's sister," Maren said succinctly.

"Been eventful?" Audrey inquired.

"She's not as bad as everyone makes her out to be, including Steve. Funny after ten years, they're still proving points over stupid stuff," Maren told them. "And yes mother, Steve can score high on stupid."

"Maren," Audrey said as she watched her daughter lean back.

Jack sized up Pam's red one-piece scooped to show enticing cleavage. "Their little girl is awfully adorable," Jack said. All men admired; only dim-witted ones broadcast it.

"Dylan seemed to like her." Maren finished her water, smiling. "I don't know if it's because I'm dating, but Dylan has taken a fondness to girls suddenly."

"A regular guy," Jack joked.

"There's Steve with him," Audrey said. "Now be nice, Maren."

The two of them approached the table. "We're ready if you are," Steve said. "Hang on Dylan, I'll get you some water. I think we can get to the boardwalk over there." As he turned from pointing, he spotted Pam steps away at the bar.

She stood in bare feet, with a beach towel wrapped as a skirt. He'd heard her say "Dr. Morgan." Clearly she'd taken a call on her cell.

"Shelly…how ya feeling?" Pam paused. "It's not even 24 hours. Give it time." The call continued. Dylan impatiently started to the bar where there was serve-yourself water. In the process of pouring he got the water nozzle stuck leaking a continued stream to the pavement.

Pam noticed, waving off Maren who came to the rescue. With her free hand, Pam fixed the nozzle for Dylan, offering a smile most moms recognize.

"Lay off the alcohol. Water. Cranberry juice. I gave you 500 mg plus the second script for pain," Pam said. "If I could run this through a lab, I could be sure it's right. But I'm here. Where are you anyway?"

Maren came up alongside Dylan, mouthed a thank-you to Pam, and started to steer him away. Pam covered the receiver with her free hand. "No problem," she said to Maren before resuming with her sister. "Oh really…"

A devilish grin crossed Pam's face as she shook her head. "How generous of Eric's brother." Pam appeared antsy. "Shelly, gotta run. Three scripts, right? You should be better by Christmas. Call me if you aren't." She lowered her cell to her side as she leveled Steve a stare.

"With a look like that I need a beer, not water," he said, stepping forward for a drink himself. "Pam, have you met Maren's parents?" Maren did the introductions. Audrey seemed pleased that Maren went easier on Steve. Even more pleased to finally lay eyes on Pam.

"Nice to meet you," Pam said, turning to Steve. "I thought we agreed we weren't encouraging Shelly and Eric."

Steve mildly choked on a gulp of water. "*We*," he said, motioning with his index finger between Pam and himself, "never agreed on anything other than being surprised. What's with Shelly? She alright?"

"She's got all the symptoms of a perfectly horrible UTI so I called in scripts. Not improved yet, and if I had access to a lab…" She stopped. "Do you think Paul could run a lab for me…for Shelly?"

"Paul's in Pittsburgh. It's Monday. I'll call Suzanna and tell her or my PA to run it through my office." Steve reached for his Blackberry leaving the message. "Here's my card. You heard what I said. She'll get the results to you. Tell Shelly to get there today. Tomorrow, they're out."

"Thanks, seeing as how she's so close, shouldn't be a problem." Her mood turned. "You gave them your apartment?"

"Pam, come on…they're on holiday break and Eric wouldn't let up."

"So you caved," she said, narrowing her eyes. Pam turned to Maren mumbling something about a keg party, Eric's band practicing until two in the morning, with a little weed added in.

"You're making that up just to pi..." Steve stopped mindful of present company. "Just to get me going."

"Mildly embellished and amused that it worked," Pam chuckled. She crossed her arms. "I'm not the one who has to go home to remnants of nearly a dozen college kids. You are."

"They're in graduate school," Maren offered.

"Still, 20-something-year-old minds," Pam asserted. Her eyes, Steve's eyes suddenly locked uneasily remembering where their minds had traveled at that age.

"What's happening over here?" Jerry asked as he ordered lemonade and a beer at the bar. Jerry, in swim trunks and a polo shirt, extended his hand to Steve and Maren, who introduced him to Audrey and Jack.

"Your wife's all over her sister and my brother...becoming Scrooge by the minute," Steve told him.

"He loaned his place to the happy couple," Pam scoffed. "Steve, while we put in 15-hour days, Shelly and Eric ran wilder...remember that." Anyone listening could hear her resentment.

Jerry interrupted. "She just learned about the upcoming 80-hour limit," Jerry said. Steve knew medical training would be capped soon, far from the grueling weekly schedules he and Pam faced.

"Let me guess." Steve turned to Pam, "You consider that slacking."

"She always considers her sister a slacker," Jerry added.

"Slacking at your apartment I'll bet," Pam said. "If your sense of organization still aligns like the Dewey Decimal system, schedule a cleaning before you unlock the front door."

"My apartment barely fits a small herd of residents on rounds," Steve said. "Any clean up is my problem, not yours." Jerry smiled. He knew his wife could instigate back and forth, and her former flame had just won this exchange.

"This is for Chloé," Jerry said, handing the lemonade to Pam. Hinting she take it there. Dylan ran ahead. As Chloé sat on the pool chaise, Dylan rushed up hugging her goodbye.

"Oh no...Dylan," Steve mumbled. His face snapped to Pam. Shared dread.

Pam heaved a sigh. "Not singing 'Joy to the World' to another love fest."

"Last month it was Steve's niece," Maren said. "Next month, who knows?" That brought a laugh.

"Like Paul…years ago." Pam qualified this after Steve eyed silence-it.

Time to walk away Pam determined. "It was a pleasure meeting you," she said to Jack and Audrey. "Enjoy the rest of your vacation, Maren."

"We will…thanks," she replied. "Please send Lovestruck back over. We need to have lunch."

"Merry Christmas, Pam," Steve offered.

"Scrooge thanks you…for your help with the lab." Pam smiled as Steve put his Ray-Ban specs back on and his palm on Maren's back.

Jerry had asked her a question, one Steve hadn't heard from the start.

"Well, yes, he is Dylan's grandfather," Maren answered.

"Do you think you'll take the job," Jerry asked.

"Just got the offer. It's on my list to review." Maren took full benefit of Steve's nudge toward the brick archway. "We're headed to lunch, then checking out. Have a good week, Jerry."

"You folks do the same. Watching the game tonight, Steve?"

"Wouldn't miss it." With that, Steve steered Maren and led the way.

"I thought they lived in Philly, as in the Eagles," Maren said out of earshot.

"Just conversation. Vacation starts now. I need that beer."

As they entered the restaurant, Jack pointed out the bar. "Order one, I'm driving."

"Hell yeah," Steve muttered back.

Dylan chatted with Audrey sharing that if he could be Water Goofy, it would be his ideal job someday. Maren and her mom ordered tropical drinks since they weren't driving either. With what Jerry brought up, it seemed as needed as Steve's Blue Moon ale that he sipped as soon as the waiter set it down.

"So what's this about a job offer?" Steve asked.

Maren uneasily looked over at Jack, who quickly caught on that his daughter hadn't yet shared the Walter Mitchell epistle with Steve. "I was going to mention it, but you were preoccupied before we left, and I really didn't want to dampen the mood."

"Dampen any more than a former girlfriend and the guy she dumped me for," Steve said humorously taking another hefty swig from his glass.

"You handled it well, Steve," Audrey offered. She turned to her daughter.

Maren motioned that with Dylan at the table, she'd keep this short. "Amid several concerns about my life, Walter offered me a job with the firm and a January deadline to reply."

"Those things she mentioned you and Maren are better off ignoring," Jack said. "I got steamed enough for you." That only piqued Steve's curiosity. Maren exhaled slowly. She leaned over, whispered into Steve's ear about being chastised for overnights, men and more.

"Your character?" Steve asked, incredulously. He swiped a caressing hand over her forehead, down her hair pulled into a ponytail.

"They have real nerve," Jack volunteered.

"You're not seriously considering this?" Steve asked.

"Stalling," Maren said. "The marketing world isn't as huge as one thinks. Jerry asked me before if we were related...I evaded the question. He must have seen Walter, asking him."

"How well do you think they know one another?" Jack asked.

"I certainly wasn't going to get into it today," Maren replied.

"Hell no," Steve said. "You don't owe Jerry any explanations."

"Steve...Dylan's right here," Maren chided. Jack's eyes told his daughter to let these things go as as she had so many other fears this past year.

"I wouldn't worry about Jerry," Steve said. "As smart as Pam is— her GPA trumped mine ever so slightly—Jerry has more common sense. Not like we're buddies. Just my casual assessment."

Their salads then entreés arrived. Topics purposely transitioned to Maren's cousin Courtney and her husband Josh, Aunt Nora and Uncle George, with whom Audrey and Jack would visit while Maren, Steve and Dylan stayed at Courtney's.

They arrived there by mid-afternoon in the suburbs of Orlando. Courtney was two years older than Maren having turned 34 that fall. As a special education teacher, she was off for the holiday break. Her bare arms quickly enveloped Maren as Courtney greeted her favorite cousin.

"Don't you look toned?" Maren kissed her on the cheek. "And tanned. I'm jealous." A light brunette, standing about the same height as Maren, she looked like living in Florida suited her fine.

"Love the hair, Mair." Courtney bobbed at the ponytail holding Maren's long locks. "Hopefully, you'll return with a little glow yourself," she said.

"Workin' on it." Maren introduced Steve and made a fuss over Adam, who was now three, toddling as they brought in their bags. Maren had not seen him since he was an infant, though Jack and Audrey had visited Audrey's sister Nora and her husband George almost annually, barring the year Mark died.

"Josh will be home by six," Courtney said. "The wellness center closes tomorrow and Christmas Day. No one wants massages then."

Maren explained to Steve that Josh, who had a master's degree in kinesiology and worked as a trainer, was also a licensed massage therapist and had been for more than ten years. "Darn, I was hoping he could fit me in," Maren lamented.

"Funny you should mention that," her cousin said. "We'll discuss massages later." Both women were surprised when Steve revealed that while his major in college was pre-med, he'd transferred in a hefty load of kinesiology credits from two summers at another school.

"You think Josh could teach Steve a few massage moves? I need to get rid of the knots back here," Maren said, curving her arm to her neck. "Keeping with the theme of Mickey making Minnie happy."

"Ah, we left that theme on the boardwalk," Steve said. "Minnie has to massage Mickey's tight traps."

"Josh sees an uptick in appointments with people overdoing it. Anyone working at a desk or using their upper body ends up on his table."

"I think these two will have a lot to talk about," Maren said, helping Courtney assemble a casual dinner. Later the guys would enjoy football while she and her cousin cloistered themselves by the fireplace, wine in hand, once Adam fell asleep.

Dylan and Adam played in the heated pool. Steve and Jack caught up, as they kept an eye on the kids. Steve looked back on nearly four months as chief of surgery, regretting that OR time got sacrificed to administrative details. Some of his conference colleagues weighed in on how to mitigate that by manipulating his schedule.

Audrey lounged with a Grisham novel. By early evening, Nora and George arrived. Uncle George had always encouraged Maren. The wide-open arms and thumbs-up gestures he gave her validated the tender spot she still had with him.

She'd last seen Nora and Courtney in the worst of circumstances—at Mark's services. Her relatives seemed settled into their retirement. Uncle George could use a few fitness sessions by the size of his belly he'd pulled Maren up against, but he wasn't obese. Fewer beers and more rounds of golf, which he and her father planned to partake of tomorrow, seemed perfect. After dinner, Audrey and Jack followed Nora and George to stay at their home, 20 minutes away and where they'd all celebrate Christmas Eve tomorrow.

"Tell me, how serious is this?" Courtney asked, pouring them pinot grigio beside the sofa that faced the fireplace. "Aunt Audrey can't say enough about Steve. Spill, Cuz."

Maren curled her legs, clutching the sweater she put on as the air outside dipped into the 40s. The fire offered warmth. "You already know from our weekly calls and emails, we met when Dylan got sick, and I took this job. We dated all fall. What else is there?" Maren sipped her wine.

"A man that good looking, single...he's 39, right, with a few girlfriends behind him, has to excel at a few things." Leaning toward Maren, Courtney's wide eyes added visual punctuation.

"That's what you want me to dish, isn't it?"

"Well?"

"I have no complaints, Courtney, not in that department." Bashfully, Maren grabbed her glass, holding it to stave off further inquiries with a quick sip.

"Other departments don't stack up...to the bedroom, that is?"

"In the kitchen, he shines. Has a boat and knows how to operate it well, too."

"I overheard Uncle Jack say he sails."

"Yes, culinary, nautical, obviously surgical, and naughty." Maren took another sip. "He's great."

"You're in love. I can tell."

"How so?"

"The way you light up talking about him. I couldn't get that from email, but I do now," Courtney confided. "And the way his eyes, not to

298

mention his hands, roam over you, it's mutual." She poured them each a second glass. "There's something you're not saying though."

"Courtney, I can't explain it. Dating? Seems strange; other times, so natural."

"Dating is different when you're older. You've lived life. So has Steve. Go with your gut." She regarded Maren. "When was the last time you told him he rocked your world?"

"I don't know," Maren answered. "I don't think I have."

"Well, with a former girlfriend inviting verbal debate and that bar chick who sounded like his booty call, I think you better."

"Courtney!"

"Mair." She continued, using her nickname. "He's 39, with options. That's all I'm saying."

Maren realized the football option had already extended Dylan's bedtime. "Come on Dylan, let's go upstairs."

"But Mom, the Steelers put points on the board. Can't I stay with Steve and Josh?"

"Your call Mair," Josh said. "I ought to call it a night. This score sucks." Steve whipped his head. Snickered. Maren wasn't sure if it was on account of the 17-0 lead or that Josh committed the proverbial sin.

"You said a bad word, Josh," Dylan announced. "Steve gets in trouble when he says 'sucks.' Really, he does. I got grounded."

Maren momentarily forgot what her father conveyed about lightening up. "Josh…and Dylan! We don't like that word. Right, Steve?"

"Whatever you say, Mair." He smiled. Steve had never shortened her name before. "I like that, Mair." Maren sat on the arm of the sofa near him, as he reached to pat her on the behind.

"Oh no, she's got you at the 'yes dear' stage," Josh commented on their playful affection. "Seriously, it's good to see you happy, Cuz."

"I am," she agreed, rubbing the nape of Steve's neck. "Man you are tight. Good thing he's giving us massages tomorrow." She turned to Josh. "That's the best gift."

"You bet," Steve added. "Much needed." Long surgeries and hunching over his paper-pushing promotion had left him with a few extra kinks.

"I don't normally teach couples how to massage, but since you've had a few more anatomy and physiology classes than I have, I can teach you a few moves on our Mair," Josh said.

"That'd be great." Steve rested his arm at Maren's waist. "I'll do my best not to go for her carotid. Better watch my language or she'll go for mine."

"Hey, that's not nice." Maren pulled away, feigning offense. "Maybe I won't stay and watch with you."

"It's all about the chase," Steve said, reeling her back in, motioning to the next play on the screen.

"Come on, Dylan. Let your mom stay," Courtney said. "I'll tuck you into Adam's room."

Dylan whined but left holding Courtney's hand as Maren scooched Steve over, joined the guys, and crunched on his chips. The Buccaneers put a mere seven points into the game, leaving the Steelers victorious for the holidays with a 17-7 score.

Like most preparing for Christmas Eve, Courtney's house epitomized multi-tasking at its best. With the massage table set up in another room, Josh kneaded deep into Steve's deltoids, traps, and rhomboids, spending 90 minutes. Steve told him to go as deep as he had to, realizing that Santa might surprise him with soreness.

They broke for sandwiches around the pool. Steve watched the kids swim while Courtney made a side dish to take to her parents, and Josh gave Maren 90 minutes. At the end of her massage, he told her, firmly implanted in the face rest, to enjoy the aromatherapy and new age music.

Maren breathed in lavender and let out a cleansing breath contemplating how her cousin had snatched Josh. The perks Courtney must get. Josh's hands were meant to massage. Firm and sturdy, they fit the rest of his six-foot frame with the upper strength to ply tension out of a client's body with the weight of his. Strong wrists and hands withstood hours of constant use.

Like Steve, Maren thought, but his patients were asleep when he did his best work; Josh's lay fully awake, with dim lights, soft music and carefully selected scents. Maren wondered how many of them dreamed later about his faint resemblance to the actor Tom Cruise, only with tawny-gold hair, eyebrows, and that boyish smile.

"Relaxed?" Steve asked as he ran his right hand over the sheet, down Maren's back. All kinds of thoughts stirred, the least of which focused on her neck and shoulders, as he realized she wore nothing under the sheet.

"She's most tight right here at the levator scapulae," Josh told him, showing him how to ease out her acute tension. Steve took over.

"Yeah, right there," she said. Maren let out a pleasant little moan.

"Ever since watching *When Harry Met Sally,* Mair's perfecting vocal output."

"Stop teasing me," she said, reaching to slap Steve's hand. "If I turn over Josh, show Steve how to rake your hands under my shoulders up to my head. I love that move." Maren repositioned herself scooching lower on the table. "I could stay here all day."

"That's what I'm afraid of, Cuz." He laughed, removed the face cushion, and demonstrated to Steve, who took the stool to try it. "OK, Mair. We don't want to feed your threesome fantasies so I'm stepping out, and when you're dressed, I'll show you how to ply Steve. Though I think you've already reeled him in good."

"She sure has," Steve agreed. He waited for the door to close. Maren took another cleansing breath. Steve offered her a hand as she sat up, letting the sheet fall. "Dangerous in here," he said, admiringly.

"Hand me my clothes, will you?" In yes-dear mode, he complied. Reluctantly. "Josh reminds me of Paul."

"Oh yeah." Steve laughed, pulling his polo off, smoothing the sheet back over the table and lying face up. Fastening the last of her buttons, Maren opened the door. "She wanted me naked but I refused."

"We'll start her on the hard stuff after dinner, since she polished off your beer and chips last night," Josh teased. "Then she's all yours. I'm building a tricycle so keep it down." Josh spent more time educating Maren on how to maneuver Steve's muscles. "Have you even had an anatomy class?" he asked her.

"Only the informal kind," she said. "More fun that way." Steve wasn't sure if he should love that or worry about her killing him, but he went with his first thought.

"When we're done, I'll show you some stretches, using the doorjam, the mats, and well, I don't have a pole, but that'd be great for those muscle groups." Josh turned his head to Maren's giggle. He felt Steve's chest rise and fall on the table. "What?"

"Show her, Josh. I'm all for it."

301

By the time Josh finished, Maren and Steve showered off the massage oil before swimming an hour. They got dressed for church, making the family service, where they met Audrey, Jack and Courtney's parents, returning to their place for a four-course dinner. It ended so that they could get the kids to bed by 9:30 at Courtney's house.

They managed to settle Dylan and Adam only by telling them that Santa visited the warm weather states earlier than those with snow. She and Courtney had always promoted the nativity, embellishing the religious wonder by telling their kids that Santa brought some, but not all gifts.

Steve helped Josh assemble the tricycle in half the anticipated time. He tip toed the stairs and quietly closed the door behind him. The guest room had its own bath where Maren had left a nightlight. She stirred as Steve stretched underneath the covers.

"Our first Christmas together," he murmured, nuzzling her with the possibility of sex. Steve slid down the straps of her nightgown. "Did you think we'd last this long?" Her nightgown slid lower still when she arched her back.

"I wasn't sure," she said, offering her lips, her hands running up his back and down to slip off his boxers. "But you're the best thing that's happened to me this year."

"This Christmas is getting merrier, Mair...by the minute."

Steve didn't shave the next morning. Even with their late-night romp, they woke before Dylan, and Maren reached for a package tucked under the bed.

"Not something I want you to open with everyone," she admitted, elbow propped on her pillow.

Steve eyed her suspiciously. It felt firm, boxed. He tore off the wrapping, untucked an edge of cardboard. Sliding out the gift, his lips curved.

"You?" He had a hunch. The framed image, professionally taken, showed a sofa with plush, inviting pillows. In the foreground, in a snug black dress was a woman's unmistakable derrière ending in stockings as she crouched down onto a table in patent leather black high heels. Maren shook her head acknowledging she was indeed the model.

"Certifiably hot. Tasteful. I love it." He kissed her. "Goes on my desk."

302

"It's boudoir photography," she told him. "Not at work, you won't."

Maren had selected small presents shipping a box to circumvent security hassles. She chose the DUPLO hospital for Adam, leaving one at home for Hannah. They shopped for the LEGO Island Xtreme sets, the largest one to Dylan, shipped ahead from Santa.

"How'd you get the rest without him seeing," Maren demanded wading through wrapping paper. "Dylan needs a separate suitcase for a hundred pounds of plastic pieces."

"Hotel delivery," he assured her. Since Steve spent half Christmas Day assembling creations Maren vowed he could also pack them.

Nora, two years older than Audrey, gray temples proving it, sat back with her sister Christmas Day enjoying two younger generations. Audrey whispered, "Doesn't Steve stand out with stubble?" Nora's appreciative nod validated Audrey the rest of the holiday.

Chapter 20

The next morning, as Adam and Dylan played with their newly acquired loot, Maren and Steve gathered belongings for their get-away. Steve held up his smartphone. "I snapped a shot of the image. Savoring this will forever ease my stress until I can get to you," he said. "Speaking of which, make sure you pack the black sexy number." He'd surprised her after he opened the photograph. He leaned in closer, grabbing her hands while he commandeered her ear. "And the fuck-me high heels."

She surprised him. No scolding. No pinching or swatting. Just eyes that said she wanted him as much as he wanted her. "I hope wherever we're going is warm." Steve promised to take care of that concern, also.

By nine, Maren hugged Dylan and told him that his grandparents were in charge, along with Courtney and Josh. Audrey & Jack were taking him for the day but he'd spend the night right back here.

"Mair's make-up bag?" Josh asked, hoisting the larger case into the trunk. She scrunched her face into a jeer. "Unless Santa sent fun toys yesterday."

"She left those for New Year's," Steve joked. On his way to work, Josh would take them to pick up a rental for their trip to the Gulf Coast.

"Steve, you packed the book I got you? The Chesapeake one." Maren let a tote bag fall from her shoulder into the trunk then opened the back door.

"Yes dear. And a stack of journals for our one night alone without your son." Steve looked at Josh, who shook his head.

"Where are you going?" he whispered to Steve.

"You'll find out. I slipped Jack the itinerary. Call it a legal kidnapping. We won't be reading books."

"Didn't think so," Josh said as he slammed the trunk.

The drive gave them a chance to talk. "You look content," Steve said. "I'm glad we did this."

"It's been great to see you with my family," she replied. "Josh's upping the joke volume tells me he feels comfortable with you." Maren looked out at the highway and shifted to him again. "Outside of the surprise of…her." She paused. "Seems you had a fun time. You had a couple of tense weeks."

"Pam's coming in for her father seems like a blessing now," Steve said. "Your minister used some analogy about casting things off so that you can be who you genuinely are." Steve focused on the road, adjusting the air vents as the sun warmed them. "Chatting with Jerry on this trip didn't seem as awkward…that word again."

"Obviously. It was nice to see you help Pam help Shelly." Maren smiled. "I was proud of you."

"Oh gee, thanks." He glanced sideways. Turning more serious, Steve asked Maren about the church service when they sang the last hymn.

"Silent Night?" she asked. Had to be. Steve ran his hands over her shoulder when she choked on the lyrics. "Just flooded by emotion. It happens, Steve."

"I know. I'm proud of you, too. Looks like your family shares that." He removed his right hand from the wheel and quickly patted her long, flowing mane.

As they pulled into the parking lot, somewhere along Tampa Bay, Maren saw boat masts, piers, gulls soaring. Temperatures predicted to climb no higher than 70 degrees with clear skies, she'd worn a nautical jacket as had Steve. They tried theirs out since they'd given a slightly different set to Maren's parents yesterday and promised to take the whole Florida crew to dinner Friday night, before flying back Saturday.

"This is why you told me to wear my sneakers. But it's deserted."

"It's a private charter, Maren. Merry Day After Christmas," he said. "Just you, me, the captain and his wife." They got out of the car. Maren blinked. "We sail this afternoon, eat a light lunch, and moor around a barrier island," Steve continued. "They fix dinner and…leave us alone. Our cabin is forward. Theirs is aft." He smiled.

"But no one knows where we're going…what if Dylan…"

"Took care of that. Your mom will pry the few details I gave your father by evening." He got that right, Maren thought. "Any other concerns?"

"When do we set sail?" Fingers pressed to her cheeks, her excitement resembled Dylan's boarding his favorite rides. They got their bags—a rolling carry-on, Steve's small duffle, and the tote Maren brought along. Steve peaked inside. The paperback amused him.

Without strong gusts, they savored the sunshine and gentle sail. If they felt like helping out, Captain Tony and Trish lent them the ropes; if they sat back, holding hands or chatting, no one cared. The day was theirs.

Maren nibbled on croissants with chicken salad and roasted vegetables, and sipped hot tea that afternoon. She had worn navy blue slacks, a long-sleeved blouse, and her sneakers. Steve had worn practically the same attire, only in different colors. Tony dropped anchor by four, and shortly before five, Trish asked Steve if they were still on for dinner around seven.

"Yeah, I think we'll hang out for sunset...thanks," he replied. She asked if they preferred wine or suggested champagne she could put on ice for an early New Year's toast. Steve looked to Maren. "Why not?"

"Darn, I forgot my camera and wanted to check my phone."

"Go do that. I'll do the same. Let's make it as gadget free as possible. It's perfectly beautiful out here."

"Steve when you're a parent, you'll understand."

"Maybe...in due time," he said with a slight curl to his lips. "When we can communicate...really well." He could be such a clown, she thought. That topic was hers to hound, not his.

The sky was a perfect backdrop for the soft sounds Trish put on the boat's stereo, playing faintly in the air. Maren sat on a bench in the cockpit. Steve shimmied beside her when he returned from the cabin. "This is gorgeous," she told him, leaning against his shoulder. "I love it. How did you ever find this?"

"Something I've always wanted to do," he said. He shifted so that he could face her more than hold her. Neither wore sunglasses, having left them below as the sun started to fade.

"I've waited a long time for someone like you, to love a setting just like this." Steve stroked Maren's hair, worn down, flowing off her shoulders. "You're a woman who loves life, knows how to meet challenges, when to let the sails out, when to trim them."

"I didn't do very much of that today. I was lazy," she said sheepishly.

"But you can, and I love that about you," Steve said. "Maren, you're beautiful, smart, sexy. Then, with the name that signifies the sea. That's incredible." Steve brushed a strand from her forehead. "We

306

need more evenings like this. To have fun, go to bed, and wake up each morning, like we did this week."

Steve cupped her chin in his hand. "Marry me, Maren. Without a doubt, I want to spend the rest of my life with you." Maren's eyes widened. She moistened her lips before she made a hard, obvious swallow.

"Is this really happening?" Maren's hand stroked Steve's hair.

He shifted off the bench, motioning her to look at the array of orange, pink, purple and blue behind them.

"Oh, this is so real." A slightly parted mouth meant she took in more air, but the words weren't freely escaping. When she turned around she saw the Tiffany Blue Box with a white bow as Steve knelt beside her. "I'm just…so surprised. Not totally, but…"

"One of us is supposed to open this, I'm pretty sure," he said, arching his brow. Anticipation robbed his breath, but his eyes never left hers.

Finally, she tugged on the bow. Steve opened the outer box, popping open the inner one. Her eyes bulged at the round diamond, just under two carats, gleaming in the classic Tiffany setting. Steve took her left hand and slid it down her ring finger. "Marry me."

She stretched her arm out for a good look. A perfect fit, no less. "You planned this all along?"

"Ah, I was going to wait into next year, but when I planned this getaway, this setting…it felt right."

Roberta Flack's "The First Time Ever I Saw Your Face" played on the CD collection. "You've intrigued me since the night we met, Maren. I've watched you these past few months…grow, adapt. You're a fantastic mom. I want to build a life with you, make babies together. This whole idea is newer to you than me…I know. We've had different paths, purposes…different directions. But I want you, forever."

"I love you so much," she said, wetting her lips again. She took his face with both hands and kissed him. Lingering. She pulled back looking at her hand.

"I'll ask the question again, if you need me to…'cause I'd like an answer."

"No…yes," she corrected quickly. "I mean, say it again."

"Is this like getting to our first date?" Steve's blue eyes danced with her brown ones. "Maren, will you marry me?"

"Yes…yes, I want you, too. Oh my God." She closed her eyes. "Oh Steve…" She looked around, the sun fading faster. "I can't believe this. I'm in shock."

"If you took but a few more minutes I might have been, too. You really don't do anything fast, do you?"

"I'm sure that's not on the list of what you love about me, you quick and decisive surgeon."

"No. Only a future husband, happy to have found the love of my life…at last."

Maren crossed her arms as the chill set in. Steve shifted next to her, offering warmth. "Let's stay another minute, savoring this. Then, appetizers await."

"They knew. Tony and Trish knew you were proposing to me?" She stood up, studied him. Steve reached for the box and bow, zippering them into his jacket pocket. He took her gleaming hand in his.

"They specialize in private charters…even custom occasions. They had suggestions, asked a lot of questions."

"Which you didn't have to think about…or did you?" Maren narrowed her eyes. "The music…did you pick the music?"

"Some of it. The menu. The evening's not over, babe."

"That's one of the many things I love about you." She mellowed more. "Her asking about champagne? Where is it by the way?"

Steve laughed and clutched her hand tight. "Let's go see."

After champagne, baked oysters and shrimp cocktail, Maren and Steve feasted on pan seared Florida Snapper encrusted with pecans garnished with mango chutney, served with rice and a fresh vegetable medley. Red roses greeted Maren and small votive vases with tiny LED lights lit the galley illuminating the rose-petal trail to the forward cabin with more lights.

When Steve asked if she saved room for dessert, Maren clutched her stomach, leaning against the woodwork. "I thought I was your dessert?" She giggled.

"Two glasses does this…really?" Was she that much of a lightweight? Good thing they alternated between coconut water picked from the list Tony emailed.

"I snuck more while you weren't looking," she said. "I'll change...while I can stand up." She kissed him, splaying her hands to his shirt, unfastening buttons. "What is the *official* dessert?"

"Chocolate covered strawberries, I believe."

"Mmm...I'll try some."

When Maren opened the cabin door, Steve saw just how Mickey-sexy Maren had become. She stood in high heels showcasing the teddy he bought falling along her thighs. "You look ravishing."

He fed her a strawberry from a tray he set on the bed. "I'll get our glasses." Her giggling made him wonder if he ought to cut her off.

Maren lay down, flipped onto her stomach, helping herself to the tray as she held one leg, one stiletto up in the air. Steve saw the heel, followed it to her grin at the sight of his parted shirt. He felt incredibly lucky.

"You're primed without another. It's been a perfect day. A wicked headache could ruin our sail back tomorrow." He hesitated handing over her glass.

"Won't ruin anything now." Maren pulled him closer. Another sip lapsed her into a cascade of laughter convincing Steve to take it away. "I can't believe everything you made happen to pull this off. I love this ring," she said, displaying her left hand as she'd done several times already. Maren stood up. She pressed into him and immediately felt how primed he'd become.

"I love you so much." As she kissed him, Steve's arms slid the length of her. "And that you got down on one knee, I wouldn't have imagined...so maybe?"

Maren unfastened his belt, pulled his shirt out, and with his help, got him how she wanted him. As she lowered herself, she looked up. "Women always dream of a man on one knee. How is it you guys always seem to want, and get us, on both?"

Maren woke with a slight headache, which a cup of coffee and a tall glass of ice water helped considerably. With an I-told-you-so look, Steve hugged Maren in nothing but the teddy.

"You made out really well on account of champagne." Maren realized that sounded as if she only wanted sex when she got sloshed. "What I meant..."

He pulled back, granting her a devilish grin. "You're a sure thing, you mean to say...becoming a surer thing with this." He kissed the hand with her ring. "If a little champagne gets you to talk like that, commanding me with those words, I'll just help with the occasional headache."

"What did I say?" Maren asked.

His grin grew wider. "No, I'll get the Kramer-woman look."

"Well, I'm almost one."

Steve laughed out loud. "Hint: What are those shoes to most men?"

Maren remembered what he called them while packing. "I didn't. I said that?"

"Two great words, babe." He kissed her passionately. "Said several times, with such demand." He smiled.

Steve and Maren finished breakfast having their second cup of coffee in robes provided by the charter company as they sat on deck. They showered, got dressed. Then, Captain Tony set sail back to the pier.

"We have to tell Dylan first," she told Steve, calling her mom, giving no details away. Her white lie seemed harmless enough when she asked if they could meet at Downtown Disney for a light lunch, and Dylan could use his gift certificate to the LEGO store.

"I thought you already had too many to pack," Audrey reminded her.

Maren stumbled, but recovered. "What's a few more?"

Once there, they took Dylan on a quick stroll while Jack and Audrey secured a table and ordered an appetizer. Steve had surreptitiously asked the waiter to prepare a bottle of champagne on ice once they returned.

"So how was your trip," Audrey asked them both as Steve pulled the chair out for Maren, and she took her seat. Dylan moved on his so much that Audrey stopped. "Your dad just took him to the restroom not long ago." Maren told Dylan to contain his enthusiasm, and he was trying.

"Perfectly lovely," Maren answered, her left hand pocketed.

Steve sat up straight as the waiter filled four glasses. "Dylan...go ahead."

"Grampy, Grammy...guess what?"

"You need a charter plane now for your LEGO collection?" Jack teased.

"Well, yeah." That threw Dylan off. "I'm getting a stepdad!"

Jack eyed his wife, who gasped as Maren's left hand slowly picked up her champagne glass and met Steve's. Sparkle and clang competed with one another.

"To grandparents who make getaways possible…and to my fiancée who, finally, said yes." Steve kissed Maren after they toasted. He turned to Audrey. "She really doesn't do anything quickly. You warned me."

Jack stood up from the table, moving to clasp Steve's hand, but pulled him in for a hug. The first he'd ever given Steve. "She made you squirm?"

"A little," Steve answered, moving to Audrey. If Jack got one, she wasn't going to miss hers. Kiss included with her hug.

Maren finished embracing her father. They sat back down. "I wasn't expecting it, that's all…not yet, anyway," she justified. "Steve absolutely amazed me with the details." Her eyes bore into him. "How did you know my ring size?"

"Give away all my detective work?" Even Audrey wanted to know. "You showed me where you hid your rings, if you recall."

"And you asked me to try them on," she said. "Come to think of it…the stop in Chevy Chase…at the jewelry store. In October." Maren's mouth fell open. "You thought about this back then?"

"I wasn't 100% certain," he answered honestly, taking another sip. The waiter took their orders, but Maren's hand on his wrist made him continue. "Of course, the day after I got it, I had second thoughts."

"When?"

"The day you shut the door on me," Steve said with an I-got-you smile.

"Oh…" Maren's eyes traveled the table. "I really don't lose it that often."

"Well, clearly the appeal hadn't worn off," Steve said. "But with us generally growing closer, it felt right, especially turning another landmark birthday this spring, which we won't talk about."

Jack laughed. "Steve, there's life after 40. Plenty of it." He winked at his wife. With romance in the air, he leaned over to kiss Audrey.

"I'll get cousins," Dylan said. "Since I don't have any. Except here." His annoyance with that minor detail—and distance—came through in tone. "But I was going to marry Hannah."

"Dude…she'll be more fun as a cousin." Steve was resolute.

"Brides wear white. Mom, will you wear white?"

That brought up a host of questions Maren hadn't even begun to think about. "I don't know, but we're not having a huge wedding."

"I love you even more," Steve said, leaning back. "We have so much going on this next year. That said, if we elope my mother would never forgive me. She's waited a few years for this, you can imagine."

"I was thinking simple, elegant, involving water," Maren offered.

"I'll pick simple and happy over any more stress in my life," Steve said.

"Some may not be thrilled, you realize."

Uneasy eyes traveled the table. They all knew the Mitchells would have a fit. They also understood too well that this next year posed more change and challenge.

Maren wasn't worried. Anxiety—real and irrational—seemed a thing of the past. She had Dylan. She had two people who had always remained her solid rocks of support and encouragement. She had Steve, especially today…and forever.

The End

Acknowledgments

This being a first novel, I cannot begin to thank my supporters enough. From the beginning drafts, Patty and Kathy have read and re-read with content comments and line editing that they could have another line of work themselves doing this! Sue, Audrey, Bobbie, and Bill were other early readers sharing their thoughts and encouragement also. Karen, Alyssa, Lara, and Jim added expertise that made my research much easier, and for their time and thoughts I'm most grateful as well. Members of the Eastern Shore Writers Association have lent their wisdom and support, and I'm privileged to be a part of this group.

Without my technology go-to person Peter, who rescued the decades-old original manuscript in electronic form, I'm not sure any of this would have been possible. My husband Bob and family deserve credit as sharing one's life with a creative type means moments stolen to write down ideas, process out loud, and countless hours at a keyboard. I love you all for accepting me for who I am and taking that journey with me!

Finally, my thanks to every one of my readers for without those who wish to lose themselves in a story for a few hours, none of this would matter. Your spreading the word to friends and the reading public, through reviews and "likes" on Facebook, is much appreciated.

About the Author

Lauren Monroe is a novelist residing on Maryland's Eastern Shore. A native of Pittsburgh, she grew up around boats and beautiful scenery in Western Maryland, later moving to the Washington, D.C. suburbs before settling across the Bay Bridge. Various experiences shape her writing including marriage, family, friendships, a graduate degree in the social sciences, and her career paths. In her spare time, she enjoys reading fiction and non-fiction, boating, swimming, biking, good food, and travel. Lauren Monroe is a pen name for her fiction projects.

Readers' Guide

Letting Go

Book One of The Maryland Shores

When Maren Mitchell lost her husband, she felt adrift in choppy waters. Buoyed by her young son, her work, and family, she adjusts course as she's not one to ever act quickly. The handsome and decisive surgeon Steve Kramer devoted decades to advancing his medical career, but his personal life sailed past him...until Maren cornered his curiosity. He encourages her to become a co-worker, but will she become more?

The intensity that fills Steve's days drives Maren to anxious uncertainty. Will a left-brained, logical man and a creative, cautious woman get tangled in their differences and past hurts...or surrender what they must to live fuller lives and forge a future together?

For Discussion

• Readers encounter Maren Mitchell as she's grieved her husband's unexpected death, all while she and the country face a powerful anniversary reaction. What initial impression does this make? What unanticipated ordeals might you, as a reader, have witnessed, and what was meaningful to your grieving or overcoming them?

• Steve Kramer's life seems so different from its prior path and current calm, confident exterior. How do two people initially very different attract one another? Discuss your experiences with this phenomenon.

• When we live through stressful times, we make adaptations to survive day by day. The characters face two historical incidents. Many people have memories of at least one of these. Talk about these trying times. If you lived through these, discuss how you dealt with daily worry and fear.

• As the story develops, several characters must face past behavior and choices. What are the ingredients of forgiveness and moving forward? Is it easy or difficult for us to grant a do-over to someone significant in our lives? What occurs when grudges, or even resentments, remain? How does this influence having good boundaries?

• By the end of the story which characters have changed and in what ways? On a lighter note, how have their passions and favorites reflected any of your own, as a reader?

A Conversation with Lauren Monroe

What inspired your writing this story?

I wanted to write about people overcoming things in a positive way. Originally, I drafted this in the early to mid-1990s. I wrote too much like a journalist back then, and in hindsight (always the best, right?), I don't think I had as much life experience and confidence to pull it off. I tossed the hard copy that I saved all those years into the Montgomery County recycle bin upon moving across the state. Foolishly, I might add. But in 2013, keeping with my goal to get back to the keyboard, I revisited everything about the project, deciding to break the original into a series, develop the characters more, and change the setting to involve Maryland, the Chesapeake, and nautical elements.

Why did you select this particular time frame for the book?

The main character always grappled with anxiety. I expanded this, and the historical episodes nationally and regionally, seemed to fit as a worry-inducing backdrop to the overall plot. After choosing the year, I maintained some Pittsburgh influence as my hometown because I had also changed the geography. I had much fun pulling in a few favorites as my tributes to and connection with Pittsburgh, Pennsylvania.

How did your background, education, and work help with this type of writing, or more specifically, this book?

Growing up, *Medical Center* was my favorite TV series, followed by *ER* in the '90s. Healthcare has always fascinated me, followed by a graduate degree in mental health and work in that field. All of that—coupled with decades of non-fiction writing and research—enabled me to tackle this. A friend reminded me that being away from writing for a while surely cleared my mind such that fiction didn't seem as foreboding to me. Living life, understanding family systems, and learning what fosters and impedes relationships certainly made a difference, too. I set out to create genuine people, with authentic problems and real traits, because without good characters, and ones we like, it's hard to keep reading.

As an accomplished writer, you used a pen name for fiction. What goes into writers using a different name or pseudonym?

Honestly, it doesn't need to be any high-security-clearance secret. I merely wanted to keep my professional life and non-fiction separate from fiction work. About two-dozen colleagues and fellow writers agreed with my choice. The pen name itself is symbolic. A very close childhood friend selected names I admired. One I chose for my son also. She never let me live it down! So I figured…what's one more, and I chose her daughter's first name. Monroe is short for Monroeville, a town in which I grew a lot as a writer.

What can readers look forward to in Book Two?

The main characters—Maren and Steve—will be involved in the story, and some of the minor characters will take center stage. I'll add new figures into the drama also. I don't give out titles ahead, for various reasons. I have a general idea of the plot, but one never knows what turns it will take. Looking historically, there are elements to pull into the plot and drama as well. Stay tuned for those twists.

What can readers do to connect more with this series and book?

Email: shorethingpublishing@gmail.com

Positive reviews, discussion online or in places such as Good Reads helps spread the word. Please "like" this on Facebook and share with friends who might also enjoy an escape with women's fiction and contemporary romance.

https://www.facebook.com/lauren.monroe.novels